Gotta Have

FAITH

SEVEN VIRTUES RANCH ROMANCE BOOK 1

BECKY DOUGHTY

BraveHearts
Press

GOTTA HAVE FAITH: Seven Virtues Ranch Romance Book 1

Book Cover by BraveHearts Press Designs

Author Info: BeckyDoughty.com

ISBN: 978-1953347213

FAITH

Now faith is the assurance of things hoped for,
the conviction of things not seen.
Hebrews 1:11 ESV

ONE

"Nothin' finer than a hardworking woman in a worn pair of jeans and a Stetson."

Faith Goodacre straightened and turned slowly. She'd know that voice anywhere. Even after all these years. She removed her safety glasses, wishing she'd worn her shades instead, and narrowed her eyes against the brilliant sunlight. It was uncommonly warm for early May, but the weather could still change on a dime this time of year. She settled her hat a little firmer on her head, then lifted her chin a notch so she could look down her nose at the man who'd just rounded the end of the barn to park across the gravel driveway behind her. Hooking her thumbs in the belt loops on her jeans, she watched as Cordell Overman took his sweet time getting out of his big Cajun Red Silverado, grinning at her all the while.

He stopped several feet from her, thank the good Lord above, because even if she could get her feet to move, she wasn't about to retreat. He was on her turf, and she hadn't yet decided if that was a good thing or not.

She widened her stance and squared her shoulders. "Sure beats a city slicker with soft hands and a sunburnt scalp, kicking up dust in a shiny new truck, to boot," she said, letting her sweet tea drawl lace the words with just enough sugar to take the edge off.

"Ouch!" Cord clutched his chest and staggered backward a step or two. But he kept his eyes fixed on her face, and his smile didn't waver, making it somewhat difficult for her to maintain her disdainful expression.

Holy smokes, he looked good. Not that she was looking.

Okay, yeah, she was.

"You're looking good, Cord." Dang it. She hadn't meant to say it out loud, but at least she sounded unaffected by his sudden appearance.

"Even with this sizable hole you just blasted through me?" He lifted his hand and peered down as though to gauge the extent of the damage, then looked back up at her again, his eyes sparkling with humor.

"Looks to me like you'll survive," Faith quipped.

He held his arms out at his sides, making his already snug gray t-shirt stretch even tighter across his chest. "Then how about a welcome back to the holler hug for an old friend?"

She forced her gaze to stay on his face, but looking into his November sky eyes was proving just as troublesome as ogling his impressive physique.

Old friend. So that's what they were calling it these days? "Believe me; you don't want a hug from me."

"Sure, I do." He took a step toward her, but she held up a hand.

"As you so eloquently put it, I'm working. Hard." She tapped the shield of the chop saw she'd been using, then lowered the blade and knocked the safety into place. "I'm not exactly in the mood to cuddle right now." With the back of her wrist, she swiped at a drop of perspiration that trickled down the side of her face and clung to her jawline. She was sweating like a sinner in church, covered in sawdust, and her hair was plastered to her head under her hat.

Cord, on the other hand, could have stepped right off the cover of *American Cowboy.* Except he didn't have a two-day scruff, he wasn't wearing a hat, and he likely didn't even own a horse anymore.

"Cuddle is your word, not mine," he said, flashing his pearly whites at her. "I wasn't asking you to snuggle up to—"

"Semantics, Cord." She rested her hand on a cocked hip and exchanged his grin with a grimace. *Speaking of pearly white...* She imagined a holster slung low at her waist, complete with a pearl-handled Colt .45 poised for the draw. Heck, her little Glock would do the job just fine—.

Good grief, Faith. What job are you considering using a gun for? She cleared her throat, hoping he couldn't read her uncharacteristically violent thoughts.

"You're a long way from home. What brings you to our neck of the woods?" What she really wanted to ask him was what had brought him to Seven Virtues Ranch. And couldn't he have at least called first? Given her some kind of heads up? Wasn't that just common courtesy?

Cord turned his head briefly in the direction of Seven Virtues' closest neighbor, Whispering Hills Ranch. Although nothing was visible through the wooded tract that marked the property line between the ranches, Faith was pretty sure he was picturing the abandoned hay barn on the other side of the small creek that meandered through the trees. Same as she was. Not something she particularly wanted to dwell on, but his next words confirmed her suspicions. He spoke in a husky drawl. "How about a 'Welcome Back' kiss, then? Purely unselfish motives on my part, I assure you," he added, shooting her a sideways look that made something coil tightly low in her gut. Then he chuckled, making light of his request. "In honor of Uncle Judge, God rest his soul."

"I never once kissed Judge Flanner," Faith retorted, hating that he could still get to her so easily. She crossed her arms and dipped her head, hoping her hat would hide the flush coloring her cheeks. Just the thought of kissing Cordell Overman again made her blood run hot. "Besides, he was a married man, so there'd be nothing honorable about it," she added, narrowing her eyes at him. Judge had been, in fact, a widower, but he'd been married to Cord's aunt for more than fifty years before she passed away. "So, what did you say you needed? I really am busy, you know."

Cord gave a low whistle. "Miss Goodacre, when did you get so prickly?"

Prickly? She tried not to be offended by his question, but coming from Cord, the barbed word smarted. It was self-preservation, as far as she was concerned. "Why, Mr. Overman, how do you know it's 'Miss'?"

"Because I made certain of it before I headed out this way to see you." The grin turned into a bold, piano key smile, one he'd used to charm her to his will a time or two—or two hundred—back in the day.

Even before he'd had his teeth straightened and bleached. Mercy, they were white. *City boy.*

"And I brought you something." He spun on his boot heel—at least those weren't new, she noted. He'd always preferred the Western work boots over more traditional cowboy boots. He reached into the open driver's side window of his truck to withdraw a pale blue mason jar spilling over with red and yellow columbines, the delicate star-like blossoms bobbing their heads in greeting as he approached with them. Holding them out to her, he said, "For you, Fair Maiden."

Faith couldn't help it. She smiled.

"There she is," he murmured appreciatively, dipping his head to look her in the eye. "There's that pretty smile I know."

She pressed her lips together, trying desperately not to be impressed that he'd remembered about the columbines, then she shook her head in surrender. Man, he was good.

She'd once pointed her favorite flower out to him where they grew in her mother's gardens. She'd told him the fiery wildflower with its flared petals, and backward facing spikes, made her think of fairy tale dragons. He'd plucked a small handful, dropped to one knee, and offered them to her, declaring he was her knight in shining armor, ready to slay dragons for her. Faith still carefully tended the bushes that grew in riotous disarray at the top of the long drive up from Carpenter Road. She had the sneaking suspicion that Cord had helped himself to them on his way in.

Except she remembered, too. She remembered just how not ready he'd been to fight for her when it came right down to it. Almost a decade ago, he'd kicked the dust off a pair of Ropers just like the ones he wore now, forcing her to armor up and fight the dragons herself. The fact that he stood in front of her today, that pie-eating grin on his face, told her he had no clue about the damage he'd left in his wake.

After a moment's hesitation, she took the jar from him, careful not to let her fingers do any more than graze his in the exchange. It didn't matter; the jolt was still there, sending a current of electricity coursing through her veins. She resisted the impulse to shiver and turned away to set the flowers on the stacked stone retaining wall nearby. "Thank you. They're lovely. But then, I do grow the finest columbines in town."

"You do, indeed," he agreed, not denying her assertion that he'd snagged them from her flower beds. "Only the finest for Faith Goodacre. That's what I always say."

She lifted her hat and fanned her face with it, turning away from him to gaze at the blossoms that now seemed to mock her. She had no clue what her hair looked like, and even though she shouldn't care what he thought, she did. "And I always say, 'If I want it done right, I'll do it myself.' As evidenced by those flowers."

"Only because you never did know how to ask for help." His words were gentle, but they practically knocked the breath out of her anyway.

She clapped the hat back on her head and spun around to glare at him, her eyebrows raised in indignation. "That's not how I remember it."

Cord shrugged. "Maybe you remember it wrong." His tone remained casual, but she saw the tension in the set of his shoulders, in the way he cocked his right hip just a little higher than the left. They were like a couple of gunslingers settling in for a standoff. She imagined his trigger finger twitching in anticipation, just as hers had a few minutes ago.

But Faith wasn't interested in going toe to toe with him. Not today. Not ever. It had taken some doing, but she'd let go of what might have been a long time ago, and up until this moment, she'd assumed Cordell Overman had moved on as well.

So, what in the Sam Hill was he doing showing up here at Seven Virtues Ranch, bringing her fairy tale dragon flowers, and smiling at her as though the last decade had never happened? It was bad enough that he was back in the hollow; did he have to try to breach the sanctuary of her heart as well?

"No, Cord, I remember it all perfectly well." She glanced pointedly down at the watch on her wrist. Her sisters teased her about it, but she refused to whip out her phone every time she needed to check the time.

Every minute of her day was allotted for something, and none of those minutes were set aside for the man in front of her. She'd erased his name from her calendar and had no plans to put him back on the schedule. She gave him a pointed look. "If you'll excuse me, I have to get back to it." She stepped up to the saw, removed the safety, and slipped her safety glasses back on. She bent to pick up a two-by-four.

He beat her to it. "Let me help."

"But I don't need your help." Faith didn't even bother trying to convince him to hand the board over. Instead, she grabbed another one. She swung one end away from her, nearly clipping him in the hip, and balanced it on the rock wall, then slid the other end into place under the saw blade. She made a quick cut, then stacked the two pieces on the other side of her workstation with others she'd already cut.

"I was only asking." He offered her the board he held, but she didn't take it. First of all, she wasn't going to risk touching him again. And second, now she was stuck standing on principle and couldn't accept his help, even if she wanted it. Even if he offered it with no strings attached.

Except she wasn't so sure there were no strings attached. "Actually, you didn't ask. You demanded that I let you help. Two very different things."

"Semantics, Faith," he said, tossing her word back at her. But he set the two-by-four back on the pile, then leaned his backside against the stone wall, bracing his hands on either side of his hips. The pose was casual enough, but she didn't miss the subtle shift in his demeanor, the slightly deflated posture, and furrowed brow.

The uncomfortable burn of shame made her skin crawl. She really was being prickly today.

And to give him credit, he did seem to be trying to make the best of a situation that was bound to be difficult, no matter how they approached it. A phone call to warn her of his visit may have proved just as volatile, truth be told.

"Where's Jack?" she asked, suddenly realizing that her dog hadn't alerted her to Cord's approach. Usually, the tri-colored Border Collie went out of his way to let everyone on the ranch know when visitors arrived. "Jack?" she called out before pursing her lips and letting out a piercing whistle. With a certain satisfaction, she saw Cord flinch.

The dog, however, remained AWOL.

Cord spoke casually. "I met up with Prudence and Jack at the front gate down the lane. She told me where I could find you."

Faith spun to look at him. "What was she doing down there? And why did she have my dog?" A momentary bout of irritation rose inside her. Prudence, the sixth of the seven Goodacre sisters, was constantly off indulging in some whimsy or another. Faith had corralled her at the chicken coop a little earlier where the girl was collecting eggs and padding the nesting boxes with fresh straw. She'd given Prudence strict instructions to check in as soon as she was finished, as Faith would need her help framing up the new chicken tractor she was making. Their chickens free ranged in the pastures behind the cattle, and the portable chicken housing kept the flock safe from predators.

"She was taking pictures," Cord said with a soft chuckle. "She'd put together a makeshift nest with weeds and flowers and chicken eggs and set it up on top of that old stump next to the Seven Virtues sign. She had your dog posing with it."

"Poor Jack," Faith said with a snort, as she settled the board onto the saw. "She's always making him model for her. Then again, he doesn't seem to mind." She made quick work of the last three two-by-fours waiting to be cut, then brushed the sawdust off her hands and removed her glasses again. She really should be wearing gloves, but her daddy never did, so neither did she. Oh, she paid for it with calluses, ugly nails, and rough skin, but Prudence had a knack for whipping up amazing herbal salves, and Faith was one of her best customers. "Did she say she was coming up soon? I asked her to help me with this thing." She waved at the cut lumber and rolls of chicken wire nearby.

Cord shot her a dubious look, his eyebrows raised.

"See? I do know how to ask for help." She grimaced; she sounded like a two-year-old, even to her own ears.

"Right. I see." Cord nodded slowly, that stupid grin back on his face. "So, speaking of Judge Flanner—"

"But we weren't." Faith cut him off, glad for the change in subject, but not liking his patronizing tone. "We were talking about why you're here."

Cord continued like she hadn't spoken. "Frankie's selling the old place."

She frowned. He seriously didn't think she already knew about that?

Frank "Judge" Flanner—so named because he'd held the title of head judge at every Plumwood Hollow pie contest as long as anyone could remember—had died last fall, and although she didn't really miss the grouchy old rancher, Faith hated what had become of Whispering Hills over the last several years, and especially since his unexpected passing. Frank Junior—Frankie to his family and friends—was career military and had little inclination toward picking up cattle ranching where his daddy left off, and no one else in the nearby area was in any position to purchase the huge property and its dwindling herd of cattle. Which inevitably meant some stranger from out of town would be moving into the close-knit community, something that always took some adjusting to.

Once again, Faith locked the saw blade down, and this time, she unplugged it from the bright orange extension cord snaking around from the front of the barn. "So, you're here about your uncle's place? If you're hoping for an inside scoop, I don't really have much of one. I know Frankie wants to move it quickly and all in one piece, and he's priced it accordingly." She knew this because she'd contacted him about purchasing some of the acreage to expand Seven Virtues. "The big house is sitting empty right now, but Jordan Binks—you remember him? He lives on site in that cowboy cabin and keeps an eye on the place. He's a good guy, and he knows that place better than your uncle did, I'd wager, but he's old, and he's worried he'll get ousted when a new buyer comes in. He loves that place and is good with the herd. Granted, he lost a few calves and two first-calf heifers this spring, just because he was trying to manage what he could on his own. We helped out as much as we were able; Hope spent a fair amount of time over there early April." Faith frowned. "I hear he's considering keeping the bulls from breeding come fall if they haven't sold the place by then, but otherwise, he's been operating as though Judge was still calling the shots."

"Poor bulls." Cord winked at her.

Faith kept talking, ignoring his juvenile comment. "Which means unless Frankie finds a buyer soon, the place is going to start losing some serious revenue." She worried about Binks. The old cowboy had made Whispering Hills his home for more than fifty years, and the thought of him having to make a new start this late in life just about broke her heart. "Anyway, it's a real steal for all that land, the house, and the outbuildings. What's left of the herd, too, I believe. I know Judge downsized pretty extensively in the last few years, but last I heard, he was still running a good two hundred head. Oh, and he's currently got eight or nine bulls, too. There are the two good-sized ponds, and a 5-acre lake—" She broke off, waving a hand as though batting away her words. "But then, you probably know that ranch better than I do. It's gotten a little run down, but otherwise, it hasn't changed much since you left." She swallowed hard, the words stinging the back of her throat on their way out.

For a few moments, he said nothing, just studied her. Faith held his gaze, even though it about killed her to do so. Her skin prickled with the urge to squirm, but she maintained her dignity and kept it together.

"You interested in the place?" he finally asked. "You looking to expand Seven Virtues?"

She shook her head. "I couldn't take all that, even if I wanted to or had the resources to do so. It's all I can do to keep up with what we've got going here. I know of several folks around here who'd love to have just a piece of it—Seven Virtues, included—but Frankie doesn't want to parcel it out if he doesn't have to. And at the price he's selling, he'll move the package deal without too much trouble." She shrugged again like it made no difference to her, but she'd been acutely disappointed when Frankie had explained that he already had a potential buyer.

Cord nodded slowly, but when he brought a hand up to rub the back of his neck, she tensed. He was nervous. That neck grab thing he did, while awfully pretty the way it showed off his muscular arms, was as sure a tell if ever there was one, at least when it came to Cordell Overman. And one she recognized, even after all these years.

A rogue breeze whispered against the damp tendrils of hair clinging to her neck, and Faith lifted her face to it, releasing a long sigh of pleasure. She reached up to hold her hat on, closing her eyes against the brilliant sky, and shot him the same question he'd asked her. "Why? Are you interested in the place, city boy?"

The moment the words left her mouth, she wanted to suck them back in. She suddenly and acutely did not want to look at him for fear of what she might see on his face. She'd asked the question in jest, but now that it was out there, it struck her that Cord's arrival in Plumwood Hollow was quite a coincidence. What if he was back to take a look at his uncle's place?

Have mercy. What if Cordell Overman moved in next door? The thought made her knees go weak.

TWO

Cordell Overman had a really good idea of how a thirsty man felt staring at an oasis in the desert. The moment he laid eyes on her, his mouth went so dry, it almost hurt to swallow. When he tried to speak, he experienced a moment of sheer panic, because his tongue refused to cooperate. His pulse had been racing for two days at the mere thought of seeing Faith Goodacre again, but the real-life version of her literally took his breath away.

The beautiful girl he remembered—dreamed about, pined after, ached for—had become a beautiful woman. Her curves, already lush and feminine back in high school, had filled out in a way that made his palms sweat, and the upward thrust of her chin exposed the pale hollow under her jaw where he used to plant kisses just to hear the sweet noises she made. Those lips—

"I'm going to grab a glass of sweet tea," Faith said abruptly. "Can I—" She stumbled over the words, her cheeks growing pink when she caught him gawking at her. "Can I offer you a glass?"

Was he drooling? He wouldn't be surprised. He ran a hand over his mouth and along his jawline, just in case. He wasn't thinking about Whispering Hills, that was for sure, and from the look on her face, he could tell that *she* could tell exactly what he was thinking.

He glanced away, corralling his wayward thoughts. *I know, I know. But I am just a man, Lord, and you made Faith Goodacre a very fine woman.* He took a slow, steadying breath and counted backward from ten. At four, he braved looking at her again.

She kicked at a clump of tenacious fescue that had rooted itself in the gravel, her head down, her arms crossed tightly over her chest.

Don't shut me out, Faith. "Sure. I'd appreciate a cold drink." His voice held just the slightest rasp, but he cleared his throat, hoping she hadn't noticed. He took a step toward her, and she flinched, shifting backward and tripping over the leg of a sawhorse. When he reached out to steady her, she put an arm up as though to ward off an attack. Withdrawing his hand, he wasn't sure whether to be offended or not. "You all right?"

"Of course." She gestured down the driveway ahead of her. "Shall we?"

When Cord reached out again, she side-stepped a little and glared up at him. "What are you doing?" she asked.

"Just grabbing the flowers." He picked up the jar from where it sat on the rock wall, grinning in spite of her indignant tone. He kinda liked the fact that she didn't seem any more immune to him than he was to her. "I'll carry them for you."

"Oh. Right. Thanks." She turned on her heel and started toward the house, not waiting for him.

He didn't mind, no, indeed. Not when she filled out those jeans the way she did. He paused to take in the wonder of it all.

He was having a hard time remembering why he'd walked away from her in the first place.

"You going to join me, Cordell Overman, or are you just going to stand there ogling my backside all day?"

Cord laughed out loud and caught up to her quickly, his strides sure and long. "How did you know?" he said, intentionally crowding her just a little. He held the jar of flowers out in front of him, careful not to slosh the water on their toes. "You got eyes in the back of your head or something? And here I thought that was just a mom thing." He nudged her with an elbow.

A strange look crossed her face, quickly followed by a scowl. "You were practically burning a hole in my Levis. Cut it out."

"I apologize. You're right. Totally out of line." He meant it, too. Oh, he wanted to stare at her all day, and not just her backside. He wanted to pull her up against him and kiss her until her eyes rolled back in her head. He wanted to— "Stop!"

"What?" Faith jerked to a halt and planted her hands on her hips, glaring up at him once again.

Cord squeezed his eyes shut and shook his head before opening them again. "Never mind. Sorry."

"Wow. Really?" When he only shrugged, she said, "You know, maybe you should just tell me what you need, and we can forget about the tea." She narrowed her eyes at him and waited for his response. "I really do have work to do." The toe of her right foot tapped impatiently, making him smile again.

"And I really could use that sweet tea. Might cool us both down some," he replied, appreciating the high spots of color in her cheeks. "You taking back your offer of hospitality, Miss Goodacre?" He lifted the columbines pointedly and cocked his head to give her a cajoling look. "Even after I brought you your favorite fairy dragon flowers?"

The right side of her mouth twitched just the tiniest bit. She was fighting back a smile, he could tell. A rush of satisfaction coursed through him and he reached out to tweak the brim of her hat. She leaned backward, pulling out of his reach, but her glare had softened. He was getting through to her.

"Then let's go. I don't have all day." She took off again, not bothering to check if he was following or not.

He did not look at her backside. Not directly.

THREE

THEY'D SIT OUTSIDE, FACING the lane so she'd be able to see Pru and Jack coming. With Abby and Jasmine in school for a couple more hours, and Charity and Daddy over in Bowling Green for the day to watch the twins perform their trick riding show for a fundraiser event, the place was quieter than usual on a Wednesday afternoon. Faith didn't want Cord to get any false notions about the two of them being alone.

She knew he was close on her heels, but she didn't wait for him. Sure, it wasn't polite charging ahead like an offended hen the way she was, but Cord had put her off her pace, showing up unannounced like that. Especially when he stood so close that she could smell the cologne he wore; something clean and crisp, like sweet lemonade combined with the tang of fresh cut hay on a hot summer afternoon. She couldn't let him get so close to her again; he was wreaking havoc on her defenses.

She hurried up the wide porch steps and pushed through the screen door into the kitchen. When Jedediah Goodacre moved his troop of women to Plumwood Hollow, he built his home with them in mind. The front door that faced Carpenter Road opened into a large, comfortable family room with exposed ceiling beams and a massive brick fireplace. Four bedrooms and two bathrooms for the girls to share flanked a wide hallway, while Jed and his beloved Caroline's master bedroom had a three-quarter bath so they wouldn't have to fight their way through the throng of daughters to get to the john. But the enormous country kitchen and dining room that took up the whole back section of the house was where the majority of Goodacre home life took place. Sure, they enjoyed their evenings in the family room with its rustic furnishings, books, and these days, the large, flat-screen TV, but any work that needed doing, be it schoolwork, church work, or ranch work, not to mention all the cooking and eating that went on, happened in the kitchen.

Faith tossed her hat on the butcher block island and pulled open the freezer door. Shoving her head inside, she sighed at the blast of chilly air, fervently praying that Cord would mistake the high color in her cheeks for too much time in the sun.

"Do you need any help, or shall I wait out here for you?"

She jerked in surprise, bumping her head on the top of the freezer. "Sweet cheese and crackers!" She rubbed the spot with one hand while she grabbed the ice bin with the other, letting the door swing closed as she turned to look at him.

Cord stood framed in the doorway, the screen softening his features a little. It didn't matter; she knew every angle, every groove, the line of his jaw, the arch of his brow. Sure, he'd matured, and those same lines and angles had become more chiseled and defined, but it was still the face of the man she'd once loved even more than herself. A thousand times, and a thousand more, she'd imagined him standing just so, grinning at her the way he always did, waiting for her to open the door and welcome him into the heart of the Goodacre home.

"Sweet cheese... and—?" He left the phrase hanging for effect.

She shrugged, trying to pull off nonchalance. "You know we don't cuss in this house." She rubbed the top of her head and added, "That hurt bad enough to warrant one, though. Knocked my teeth together."

"I'm sorry. I didn't mean to startle you," he said.

"Never mind." She shooed him off. "Go grab a seat. If I want help, I'll ask for it." The second the words were out, she wanted to suck them back in.

To his credit, Cord didn't even shoot her a what-did-I-tell-you look. Instead, he simply said, "Holler if you need me," and ambled off toward a grouping of patio furniture, the same table and chairs that had been there since shortly after the porch was built. She and Cord had whiled away many long summer hours at that table.

Assaulted by memories, her traitorous heart hollered in need of him, all right. But thank the good Lord above, she was the only one who could hear it.

She needed to get her wayward thoughts and roller coaster emotions in check, and puttering around the comfortable kitchen always grounded her, even if she wasn't much of a cook. Faith took her time loading a pretty painted tray with a pitcher of the amber brew and three glasses—one for Prudence, she'd make a point of saying—along with several napkins and a plate of Charity's hearty oatmeal applesauce muffins.

An old oval mirror hung on the wall next to the refrigerator, and she checked her reflection before picking up the tray and heading out. To her surprise, she didn't look too awful. In fact, the flush of color in her cheeks accented her bright green eyes quite nicely, if she said so herself.

With her hip, she nudged the screen door open and crossed the porch to the table where Cord waited. All good manners and charm, he stood when she approached, studying her openly, making her nervous all over again.

"What?" she said, feeling awkward under his perusal. "Do I have something in my teeth?"

Cord shook his head slowly, one side of his mouth curving up. "It's just good to see you, Faith. I mean it in all sincerity. Really good."

"Oh. Well. Thanks." She felt a rush of heat that turned her cheeks warm. Settling the tray on the table, she deflected his focus from her to the treats. "Don't worry; Charity made the muffins, not me. And of course, they're delicious. A staple around here."

"I'm not worried." Cord accepted the glass she handed him, not saying a word when she fumbled a little in her attempt to avoid touching him. Was he truly as unaffected by all this as he seemed? "Thank you, Faith." Even the way he said her name; it was like he'd wrapped the single syllable in seduction.

"Of course. Please, sit." She pulled her chair in a little closer to the table, grimacing when she knocked her knee into one of the table legs. The flowers bobbed and dipped playfully, almost like they were laughing at her. "Help yourself," she said, waving at the muffins. She'd probably drop one in his lap if she tried to dish him up.

Cord waited until she chose one first, then took a bite of his own. "Wow," he said after a few moments. "These are amazing."

"Yeah. I swear baking is Charity's spiritual gift."

"Baking is a spiritual gift, hm?"

"Sure, it is. If you read your Bible, Mr. Overman, you'd know that," she teased.

"That's the thing, Miss Goodacre. I do read it, and I don't recall baking being on any of St. Paul's lists."

"Well, suffice it to say that if it were a spiritual gift, it would be Charity's." She shot him a sidelong glance. "So does that mean we'll be seeing you in church on Sunday?" In spite of her light-hearted tone, she desperately hoped he'd say no. This Sunday was a big day for their family, and Faith wasn't sure she could handle the strain of having him show up. She was so distracted trying to come up with a good enough reason to play hooky from morning worship—one her father would accept, at any rate—that she almost missed his response.

"Actually, I'm heading home this weekend. Spending Mother's Day with my mom." His features softened as he looked past Faith in the general direction of Louisville. In the best sense of the word, Cord was a Mama's boy. Faith had never heard him speak a negative word about his mother, and although she'd only met the woman once, seeing their mutual love and respect for each other had made her heart ache over the loss of her own mother in her life.

"Does she know you're here?" It was only a few hours' drive to Louisville, so it made perfect sense for him to head home to spend the special day with her.

"She does." He didn't expound, and although she was becoming more curious by the minute about his reasons for being in town, Faith kept her questions to herself. The fact that his mother knew he was there, however, made his visit feel all the more official.

"I'll be back next week, though," Cord added. "And you'll be seeing me in church on Sunday, sure as sunshine. Eighth row back, just like old times." He took a long draw on his tea, then asked, "Will I see you there? Or are you going to boycott church if I show up?"

Had he read her mind? "You know the Goodacres. There every Sunday, come Hell or high water." She smirked. "Or downed fences, sick calves, coyotes. You know how it is."

He nodded. "I remember. It's good to know there are some things in this life a man can always count on." He smiled warmly at her, a slow, country boy smile, drawing her attention to his well-defined lips, and the way the top one protruded just the slightest bit over the bottom. She knew deep in her heart that his words were meant as a compliment, but the emotions they stirred up in her were making her want to crawl out of her skin.

Or crawl across the table and scratch his eyes out.

Or crawl across the table and kiss him until she forgot all the misery she'd suffered since the last time they'd sat on this porch together.

She would not think about kissing him. She tore her gaze away from his mouth.

She would think instead about those weeks, months, *years* of sitting in church between her stern father and one of her sisters, offering her broken and battered heart to Jesus, knowing that Cord's seat in the row right behind hers remained empty.

At that moment, Jack came into view, bounding up the lane toward the house. Faith stood, relieved at the distraction, and moved to stand at the top of the porch steps. She clapped her hands in greeting. "Hey, Jack!" she called out. "Here, boy!"

The dog kicked it up a notch, lengthening his stride and barking joyfully in response. Behind him, several yards back, came Prudence, dawdling along at her own pace, her egg basket looped over one arm as she walked along the edge of the lane. She paused now and then to pick a flower or collect a stone.

Prudence glanced up toward the porch when she heard Faith's call. She waved enthusiastically. "Hello!" she called out. "I see you found her, Cord!"

After greeting Jack with affectionate ear scratches and baby talk, Faith stood again, eyeing the slow progression of her sister. Pretty as a picture, Faith thought. A colorful ring of greenery and flowers perched on the girl's head, and her bright yellow sundress swished from side to side as she moved. Even her worn cowboy boots looked whimsical and artsy, simply because of the person who wore them.

Faith glanced down at her own feet and frowned. She could see a clump of cow manure clinging to the side of one of her boots. Nice. Hopefully, she hadn't left bits and pieces of it in the kitchen; Charity would have her hide for it.

Jack headed for his water bowl and loudly lapped up a drink before crossing over to nudge Cord with his wet snout. It was apparent that the dog had already taken stock of him today since he didn't perform his usual circuitous sniffing ritual with which he typically greeted newcomers.

"Hey, boy." Cord didn't push the dog away, even though Jack left a slobbery patch on his jeans.

The man was getting too comfortable. And as much as Faith wanted Prudence around to ease the tension in the air, her younger sister's presence would also make it more difficult to get to the bottom of why he was here in the first place. In a low voice, she asked, "So is that really all you came here for, Cord? The current goings-on over at Whispering Hills Ranch? Or did you just come over here to rile me up?" She needed to know.

"Truth be told, that was just polite conversation," he said, rising to his feet and coming to stand beside her. She could feel him looking at her. "I figured you already knew about Whispering Hills."

"So, you came all the way out here just to rile me up, then." She widened her stance in an attempt to look immune to his nearness. Too many emotions were jockeying for position inside her, and she knew there was nothing like manual labor to set her mind straight. She'd leave her sister to entertain him, and she'd ride hard for the far pasture to check on the upgraded watering system. She'd put in some new pipe last week, extending the line a good hundred yards beyond where the old one capped. Getting water farther out allowed for better use of that section of pasture, and so far, there were no leaks, and the water pressure seemed unchanged. "Fine. You've succeeded. Now I've got to get back to work. Prudence is a much better hostess than I am; she'll make you feel welcome." She elbowed him in the side, then berated herself for touching him again. "She might even give you that hug you were hoping for."

"She already did."

"Right. Of course, she did." The thought of the pretty Prudence enfolded in Cordell Overman's embrace caused a bittersweet taste in her mouth.

Cord crossed his arms and added, "But hers wasn't the hug I was hoping for."

There went another one of her hard-won defenses, crumbling to ruins around her heart. "Don't do that," she murmured. She spun away from him and headed inside the kitchen with her empty tea glass. She'd leave the rest of the tray for Prudence to take care of. Taking a deep breath, she snatched up her hat from the butcher block and shoved it down on her head, then gave herself a bolstering look in the mirror before heading back outside.

Cord was still standing at the top of the steps where she left him, and when she drew near, he said, "So you're saying I got you riled up, then." There was a cocky grin in his voice, but to her surprise, the sound of it soothed her spirit. Trust Cord to take the awkward edge off the situation by making light of it. She bit her bottom lip to keep her own smile from making an appearance.

"So, you're saying you want me to kick your backside into next Thursday, then?" she shot back. She had to look away; he knew her too well, and he'd do his best to goad a laugh out of her, especially once he figured out how close she was to breaking.

Prudence approached the porch and smiled back and forth between them. "I'll put these in the kitchen," she said after a moment, holding up her egg basket, apparently sensing that she'd interrupted something. She brushed by Faith and mouthed, "You okay?"

Faith dipped her head quickly in response, then flashed a bright smile at Cord, hoping he hadn't caught the exchange. He seemed unaware, his attention on Jack who lay sprawled on his side at his feet, legs akimbo. Cord obligingly rubbed the dog's belly with the rounded toe of his boot.

He waited until the screen door thwacked closed behind Prudence, then moved to lean against the porch rail, his arms crossed loosely in front of him. He grinned at Faith, his deep-set eyes crinkling with mischief and challenge. "Next Thursday, hm? Those are fightin' words, Miss Goodacre. Think you can take me, do you?"

"You know it, Mr. Overman. Any time. Any day. Any place. Any way."

He nodded along with her chant; it was one he'd heard her spout a dozen or more times when they were younger. But back then, he'd been acknowledging her hold on his heart. Now, she was pretty sure he was only pushing her buttons.

"You'd best take her seriously, Cordell Overman!" Prudence sang out from inside the kitchen. "Tough as nails and meaner than bootstrap moonshine, our Faith. And with six sisters to back her up, you don't stand a chance. She can take you, all right." Her bubbly laugh drifted out to them, but the sound of running water indicated she wasn't in any rush to rejoin them.

"Thank you, Prudence. I'll remember that," Cord called back to her. Then he straightened, stepped right up close to Faith, and lowered his voice. "Cuz you should know, Faith Goodacre, that I'm back in Plumwood Hollow to stay, and I'm here for the taking."

Faith couldn't breathe. She couldn't swallow, and she couldn't come up with anything even remotely flippant to say. But she stood her ground, refusing to be intimidated. Or to let him know that she was.

Cord nudged the brim of her hat up, but when he brushed her cheek with the backs of his knuckles, she turned her face away.

Why did he have to seem so… so blatantly interested in her? And not just like he was interested in what she'd done with herself since they'd last seen each other, or curious about her take on his uncle's place next door. It wasn't even the look of a man sizing up which parts of her well-endowed body were real or not; *that* kind of expression she was accustomed to and could dismiss for the ignorance and bad manners it was. No, he was staring at her like a hardworking man eyeing a bowl of Charity's hearty beef stew after a long winter's day spent in the saddle. Every nerve ending in her body was buzzing with awareness.

"Cut it out, Cord," she said, her voice soft and serious. He'd been gone too long, and too much had changed. "I mean it."

In a quandary, she waited to see what move he'd make. If she turned away, he'd get a clear shot of her hindquarters, and although she wasn't ashamed of the extra bit of cushion the Good Lord gave her, she knew better than to turn her back on a hunter. Especially as it seemed she was the prey. But if she just stood there, he might think she welcomed his advances, and she knew better than to open that door again.

To her surprise, Cord moved to settle into the chair he'd occupied before Prudence showed up. "I'm not here to force myself on you."

"That's good of you," she said, rather dryly.

He kept smiling, ignoring her sarcasm. "But you should know that I plan on doing my best to win back your heart."

Faith's eyes widened at his bold statement, but she kept her teeth clenched so her jaw wouldn't drop.

As casual as Sunday afternoon, Cord topped off his sweet tea and filled the third glass Faith had brought out for Prudence. "And I'm not ashamed to make a fool of myself, if that's what it takes."

"Well, you're doing a fine job of it, that's for sure," she retorted.

He kept right on going. "And you should also know that I may not be as—what did Prudence call you? Bootstrap moonshine mean?—as your reputation claims you are. All of which I have a hard time believing, by the way," he added, reaching over the arm of his chair to scratch the top of Jack's head.

"This is the most ridiculous conversation ever." She was practically sputtering.

"You might as well let me finish, because I intend to, one way or the other," Cord drawled. "Cuz I'm as stubborn as the day is long."

"I won't argue with—"

"Faith Goodacre," Cord interrupted, shaking his head. "You'd still argue with a fence post, wouldn't you?"

She glared at him, her mouth opening and closing like a sunfish stranded on a riverbank.

He leaned back in his chair and cocked his head to look at her, that slow smile softening his features.

"Well, you'd still aggravate a rock!" she fumed, her fists clenching at her sides. "That certainly hasn't changed one bit."

"And you're still beautiful when you're riled up. Something else that hasn't changed."

"Come on, Jack." She slapped her thigh, and Jack leaped to his feet to frolic in anticipation around her legs. "We're leaving." She had to sidestep quickly to avoid tripping over him as she headed down the steps.

"And I'm staying," Cord shot back, his voice ringing in her ears even as she hurried away. "That's the real reason I came all the way out here. I thought it only right that you should hear it from me."

FOUR

CORD WATCHED HER WALK away. Or rather, flounce away. Surely, that's what it meant to flounce. Her full hips swung wider than usual, her arms practically flailing from the momentum, and her shoulder-length brown curls bounced angrily from under the rim of her hat. Oh, yeah. He'd riled her up good.

Just like she'd done to him.

Even though he'd spent the last few days working up the guts to pay a visit to Seven Virtues Ranch, Cord hadn't been prepared for his reaction to seeing her in person. When she'd turned around to size him up, her shoulders glistening in the sunshine where they were exposed by the tank top she wore, and her chin lifted like the queen of Sheba, it had felt like a mule kick to the chest. He'd taken his time getting out of the truck just to recover, both from the impact and from the shock of his inappropriate greeting.

He grimaced as he gazed down into his tea glass. Why in the blazes had his first words to her been so crude? A hard-working woman in a worn pair of jeans? He sounded like an arrogant, chauvinistic pig. A class act buffoon.

It certainly wasn't what he'd planned to say. Oh, he'd waffled between a few variations of "Miss Goodacre, it sure is good to see you again," but he'd secretly had every hope that she'd throw herself into his arms and kiss the need for words right out of him.

That's the way it might have happened in the past.

Because Faith Goodacre knew how to kiss a man senseless.

He wasn't stupid enough to believe it would go down like that, but he'd secretly hoped for it, nonetheless.

That said, he wasn't completely disappointed, either. Clearly, the past they'd shared still sizzled between them. Oh, it might have lain dormant inside her for the last ten years, but he'd seen it spark to life in her eyes the moment she recognized him.

The look on her face had taken his breath away. And filled his chest—that place that had been so empty for too long—with hope.

"You blew it, didn't you?" Prudence asked, pushing open the screen door to join him at the table. The young woman was pretty as a picture with her spiky hair framing her wide, gentle eyes. They weren't sun tea colored like Faith's, Cord noticed; Prudence's were the color of a pale winter sky, and tilted up a little, giving her a dreamy, otherworldly appeal that soothed a person's spirit just looking at her. The last time he'd seen Prudence, she must've been only eight or nine years old. She still looked more child than woman, but something about the straightforward way she watched him led him to believe she had wisdom beyond her years.

He handed her the glass of tea he'd poured for her. "I hope not," he said with candor. Faith's reaction made him think of a Midwestern summer storm, blowing in and blustering through, only to leave crystal clear skies and rain-drenched refreshment in its wake. That's what he was hoping for—praying for—with the eldest Miss Goodacre. He longed for the washed clean second chance that would surely come if he waited out the deluge.

Prudence dropped into a chair opposite him. "Did I hear you right? You're back in the hollow to stay?"

"That's my plan." He wasn't sure how much to share with her; he didn't want Faith to hear about his plans from anyone but himself.

Prudence nodded, but like her sister, she didn't push for details. She slid the plate of muffins close and took great care selecting which one she wanted. She studied him openly as she methodically broke off and ate one tiny piece at a time.

Finally, unable to bear the weight of her stare any longer, he cleared his throat and said, "So what are you up to these days? You going to college?"

She smiled brightly and shook her head. "Oh, goodness, no. I don't do so well in a classroom setting. I'm a hands-on girl, you know? I need to touch and taste and smell, to take things in if I'm going to learn about them. Quite literally," she said with a smile, plucking one of the columbines from its stem and popping it into her mouth.

"Whoa." Cord's eyebrows shot up. "I thought those were toxic."

"The flowers of this species are quite tasty, especially when you get some of the nectar. A spicy and sweet combo, they're best early in the blooming season. But you're right about the rest of the plant; definitely, don't eat those leaves. Your gastrointestinal tract won't thank you."

"I'll remember that." He found it easy to relax in the girl's presence. She was still the little imp he remembered, but with a whole lot more depth and self-assuredness, the kind that comes with reaching adulthood not completely unscathed, he thought. He wondered what had put that fathomless look in her eyes. He wondered why a girl like her would choose to hide away on her daddy's land, especially when she obviously wasn't in love with ranching, at least not the way Faith was.

As though she'd read his thoughts, she sighed softly and looked past him to the expanse of the pasture that dipped away from the house beyond the barn. "Right now, I'm just making myself useful where I can. It's keeping me busy enough while I try to figure out what I'm going to do with my life." She said it as though she had all the time in the world to do just that.

To Cord, the notion was completely foreign. In the world he'd been raised in, there were no handouts, no freebies, and no waiting around to figure things out. His father, Dalton Overman, had amassed a fortune in the corporate world of fast-food chains, and he'd done it with hard work and savvy business dealings. He expected no less of his son. He'd required Cord to work every summer once he started high school. After graduation, he'd had two options; go to college full time or go to work full time.

The long hours of working those summers on his uncle's massive Whispering Hills Ranch, however, had been some of the best times of his life. Not only had he fallen in love with horses and hard labor and teamwork, but he'd also fallen in love with Faith Goodacre.

Prudence drew the jar of columbines closer to her, turning it this way and that to study the flowers. "You know, Faith says these remind her of little dragon faces. Don't you love that?"

Cord chuckled softly. It was rather unsettling the way she seemed to follow his train of thought. "She once told me the same thing."

"She did?" Prudence grinned at him, apparently surprised that her sister had divulged as much to him. Maybe she couldn't read his mind after all. "She's such a realist, you know? A ducks in a row, just the facts, bullet points kind of girl. So, it's nice to see a little whimsy from her now and then." She bent forward to smell the flowers. "It's pretty rare these days," she added.

He frowned. "That doesn't sound like the Faith I know." Nights out under the stars, imagining faraway lands and alternate universes. Long, meandering rides as they talked of adventures that they might one day share. The home they would build together, the life they would create together, and the world they would change together. Dragons, knights in shining armor, and galaxies far, far away, were standard fare for Faith Goodacre.

"Maybe the Faith you knew," Prudence offered, her tone gentle, but the look in her eyes had grown quite serious. "Sometimes people change, Cord."

"Not that much," he countered, refusing to believe that the girl he'd fallen for no longer existed. "Circumstances may motivate a change in behavior, but that's not the same thing."

She popped another piece of her muffin into her mouth and chewed slowly, as though seriously contemplating his words. "I don't know that I agree with you," she finally said. "It's the circumstances in our lives, the things beyond our control, especially, that bend us, mold us, and redirect us. If we don't break, we change. We have to."

She spoke from experience, Cord was certain, and it made his chest tighten in sympathy. What had happened to her? "I'd like to think the Faith who saw sailing ships in clouds and dragon faces in flowers is still alive and well."

"Oh, she's there, all right. It's just not who she is anymore." Prudence emphasized the word 'is' as though that explained everything. After a few moments, she expounded. "The way I see it, we're all made up of bits and pieces of ourselves, like a big jigsaw puzzle. That Faith you once knew, the teenager who looked for magic and miracles? That girl is just one piece of the puzzle of who Faith is now. You can't say you know a person just because you know that one piece really well. When you step back and see the whole picture, and where that piece fits into the grand scheme...." She shrugged, letting the words trail off.

"I think I understand." Cord nodded and slid his chair back, suddenly unsettled by the candid conversation. It occurred to him in that moment that he was missing something, an important piece to the puzzle that was Faith. Yesterday at the bank, he'd run into Tanner Baucom, one of the guys who'd worked alongside him at the ranch that last summer after high school. He'd barely gotten a greeting and a handshake out before Tanner had asked if he'd been by to see Faith yet. And when he'd said no, it hadn't taken a genius to tell that Tanner was doing his best to wrap up the conversation in short order.

Then later that afternoon at the gas station, old Harv had greeted him with the same snaggle-toothed grin he'd had a decade ago. "Well, hey there, Cord. What brings you back to the holler?" Without waiting for an answer, he'd started filling Cord's fuel tank, then nodded in the general direction of Seven Virtues. "You talk to that Goodacre girl since you been back?" Cord had assured the old guy he had every intention of doing so the next day, and Harv had nodded sagely. "Good for you, son. It's about time."

Cord hadn't connected the two exchanges until just now, sitting across from Prudence, the look on her face indicating there were things not being said, things he should know about. He knew just the person to ask.

"I'd best be going," he began, sweeping a few crumbs from the table into his cupped palm, then brushing them off onto his plate.

Before he could rise, Prudence said, "I remember you better than you think I do, Cordell Overman." Her tone remained genial, her posture relaxed, but something in her voice made him pause. She took her sweet time finishing her last bite of muffin and wiped her fingers on a napkin before taking a sip of tea. Everything she did was so precise and intentional, and her behavior seemed at such odds with the free spirit he'd thought she was. "I may have only been a kid, but I remember the way my big sister looked at you. The way you looked at her."

He tried to relax back into the seat again, wondering where this was leading. He nodded and chose his words carefully. "I remember you, too, Prudence. You may have grown up, but to me, you still look the same." He grimaced. That didn't come out quite the way he meant it to. What was wrong with him? It wasn't like him to be so crass and insensitive. He opened his mouth to clarify, but she spoke first.

"Rather ironic. Because to me, you still look the same, too." She smiled, but her words were weighted and sober, belying her casual expression. "People do change, Cord. At least, they should. It's called growing up. Have you? Because I assure you; Faith is not the girl you walked away from all those years ago."

"Whoa. You know, that's not exactly—" He broke off, rethinking his response. Apparently, Faith wasn't the only one who remembered things differently than he did.

"A whole lot has changed around here," Prudence added.

Was Cord only imagining things, or was there a hint of warning in her tone?

He nodded slowly, taking a few extra moments to try and decipher what she was really saying. Sure, folks had gotten a little older, the surrounding farms and ranches had adjusted to the whims of mother nature and the ever-shifting economic climate, and there were two new shops in the little town square that he didn't remember from before, plus a few that had closed down. But in general, as far as he could tell, the hands of time in Plumwood Hollow moved a lot slower than they did in Lexington, where he'd called home for the last decade. The fact that all but one of the good-looking Goodacre girls were still single was either a testament to the pace in the hollow or perhaps to the sternness of the family patriarch, Jedediah Goodacre. Regardless, from what he could tell, remarkably little had changed in this neck of the woods.

"Why haven't you been back before now?" Prudence asked, the strange inflection still there, her clear gaze locked on his. "I mean, you didn't even show up for your uncle's funeral, as I recall."

"No, I didn't. I was—detained." Off in the distance, he heard a familiar burst of sound—Faith's warrior princess battle cry, he used to call it—and an answering volley of barks that could only be Jack. He caught himself scanning the pasture for a glimpse of her, half-expecting her to come sweeping across the open field into view. He shook his head and turned back to Prudence. "Unavoidably detained."

"So, it had nothing to do with my big sister? You don't still have a thing for her?"

"Aren't you direct?" Cord chuckled softly, and then he stood. It was definitely time to go. But he smiled down at her when he said, "Truth be told, Miss Prudence, every decision I have made since meeting her has had at least a little something to do with your big sister." He shook his jeans down over his boots, took one last long swallow of his tea, and returned the glass to the tray. Prudence just watched him, her fingers moving slowly, hypnotically, as she traced invisible circles on the tablecloth. "Thanks for the company. Would you like me to take this inside?"

Prudence stopped him with a wave of her hand. "Leave it. I'll sit here and wait for Faith to get back from wherever she rode off to all helter-skelter. We've got a chicken tractor to construct."

Oddly enough, when Prudence turned down his offer to help, it felt nothing like when Faith did.

She reached out to tap the Mason jar of flowers with a metallic blue fingernail. "Tread lightly, Cord. For your own sake, as well as Faith's. There's more at stake here than you know."

He nodded slowly, touched his forehead in a two-finger salute, then headed back to his truck.

FIVE

THE WIND WHISTLED PAST her ears in a rush of sound that didn't quite drown out Cord's words of... of what? Warning? Threat? Promise? What did it all mean? Was it possible he'd only come back to the hollow for her? Or was he here, as she suspected, for another reason altogether, and simply hoped to rekindle things between them for the sake of having a good time while in town? She knew all about reputations, and his wasn't any prettier than hers used to be. A player, the media called him. In every aspect of the word.

She'd worked hard to clear her name of the sins of her past. The last time she'd allowed herself to look him up online, Cordell Overman was working hard to keep his bad reputation in good standing.

Faith's heart raced at the thought of having to fend off his advances, especially since it had just become abundantly clear that she was no more immune to them now than she'd been back in high school.

She followed the tree line, staying to the outskirts of the first pasture so that she wouldn't draw attention from anyone at the house. She assumed Cord and Prudence were still sitting on the porch. "You'd think I'd be used to folks talking about me by now," she grumbled into the wind. Shoving her hat down tighter on her head, she gave Watson a firm nudge with her heels, urging the quarter horse to lengthen his stride, now that they were out of the line of sight of the house. They cut across the end of the pasture at full gallop to circle the largest of their three ponds. Bending low over Watson's neck, Faith whooped with exhilaration; there was no way anyone could ride a horse in a flat-out run without experiencing elation.

Jack fell behind, barking in frustration as he, too, lengthened his stride. "Come on, Jack!" she hollered, encouraging the dog to follow along, even when she and Watson crested the knoll overlooking the next pasture, and started down the other side. The dog barked in response, and Faith whooped again.

This was where she belonged. These wide-open spaces and rolling pastures interlaced with fingers of woodland that turned the land into an earthen quilt. Where she and Watson and Jack could run and ride and forget, even if only for a few minutes, all the ups and downs, the hills and valleys that made up her life. Where she could keep at bay the memories that encroached on the edges of this little piece of heaven that she'd worked so hard to forge for her sisters, for her stern, but beloved father, and for Jasmine.

Especially for Jasmine.

And she would move heaven and earth to defend their little kingdom. Or queendom, according to Jasmine.

She smiled at the sight of the healthy herd of Dexters grazing peacefully in their cordoned-off paddock. It had been a stellar spring calving season, and the last cow had finally delivered just yesterday. Having a veterinarian in the family was a major coup, and because of Hope's quick, capable hands, they hadn't lost a single baby this go-around. It was one of the busiest times of the year for Hope; calving season meant little sleep for any rancher, but especially for a rancher who also happened to be only one of two big animal vets in a hundred miles.

Two of their first-calf heifers had initially rejected their little ones, and the pairs had been isolated in a couple of paddocks close to the barn so they could be monitored and helped along as needed. One duo took no more than twenty-four hours to acclimate to each other, and they'd been released back into the herd a few days later. The second pair proved to be a bit more troublesome, the new mama something of a bully at first, head-butting and kicking at the calf when it approached to nurse. Faith had resorted to tying the cow up and feeding her as a distraction so the calf could get to her mama's milk-swollen udder without injury. Up until just yesterday, Faith had been considering the possibility of bottle-feeding the calf, which would mean hours of extra work every day with round-the-clock feedings. But last night, when she'd gone to check on them, she'd been elated to see the baby nursing boisterously and the new mama turning her head to nudge and encourage the little thing. This morning, the two were inseparable. Faith would give them another few days to solidify the bond, then incorporate them back into the herd as well. She felt like a proud mama, herself.

She was also glad to be finished with banding and ear-tagging, one of the less appealing aspects of calving season. Although Faith and her sisters did not enjoy the process of tying off testicles or punching tag pins through tender little ears, they were quick and efficient about it, and Faith loved to look out over the herd and see all their prized Dexters clearly labeled and accounted for.

Faith had made a name for herself with her Dexters, a small, but hardy Irish breed with a huge meat conversion rate. She'd become the quintessential craft rancher, and she now sold her organic grass-fed cattle primarily to whole-beast butchers and private buyers who wanted to know exactly what they were selling, serving, and eating. Some of her favorite customers, however, were the families who stopped by her pens during the fall festival looking for a family milk cow. Because Dexters were considered dual purpose, they were a terrific choice for those customers. They weren't huge producers compared to the popular dairy breeds like Jerseys or Guernseys, but the Dexter cow's one-and-a-half-to-two gallons daily production was just perfect for a family, and the diminutive size and friendly personality of the breed made it ideal for children.

Seven Virtues Ranch had come a long way since Jedediah Goodacre moved his family to Plumwood Hollow. The man grew up on a cattle ranch in Texas, where land was plentiful, and pastures stretched on for as far as the eye could see. Ranches consisted of acres by the thousands, only a few trees now and then to break up the uninterrupted vistas of grassland.

Or to draw down the lightning during the rampaging summer storms.

It was after a long stretch of drought years in Texas, coupled with rising medical bills for his wife, however, that Jed decided to cut his losses and sell his barren land and stock for what he could get out with. Then he uprooted his wife and children — there were five daughters at the time — and moved them to a part of the country where land was a little harder to come by, at least in large quantities, but the grass truly was greener, and they'd live close to a doctor who thought he could help Caroline. Through a ranching connection, Jed purchased a decent piece of land and a few starter cows from Judge Flanner, and over the first couple of years in Plumwood Hollow, he slowly built up his herd by purchasing bred cows from local auctions and private sellers.

He had a good eye for prime stock, and a lifetime of knowledge about the care and feeding of beef cattle, but Jed brought with him his great big Texas methods to the small West Kentucky farm country, and for years, he struggled to make things work in his new, scaled-down world. When his beloved Caroline, already weakened by her deficient immune system, died from complications a year after the birth of their seventh daughter, Jed just about hung up his hat. Over the next few years, it was all he could do not to buckle under the burden of his heavy load and heavier heart.

Faith, the eldest daughter, was twelve when her mother died, and already far too mature for her age. Accustomed to helping out with all her younger sisters because of her mother's prolonged illness, she refused to let the family come apart, assigning duties militarily to each of the girls to keep Social Services from knocking on their door.

Betina Flanner from Whispering Hills next door made it her personal mission to see to the girls' welfare—that's what neighbors were for—and every time she came visiting, it never ceased to amaze her how well things ran at Seven Virtues. She had no reservations about telling the caseworker to mind his own business, and for that, Faith was grateful. She could handle caring for her grieving father and six sisters, but she wasn't quite old enough or brave enough to tell off the nosy government official.

It was a research project during Faith's senior year in high school where she discovered the merits of rotational grazing and her whole perspective on raising beef cattle changed. She knew she'd found a way to revive Seven Virtues Ranch, if only she could convince her father that her methods would prove far more fruitful than his more traditional ones, at least on the smaller acreage on which they operated in the Midwest.

It had taken her two years to sell him on it, and he'd been skeptical at first, even a little derogatory, but when she wouldn't give up, he finally allowed her to experiment... but only with cows she purchased with her own money.

It wasn't long before he saw evidence that her methods worked; her results were phenomenal in comparison to his. Not only were her animals happier and healthier, so was the land her small herd of Dexters grazed.

It was when she discovered dung beetles in the part of the ranch that she managed that had finally convinced Jed; it had been years since they'd seen the industrious, highly beneficial little creatures in his pastures, and their return signaled a return of nature's balance to their land.

But that fall, right after Faith turned twenty-one, tragedy struck. While clearing brush from around the edge of the east pasture, the front wheel of Jed's tractor climbed up a too tough sapling, and the machine rolled, taking him down under it. Faith found him a couple of hours later, his left arm resting against his abdomen at an odd angle because of a dislocated shoulder, and his right leg pinned beneath the tractor. The shattered thigh bone required a series of surgeries to repair the extensive damage, followed by several weeks in a rehabilitation facility before he was released to come home under strict guidelines and limitations. It was during this time that Faith took over running the ranch.

Much to her surprise and pleasure, Jed encouraged her to aggressively implement her methods in his absence. "The way I see it, Faith, the good Lord might have knocked me off that tractor Himself just to get me to shut up and listen to what I already knew in my heart. I can see that you know what you're doing—you're a smart girl, just like your mother—but I was too busy being a stubborn old man to admit it outright. So, He took me out of the picture in order to give you a chance to take Seven Virtues for a spin." He insisted that she keep him apprised of every detail while he convalesced, but each change she incorporated came with heartfelt support from her father.

By the following spring calving season, Jed was up and around enough to participate in some of the less strenuous activities, such as taking shifts in the round-the-clock bottle-feeding of an orphaned calf, record-keeping, and making sure his daughters were fed and watered themselves. Faith took great pride in showing her father all that she'd accomplished in the months he'd been out of commission.

Over the next few years, they worked together to methodically transition their herd from a mix-and-match selection of standard beef cattle to the purebred Dexters, fine-tuning the whole operation to maximize pasture yield while minimizing stress to both the herd and the land. Although her system required more time spent with the cows on a daily basis, that consistent interaction allowed for much easier management of their stock. She was familiar with each animal by sight and could immediately tell if anything was wrong, and the herd was accustomed to her and her sisters on their horses, moving in and among them, accompanied by Jack. The cows even came when called. When it was time to move the herd from one paddock to another, Faith simply opened up the temporary fencing, hollered out for a fat old girl named Sassy, the first breeder that Faith had purchased with her own money, and once the dame started heading for the new grass, the rest of the herd followed. Sure, every once in a while, Jack got to show his colors when the cows decided to do their own thing, but most of the time, Faith's system ran like clockwork.

The benefits of the system weren't just evident to Faith and her family, and over the last few years, she'd been asked to share about her techniques with local farming and ranching communities, at high school career days, FFA and 4-H events, and more.

No longer did people point and whisper, their lips pursed in censure at her and Jasmine; they smiled and waved, calling out warm welcomes instead. When Judge Flanner, himself, came over one gorgeous Sunday afternoon last fall and asked her to explain her grazing system to him, Faith felt like she'd won the lottery. But a few weeks before Thanksgiving, Judge suffered a fatal heart attack, and the community grieved his loss as though he were royalty. The man was, indeed, a pillar in Plumwood Hollow, as much a landmark as the post office or the Glory to God Community Church downtown.

Unfortunately, Judge Flanner's passing left Whispering Hills Ranch without a rancher. Frank Junior's name was on the will, to be sure.

However, Frankie was a good man who happened to be a decent rancher, but a far better soldier.

Although Faith understood Frankie's desire to sell the ranch as a single unit, it still frustrated her to no end that she couldn't take a couple of dozen acres off his hands. Her herd was pushing capacity for what she felt was reasonable on the acreage the Goodacres had, and Faith ached at the thought of the Flanner land next door slipping through her fingers.

Especially if it was going to go to some big-money outsider who had the means to purchase the place outright. She couldn't help wondering what kind of neighbor they'd be getting; it was the stuff of nightmares, truth be told.

The possibility of it being purchased by Cordell Overman didn't make it any less terrifying.

SIX

CORD PULLED INTO THE parking lot of the church he'd attended with the Flanners every summer during his high school years. He hadn't seen Reverend Treadwell or his ageless secretary, Trudy Huckster, since he'd left town almost a decade ago. But according to the marquee out front, both of them were still at it. Below the pastor's name and the church service times were the words, "Forbidden fruit creates some nasty jams." Trudy loved her cheesy church marquee sayings; the sassier, the better. Cord was looking forward to seeing them both, and hoped he'd get a warmer reception in God's house than he had at the Goodacre place.

"Glory be, if it isn't young Cordell!" Trudy clapped her hands in delight when he entered the church office. "Get over here and give me some sugar!" She pushed to her feet with no little effort—the woman was about as round as she was tall—and bustled around her frighteningly organized desk to throw her arms around him. She smelled like wild honey and shortbread, the same as she always had, and Cord felt his shoulders relax a little. One more thing that hadn't changed. "Toby! Get out here and see what I got!" she bellowed, making Cord flinch, her voice reverberating around the room in exclamation marks. That hadn't changed, either.

"What is all the ruckus out here?" The reverend came through the door of his office, reading glasses still perched on his nose. When he saw Cord, his concerned expression dissolved behind a wide smile of welcome. "Well, well, well. Cord Overman. What a pleasure it is to see you, young man." He removed his glasses and stepped forward, but instead of taking Cord's outstretched hand, he, too, enveloped him in a manly hug, complete with three solid back slaps. Reverend Tobias Treadwell was quite tall, but skinny as a whip. Even so, Cord could feel the tensile strength in the man's lean stature, and he returned the hug without reservation. "What brings you to our little hollow?"

"It's been too long, young man," Trudy quipped before Cord could respond, then she took his hand and squeezed it with her soft, plump fingers. Shaking her head hard enough to set her steel gray afro to trembling, she said, "I'm so sorry about your uncle. He was such a lovely man, a real asset to our community, and we miss him terribly." Trudy continued shaking her head, and now that she'd stopped talking, her jowls jiggled, too.

The phone rang on Trudy's desk, and she excused herself, shooing the two men toward the pastor's office. "I'll bring you something to drink when I get off the phone," she said, already picking up the old-fashioned handset and holding it to her ear. "I was just getting ready to brew a fresh batch of coffee for Toby—Oh, hello, Susanne! Guess who's visiting, even as we speak!"

Cord chuckled as he followed the pastor into his office. Well, that was one way to get the word out, he thought. A church secretary was a force of nature in a small town like Plumwood Hollow.

Rev. Treadwell indicated that Cord sit in one of the dated, but comfortable chairs in front of his large oak desk. Without preamble, he said, "We missed you at Judge's memorial." His eyes were kind, his expression caring, but his words were brutally direct.

If Cord hadn't wanted to be challenged, he shouldn't have chosen to pay visits to the two people in town who would hold his toes to the fire. Between Faith and the pastor, he was feeling more vulnerable than he had in a long time. Well, at least in the last six months. "Right. I know. I should have been here."

The good reverend stayed quiet, waiting for him to expound, and it reminded Cord a little of Prudence. Maybe everyone in the hollow was like this, he thought. Maybe people here didn't mind leaving the silent places in between the important words, and he just hadn't noticed when he'd been a teenager too busy filling up those silent places with his own importance.

Clearly, the man expected more, but when Cord held his tongue, Reverend Treadwell leaned back in his chair and said, "Acknowledgment is a good place to start. So what brings you to the Lord's house today, son?"

"Well, actually, Uncle Judge, in a roundabout way." Cord decided to get right to the point—it seemed the man across the desk from him preferred it that way, anyway. "I'm buying the ranch from Frankie. House, barns, equipment, horses and cattle, chickens, the whole package deal."

"I see." Rev. Treadwell nodded slowly, but he didn't voice the questions in his eyes. He just waited for Cord to continue.

Cord cleared his throat, trying to figure out the best place to start. Just then, Trudy bustled in with a tray holding steaming mugs of black brew and set it on the desk between the men. "Do you take cream or sugar, Cordell? Our good shepherd here prefers it black as sin and strong enough to set the devil himself on his backside."

Cord chuckled and shook his head. "If Rev can handle it unadulterated, then so can I."

"Don't say I didn't warn you, sugar." She squeezed his chin and added, "It's just so good to see you. And I have a carton of creamer in the kitchen if you change your mind, alrighty?"

"Thank you, Trudy," the reverend said after taking a careful sip from his cup. "This is perfect."

"My pleasure. You boys give me a shout if you need anything else." Then she swept back out of the office, pulling the door nearly closed behind her.

Open just enough, Cord assumed, that she'd be able to catch all the important bits of their conversation.

He blew on the surface of the hot liquid in his mug, tested it, then grimaced appreciatively. "Wow. She wasn't kidding. This stuff is pretty wicked, Rev."

"It'll get your blood pumping, yes indeed. So, go on. You were telling me about buying your uncle's place, but back up a little. Tell me about football. I know you retired a couple of years ago—a few too many concussions, right?"

"Yes." Cord nodded slowly, then took a sip of his coffee to soothe the lump that had risen in his throat. "I didn't make the draft, but right out of college, I signed a three-year rookie contract with the Bengals and thought I'd died and gone to heaven."

"Who dey!" The pastor chanted in a loud bellow.

"Nooooobody!" Trudy Huckster's response from the other side of the door made both men chuckle. The secretary was as big a fan of the Cincinnati football team as Reverend Treadwell, and everyone in the hollow knew not to talk smack about the Bengals in church. At least not in Plumwood Hollow's Glory of God Church.

"I don't really know what happened, Rev." Cord picked up his tale again. "But by the middle of my second year, I'd started to lose my edge, and no matter how hard I worked at it, I couldn't get it back. I could feel myself slipping, but there was nothing I could do to stop the decline. Then my third year, I took some bad hits." He held up four fingers. "My fourth concussion is what did me in. When I came around, I didn't know what day it was, couldn't recall even suiting up to play. It took me almost a week before I remembered the game, and then a couple more before I remembered the play that took me out."

"There were a lot of prayers being said for you, Cord."

"I know. Thank you. I'm good these days, except I periodically get migraines, something my doctor says may never go away. Even now, they can lay me out for a day or two, sometimes longer. Anyway, when the doc gave me a stern warning—felt like a threat at the time—that another hit to my head like that one would cause permanent damage, I made the decision to hang up my jersey." Cord lowered his gaze again and added, "The worst thing about it was the pressure I got to stay in the game, to keep playing in spite of the risk. I walked away feeling like a quitter." Cord grimaced as he said it; the word still stirred up some fairly raw emotions in him, especially compounded with his recent decision to leave scouting after only a few years. Did he have what it took to commit long term to anything? Would he walk away from Whispering Ranch after a couple of years of playing rancher, too?

"I've seen many a player wait too long to quit and pay dearly for it," Reverend Treadwell said.

"Yeah, and truth be told, I don't begrudge a single person for leaning on me to stay; really, I don't. It's the nature of the game, isn't it? Injury, I mean? You can't have a bunch of us hurtling ourselves at each other without someone losing an eye, or at least a brain cell or two." He chuckled dryly in an attempt to make light of it, but then said, "I think if I had been showing up with my A-game all along, I would have found the motivation to stay. In fact, if I'd been bringing my A-game all along, I doubt I would have gotten at least the last two concussions. By the time my rookie contract was up, I knew I'd lost it, Rev. The Bengals were ready to release me, and although I figured I could land another contract somewhere else, my heart wasn't in it, and I didn't want to be *that* guy, you know? The teammate who couldn't carry his own weight. So, when my term ended, I made it official and retired. Three years, Rev. That's all I got out of the game. Three years, a bruised brain, and a chunk of change burning a hole in my pocket."

The pastor nodded sagely. "Sounds like a tough decision for any man to have to make."

"It was. One of the hardest." He scratched his jaw absentmindedly. "When I walked out of the Bengal locker room for the last time, my pride nearly had me tucking my tail between my legs and skedaddling back to Mama. But something a buddy said to me stuck in my craw—he said I had a knack for firing up the other players, motivating them to get the job done, and done well."

"I can attest to that," the pastor confirmed. "You have the gift of exhortation." He took a sip of coffee and added, "Encouragement. Persuasion." The last word he said with a slightly sardonic grin. "You could persuade fish out of the water and birds out of the skies, son. Not to mention convincing your friends to go along with every wild hair of yours, no matter how much trouble it got you into." The pastor chuckled, taking the edge off his words. "Those were the beginning stages of exhortation, I believe. You were just testing out the height and breadth of your spiritual gift."

Cord let the pastor's words sink in. "Thank you. You've always said that, but until now, I never made the connection. Guess it makes sense." He sat back in the chair, the mug held loosely between his big hands, relishing in the fact that he was here, back in Plumwood Hollow again. A place he desperately wanted to call home.

He hadn't realized just how much he'd missed it until coming back. He knew exactly how badly he ached for Faith, but he'd always assumed the hollow was simply the backdrop of their relationship, not an entity all its own. Being here now, he realized differently.

Could he stay, even if she rejected him? Could he make a life for himself at Whispering Hills Ranch right next door to Seven Virtues if she refused to have him?

Could he convince the good folks of Plumwood Hollow to embrace him if Faith didn't?

He'd spent his first day in town just driving through the community with his windows up and his shades on, staying incognito except for a few necessary stops for fuel, food, and a little cash. He'd gone to Nesbit's Grocery last night and run into a few people who remembered him. Phil Braxton's family owned the hardware and feed store, and one day he and his wife, Leslie, a woman Cord vaguely remembered by face, if not by name, would take over the business. Phil, one of those all-around nice guys even back in high school, had greeted Cord warmly, but now in hindsight, Leslie had seemed a little standoffish, albeit quite polite. Cord had chalked it up to her being shy and thought nothing more of it.

Russ Timmons, an oak of a man who'd worked the checkout line as long as Cord could remember, greeted him like he'd been in just last week. Even so, Cord had sensed some reservation. Was it just because he'd been gone so long, or because he'd missed his uncle's funeral? Or did it have something to do with Faith?

Then there was Jenny... Jenny Stewart? Jenny Stanton? She didn't seem to have a problem accepting his presence in town. She'd planted herself in his path in the produce aisle, and he definitely remembered Jenny, even if he couldn't recall her last name. He congratulated her politely when she flashed the ring on her finger at him, even when she stuck out her bottom lip and said, "Why didn't you come back sooner, Cord? I'm off the market now." Then she sent him a coy look and gave him a suggestive hip bump. "For now, anyway. But you know what they say. Third time's the charm." He didn't ask for an explanation and was glad when she moved on, having remembered she was in a hurry to get to her next stop.

He had been surprised that Faith hadn't already at least heard he was in town, what with the way news of any kind, good, bad, and everything in between, seemed to spread like wildfire on a hot and windy August day.

He was staying out at the Flanner place—Frankie had insisted—only one driveway down from Seven Virtues on Carpenter Road, but he supposed that unless someone saw him coming and going, it wasn't likely they'd know he was out there.

Or if Jordan Binks talked. But then, like most folks who preferred livestock to people, Binks wasn't much of a talker, at least not in the way of gossip. And knowing Faith, it wasn't likely she'd set foot off Goodacre land in the last few days, either. The way he remembered it, she rarely left Seven Virtues except for social events or church, or to meet up with him.

If that even counted. The two of them usually stuck pretty close to home. That big old, empty hay barn just the other side of the tree line held some of the sweetest memories of his high school years. Some of the most shameful memories, too, but that was something he hoped to rectify in the weeks and months—hopefully, years—to come.

He cleared his throat in a futile attempt to knock loose those thoughts. Especially since he was sitting across a desk from Faith's pastor and the man who had come alongside Cord when he was sure his heart would simply stop beating from the pain of losing the woman he loved.

Again, not something he wanted to dwell on.

"Anyway, so I contacted the folks back at Kentucky University, and within a year, I was scouting full time, and consistently handpicking winners."

"From what I know about it, scouting requires an awful lot of traveling. Long hours on the road."

"It's an insane amount of traveling," Cord agreed, his eyes wide in emphasis. "Driving mile upon mile into tiny communities that barely show up on Google Maps, sleeping in cheap hotels, existing on fast food and truck stop fare." He rubbed his stomach and grimaced, then held his mug aloft. "Many a time I could have used some of your black-as-sin coffee."

Reverend Treadwell chuckled and lifted his own mug in a return salute.

"It wasn't so bad, though," Cord continued. "I was young and unattached, for the most part, anyway."

"You always seemed to have someone on your arm. What happened to that Brianna Peters you were said to be getting serious about?"

Cord shook his head, pressing his lips together. "Nah. That never went beyond the thinking about it stage. We were on again, off again, starting back in college." He chuckled self-deprecatingly and shook his head. "To be honest, it was always more off than on. She stuck around for a little while after I left the Bengals, but she wasn't happy with my decision to retire—she was one of those pressuring me to keep playing. Anyway, last fall, she got engaged to another teammate who signed on a year after I did. He's still in the game." Brianna had called Cord to tell him about her engagement, her reason being that she didn't want him to hear about it on social media. Something in the way she sounded, though, made him doubt her intentions were exactly honorable. She was either rubbing his nose in it or hoping he'd try to talk her out of it. Neither option sat well with him, and the conversation had been short. There'd been a few half-hearted attempts at relationships before and after Brianna, but none had lasted very long, especially not with his crazy scouting schedule.

Reverend Treadwell spoke slowly, contemplatively. "So why scouting? I'd think it would be difficult recruiting young men to go do what you couldn't do yourself."

Cord chuckled dryly. "Believe it or not, I wanted to help good players get the best opportunities in a game I love. It was rewarding to see a name I championed go out there and prove me right."

"Cordell Overman. The champion of champions," the reverend stated.

"I liked the job, Rev," Cord continued. "It suited me just fine. Until it didn't."

The pastor's brows lifted in question, but he only repeated, "I see."

Cord ran his palm down the curve of his jaw before he continued. "I gave them six months, then planned to head home to Louisville to a job working for my dad. Normal hours, affordable health insurance, a pension plan, the works."

"That's what you were looking for?"

After a moment's pause, Cord said, "I thought it was what I was supposed to be looking for. The kind of job on which to build a future. But when Frankie called and asked me if I'd be interested in buying his ranch, it took me all of about thirty seconds to make up my mind about it." Cord stretched his legs out in front of him and chuckled. "Funny thing is,

I know the hours are going to be just as insane as scouting, even if it isn't as much driving and crappy food. I also know the pay may never measure up to what I could be making had I taken that job with Dad." He tapped his sternum emphatically. "But I'll be working those long hours at crap wages for me. On my own land, with my own stock. And I'll be going home to my own bed every night."

"I see," the reverend said again. "Well, it's prime property, Cord, and I know a lot of folks in this area and beyond who were hoping for a piece of it. They'll be glad to know it's not going to a complete stranger."

Cord nodded. "Yes, I've heard. I spoke to Faith Goodacre today." Just saying her name out loud made his pulse quicken. "She told me the same thing, that she'd even tried to buy some acreage off Frankie for Seven Virtues."

"You've seen Faith, then?" The look on Reverend Treadwell's face made Cord frown.

"Yes. Right before I came here."

"I see."

"You see? You see what? That's about the fifth or sixth time you've said that. I get the feeling you say it instead of saying what you're really thinking," Cord began, not liking the way the pastor had carefully modulated his expression to one of such blandness, that they could have been talking about the weather. "In fact, I get the feeling there's something pretty important that you're not telling me. That a whole lot of folks in this town aren't telling me. Which is one of the main reasons I'm here to see you. Is something wrong with Faith? She sick or something?" He tried to sound casual, but the thought made his stomach lurch. She'd told him all about her mother's illness.

"No, no," Reverend Treadwell assured him, shaking his head vehemently. "Not that I'm aware, anyway. But I get the impression your visit with Faith might not have been very... well, informative, I guess."

"Informative?"

"Did you two talk about your past?"

"You like to get right to the point, don't you?" Cord muttered.

"No use beating around the bush," the reverend said as casual as cotton.

"We didn't. But that's definitely our next conversation." Cord licked his lips, his mouth uncomfortably dry. "Not just about our past, either, Rev. I'm here to talk to her about our future. Together. After seeing her today, I believe we still have one."

"I see—" Reverend Treadwell broke off when Cord narrowed his eyes at him. He put a hand up to deflect his irritation. "Forgive me. What's your motivation for pursuing her, Cord? You've been gone a long time. Do you think it's going to be as simple as riding back into town and sweeping her off her feet?" Coming from anyone else, his words might have been sarcastic, but the pastor asked with all sincerity.

Cord considered carefully before answering with a question of his own. "You're a praying man, right?"

"You and the rest of this church had better hope I am," Reverend Treadwell said with a chuckle, then grew serious when Cord didn't join in. "I am, son. Very much so. Prayer is my lifeline."

"A lifeline. Yes." Cord nodded, hesitant to say his next words out loud, lest he sound like he was going off the deep end. He squared his shoulders and forged ahead. "Over the last year or so, I've become something of a praying man, too. It's like I'm conversing with God all the time, you know? And sometimes I think—well, I think God is talking back." He glanced down into the dregs in his coffee cup. He hadn't realized he'd downed the whole thing. "I'm supposed to be here, Rev." Cord shifted in his seat and met the pastor's eyes. "I believe it in my gut. I can't tell you exactly why or how I know. Call it a hunch, a spiritual nudge, or the Good Lord leaning down to thump me in the back of the head, but I know this is where I'm supposed to be. I'm here to win back her heart. Or as you put it, to ride into town and sweep her off her feet." He nodded, as though agreeing with himself. "I'm not leaving. I made that mistake once, and I'm not making it again."

"It may not be as simple as that." Reverend Treadwell's eyes were sympathetic, and that worried Cord more than the banal expression had.

"And just why is that, Rev? You're not the first person who's said so to me. Is she secretly married? Engaged? Because by her own admission, she's single." He leaned back in his chair, a sense of foreboding welling up in him.

"A person who is single isn't automatically available." The pastor eyed Cord thoughtfully for a few moments before continuing. "People change, son. I think you know that. Some more than others."

Again, Prudence had said essentially the same thing to him only hours ago. "Faith is still Faith." The moment the words were out, he regretted speaking them out loud. He sounded like a dogmatic windbag.

"She is, indeed. But I assure you, she's not the same Faith you walked away from all those years ago."

"I didn't walk away from her, Reverend Treadwell. Why does everyone think that?" Cord frowned in frustration. "She was supposed to come with me. She's the one who changed her mind, not me." He hated that he sounded so defensive, but he kept getting the vibe that he'd been painted out to be the only bad guy in this picture. He was more than willing to take responsibility for his part in the demise of the relationship, but when all was said and done, it had been Faith - not him - who cut things off.

"I'm not pointing fingers, Cord." Reverend Treadwell braced his forearms on the desk and leaned in. "But if you knew the girl like you say you did, then you would have known she'd never leave this place. This is her home. This is where her heart is. Her family. Her life."

Cord shook his head, not because he didn't agree, but because he knew the man across from him was right. He'd always known Faith was a rancher, a cowgirl from the holler, through and through. But when she talked about traveling with him, about leaving behind the small-town life and seeing the world together, he'd believed her because it was what he wanted to hear. He'd thought that as long as they were together, they'd be home, no matter where they ended up.

"As far as Faith is concerned, son," the pastor continued, his voice kind, "you did leave her because she's the one still here. And when push came to shove, you settled for a future without her rather than choosing to fight for one with her. I'm not saying you would have gotten your girl in the end - I know both Faith and Jed well enough to make no guarantees on that count - but when things didn't go the way you expected, you simply moved on with your life without her."

"Wow. You know, that's not really the way it happened, Rev. Why does everyone around here remember it so differently than I do?" Cord slumped in the chair, reeling a little from what felt like a sucker punch. And from a trusted friend, too.

"I can't speak for other folk, mind you, but I remember it the way I do, Cord, because I watched that girl become a woman as she picked up the pieces of her broken heart. Faith pulled up her bootstraps, quite literally, and made a new life for herself and her—well, for her family, after you stopped coming back." He lifted both hands to ward off Cord's rebuttal. "You also should know that Faith chose well when she opted to stay here in the hollow."

"What is that supposed to mean? You don't think I could have made her happy? You don't think we had a chance anywhere else?"

"I think she chose well under circumstances you weren't around to witness."

Cord sat forward and narrowed his eyes at Reverend Treadwell. "Why all this beating around the bush, Rev? Folks all over town are ducking and dodging me like I have the plague. Oh, they're nice enough, but I've never felt more like an outsider in my life." Cord rubbed a palm over his face, then shoved his fingers through his short hair. "What are you not telling me?"

The older man shook his head, his brow furrowed. "It's not my place to mend this bridge between you, Cord. I can only be here to support each of you as you do the work yourselves."

Cord squared his shoulders. Whatever it was, he could handle it. He would handle it. "Well, you should know that I've come ready to fight for her. Ready to win her heart again. Seeing her today—" His voice cracked. He tried again. "I know being here is the right thing."

"I believe you may be in for the fight of your life if you really intend to win her heart."

"I do."

Reverend Treadwell smiled. "Careful there, son. Braver men than you shy away from those two little words."

"I don't."

The pastor nodded slowly. "I see."

SEVEN

For the next several days, Faith walked around on eggshells, half expecting Cord to appear around every corner, around every bend. She found herself snipping at her sisters over silly things and fighting off the urge to bury her head under her pillow at night so she could give in to the tears that waited just behind her eyes. She was an emotional wreck, and everyone in the house seemed to go out of their way to avoid her.

Even Jasmine noticed. "What is wrong with you, Mama? You act like you want to kick a brick."

"Oh, baby. I guess I'm just tired. You know how it is during calving season. I never get quite enough sleep." Faith sat across from the child. On the table before her was a stack of bills she was working her way through, a task that didn't make her mood any better.

"Yeah, but the last calf was born a couple days ago, and you weren't this cancerous until now." Jasmine was busy with a pair of scissors, markers, and a stack of colorful craft paper. She was making a Mother's Day card for Faith, so she'd propped an oversized *Where's Waldo* book open in front of her to keep her mother from seeing her project.

"Cantankerous," Faith corrected. "Cantankerous means cranky and mean. Cancerous would mean I have cancer."

Abby sat at the other end of the table doing homework. She didn't even bother lifting her eyes from the Economics textbook she was studying. "Or it means you act like cancer. You know, making everyone sick and miserable. Making everyone want to zap you out of existence."

"Thanks," Faith said, her tone matching her little sister's snarky sarcasm. But the girl was right. Abby and Jasmine were stuck in the kitchen with her that Friday afternoon doing homework, but there was a reason the rest of the family weren't wandering in and out of the large room the way they usually did. Even her father had opted to take his afternoon coffee out to the large kitchen garden where he grew his prized tomatoes every year. They were still about a month from even flowering, but Jed looked for blossoms every day once the weather warmed up. "I'm sorry, girls. I'll snap out of it, I promise."

"That's probably a good idea, Mama. Right now, no one wants to even celebrate with you on Mother's Day," Jasmine explained with the transparency of a child. "Justice said she'd celebrate if you slept in, missed church, and then took a Sunday afternoon nap."

"I'd celebrate if I got to do that, too," Faith said with a dry chuckle. "I can't remember the last time I slept in, at least not since you've been born, Jaz. And a Sunday afternoon nap? Wouldn't that be glorious?"

"We could give you a Sunday afternoon nap for Mother's Day," Jasmine suggested.

"Hear, hear," Abby quipped from the end of the table. "And because we love you so, so much, we'll leave you here in peace and quiet while we all head over to the Smokehouse Grill for ribs and mac and cheese."

"Hear, hear!" Jasmine echoed, a dreamy look in her eyes. "Mmm. Ribs. I could eat those babies every single day of my life until I die."

Faith nudged her daughter's foot under the table. "You are your grandfather's granddaughter, you and your rib addiction."

Jasmine peeked over the top of the book at her. "At least I'm not addicted to ciggies or tobacco."

Faith burst out laughing. "Ciggies? Where did you hear that?"

"That's what Nona calls her gross cigarettes." Jasmine lowered her head behind the book again, returning to her industrious crafting. "Yvette's daddy says they're cancer sticks, but Nona doesn't have cancer. She just smells like a burning rug."

"I'm curious as to how you know what a burning rug smells like," Abby said, closing her textbook and shoving it into her backpack.

"I didn't burn anything," Jasmine retorted rather defensively. Faith eyed her dubiously, now curious herself, but the little girl went on. "It's only that Nona looks kind of like a floppy, rolled-up rug sitting in her chair. You know, all lumpy and crumpled up. And when she smokes...." She let the words trail off, but the visual she'd created needed no more explanation.

Naomi "Nona" Valiente moved in with her son, Levi, after his wife abandoned him and their baby daughter, Yvette, when the child was not even six months old.

Faith and Levi had become friends over their shared single parenthood status, and although they'd dated a few times, they'd opted to remain friends after a disastrous-turned-hilarious attempt at a make-out session after a night out without their toddlers. Faith had still been nursing, and the kiss had triggered a letdown of her milk, soaking the nursing pads she wore, through her pretty pink top to wet the front of Levi's black pearl-button shirt, too. After a few moments of mortifying awkwardness, they'd both laughed until they could hardly breathe. It had been the beginning of a beautiful friendship and the end of any misguided notions that there might be more between them.

Nona, in spite of her ciggy habit, had been a huge blessing to the scared young father and his tiny daughter, and by extension, to Faith and Jasmine, too. The old woman was generous with her love and treated Jasmine with the same grandmotherly affection she gave to Yvette. Faith had never had any reservations about leaving her daughter in Nona's care, cancer sticks notwithstanding, but she only smoked outside, well away from wherever the girls were playing.

"But don't tell her I said she looks like a rug, okay, Mama? I love that Nona something fierce, and I wouldn't want to hurt her feelings."

"Of course not, sugar pie." Over the top of the open book, Faith tapped her daughter's head with the end of her pencil. "You're a sweet girl."

"Don't peek!" Jasmine shrieked, grabbing the book and sliding it a little closer. She glared at Faith from behind it.

"I can see what she's making. Want me to tell you about it?" Abby rose and came around the table to stand behind Jasmine, who slammed the open book down on top of her artwork. Faith grimaced, hoping the markers all had lids on them and that the Elmer's glue was dry.

"Don't you dare, Abby Goodacre," Jasmine warned, glaring at her youngest aunt. "Or I'll tell her I saw you kissing that Mike boy yesterday." Then her eyes widened, and she slapped a hand over her mouth. "I'm sorry, Abby. I'm sorry! I didn't mean to snitch; I promise."

Abby flicked her niece in the side of the head, and Jasmine, suffering the shame of having spilled a secret she'd promised to keep, took the punishment with barely a flinch. "Thanks, you little blabbermouth."

"I didn't mean to, Abby. It was an accident!" Jasmine wailed, pushing up from her seat, and hurrying to follow Abby from the room.

Faith stared after the girls, but after a moment's consideration, decided to let them work it out. Abby had just turned seventeen last month. She was more like a big sister to Jasmine than an aunt, and tiffs like this were common between them. They were usually resolved quickly, too.

In fact, tiffs like this were common, period, in their house of seven sisters with only their hard-working father to run interference. The family of girls had learned early on that making peace made living together a lot easier than holding grudges.

Besides, she needed to get through the stack of paperwork in front of her, and maybe she could focus better without any distractions. She eyed the book still face down over Jasmine's project. The child would be heartbroken if things were stuck to the pages, so without looking so she could say she'd seen nothing, Faith carefully propped the book back up as it had been before and hoped for the best. With a sigh, she settled back into her seat and returned to balancing the checkbook.

The quiet was short-lived. Barely five minutes had passed when Charity bustled into the kitchen, Prudence right behind her. The two were talking animatedly over some recipe, Prudence reading from a list of ingredients on her phone as Charity opened the pantry to peruse the contents.

Prudence glanced up and caught Faith's eye. "Hey, Faith," she said, offering her greeting tentatively. In a sing-song voice, she drawled, "How's it going?"

"You act like you're afraid to talk to me," Faith returned, frowning.

Prudence shrugged one shoulder. "I kinda am. You've been pretty scary since Cord showed up here." She leaned a hip against the end of the table and crossed her arms as she studied Faith. "Do you still have a thing for him?" she asked.

"Wow. Presumptuous, are we?" Faith asked, shuffling her papers into a neat pile. So much for getting through the bills today. At least not in the kitchen.

"Funny thing. That's essentially the same response he gave me the other day when I asked him the same question," Prudence shot back, but her tone wasn't mocking.

"Whoa. Hold up, now," Charity interrupted, her hands stilling on the handles of a large stockpot. "You and Cord Overman? After all this time?"

Faith's impulse was to quote the famous line from Harry Potter, the one so simply delivered by the brooding Professor Snape, but she couldn't bring herself to utter the single word. 'Always' was too close to the truth, and even the thought of admitting it made her feel a little queasy. "Drop it, you guys. There is no me and Cord."

"I don't know about that," Prudence countered. "He seemed pretty set on the idea, from what I could tell."

Charity gawked at Prudence. "Wait. Did he actually say that?" Her eyes, alight with her gregarious nature, darted back and forth between her sisters. "I'd heard he was back, but I hadn't heard he was back for you, Faithy." Her brows lifted higher, disappearing behind her thick blonde bangs. "Does he know about—" She broke off and pointed toward the hallway, then mouthed Jasmine's name.

"There's no way he knows," Prudence said before Faith could respond. "He wouldn't have been sitting here so casually the other day if he did."

"Or maybe he's known all along and just didn't care enough to do anything about it," Faith snipped.

"You don't really believe that," Prudence said. "He's not like that, and you know it."

Faith stood abruptly, grabbing the back of her chair to keep it from toppling. "I don't know what he's like, Prudence, and neither do you. It's been ten years since he last set foot in the hollow, remember? A person can change a lot in that amount of time." Then she scooped up her paperwork and started for the screen door. She'd find a quiet spot in the barn.

"He has the right to know." Prudence's words stopped her. "And I think he has the right to hear it from you, Faith. He was pretty clear about his intentions where you're concerned. I heard him tell you he was here to pursue you."

Faith eyed her with almost the exact expression she'd seen on Abby's face when Jasmine had talked too freely a little earlier. "You know, Prudence, for someone so young and inexperienced, you sure seem to think you have it all figured out. Maybe you should try keeping your opinions to yourself for a change." Then she spun on her heel and shoved the screen door open so hard it slapped against the outside wall and bounced closed with a reverberating slam.

She really did want to kick a brick right about now.

In fact, if Cordell Overman appeared before her at that moment, she'd just kick him.

Or she'd throw herself into his arms and kiss him.

"Hells bells, Faith Louise Goodacre," she snarled as she practically launched herself down the porch steps. "Get your act together, woman."

"You owe the cuss jar a dollar, Mama!"

Faith spun around, her mouth open in surprise. Oh Lordy, what had the child heard? The screen door was no sound barrier, and Faith and her sisters hadn't exactly been keeping the volume low. Jasmine should have been down the hall in Abby's room trying to win back her favorite aunt's affections, not outside the back door to the kitchen. Faith wracked her brain, trying to recall what had been said. Had they used her daughter's name in reference to Cord?

Jasmine was tucked into the crawl space under the porch. Years ago, the girl had claimed the little area behind the steps where it was protected from the worst of the weather. She'd furnished it with a child's lawn chair and an old sleeping bag for Jack, who often utilized the space even when Jasmine wasn't around. A small metal cabinet she'd rescued from the barn was wedged into the space, too, and in it, she kept a stash of books, a flashlight, a jar of gummy bears that was empty more often than not, and a jar of dog kibbles that was also empty more often than not.

"Hey, baby." Faith crouched down so she could see the girl's face. She wasn't sitting in the chair, but instead, was curled up against Jack's side on the blanket. "Remind me to put one in there tonight, okay? I need to run out to the barn right now."

"Why were you and Aunt Prudence fighting?" Jasmine asked. There were traces of tears on her cheeks, but she didn't appear to be crying now. Surely, she would be asking something else if she'd made the connection between herself and the man the women had been discussing in the kitchen. "You sounded really mad when you came out."

"I was mad," Faith admitted. "I'm sorry. I should have controlled myself better."

"Me, too," Jasmine muttered. "I should have controlled my stupid mouth better. I hurt Abby's feelings."

Faith sighed and hung her head. "Yeah, well, I should have controlled my stupid mouth better, too."

"You owe the cuss jar another dollar." The girl snorted behind her hand. "You said stupid."

"Yeah? Well, so did you," Faith shot back, reaching out to tickle her daughter in the ribcage. "And who says stupid is a cuss word?"

"Grampa. He said it's a foul word, even if it isn't exactly cussing, because the only time people use it is to tear someone or something down."

Faith nodded. "You know, sugar pie, your grandfather is a wise man."

"Are you going to apologize to Aunt Prudence?" Jasmine asked after a moment. "Because I think you should. I apologized to Abby, and even though she's still mad at me, she said she forgives me. I think Aunt Prudence would at least forgive you, too." Jasmine called all her aunts by the title, except for Abby, but that had been Abby's preference.

"If Abby forgave you, then why are you out here?" Faith asked, shifting her weight a little. The crouch was getting uncomfortable. Jack's tail thumped against the ground a few times. He lifted his gaze to look at her, but he stayed put, content to offer comfort to the person who needed it most at the moment. "I thought you would be in Abby's room with her."

Jasmine shook her head. "She wouldn't let me come in. She said she forgave me, but she told me she needed her space." The girl sighed deeply, as though the weight of the world rested on her narrow shoulders. "I came out here to hide until I felt better." She stroked the dog's head, scratching absentmindedly between his ears.

Faith lowered her gaze to the toes of her boots before responding. "I will talk to Pru, Jasmine, but not right now. I think I need a little space as well. Sometimes people do things that make us go a little batty, and the best thing is to spend some time apart so we can set things right in our own heads first. I love Prudence very much, but—"

"Does Aunt Prudence know that?" Jasmine interrupted.

"That she made me batty? Yes," Faith began, but stopped when Jasmine shook her head.

"No, I mean, does she know you love her?" The girl sniffled loudly. "Because even though Abby said she forgives me, I'm pretty sure that girl hates my guts."

"Oh, sugar pie, she does not hate your guts, I promise." Faith crab-walked a little closer so she could take Jasmine's hand. "She loves you very much."

Jasmine's shoulders hunched even more, if that was possible. "But that's not how it feels right now, since she won't talk to me."

"Hey, squirt."

Startled, Faith jerked in surprise and toppled backward onto her rear, but she held tight to the pile of paperwork in her hands. She scowled up at Abby behind her.

"Sorry, Faith. Didn't mean to scare you." Abby said with a smirk. She leaned in toward Jasmine. "I'm sorry I wouldn't talk to you. I don't hate your guts. I love your guts. Your greasy grimy gopher guts."

"Ew." Jasmine snickered and made a face. "I love your greasy grimy gopher guts, too. I'm sorry I squealed on you."

Faith held out her free hand to Abby. "Help me up, then tell me which Mike we're talking about. Does Daddy need to oil his shotgun?"

Abby rolled her eyes, but said nothing, and Faith grinned when she saw Jasmine do the same. She brushed off her backside and stepped back so her daughter could crawl out of her hidey-hole.

Once clear, Jasmine stood with her feet braced apart and flexed her scrawny arms. "He's not a kid, Mama. He's a man. A really, really hot man with beeee-you-tee-ful lips and really big guns." The girl wiggled her eyebrows exaggeratedly. "You should see his muscles."

Faith turned a sardonic look on her little sister. "I take it you're teaching her everything you know about really, really hot men? And has she actually seen Mike's big guns?"

Abby shrugged. "Maybe. He does like to show them off. And he is pretty da—stinkin' hot," she assured Faith. "You should see him."

"I'll take your word for it—not *that* word, mind you. I should make you stick a dollar in the cuss jar just for thinking it," Faith said with a shake of her head.

"I can't help the thoughts that fly into my head. It's what I do with them that counts," Abby defended herself. "I stopped myself before it made it all the way out. That should count for something. Isn't self-control a fruit of the Spirit?"

"For as he thinks in his heart, so is he." With an exaggerated finger wag, Faith quoted the over-used verse from Proverbs. "But will you do me a favor? Please resist the urge to exchange saliva in the presence of your pure-as-new-fallen-snow niece."

"Exchange saliva. Gross. What does that mean?" Jasmine frowned, her brain working overtime to figure it out. "Exchange saliva. Exchange saliva. Exchange—"

"Stop saying that, you freak," Abby interjected. "That's a nasty, disgusting way to say kissing."

"But how—"

Abby closed her eyes and waggled her tongue in an obscene pantomime that was supposed to look like passionate French kissing.

Jasmine's reaction said it all. "Disgusting!" the girl hollered in a strong cockney accent. Then she performed her own pantomime by opening her mouth and pretending to stick her finger down her throat, followed by nasty gagging sounds.

"Abby, did you show her that meme?" Faith narrowed her eyes at her sister, having seen the ridiculous thing herself. "It's rife with foul words."

"Of course I did," Abby said with feigned innocence. "It's a precious mother-daughter moment caught on camera." She turned back to Jasmine. "And believe me, Jasmoney Baloney. You'll think otherwise about exchanging saliva one day."

"No, she won't!" Faith declared, biting back a smile. Faith knew Abby's brassy behavior was primarily just to get a rise out of everyone, not because she was a rebel wild child. It had to be tough being the youngest of seven sisters, no matter how mellow their father had become over the last several years. To her daughter, she said, "Jasmine, you just go right on thinking all that mushy gushy gunky stuff is disgusting, you hear?"

"Mushy gushy yummy stuff is more like it," Abby retorted. "Like chocolate mousse cheesecake. Mmmm."

"Shush, little sister."

Jasmine sent a skeptical look at her mother. "Maybe I might like it just fine when I get a little older, Mama. Will that be okay? Cuz I sure do like cheesecake." She frowned in bemused contemplation. "I'm not sure about cheesecake made from moose, though. There might not be enough chocolate in the world to make moose antlers taste good, even on cheesecake."

"Mousse is a fancy French word," Abby explained. "Since we're talking about French kissing and all."

"Abby," Faith warned in an ominous tone.

"What?" Abby blinked innocently at Faith, then said to Jasmine, "Mousse is dessert stuff that's kinda like pudding and whipped cream mixed together. It's that stuff Charity made at Easter, remember?"

"Oh. Then I could go for some of that." Jasmine's eyes widened, and she nodded slowly while licking her lips. "Oh, yeah. Mmmm."

"And that, wee Snazzy Jazzy, is exactly the way I feel when I look at Chocolate Mousse Mike," the teenager said, nodding slowly. "Oh, yeah. Mmmm."

"Abstinence Caroline Goodacre!" Faith reached over and flicked her sister in the side of the head, just like the teenager had done to Jasmine in the kitchen earlier.

Abby tried to dodge, but she wasn't quick enough. "Ow!" She was laughing, though, and as she rubbed the spot above her ear, she said, "He likes to flaunt his wares, but he's harmless. I promise. It's Mike Nesbit."

Of Nesbit's Grocery, of course. Well, at least the kid came from good stock, Faith thought. "We'll talk about it later tonight, okay? I need to get some work done."

"Maybe we will, maybe we won't," Abby tossed back. "We're just having fun. Nothing serious. I mean, we're friends, but I don't really *like* him, like him. He doesn't seem like boyfriend material, you know?"

Faith nodded. She did know, and part of her wanted Abby not to be too worried about finding the perfect guy right out of the chute, to enjoy being young and flirty and fun for as long as she could. But she also knew how easy it was to take things too far, to make a wrong decision in the heat of the moment, one that had the potential to change the course of one's life. "Still, Abby, tread softly, okay? For his sake, as well as for your own."

Abby nodded. "I am being careful, Faith. I promise. And you know good and well that Mr. Nesbit would take a bander to that boy if he so much as heard a whisper of Mike messing around."

Jasmine's eyes went wide again, this time in horror. "Mr. Nesbit would castrate his own son?" The girl had grown up around the cattle and knew quite well what banders were used for.

Faith, with the lightning quick speed of a mother defending her child, flicked her sister in the side of the head again. This time, Abby didn't even see it coming.

"Ow!" Abby moved to stand behind Jasmine. "Protect me from your scary mama and her jackhammer fingers, little girl."

"No, sugar pie," Faith quickly assured her daughter. "Mr. Nesbit would never do any such thing. Your Aunt Abby here is full of malarkey. Don't you believe a word of what she says."

"Hey, Jasmine." With a capricious grin, Abby leaned in over the girl's shoulder to murmur in her ear. "I think my oldest sister is the finest, sweetest, prettiest, most God-fearing woman in all of Kentucky. You are one lucky little girl to have her for your mama."

"But that's true, Abby." Jasmine's brow furrowed, and she cocked her head at Faith. "Mama, that's true, isn't it? So, I have to believe her sometimes."

Faith threw her hands up in surrender. "*You* make me a little batty," she said, glaring at Abby. "A *lot* batty."

"Then my work here is done," Abby said, brushing her hands together and draping an arm around Jasmine's shoulders. "Come on, squirt. Let's go see the baby ducks."

Faith watched the two girls walk away again, but instead of heading out to the barn as she'd planned, she sighed deeply and made her way back up the porch steps. Through the screen door, she could see Prudence sitting at the table cutting hearts and flowers out of some of the colored paper Jasmine had left behind. She'd likely heard the whole conversation Faith had just had with her daughter.

"Hey," Faith began as she entered the kitchen.

"Hey, yourself," Prudence said, not looking at her.

"I'm sorry. That was really unkind of me."

Prudence kept snipping away, her cutouts perfectly symmetrical, even though she freehanded each one. "Maybe so, but you're right. I do tend to give my opinion a little too freely."

Faith pulled a chair out and sat down close by. "That's just it, Pru. You don't. You are always so sensitive and gentle. It's one of the things I love about you." She leaned forward and put a hand on her sister's to still the scissors. "And I do love you. I hope you know that."

"I know you do." Prudence's shoulders slumped a little, and she laid the scissors aside, lacing her fingers together tightly. She did look at Faith then, and although her eyes seemed almost bruised with misery, she didn't shed a single tear. "And I love you, Faith. That's a fact, not an opinion. I love you, and I want you to be happy. And I don't want you to—well, to miss out on something because you're afraid."

Faith felt her hackles begin to rise, but she pressed her lips together, putting into practice the self-control she'd touted to her daughter.

"And I know I'm pushing it by not just closing my mouth right now and keeping my thoughts to myself," Pru hurried on. "But I think you should give him a chance."

"Prudence." Faith didn't have to ask who her sister was referring to. "Stop. You don't know anything about—"

"But I do, Faith," she interrupted, her voice tender but firm. "You want to hear something crazy?"

"Probably not." Faith shook her head and picked up one of the paper hearts from the table. She toyed with the edges of it until it looked as tattered as her own felt. "I'm thinking you might be on the verge of sharing your opinion with me again."

"Actually, I'm not. This isn't my opinion; it's a fact, too." Prudence shifted in her chair so she could look more directly at Faith. "I said the exact same thing to Cord as you just said to Abby. I mean, pretty much word for word. Tread lightly, for his sake and yours."

"Sounds like good advice. I don't need him over here stomping around, making his presence known, if you know what I mean. This is my turf, my daughter. He's had no part of this, and he can't just barrel back into town and expect to be received with open arms and a round of good ol' boy drinks."

"How can you say that? He had a pretty significant part in creating that little girl, wouldn't you say?" Prudence shook her head in frustration, her spiky hair animating her agitation. "And I don't think it's fair to hold him responsible for not participating when he doesn't even know she exists."

"You know what?" Faith leaned back in her chair, shaking her head. "Enough. I came in here to apologize for falsely accusing you of something, but it seems to me that maybe I was right about you, after all. The way I see it, what is or isn't between Cordell Overman and Jasmine and me is none of your business."

"But it is, no matter how hard you try to deny it. The way I see it," she said, pressing a hand to her chest demonstratively. "Jasmine makes Cord part of our family. And really, that's fact, not opinion."

"Shut up, Pru." Once again, Faith pushed to her feet quickly. This time, she didn't catch her chair in time, and it hit the floor with a loud crash.

"Actually, I think that's part of the problem. I think we all have kept quiet just a little too long." Prudence pushed to her feet, too. "In fact, I have a feeling if you don't open your mouth and speak for yourself, someone else in this hollow is going to do the speaking for you. Folks aren't blind, and they're not stupid, either."

"What is that supposed to mean?" Faith said, picking up her chair and shoving it back under the table with a little too much vehemence. She gripped the top rung of the chair back tightly.

"Come on, sis. People have always assumed she's his, even if they don't talk openly about it. All anyone has to do is look at the two of them side by side to know the truth of it. She has his eyes, and that cleft in her chin is his, too. She even has his smile; something about the way her top lip sticks out over her bottom one. It's literally as plain as the nose on her face!" Prudence never raised her voice in anger, but she trembled now with bottled up emotion. She wrapped her arms around her middle and added, "Like I said, folks here aren't blind. But they're not stupid, either. All along, they have believed he abandoned you when you were pregnant; however, that's not true, is it? Because you never told him. You never gave him the choice. Somebody's going to figure it out soon enough."

"Figure out what?" Faith asked. "According to you, they already know he's her daddy."

"Figure out that you might be the bad guy here, not Cord."

"How dare you?" Faith snarled; her fists clenched at her sides. "You know nothing about the kind of choices I had to make back then. What were you—five?"

"I was almost ten, Faith, your daughter's age." Prudence's voice broke, but she pushed on in a half whisper. "I worshiped the ground you walked on, just like Jasmine does with Abby. Which meant I was half in love with Cordell Overman because you were. And when he left, my heart broke, too, remember?"

Her words struck a chord of truth in Faith, but she ground out, "You have no clue what it's like, Pru. You can't even imagine how hard it is to stand back and let the man you love walk away because you believe it's the right thing to do. This conversation is over."

Prudence swallowed hard and looked away, and for a moment, Faith's confidence faltered. She knew something had happened to Prudence the end of her senior year of high school—the girl had gone from dreamy-eyed to hollow-eyed almost overnight. But when asked, Prudence simply explained she was growing up, that it was time to stop living in the dream world of her childhood. It had been nearly two years since she'd graduated, and although she'd regained some of her whimsical spark, Pru still bore the marks of having walked through some shadowy places.

Now, however, as their words hung like a toxic cloud between them, Faith wondered again what had happened to her little sister. Because she recognized the haunted look on Prudence's face as one that she herself had worn long after Cord left Plumwood Hollow all those years ago. Had Prudence, too, been abandoned by someone she loved?

Faith shook her head. No. If Pru had loved someone so deeply, Faith would have known about it. She opened her mouth to tell her sister to keep her nose out of things, but Prudence spoke first, her tone almost pleading.

"I don't want you hurt again, Faith, but I have a feeling you might hurt even worse if you don't at least give him a chance. I think he's willing to tread lightly—I really do—if you'll open your heart to him. If you'll try trusting him again." She reached over to cover Faith's hand with her own slender one. "He does deserve to know her, just like she deserves to know him. And they should both hear it from you before they hear about it from anyone else."

Faith closed her eyes and took a deep breath, then let it out slowly. She may not want to hear the things Prudence was saying, but that didn't make her sister wrong. And Pru, of all people, would never intentionally hurt a single living creature, especially not any of her beloved family.

"You're right." Faith nodded, lifting her gaze to meet her sister's. "I know that. I'm sorry." She threaded their fingers together, Prudence's hand so soft compared to Faith's work-calloused one. "It scares the living daylights out of me, but I know it needs to be done, and that it needs to be done right." She tightened her grip. "He's going to see his mom this weekend, so I have some time to figure out how, but I know I have to make it happen soon." Her pulse fluttered erratically, and she added in a croak of a whisper,

"I have a feeling he's back in the hollow because he's going to be the new owner of Whispering Hills Ranch. Right next door."

"I have a feeling he's back in the hollow because of you," Pru said, squeezing Faith's hand. "His uncle's ranch was just the providential excuse he needed to make it happen."

Faith wanted to argue, but in the back of her mind, she thought perhaps her sister might be right about that, too.

But why had it taken Cord a whole decade to come back for her was anyone's guess. It was no secret he was no longer the rising star running back he'd been when he left for Wildcat football camp the summer after high school. So why hadn't he come back to her when the game hadn't wanted him three years ago?

After a few moments of silence, she simply said again, "I do love you, Pru. I hope you know that."

"I know that. I love you, too."

EIGHT

So, the reverend thought Cord was in for the fight of his life, did he? Well, he'd already faced down death and walked away. A couple of times. He had a few scars to show for it, yes, but he was on his own two feet and still ready to fight for what he believed in. And Cordell Overman believed in the love he still harbored for Faith Goodacre.

He also believed in what he'd seen in Faith's eyes sitting across that old porch table from her. It was far more than a spark of attraction, he decided. No, what he saw there was powerful, and it scared her. That's why she ran.

From the moment they'd met as teenagers, they'd been drawn to each other like magnets.

He'd seen that same kind of connection between his parents, that light that shone from his mother's eyes when she looked at his father, the gentle way his father touched his mother, as though he couldn't be near her without reaching for her. Theirs was a deep, abiding love that they intentionally nurtured and protected, and their relationship came first before anything else. They'd modeled the kind of commitment Cord wanted in his own marriage, and the only woman he'd ever imagined sharing forever with was Faith Goodacre.

He'd been one hundred percent ready to take his father's job offer, but the moment he learned about Whispering Hills, something in Cord's chest expanded, decompressed. In a vision clear as day, he saw himself filling the big ranch house with a wife and family, their children being raised feeding pigs and chickens, riding horses, rounding up cattle, planting gardens, and skinny dipping in the lake. As though he'd received a vision of the future, he knew, without a shadow of a doubt, that he would do everything in his power to be the next owner of Whispering Hills Ranch.

Because the moment the picture came into focus, he recognized the woman standing on the wraparound porch beside him. Faith Goodacre. It had always been Faith. Not Brianna Peters. Not Mallory Walther. Not Ramona Blythe.

Faith Goodacre. If God was merciful, Faith Goodacre Overman.

Even after all these years, that connection between them hadn't changed, and seeing her again had only made him more certain of how much he needed her in his life again. All he had to do now was convince her that she needed him just as much.

This weekend, however, was all about his mama.

Except for the bouquet of red Gerbera daisies he'd ordered from Trilby's Blossoms and Books downtown. Trilby, herself, promised him they'd be delivered to Faith this afternoon around three o'clock. There was also the box of bonbons and truffles he had ordered from Suzi's Sweet Treats. Suzi made the best éclairs Cord had ever tasted, but he knew Faith had a weakness for the pastry chef's chocolate candies. She'd receive the pretty blue box sometime on Monday. Then on Wednesday, the vase of blue Stargazer lilies and white jasmine sprays would be delivered in the evening when the fragrance of both blossoms was strongest. Then if things went the way he hoped, Cord would be back sometime on Friday to personally deliver a jar of his mother's rose petal jam, a treat Faith had practically inhaled when he'd gifted her some on their first anniversary.

He grinned at his reflection in the rearview mirror as he parked his car in the driveway of his parents' house, imagining the look of pleasure and frustration on Faith's face when she received her deliveries. He'd intentionally left everything anonymous; the gifts spoke for themselves since each one represented a special memory he and Faith had shared. He had no doubt that by the time he returned to Plumwood Hollow, they'd be the talk of the town, and that was fine by him.

"Cord, you're home!" Carmelita Overman said when he stepped outside onto the veranda where she was lounging with a book in a colorful hammock. The woman rarely took advantage of lazy Saturday afternoons, but he was pleased to see her doing so now.

"Don't get up," he told her when she started to rise, the hammock making her usually graceful movements slightly comical. "You might hurt yourself."

"Don't you laugh at me, young man," she said with exaggerated sternness, but she relaxed back into the colorful canvas swing just the same.

"I'll come to you." He pulled a patio chair close and dropped down into it. "You can hug me later," he added with another smirk, giving the hammock a nudge to set it in motion.

"What are you doing here already?" She closed the book without bothering to mark her place and tucked it against her side. "I thought you weren't coming until this evening."

"The plans I'd hoped to make this morning didn't happen, so I got on the road a little earlier, that's all."

"Faith?" she asked, her eyes soft with empathy.

"Some things just take time." It wasn't exactly a confirmation, but he didn't want to let himself get discouraged. He'd originally left the morning free on the off-chance Faith would want to spend time with him, but seeing as that wasn't the case, he wound up heading out right after breakfast.

"The best things usually do." Carmelita reached over and patted her son's knee. "You've waited this long, right?"

"I saw her a couple of days ago." He leaned his head back and stared up at the slats of the portico roof, the Carolina Jessamine vine with its bright yellow flowers, a favorite of his mother's, twining gracefully with the pale pink 'New Dawn' climbing rose that grew vigorously overhead. Both vines were in full bloom, something that happened every year right before Mother's Day. Had God planned flowers to bloom so exuberantly in spring just to honor mothers?

"And?"

"Put it this way," Cord said with a dry chuckle. "She wasn't nearly as excited to see me as I was to see her."

"Oh, dear."

Cord shook his head. "My fault, Ma. I didn't give her any warning, and I—"

"You didn't give her any warning?" His mother swung her legs over the side of the hammock and sat up, somehow making the move look far more dignified than he'd expected. "Cordell Overman. Haven't I taught you better than that?"

Cord rubbed his eyes with his thumb and forefinger, then grimaced. "I know, I know. I was going to call her first. Ask her out to dinner, you know? Somewhere neutral. But I couldn't figure out where to begin, and last Wednesday, I just sorta missed Uncle Judge's driveway, and wound up in front of Seven Virtues. And Prudence was there. You may not remember her, but she's one of Faith's little sisters."

"Seven girls altogether, right?" Carmelita shook her head slowly in sympathy; Cord had told her about Faith losing her mother, and how, being the oldest sibling at the time, she'd done her best to help her father raise the rest of the girls. "She must be such a remarkable young lady," Carmelita murmured. "I can't wait to get to know her better."

"I can't either, Ma. Sometimes I wonder, though—"

"Stop it, young man," she said, cutting him off. "I have an in with the Man upstairs; I'll have you know. I've been putting in my request for many years now, and from what I can tell, He's finally giving ear to my prayers." She shot him a stern look. "So you foil things up by showing up at her place unannounced?"

"I know," Cord said again. "I didn't plan to do it that way, I promise. But when I saw Prudence standing in front of their sign, waving at me as though she'd been waiting for me to show up, I pulled over to say hello. I felt like not to do so would have been rude."

"How odd," Carmelita said, her head slightly cocked as she listened to her son. "How did she know you were coming?"

"She didn't." Cord looked sheepishly at his mother and explained. "She'd seen my truck slow down as I drove by, um, a couple of times, and waved me down to see if I was lost."

"Oh, honey, you didn't." But Carmelita laughed sweetly. "There is nothing more disquieting than being in love, is there? It can make us do the most wonderfully foolish things."

Cord didn't bother to respond. The whole last decade of his life felt like an exercise in foolish things, but he knew for certain he was coming out of it a better man. Which meant he had more to offer Faith than he'd ever had before.

"So, what happened?" Carmelita prodded.

"I talked to Prudence—she's just a grown-up version of the kid I remember—and met Faith's dog, Jack, who seemed to like me well enough."

"There's that," his mother said, a hopeful lilt in her voice. "Dogs know good people." She'd lost her old retriever just after the new year, and although she wasn't yet ready to have a new dog, she was now able to talk about Tornado without tears.

"That's what Prudence said, which is why she strongly encouraged me to go see Faith right then."

"Strongly encouraged?" The look on Carmelita's face said she knew exactly what that meant.

"If I didn't, she'd tell Faith I'd been there and chickened out. Said she didn't keep secrets from her sister." He frowned and reached up to rub at the back of his neck as he recalled their interaction. "Truth be told, I got the impression that girl keeps a lot of secrets. Or at least one or two big ones."

"Hm." His mother nodded. "I can't imagine sharing a home with all those women and not wanting to keep a few things to myself."

Cord nodded. "True. Anyway, she told me she'd give me a half hour head start, then went back to taking pictures of the dog in front of the sign. For their website, or something."

"Would you get to the good stuff already?" his mother said, nudging his knee with her sandaled foot. "What happened with Faith?"

"Well, as I said, she didn't seem thrilled to see me."

"But?" Carmelita leaned forward, her eyes bright with curiosity.

Cord chuckled. "I feel like this is turning into some kind of high school girl's locker room conversation, Ma."

"I am your mother," she retorted. "I gave birth to you. I changed your diapers and bathed you and fed you and clothed you. You owe me, son."

Cord lifted his hands in surrender. "Okay, okay," he said around his laughter. "In spite of everything she said, it's still there. That—that spark. I saw it in her eyes."

Carmelita clapped her hands together and pushed up out of the hammock. "That is good news, indeed, for this mother's heart." She gestured for him to stand, too. "Give me a hug, you big lug. I'm glad you're home. Your father should be here any minute; he had to run out for a quick errand."

Cord swept her up in a warm embrace, but not before he'd seen the gleam of anticipation in her eyes. He knew exactly what his father was up to. Dalton Overman gifted Carmelita with a new piece of jewelry every Mother's Day, almost as much a celebration of his only son as it was the mother of his son. But Cord knew the best gift his father had ever given his mother was being a good husband who loved her more than his own life.

Dalton Overman found them in the kitchen, waiting for a pot of coffee to finish brewing. He'd met with some colleagues over golf, followed by lunch, and was just as surprised to see Cord home already as his wife had been. "Cord!" he exclaimed, his long strides covering the distance between them. Not quite as demonstrative as Carmelita, he shook Cord's hand, then pulled him in for a quick man-hug.

Broader at the shoulders, and a few inches taller than Cord, Dalton commanded respect wherever he went, but friends and family knew well the gentle nature of the man behind the custom-tailored suits. Cord couldn't remember ever being afraid of his father, not even when he was in trouble growing up. Sure, he'd been terrified of the discipline Dalton doled out—the man came up with extremely creative punishments that were difficult to forget—but Cord always knew exactly what he'd done to deserve them. He also knew, even in the middle of the worst of times, that his father believed in him and loved him, and wanted better for him.

Dalton had a knack for encouraging people to go that extra step, to dig deeper and stretch farther than they ever thought they could. It was what made him a good businessman, as well as a good father. Pastor Treadwell's words drifted through Cord's mind. *You have the gift of exhortation, son.* Suddenly, Cord realized where he'd gotten it.

"Hey, Dad." Cord gave his father an extra thump on the back, then returned to his seat at the breakfast bar.

"Just in time for coffee." Carmelita stood on tiptoe to kiss her husband.

"Smells fantastic," Dalton said, patting her backside affectionately as she practically twirled away from him.

Cord smiled and glanced away out of respect. His mother always got a little giddy when his father came home. It had been that way as far back as he could remember. Could Cord hope to stir that kind of response in Faith?

Over an early evening meal of Carmelita's chicken salad sandwiches and a rich French onion soup she'd made from scratch in her slow cooker, they talked about Cord's plans for Whispering Hills.

"It's going as smoothly as can be expected," he said, explaining how the purchase had gone without a hitch, in part, thanks to Frankie being thrilled at the prospect of handing over the Flanner home to family, especially someone he was confident would care for it with the greatest appreciation. With Cord's significant savings from his short-term football career, and his sizable trust fund for backup, there was no reason for delay. But over the few days he'd spent at the ranch, Cord had been rather shocked to see how much the place had fallen into disrepair, and he expressed as much to his parents. "I don't even think Frankie realized how badly his dad had let the place go. Did you two notice stuff when you were there for the memorial service?"

"Oh, we didn't stay at the ranch," his mother said. "We knew it was only Frankie and that lovely Mr. Binks fellow out there, and it would be asking far too much of those boys to host guests. We stayed at a darling little inn over in Muldoon."

Dalton nodded, his brow furrowed in thought. "That's right. We didn't stay at the ranch, but we did go out there to take them a meal that last day, remember, Carmelita?" To Cord, he added, "Your mother is a remarkable woman, son. She put together a basket of food for those two that would feed a whole army for a month."

"None of it was homemade, though." Carmelita waved a dismissive hand at him. "There was nowhere to cook in our hotel room. So I just went shopping for them, knowing they'd eat right out of the cans in the pantry if they had nothing else."

Dalton covered his wife's hand with his own and squeezed. "It was exactly what they needed, sweetheart. Frankie said so several times." Turning back to Cord, he continued. "We did talk a little about the condition of the place. Everything looked like it could use a new coat of paint, and according to Frankie, there was a barn with some structural damage that he thought might have to come down at some point. But you know me, son. I'll be the first to admit that I'm not the best person to ask about things like that. I have good folks who can take a look for you, though."

"Thanks, Dad. I'll keep that in mind. Frankie gave me the same list," Cord explained. "He also said the old fencing needs upgrading, some of the equipment replaced, and that there's some work to be done on the house. Binks added a few minor things to the list, too." He frowned and ran a finger around the lip of his water glass, creating a resonating hum that made his mother jump. "Sorry," he said with a sheepish grin. Then he sobered again. "It's more than that, though. Everything feels like it's... *leaning*, if you know what I mean. It's like the place just got old right along with Uncle Judge and has been slowly falling into disrepair. The deeper I dig, the more I find that needs to be done just to get everything operational again. It's pretty evident that Binks has been struggling to keep his head above water, but from what I can tell, that ship started sinking long before Uncle Judge died." He shot an apologetic look at his mother. "Aunt Betina's rose garden is nothing but a jumble of weeds and thorny brambles now."

"Oh, sweetie, I know," Carmelita murmured, her eyes growing misty. "It was like that when we were there, too." Carmelita and her sister were both avid gardeners, but they'd shared a love of roses, especially.

His father studied him for a few moments before asking, "Are you having second thoughts? Reconsidering?"

Cord shook his head emphatically. "No, no. That's not it." He sighed and picked up his coffee, downing the last of his first cup. Cord wasn't afraid of the growing mountain of work that needed to be done on the ranch. Sure, he had the benefit of having resources to hire folks to do the work for him, but he was looking forward to getting his own hands dirty, his own boots scuffed. There was something edifying and character building about laboring for even the smallest reward—a hot supper at the end of the day, a good night's rest. Even a job-well-done high five from a hard-working teammate. That wasn't what was bothering him. "Can I ask you something? I need you to be honest."

"Of course," both his parents said in unison.

"Do you think I'm entitled? Or that I think I am?"

Both of them frowned, their expressions so similar, Cord almost laughed.

"That's silly, honey. You've worked very hard for everything you have," his mother said. "Where is this coming from?"

His father said nothing, so Cord tried to explain. "I've run into a few people in Plumwood Hollow who seem to think I'm not much more than a trust fund baby who has had everything handed to him on a silver platter. Ironically, that's what Faith's dad said to me ten years ago, too. And now, I'm beginning to question myself. I mean, things have come pretty easy to me. I got a partial sports scholarship to the university I wanted, even though I know we could have paid for every penny of my education with pocket change. I didn't make the NFL draft, but I still landed a kick butt contract with my first-choice team. Even the scouting position. Do you know most guys have to intern for months, sometimes years, before getting hired on?" He paused for a moment and looked back and forth between his parents. "How many people get opportunities like that handed to them left and right the way I have? I walk away from one dream spot, and another opens before I even have to knock."

His father nodded slowly. "I can see why you might think that, but your mother is right. You've worked hard for everything that's been offered you.

You earned that scholarship, son. You played your heart out in high school and kept your grades high. It paid off. And believe me, the Bengals signed you on because of the hard work they expected you to continue putting in. Scouting, too, is the epitome of hard work—"

"Crazy hard work," his mother piped up. "Getting you to come home for a visit was like trying to win the lottery. One chance in a billion we'd get you here."

"Ironically, though, hard work didn't pay off for either position, did it? I even struggled with grades in college, to the point where they threatened to bench me on more than one occasion."

"Where is all this leading?" his father asked, a speculative look on his face. He reached for the coffee carafe in the middle of the table, silently offered refills to the others, then took his wife's hand again.

Cord pushed away from the table and leaned back in his chair, stretching his arms up over the top of his head before continuing. "It's the ranch, dad, and my—well, my preconceived notions about it. My assumptions. I guess I expected to charge into Plumwood Hollow like some hometown hero, you know?" He threw his hands wide in a magnanimous gesture, lowered his voice, and boomed out, "Good o' boy Cordell Overman buys up Whispering Hills to keep the ranch in the family, and in the process, saves the hollow from some big bad outsider." He snorted and lowered his arms. "Then amidst the back slaps and applause—Who knows? Maybe I'd even kiss a baby or two—I'd throw on a pair of work boots and a straw hat, saddle up, and start ranching."

"You forgot the part about sweeping your high school sweetheart off her feet and riding off into the sunset together," his mother said in a soft voice. She wasn't mocking him, just acknowledging his sentiment.

"Yeah." He rubbed his eyes roughly, then grimaced. "I guess I saw things go differently than the way they have. Now I'm taking stock and not necessarily liking the new version I'm seeing. I'm half afraid those folks are right. I mean, even if I'd opted not to buy Whispering Hills, I had another killer offer from you as a backup plan. I couldn't lose." He shook his head. "Talk about being served up on a silver platter. Timing, price, location." He choked out a laugh, but he wasn't feeling any mirth at the moment.

"Next door to the woman I've loved from the moment I laid eyes on her. And she's still single!" His voice rose emphatically, but Cord could feel the edge of hysteria tickling his throat. "I mean, can it get any easier than that?

His father spoke first. "Son, you need to stop beating yourself up. I don't see things the way you're painting them. That girl you've loved all these years? That football career you dreamed of? Seems to me you've sacrificed a lot in your short life. You've had to make some tough decisions since leaving home." He held up his hand when Cord opened his mouth to speak. "No, let me finish. Now, I don't know what happened between you and Faith and her daddy, but you've been living with some unfinished business for the last decade. I'd like to think the Good Lord has been keeping tabs on that situation, and it's not because of any supposed entitlement that's brought you back full circle, but instead, it's the man upstairs working his master plan in your life. Don't sell him short, you hear?"

"Amen," Carmelita interjected.

His father continued. "I warrant he knows exactly what he's doing, and he probably had a good idea that it would take you a little longer than some to figure out what you're doing."

Cord guffawed. "Who says I know what I'm doing?"

"I do," Dalton said. "I truly believe that, son." He relaxed back in his patio chair, stretching his long legs out in front of him, and peered out over the beautifully manicured lawn of their backyard. It was a lush sanctuary with splashes of color and texture, the late afternoon sun turning the sky muted peaches and apricots that faded to mauve, even as they watched. Finally, he turned back to Cord. "Your mother and I are proud of you. You've struggled through some dark times, but you've never given up. You've never stopped searching and going after the next thing."

"That's a big part of why opportunities seem to fall in your lap, Cord," his mother added, nodding in agreement with her husband's words. "You're watching for them."

"You haven't been sitting around waiting for life to happen to you. That's why Frankie called you, son. He knows you're a man of action. We all do."

"Thank you," Cord said, humbled and honored by his parents' words. "I mean it. I can't tell you how much it means to me to have you believe in me, especially after what feels to me like a whole lot of wasted years."

"No." Carmelita shook her finger at him. "You have not wasted anything. The things you have done, the life you have experienced, even the mistakes you've made—" She broke off with a chuckle, then leaned forward over the table. "Especially the mistakes you've made, son, they've all contributed to the man you are today. You have not stopped growing or searching or striving. You keep moving forward, and that is something that comes from inside of you. It is what you're made of." She tapped the table with a bright pink fingernail, the myriad of colorful bangles on her wrist jingling against the glass top. "And you have not lost sight of what is important: family. That is why you are here today, right? I know you could have used that mess of a ranch as an excuse to stay in Plumwood Hollow this weekend, but you didn't. You came home to spend this time with me. With us. That is the sign of a good man whose heart is in the right place."

"Love you, Mom. You know I wouldn't miss spending Mother's Day with you." Cord reached over and squeezed her hand.

"Exactly. And I love you, too." She lifted a shoulder in a half shrug. "So? You have your work cut out for you. Dig in, son. Put down roots." She loved her garden metaphors. "None of your other jobs could give you that. Football and scouting and even the job your father offered—marketing, right? Those jobs were all about traveling and winning and going, going, going. This ranch? My sister said the only thing she did not love about ranching was how hard it was for them to go anywhere." She smiled as some memory flashed across her mind. "But she loved it, Cord. And we all know you love it, too."

Cord nodded slowly. "I do. I always have. And not just because of the girl next door, either," he added with a chuckle. "Although she certainly completed the picture. I still love her, too."

"Then you go home, and you work your rear end off to convince her of that," his mother said, settling back in her chair and turning to smile at her husband. "You have your father's gift of persuasion, son. He had my heart in his hands before I even knew I wanted to give it to him."

"Likewise, darling," Dalton said with a tender smile.

Cord cleared his throat. "Okay, you two lovebirds. You're making me jealous." He leaned forward and rested his forearms on the table. "Uncle Judge offered me a position at the ranch; did you know that? My sophomore year at UK, he called me up and asked me to consider stepping in at the ranch instead of playing football after I graduated."

"He did?" The look on her face told him this was the first time his mother had heard of it.

But Dalton nodded slowly. "I knew about it," he said. "After the fact, anyway. Judge came to me and asked me to speak to you."

Cord frowned. "About taking his job offer? After I turned him down?"

"Well," his father began, dragging the word out. "He knew Frankie had his sights set beyond the boundary line of Whispering Hills, Plumwood Hollow, and the Midwest. That kid wanted to be a soldier from the time he was old enough to march."

"I know. He's been into camo and face paint for as long as I can remember," Cord said with a chuckle. "Strategy plans, cadence calls, digging trenches. Came in handy the summer Uncle Judge had us dig the foundation for two new bunkhouses. Frankie commandeered that project start to finish." He smiled affectionately, remembering how seriously his older cousin had taken the assignment. "His dad was really proud of him, of all of us. He hadn't expected us to actually complete the task, no less to do the job even better than a construction crew with machines would. We were all proud of that work. We kinda felt like those were our bunkhouses after that."

"I remember that," Carmelita said. "You came home after that summer with your head up and your shoulders back like you'd just survived a rite of passage into manhood."

"Your uncle told me he thought you'd caught the ranching bug that summer," Dalton said, a wry smile on his face. "We took bets on whether you'd end up in football or ranching. Looks like we were both right."

"Wasn't that also the year you fell in love with Faith Goodacre?" Carmelita asked.

Cord shook his head. "Nope. I fell in love with Faith Goodacre the first time I laid eyes on her that first summer working on the ranch." He shot his mom a crooked grin and said, "But that was the year I kissed Faith Goodacre for the first time, and let me tell you something. I caught that bug, too. Down for the count. Fever, chills, sleepless nights tossing and turning—"

"I think we get it, honey," Carmelita said with a giggle, bringing her hands up to wave off any further explanation from Cord.

"Sometimes I wonder how things would have turned out if I'd taken him up on it. Chosen ranching over football from the get-go."

"And you would have always wondered, wouldn't you?" his mother replied, her expression firm. "Enough. You've had some wonderful, irreplaceable experiences that no one, least of all you, should ever begrudge you. You gave your all to football, and it didn't pan out for you as a player. You used your gifts as a scout, but now that season has ended."

"Consider this, Cord," his father interjected. "Had you stayed on at Whispering Hills, you might be running your uncle's ranch now. Who knows? Maybe he would still be alive if he'd had someone like you working alongside him."

"Not helping, Dad."

"Let me finish," Dalton said, lifting a hand to stay Cord's words. "Instead, you are now your own man with a plan completely different from your uncle's, with a college education that has helped hone your head for business, and with a significant chunk of your own money from your football career. Your endeavors this last decade have put you in the position you're in now to make the decisions you're making now. You're a little older, a whole lot wiser, and you have a much better understanding of yourself as a man."

Carmelita nodded in agreement but said nothing.

"Buying your uncle's place free from any expectations he might have projected onto you while you worked for him gives you the freedom to make it wholly and completely yours. That, my son, is a rare gift that few ever have the opportunity to explore. Regretting how you got here? Now that would be a tragic waste."

NINE

As she did every night since she'd moved back to the ranch, Charity had the coffee pot filled and ready to go; all Faith had to do was push the red button to start it brewing. She let Jack outside to do his business, then pulled out a chair in the dimly lit kitchen while the Mr. Coffee relic gurgled and burped, the robust French roast fragrancing the air around her. She bent down to pull her socks up snug over her calves, then slipped her feet into her boots.

Steaming mug in hand, she slipped outside into the early Sunday morning. A late spring fog clung with wispy tendrils to everything as the sun broke free of the horizon, spilling golden streams of light into the haze. No one else was awake yet, and she cherished mornings like this when God seemed to welcome her out into his creation personally. "You're pretty demonstrative when we're paying attention, aren't you?" she murmured as she watched the sky shift and fluctuate like a living thing.

Seven Virtues was just large enough that once she sent the younger girls off to school on weekdays, several hours could pass without her running into anyone except the livestock and Jack, but it was rare that she was the first one awake. She resisted the urge to check on her father who was usually seated at the big kitchen table with his Bible and his first or second cup of coffee before she crawled out of bed. "Let him have a couple of extra minutes of sleep," she told herself as she shoved her hat down a little firmer on her head. He was probably awake anyway, lying in bed, wishing his Caroline were there with him.

Watson called out a greeting from the paddock he shared with three other horses behind the barn: Charity and Abby's Quarters, and

Prudence's rescued Andalusian. They all knew the sound of the kitchen door, so even though their paddock was built behind the barn and out of sight, the lot set up an excited ruckus each morning, anticipating food, love, and maybe even some riding time. Courage and Justice kept their matching white Irish Sport Horses, Flash and Fire, stabled in a separate paddock with their own small barn at the back of the indoor arena where they did much of their practicing. The pair of geldings were brothers who didn't seem to realize they weren't literally attached at the hips, which worked out well for the twins' trick riding show, Twisted Sisters.

Faith filled the hay nets for the other three horses in the paddock to quiet them down, then led Watson into the big barn where she let him munch on a small flake while she brushed him down and then saddled him. She'd let all the animals out into the horse pasture when she came back from checking her herd.

After downing the last of her coffee, still so hot it made her tongue tingle, Faith led the horse out of the barn, Jack practically dancing around their feet. Watson snorted with excitement, too.

Out in the crisp morning air, she mounted up, smiling at the way Watson's muscles bunched and twitched in anticipation. She stroked his neck, talking quietly to him as they rounded the end of the building. She'd had the horse since high school, and although he wasn't a young buck, Watson was young at heart. He loved the ranch as much as Faith did, and took his work seriously, performing it with a joy and verve that made Faith's job even more pleasurable.

Glancing over at the house, she saw a light flicker on in the kitchen. If she didn't get going quickly, someone would step outside to greet her, and her morning solitude would be broken. Leaning down over Watson's neck, she murmured, "Let's go, boy!" Jack must've picked up on her intentions, because he dashed out in front, and took off down the dirt road toward the high pasture. Not to be bested, Watson let out a challenging whinny, and Faith gave him an encouraging nudge with her heels.

The cattle seemed lazy that morning, barely paying them any mind as Faith, Watson, and Jack meandered through the herd, counting heads, monitoring the calves and their mamas, checking for any signs of failure to thrive in the new babies. She preferred the horse to the ATVs when working directly with the cows, although she used the four-wheelers for the heavy lifting tasks, like moving the massive portable watering tanks, distributing hay in winter, or repositioning the chicken tractor. Not only did the herd behave better around the horses, but it gave her an excuse to ride Watson every day.

She took a moment to make sure the water lines were functioning properly to keep the troughs full, then glanced at her watch before heading back. By now, the house would be abuzz with activity. Charity would be overseeing breakfast preparations, commandeering setting the table or peeling potatoes. Prudence and Jasmine would tend the pigs and ducks, and Daddy would be out checking on the garden. The twins were likely in the smaller barn with their twin horses, murmuring softly among themselves. It intrigued Faith to see the four of them communicating: half the time, she couldn't tell whether her sisters were talking to each other or their horses. Abby, Faith was certain, would still be loitering in her room, pushing it to the last minute before crawling out of bed to face the day. At barely seventeen, her youngest sister was all teenager, and before she got caught up in the activities of the day, her favorite place to be was burrowed beneath the covers on her antique four-poster bed. Mornings were hard for her: she was definitely the night owl of the family, just like their mother had been.

Faith wondered what Hope was up to this morning, if she and Chet would be joining them for Sunday morning breakfast, or if they'd just meet up with them at church and then come back with them after the service for dinner. Now that Charity had moved home again, Hope was the only sister who lived off the ranch. She and her husband, Chet Willis, had a lovely little home next to Hope's veterinary practice. Although she worked on just about any kind of animal folks could round up, Hope called herself a large animal vet, and she specialized in equine chiropractic care. Because of her unique skills, she did a significant amount of traveling, something Chet often complained about. But then, Chet complained about a lot of things these days.

"Happy Mother's Day!" Jasmine cried out when Faith entered the kitchen. She launched herself at her mother, squeezed her in a tight hug, then stepped back so she could shove a small gift box and the card she'd made yesterday at her. "I love you, mama," the child said. "Now open it!"

"Hold on, sugar pie. Let me get out of my gear and wash my hands."

"Did you bring your coffee cup back in with you?" Charity asked from where she stood at the sink, washing up a frying pan.

Faith smacked her forehead with an open palm. "I'll be right back." She turned to dash back out to the barn, just as Courage and Justice strode in.

"I got you covered," Daddy said, thrusting his chin toward the row of cup hooks under the cupboard. "I washed it and hung it up to dry. Happy Mother's Day, Daughter."

Faith slipped out of her jacket and boots, returned her hat to its place, then circled the table to hug her father. "Happy Mother's Day to you too, Daddy." Because their mother was no longer with them, Mother's Day was more of a memorial day, not just to remember their mother, but also to celebrate how everyone had stepped up to fill her shoes. Somehow, in spite of their great loss, they had not just survived, but thrived, and they all knew Caroline would be proud of them.

Faith made her rounds to the other girls in the room, ending with Charity. Without asking, she picked up a dishtowel and began to dry the dishes Charity washed. Behind her, the table was being set, glasses were being filled, and the chatter of a busy household ebbed and flowed as the meal came together. Just as they were about to sit down, Hope pushed through the door with a wide smile on her face and a huge basket in her arms.

She was alone. Faith exchanged knowing looks with Charity, but no one said anything, not even Abby. In fact, lately, around the Goodacre home, Chet wasn't missed nearly as much as he should be. It wasn't right, but it was true. No one said it out loud, but if it weren't for the fact that he was their sister's husband, if the man left town and never came back, there'd be a celebratory round of "Good riddance" around their table.

"Happy Mother's Day to everyone!" Hope declared, setting the basket on the counter next to the coffeepot. "I come bearing chocolate for dipping strawberries, sparkling Apple cider, and Mama's favorite, a tub of—"

"Red licorice!" Jasmine finished for her. "Can I have a piece now?"

"No, silly. It's for this afternoon when we go visit your grandma." Hope held out her arms. "Now come give your favorite aunt in the whole world a big old hug."

Jasmine planted her hands on her hips and shot Hope a reproachful look. "I don't think my arms are big enough to wrap around all six of you at the same time." She threw in a head wag and added, "Because I know you know I don't have any favorites."

"Do you need any ice for that burn?" Abby asked with a sarcastic drawl. "And I know you know that if she did have a favorite, it would be me."

Breakfast was borderline chaos as usual, especially since most of them still had to get ready for church, but they headed out the door in good time and filed into their pew with four minutes to spare.

Every year, high school boys handed out pink and red carnations to every woman, young and old, who entered the building, and Faith held hers to her nose, smelling the faint sweetness that somehow reminded her of her mother. The pastor spoke about the woman who raised Mary, the mother of Jesus, and how huge a role she would have played in helping Mary to be the mother she was. It was a poignant reminder of how important multigenerational families were, and Faith made a silent commitment to invite her grandparents, Marcie and George Oakley, out for a visit soon. They lived in Florida and had no taste for ranch life like their daughter and granddaughters, but they did enjoy spending time with the girls. Courage and Justice were performing several times over the summer, and their flamboyant grandmother did like to get all decked out in her colorful pearl button shirts and rhinestone-studded jeans. Meemaw Oakley didn't care that she looked like a tourist with her beaded and feathered felt hats; she and Pops were there to support their granddaughters in style. They hadn't been since Christmas, so a visit was overdue.

Jed, on the other hand, had been raised by a single father in Texas. He had no siblings, and his father had passed away when Faith was just old enough to remember him. In her mind, Grandpa Waylen was like the Marlboro Man. Silent, always on a horse, and with a faraway look in his eyes, as though the man lived on a different plane altogether. Her father rarely spoke of the man, except with great respect, which only served to validate her idea of him.

After church, they stopped by the house to change out of their fancy clothes, then they loaded up a cooler with barbecue sandwiches, potato salad, coleslaw, sweet tea, and brownies, and strapped it onto the back of one of the four-wheelers, which Daddy drove. He went on ahead to the small copse of woods on the east side of the ranch where, in a small natural clearing, they'd discovered a thriving patch of wild strawberries guarded by a multi-trunked eastern redbud that bloomed ferociously from right after Easter through to early June. They dubbed it Mama's Secret Garden, and over the years, they planted Caroline's beloved red columbines and some purple spiderwort from her flower garden to complement the pretty little yellow violets that grew wild in the clearing. Then, a few years ago, a brier of blackberries cropped up along one edge, and although they kept them trimmed back so they wouldn't take over, the girls watched for the ripening fruit in the late summer. Every August, they celebrated their mother's birthday there, filling buckets with blackberries, then taking them back to the house to turn their harvest into pies, jams, and syrups.

The rest of them walked, giving Jed a few moments alone to remember his Caroline before the girls showed up. Hope let Jasmine carry the tub of red licorice, allowing her three pieces to eat on the way, while she carted the basket of cider and the chocolate she'd heated up and poured into an insulated coffee carafe so they could dip the wild strawberries into it. Charity, Abby, and the twins all had fold-up lawn chairs slung over their shoulders, Faith brought the croquet set, and Prudence carried her gardening bag, intent on doing a little maintenance as they whiled away the afternoon with the spirit of their mother.

It was the perfect day for a Sunday afternoon picnic in the woods, and Faith sank low in her canvas chair, her stomach full and the drone of insects lulling her into a trance-like state of mind. Jasmine, Abby, Hope, and Justice were playing a fiercely competitive round of croquet, and Daddy lay stretched out on one of the blankets, his hat tipped low over his eyes to block out the flickering sunlight overhead. Charity and Prudence were gathering redbud blossoms to make a batch of the yummy pink jelly, and Courage sat in another lawn chair beside Faith, trying to concentrate on something she was reading for school.

The twins, both majoring in business, had very different directions in mind. Courage was leaning more toward agriculture, while Justice had a fascination with business law. She blamed it on her name—"What else was I supposed to study with a name like mine?"—but she loved the minutiae of contracts, rules and regulations, organization, and order. Their different personalities were also evident in their trick riding act; while Justice was the more technical and precise rider, Courage rode with more grace and style, playing off the vibe of their audiences. Justice handled the details of their business, while Courage catered to the crowds, designed their costumes, and decked out their horses in style.

As Faith lazily studied her family, she was reminded of one of those Renoir paintings, the Impressionist images of young people picnicking in the painter's gardens.

"I hear Frankie found himself a buyer," Daddy said, not bothering to remove his hat. So, he wasn't asleep after all. "Talk is it's going to be some kind of a dude ranch."

"What?" Faith was suddenly wide awake, herself. She sat forward, almost spilling the last of her sweet tea. Talk about worst-case scenario. The last thing she wanted was a bunch of urbanites playing cowboy dress-up, partying until all hours, scaring her Dexters. Not to mention what they would do to Judge's herd, between cow tipping dares and patty wars. And she couldn't imagine how poor Jordan Binks was handling this. "What on earth was Frankie thinking? It would've been better if he'd parceled off the land in bits and pieces than to turn it over to some Boss Hogs and his Dukes of Hazzard." Jack, who'd been interfering with the game by chasing the wooden balls, seemed to sense her distress and hurried to her side. He nudged his nose against her palm to comfort her. "Why didn't he talk to us about this? Why didn't he at least tell me that he was considering this when I spoke to him a couple of weeks ago?"

"A dude ranch? As in a bunch of city folk playing rhinestone cowboy?" Courage asked, her mind going in the exact direction Faith's had. She closed her book in her lap, the reading material no longer holding her attention.

Charity called out above the noise of the game her sisters were playing. "I caught wind of something similar, but no one seems to know anything more than that."

"I thought it might be Cord Overman," Prudence suggested, testing the weight of the harvest she held. The redbud tree had bloomed prolifically this year, and the bright pink flowers were spilling over the top of the basket. "Although, I don't think he's a dude ranch kind of guy."

The game came to a sudden halt as Hope, who was lining up a hit, straightened abruptly and turned to look at Faith. Justice, too, rested her mallet on the toe of her sneaker and shot a questioning look at her oldest sister. Abby and Jasmine paused in their ribbing of each other to look around the group with growing curiosity.

"Who is Cord Overman?" Jasmine asked, then she stepped up to the blue ball in front of her and took a swing.

"Hey! It's not your turn," Abby said, bumping the ball back to the general vicinity of where it had been.

Jed sat up slowly, returning his hat to his head, tugging the brim down low in front so that Faith still couldn't see his face. In other words, Daddy was deep in thought and wasn't yet ready to let anyone know what was going through his mind. That was even scarier than if he had reacted off the cuff.

"I heard that boy came by here for a visit the other day," he said, his voice low and even. He finally lifted his gaze to meet Faith's, but his expression told her he wasn't asking her if it was true or not.

Faith glanced over at Prudence, who shook her head. "Don't look at me," she objected. "I didn't say a word."

"She didn't have to," Jed said. "Toby mentioned it to me at church today. Told me the kid stopped in to see him, too."

"He's not a boy anymore, Daddy." She didn't mean to be rude, but she didn't like the slightly derogatory tone her father used in referring to Cord.

"Or a kid, either." Why she was defending him, she couldn't exactly say, and she lowered her eyes to focus on Jack's adoring face.

Her face flushed hotly as she thought about the bouquet of scarlet Gerbera daisies Trilby's husband, Mitch—who also happened to be Plumwood Hollow's Postmaster—had delivered to her yesterday. There'd been no note, no name, but the gregarious mailman had given her a cheeky nod and said, "Mighty nice color, Miss Faith. Matches your cheeks. I'll let young Cord know you're pleased with them." Fortunately, she and Prudence had been the only people in the house at that moment, and although her sister said nothing, Faith didn't miss the glint of satisfaction in her pale blue eyes.

Faith hadn't needed a note to know who'd sent them, nor had she been surprised when Mitch attributed the flowers to Cord. She'd painted a whole row of the bright-faced flowers inside the decrepit hay barn on the other side of the tree line. "Don't they just make you happy to look at them?" she'd asked him as she'd swirled more red on her brush. Cord had said it made him happy that they made her happy. Then he'd proceeded to grab her around the waist, pinning her arms to her sides, and he snatched the brush from her and painted a long red line down the bridge of her nose while she squealed in helpless delight.

"Whatever he is," her father replied, jolting Faith out of her reverie. "I would've liked to have heard about it from you, rather than being surprised by the good pastor." He stood and shook his creased jeans down over his boots. "You might have said something to me."

"It was just a hello. I didn't feel like it was worthy of an official announcement." Although the daisies indicated that it was clearly something more.

"Who is Cord Overman?" Jasmine asked again, this time a little more demanding. "Why is everyone acting so weird?"

"Yeah," Abby chimed in. "Inquiring minds want to know. Is he hot? You got a boyfriend we don't know about, Faith? Or is he, you know, like, your baby daddy, or something equally scandalous?"

"Abstinence!" At least three or four people cried out in reprimand.

"Whoa." Abby's eyes grew wide in affront, then even wider as the truth of her callous words dawned on her. "Whoa. Dude." She put a hand over her mouth, but when she saw Jasmine staring at her with narrowed eyes, she lowered it quickly. "Sorry," she muttered, barely above a whisper, then she crossed to the blanket and snatched up her glass, chugging the remainder of her tea. She wouldn't meet Faith's eyes.

"Mama?" Jasmine threw down her mallet, planted her hands on her hips, and glared at her mother. But the power of speech seemed to have abandoned Faith in that moment, so the child turned her November sky eyes on her grandfather. "Grampa? What's going on?"

Jed clenched his jaw, his lips pressed together to form a straight line, then shot Faith an apologetic look. "I shouldn't have brought up Whispering Hills today. It's just rumors, from what I can tell. I'm sure we'll learn more when the dust settles." He walked over and picked up the mallet Jasmine had tossed, then handed it back to her. "How about we set up for horseshoes instead? I bet Jack won't go chasing those every time you throw them."

Justice chuckled. "At least not after the first one," she quipped.

"But who is Cord Overman?" Jasmine insisted, although her voice was no longer quite so shrill. She eyed her grandfather, who was making a big show of limbering up his shoulders and shaking out his hands. "I'm not a baby anymore. I can handle a lot more than you think I can."

"He's Judge Flanner's nephew," Prudence interjected with straightforward simplicity. She stood beneath the splayed branches of the redbud, looking like she belonged on the island of Neverland. "He used to work on his uncle's ranch during the summer when he was in high school." She met Faith's eyes. "You know, I think it would be great to have someone next door who already knows and loves Whispering Hills, as well as Plumwood Hollow. He's practically family," she added, ignoring Abby's quiet squawk and subsequent coughing fit. "I mean, folks in the hollow already know him, right? And from what I can remember, he loved ranching, so even if he is thinking about a dude ranch operation, I doubt he'd turn it into party central."

"You remember him?" Charity asked, cocking her head in surprise.

"Of course, I do. I was the same age as—" Prudence began, but her father cut her off.

"Enough talk about Whispering Hills," Jed said. "We came here to celebrate mothers in Caroline's secret garden, so I'm going to do that by beating all you little princesses in a manly game of horseshoes. Ladies?"

The rest of the afternoon, they did their best to steer conversation clear of any mention of the neighboring ranch, but Faith could see there was much speculation brewing behind her daughter's eyes. She was fairly certain she'd be asked some pretty direct questions before bedtime this evening, and she wasn't looking forward to it. Maybe one of the cows was sick, and she would have to put off any deep discussions until another day.

That thought was immediately washed away by a wave of guilt; she would never wish illness on one of her Dexters just so she could shirk her responsibilities.

Ironically, it wasn't a sick cow that kept the whole gang pretty busy when they got home from their relaxing afternoon. Before they even reached the bottom pasture, Jack set up a barking that stopped all conversation and had them running for the barn.

Charity, Prudence, and Jasmine helped Jed unload his four-wheeler, while Faith and Justice pulled out the other two ATVs. Hope jumped on behind Faith, and Courage joined her twin. The horses, sensing their urgency, raced around their paddock, setting up a ruckus of their own, but the girls didn't bother stopping to calm them. Jack ran on ahead of them, leading the way, and Faith knew daddy wasn't too far behind.

They spotted what remained of the herd milling about restlessly, calling to their family members they'd been separated from. A large section of the electric fence between Seven Virtues and Whispering Hills was down, and a post knocked askew, the top three wires snapped, the bottom one still connected but lying slack on the ground. Which meant it was still hot.

Faith hollered at the twins to go shut down the power and then sent up a prayer that all her babies were safe.

TEN

"It was a downright rotten way to end a Mother's Day for that family," Binks told Cord, his voice heavy with misery, and perhaps a little censure as well. "I'm doing what I can to keep things up and running 'round here, but I'm afraid I'm just not able to get it done alone anymore. There was a time...." The old man didn't finish his sentence, but just shook his head, an expression of frustration shadowing his features.

Storm Chaser, one of his uncle's — soon to be officially his — younger bulls, a huge fellow with a chest the size of his ego, had broken out of the paddock he shared with two others, and then headed straight for the fence line between the properties. Judge still used wood fencing in some parts of his ranch, and Storm Chaser had seen it as more of a challenge than a barricade. Once through that, he'd rooted around through the small section of the wooded area until he came to Faith's electric fence line. He'd made quick work of that, quite likely getting a few jolts of electricity that, rather than deterring him, spurred him on. Once the fence was down, Faith's Dexters had scrambled every which way to avoid the rambunctious bull, the panicking cows desperate to protect their young. It had taken Binks and the Goodacres several hours to get all the animals back where they were supposed to be, fences repaired, and the herd examined for any signs of lasting distress or injury.

"I should've been here," Cord said as he examined the repaired fence around the bull paddock. Binks had done a stand-up job as usual, but he was right. Whispering Hills was too much for only one old man to manage. "This should have been my responsibility, not yours."

Not only had he not been here for the breakout, but he'd been held up in Louisville with some financial paperwork, so instead of returning to Plumwood Hollow yesterday afternoon, he hadn't gotten in until close to midnight. It had been too late to show up on Faith's doorstep then, even if he was armed with not one jar, but a basket filled with several jars of the rose jelly Faith liked so much. He hoped to get over there today; he wanted to know if she'd liked her other gifts as well.

Binks crossed his arms and rested them on top of the fence post, staring thoughtfully at the three bulls milling placidly around the round bale hay feeder. Today, Storm Chaser showed no signs of whatever spirit had spurred on his rampage last Sunday. The old foreman made a chuffing sound with his mouth, and all three bulls lifted their heavy heads in response. It was Storm Chaser who came over to see what the two men wanted, and Binks reached across the fence and scratched the flat forehead between the animal's nearly black eyes.

"They're not bad fellows, son. They just haven't had a whole lot to do lately." Then he shot Cord a sly look and a wink. "It's not easy for a young buck—or bull," he said with a nod toward Storm Chaser, "to stay on his side of the rail when he knows what he wants is just across the fence line."

Cord raised a brow at the old man, but only said, "Young bucks and bulls can be impulsive that way. Let's just hope you all got there in time to keep him from taking advantage of those girls on the other side of the fence line. That's all Faith needs; an unplanned pregnancy or two."

Binks made a sound like he was choking and then began to cough vehemently.

"You okay?" Cord asked, gently thumping him on the back. The old guy was breathing, but his face was as red as a tomato. "You need some water or something?"

"No, no," Binks wheezed, waving his hands in front of him. "I'm fine. Just breathed in the wrong way."

Cord waited while the foreman cleared his throat a few times, then said, "I should head over to Seven Virtues today. I'm long overdue to talk to the Goodacres about my plans for this place." He'd been hesitant to tell anyone anything until the property was his, free and clear, but he now realized that was because he'd been expecting folks to be pleased to see him again, and he'd wanted it to be a great big, joyful surprise for the community. Ha. He had a feeling he'd be having several conversations like the one he needed to have with the Goodacres. Conversations that started with explanations instead of congratulations.

Binks shook his head. "Not today, you won't. Far as I know, the whole family's over in Muldoon for the day. The twins are performing at some mucky-muck county fundraiser shindig." He gave the wooden fence one last kick with his scuffed boot, then turned back toward the house. "They won't be home until late this evening, according to Faith, but I'm sure they'll be in church tomorrow. Never miss a Sunday service, Jed and the Goodacre girls."

"Tomorrow at church, then." Cord caught up easily, the old man's slightly hitched gait no match for his younger, longer stride. "Hey, I think I'll ride out and start doing perimeter checks. I expect upgrading fence lines is going to be priority, so I'd like to get a jump start on that. Figure out what I need to order and get that called in first thing next week. You need anything more from me right now?"

The two went their separate ways at the fork in the drive, Cord heading for the huge equipment garage for an ATV. At the last minute, he changed his mind. "Faith would tell me to do this on a horse." As much as he'd once loved riding, especially with the girl next door, it had been a while since he'd spent time in the saddle. He needed some practice, and today, knowing there wasn't anyone next door to catch him looking like a greenhorn, seemed as good a time as any.

The purchase of the ranch came with several horses, including three older quarter horses that were all-around ranch stock, willing to tolerate almost any level of rider, and comfortable with whatever task they were asked to perform. They were the same horses he'd cut his teeth on back in high school, and he was glad for the familiarity of the animals with their pleasant natures. Fred and Ethel, the draft horses whose main job, as far as Cord could remember, was to pull the Whispering Hills Ranch float in the Plumwood Hollow Founders Day Parade every August, were kept in a separate paddock with a Paint named Hidalgo. According to Binks, the brown and white gelding was as sweet as a Georgia peach toward the much larger drafts, but he tended to pick fights with other horses closer to his size, nipping and kicking at random. Hidalgo, however, was Frankie's horse, a gift from his father, and the spirited animal had a home on the ranch for as long as Frankie wanted him there.

Cord's favorite, Capitan, one he'd finally had the gumption to stake a claim on that last summer he'd spent on the ranch, was a rather handsome black Morgan, and Cord was thrilled to find the beast still there. It made him even happier when the horse greeted him as if he'd only been away a day, not a decade. He'd take Capitan out now, hoping the old boy would sense his lack of practice and take it easy on him.

It only took a few tries to get himself seated comfortably in the saddle, and Cord found himself grinning like a madman over his accomplishment. The years had settled Capitan, and although the horse still had a glint of mischief in his brown eyes, he stood patiently while Cord figured things out.

Together, they rode out across the near pasture toward the section of woods that was the boundary line between Uncle Judge's land—"No, mine," Cord corrected himself—and the section he'd sold to Jed Goodacre almost twenty years ago. How many times had he made his way along this same route, hoping for a glimpse of the pretty cowgirl next door? He smiled as he remembered telling her as much, only to have her grin self-consciously and admit to doing the same thing on her side of the trees.

He narrowed his eyes and craned his neck to peer through the thick growth for any sign of movement beyond the trees. It was just as Binks had insinuated back at the bullpen. It had been impossible back then for Cord to stay on his side of the rail when he knew what he wanted was just across the fence line.

"Yet another thing that hasn't changed," he said with a quiet chuckle, acknowledging the intense, aching pull of her, even now knowing she wasn't home.

Capitan tossed his head and let out a quiet nicker of contentment, as though to say, "It's about time we did this again."

ELEVEN

In spite of his promise to be there, Cord did not attend church on Sunday after all. He was not seated in the pew behind her, he did not lean forward to whisper sugar words in her ear at inappropriate times, and his unabashedly off-key baritone voice did not sweep around her during the worship songs, endearing him to her in a way a perfect, beautiful voice never could.

Even though he might as well have been, for all the thoughts of him that were making her want to fidget in her seat in the worst way.

He was not there to hear Reverend Treadwell talk about forgiveness and unconditional love, nor did he get to hear Abby perform a stunning rendition of "It is Well with my Soul," while accompanying herself on her guitar.

He was not there to see how pretty Faith looked in her ankle-length peasant dress with its short cap sleeves that showed off her toned arms, and the embroidered sweetheart neckline that made her feel more like a woman than a rancher. Nor had he shown up early like he used to so she could catch him before the service started. She'd waited alone on the bench under the big Blue Ash tree until the last minute; she'd planned to tell him about Jasmine, then escape inside so he could decide what move he wanted to make. If he left, so be it. If he stayed, she'd figure out the next step then.

But Cord was not there to learn of his daughter's existence, or to see the achingly beautiful child tucked into the pew between Faith and Jed Goodacre. The girl with hair that framed her face in a mass of natural curls just like her mother's, whose bold features bore a striking resemblance to the father she'd never met.

Faith rested a hand on Jasmine's back as the worship leader dismissed the congregation with the charge to seek out ways to bless each other this week. She was beginning to feel a little claustrophobic, having thought of little else besides Cord's absence. Sure, she'd done her best to listen to the message, especially since it was so timely with Cord's return to the hollow and him already breaking promises.

She'd been so certain he'd be here today. She'd been as prepared as she could possibly be to introduce him to Jasmine, depending on the public setting to keep the questions she knew he'd ask at bay. She'd even prepared her father and sisters for the inevitable awkwardness, especially if Cord figured out that the girl who favored him was, in fact, the daughter he'd abandoned when he'd done the same to her mother.

Faith had believed him when he said he'd be there. Again. And he'd let her down. Again.

She bore up under the overwhelming urge to push her way through the crowded aisle and out the tall front doors of the little church. She was desperate for some fresh air untainted with flowery perfumes, trivial conversation, and unbearable disillusion. But there was no such thing as slipping out unnoticed at the end of a Sunday service at Glory to God Fellowship. Especially when you belonged to a family so large, you took up a whole pew. The Goodacres were practically a procession of their own, with all seven sisters in their Sunday finery, Jasmine, and Jedediah leading the way.

"Mama, Yvette is over there," Jasmine said, pointing across the aisle to the little girl who was waving frantically at them. "Can I go talk to her?"

Faith made eye contact with Yvette's father, Levi, and gestured between the two girls. He nodded, but when their line of sight was blocked by Sherman Bench maneuvering down the aisle—a man as immense as his name implied, and one who preferred to sit near the front because he'd lost hearing in one ear when he was a child—Faith grabbed Jasmine's hand and made her wait. She didn't want the girl trampled. Not that Sherman, the quintessential gentle giant, would do so on purpose, but Jasmine had a knack for getting underfoot.

Instead, Sherman Bench happened to bump into Jenny Stuben, who then stumbled into Roger Platt, a man who was not her current fiancé. Roger Platt, however, had been in a relationship of sorts with Jenny, not once, but twice, in between her previous broken engagements, and the look on his face said he might be hoping for another go at it. At that moment, Alan Triplett, whose ring Jenny was wearing at the moment, stepped into the melee, mistaking Jenny's high-pitched giggles for cries of help, and when he shoved past Roger to get to his woman, all hell broke loose.

In church, no less.

"Lord have mercy, help us all," Jedediah muttered before turning around and gesturing for the whole row of his girls to make for the side aisle instead. Ducking her head to hide her smile, Faith wanted to ask if that counted as a prayer instead of cussing since her father uttered the words in the house of God.

"But Grampa, I need to talk to Yvette!" Jasmine declared, refusing to budge.

"You'll get to her faster going around," he told her, then raised his voice to Abby, who had pulled out her cell phone and was filming the chest-thumping in the center aisle. "Put that thing away, Abstinence Goodacre, or so help me, God, I'll put it away for you."

Abby rolled her eyes at her father's use of her full name in public, and then turned her phone to snap a picture of him. "You shouldn't cuss in church, Daddy," she called out with a cheeky grin, and then shoved the offending piece of technology into her back pocket. With a flip of her long auburn hair—where on earth had she gotten those copper curls?—she turned around and led the troop out into the side aisle. It, too, was getting congested, as folks started making their way back inside the church to see what the ruckus was about.

"Grampa, that way!" Jasmine said, tugging Jed's hand and drawing him toward the front of the church. "We can go around by the stage."

At that moment, Trudy Huckster bustled out from the side door behind the piano and crossed to the podium. With her fold up fan—Faith couldn't remember ever seeing Trudy without a fan in church—she tapped the podium microphone, the amplified thwack reverberating with the punch of a gunshot through the suddenly stone still sanctuary.

Abby, grinning like a delighted Cheshire Cat, whipped out her phone again, panning the room to take it all in.

"What was that you said, Lord?" Trudy asked, her voice booming out into the room. She cocked her head like she was listening, her ear lifted toward heaven. The woman hardly needed the microphone, which was good, since she wasn't tall enough to speak into it. "Don't make you come down here, you say? I'll let them know." With another, albeit gentler thump on the microphone, she turned a stern expression on the group in the center aisle. "Do I need to repeat that, boys?"

"No ma'am," Sherman replied, although Faith was pretty sure Trudy had been speaking to Roger and Alan, not the poor man who'd inadvertently started it all.

"Good." And with that, the matronly woman opened her arms wide and headed down the center aisle herself, herding everyone out in front of her.

Had Reverend Treadwell sent her in his stead like some avenging angel? Or was he outside deep in conversation with a parishioner, completely oblivious to the shepherding going on inside? Either way, Trudy was quite capable of handling the hotheaded young studs in Reverend Treadwell's flock, and the pastor well knew it, Faith was certain.

"Jazzy!" Yvette scuttled across the aisle behind the church secretary, her father in tow, and threw her creamy mocha arms around Jasmine.

"Vetty!" Jasmine responded in kind. They acted like they hadn't seen each other in years, not just since school on Friday.

"Daddy, I need some air," Faith said, leaning in close to her father's ear so he could hear her over the screeches of the happy girls. "Can you bring Jasmine out with you? I'll be by my truck."

Jed nodded. "I'll bring her home if you like. I need to talk to Levi anyway." Levi Valiente owned and operated the local butcher shop, and Seven Virtues utilized his services regularly. He was frighteningly skilled with his blades—he could slice meat thin enough to see through, no machine required.

"Really? That would be great. I'm a little—" She fanned the air in front of her but didn't finish her sentence. If anyone knew how she felt about crowded, enclosed spaces, it was her father, a man who'd spent the majority of his life out in the great wide open. "Hey, Levi," she said to the handsome butcher. He had the best mustache in the world, Levi did, and although she usually preferred no more than a working man scruff on guys, she couldn't imagine Levi without his 'stache. It was a little like trying to imagine Sam Elliott without his.

Levi also greeted Hope and Charity who still lingered nearby, and Faith made her excuses and headed outside. By the time she got to her truck, she'd been stopped by half a dozen people, complimented on her appearance by both Roger Platt and Cedric Bennett, a man who was closer to her father's age than hers, but who'd made it clear that he didn't mind if she didn't.

She did.

With a sigh of relief, she sank into the driver's seat of her truck and braced both hands on the wheel. Squeezing her eyes shut, she leaned her head back against the seat's headrest, taking long, slow breaths to calm her frazzled nerves.

Between the rumors circulating around town about what Cord planned to do with the ranch next door to hers, and the not so anonymous gifts she'd been receiving all week, she'd been stirred up and bubbling over since he'd made his surprise visit. The daisies on Saturday, the box of truffles on Monday—her favorite caramel and cream, no nut assortment. It was the lilies and jasmine on Wednesday that sent her riding out to the woods to Caroline's secret garden, where she poured her heart out to her mother as Watson trimmed the grass contentedly nearby. She'd returned home knowing what she had to do; it was time to tell the man about his daughter. If Cordell Overman still wanted back into her life after learning about Jasmine, then she'd let him. In fact, she'd welcome him, maybe even with both arms wide open. It wouldn't be easy, she had no illusions there, but it would be right.

Although she was loathe to admit it, even to herself, she'd been looking forward to seeing him today. Once the decision was made, she just wanted to take the next step, no matter where it led them.

She'd been ready, oh, so ready.

He hadn't bothered showing up.

Sure, it was just church. And stuff happened, she knew that. He probably had a perfectly reasonable explanation for not sitting behind her like he said he would. But her gut—or was it her heart?—didn't understand the difference between reason and rejection. "I think I hate you, Cordell Overman," she ground out, torn between anger and heartache all over again.

Her passenger door opened, and Faith's eyes flew open in shock as the very man she was berating all but flung himself into the seat beside her. "Right about now, Faith Goodacre, the feeling's pretty much mutual."

TWELVE

Faith Goodacre looked just as stunning in her pretty blue dress as she did in jeans and a tank top, and without her hat to hide beneath, he could drink his fill of looking at her. But it wasn't her beauty that had his blood roaring so loudly in his ears that he could hardly think straight.

He'd arrived at church several minutes after the service began and had slipped into an empty seat at the back of the sanctuary. His internal alarm clock had betrayed him that morning, and he'd awakened with a start, knowing instinctively that it was much later than he'd planned to get up.

Cord hadn't been sleeping well, not since first arriving in Plumwood Hollow. At first, he'd chalked it up to the stress of sorting through all the ins and outs of purchasing the ranch, but something had been niggling at his brain for the last couple of weeks. Something was going on, some piece of the puzzle he wasn't seeing. People he ran into around town were pleased enough to see him, but there was an air of reservation with almost everyone he met, almost as though folks were questioning his motives for being there.

He knew he wasn't born and bred a hollow kid, but he was still family; still one of them, wasn't he? So why were people treating him like an outsider? Conversations felt stilted and guarded, and everyone and their mother asked if he'd been over to see Faith yet.

He'd noticed the girl nestled between Faith and Jed, her head resting against the old man's arm in a comfortable, possessive manner. He'd been curious, sure, but his focus had been on Faith.

Until Reverend Treadwell bowed his head to wrap up his message with a prayer. Like most children after having been asked to be still for an hour, the girl had grown fidgety, and the moment heads lowered and eyes closed around her, she started a slow scan of the room.

As though drawn in by a tractor beam, he hadn't been able to take his eyes off her, and when their gazes connected, she'd studied him unabashedly.

It was like looking at a picture of himself when he was that age. What was she? Eight? Ten? His own eyes stared right back at him, the top lip that stuck out over the bottom one. The straight line of her nose, and even the thumbprint cleft in her chin, although her feminine jawline was undeniably Faith's.

When the child cocked her head and smiled at him, a pain so bittersweet and raw tore right through his heart that he pressed his fist to his chest, half expecting to find a gaping hole that needed to be plugged. Faith Goodacre was exceptionally skilled at punching holes through his heart. The girl had ducked her head and turned away, and when the congregation rose to sing the closing song, somehow, Cord pushed to his feet and staggered out into the dazzling sunlight.

He made it to his truck parked some distance away, but his breaths were coming in short, sharp gasps, making his lungs burn. Tiny lights flickered around the periphery of his vision, and he knew he was going to pass out. He perched on the rear bumper and leaned forward, bracing his elbows on his knees. He focused his gaze on a pebble shaped like California between his feet. With his head lowered, he forced himself to take long, slow breaths, in and out, until the pinging sounds in his ears subsided and he could swallow without feeling like he was being strangled.

"I have a daughter," he whispered to California, the words burning his throat. "We have a daughter." Then he let out a manic chuckle and amended his declaration, "Not you and me, California. Faith and me."

He straightened slowly and lifted his gaze to the front doors of the church as they opened wide. Folks began trickling out behind Reverend Treadwell, who stopped at the bottom of the front steps where he could exchange greetings with everyone. "He acts like this is just another Sunday in May," Cord muttered as he pushed to his feet, gripping the lip of the tailgate until he was sure his shaking legs wouldn't give out on him. He started back across the parking lot; he had no clue what he would do or say when he confronted Faith, but he didn't care. Apparently, they both had long-overdue things to discuss with each other.

It was almost like the parting of the Red Sea as he moved through the parishioners now milling about on the front lawn. He hoped he wasn't rude to anyone, but something about his posture or expression must have given folks fair warning of his single-minded focus, because even though he was going against the flow of traffic, he made it inside the foyer of the church without one interception. He'd somehow even managed to slip past the reverend.

He found Faith and the rest of the Goodacres—surely, they all knew. They all knew. Did the girl?—still standing in their family pew near the front, hedged in on both ends by congested aisles. He started up the center aisle but was forced to a standstill as up ahead of him, the beginnings of an altercation appeared to be taking place. In church, no less. He turned back to go around, but found his retreat blocked by a surge of people coming back in to see what was going on.

When Trudy rapped her fan on the microphone up front, the crack of sound was like a bucket of cold water over his head. What was he doing? There were already two men in the building well on their way toward making fools of themselves over a woman who seemed to believe her worth was measured by the number of carats on her finger, and folks were gathering around to watch the live entertainment. Abby Goodacre—little Abby, the butterball toddler he remembered who'd just about blown his mind when she stepped up on stage as a willowy redheaded teenage songbird—wasn't the only person who had her phone out, documenting the whole event for social media glory.

He'd been about to cause a scene of his own. One that would have resulted in far worse wounds than any Roger Platt or Alan Triplett could inflict on each other, that was for sure.

But he couldn't just walk away. He ducked his head and reached up to rub the back of his neck, hard. "Get it together, man," he muttered.

Grateful for the stay he'd just been granted, he managed to finagle his way back outdoors without jostling too many curious folks still trying to get a glimpse of the hoopla inside. He shook the reverend's hand, but didn't engage in conversation with him, then made his way toward his truck again, deciding to watch for Faith from there. He'd parked with a direct line of sight on the front doors of the church, and unless she slipped out the back, he'd see her.

Sure enough, several minutes later, Faith stepped out into the sunshine and took a deep breath. Even from across the parking lot he could see her shoulders rise and fall with obvious relief. She'd always hated being trapped indoors, especially on days when the weather was like this. After shaking the reverend's hand, she sidled past a group of chattering women, greeting them all with a quick wave and a smile, then was stopped by Roger Platt, who'd been ushered out ahead of the church secretary. The man's hug seemed to go on far longer than appropriate and Cord fought the urge to launch himself across the parking lot to her rescue. But she disentangled herself and had almost made it across the lawn when another man—familiar, but Cord couldn't place him—took her hand and held it while he spoke to her. Faith nodded, smiled, and then withdrew her hand and surreptitiously wiped it on her skirt. The moment she stepped off the sidewalk, she lowered her head and picked up her pace, moving in the opposite direction from Cord.

He had no trouble catching up to her, and when she climbed into her truck and sat there for a moment with her eyes closed, it was all the opportunity he needed to circle to the other side without her even noticing. Thank goodness no one ever locked their vehicles in this town.

"I think I hate you, Cordell Overman," he heard her say.

At that moment, he thought hate was far too small a word for what he was feeling.

THIRTEEN

"WHAT ARE YOU DOING?" she squawked, embarrassed he'd heard her lash out at him, and surprised at his sudden appearance in the seat beside her.

"How old is she?" he growled, his voice gravelly with tension, the words coming out bruised and angry. When Faith didn't immediately respond, he raised his voice. "How old, Faith? How. Old. Is. Your. Daughter." He sounded like he might start hyperventilating, the way he punched out every word.

"If you're going to yell at me, you can get out of my truck," she shot back, still clutching the steering wheel, her knuckles turning white. She was glad for the console between them; for some silly reason, it made her feel a little less vulnerable. They both sat like coiled rattlers, facing straight ahead, staring out the windshield at the front entrance of the church. *Please don't come out, Jasmine. Please don't come out yet.* The thought kept spinning round and round in her head.

Like the snake she'd just been imagining, Cord's hand shot out across the console to clasp her wrist. "Look at me!" he demanded.

She sensed the thrum of energy coursing through his body, down his arm, and into hers where his fingertips pressed into the fragile skin on the underside of her wrist. She wondered if he could feel her racing pulse.

"Is that girl in there my dau—my—my daughter?" He choked on the words, his tone jagged and wretched, then he let out a sound of such gut-wrenching anguish that Faith wanted to cover her ears to shut it out. "She is, isn't she? I have a daughter." he finally managed to get out.

"Let go of me," she whispered, trying to pull her wrist out of his grasp. This wasn't the way it was supposed to happen.

"She's mine, isn't she?" he asked again. His voice was stronger now.

"Let go of me." So was hers.

"Is she mine?" His fingers tightened around her wrist. He wasn't exactly hurting her, but she felt the restraint in his grip, and she knew without a shadow of a doubt, that if he so desired—and right now, he probably did—he could snap her bones without a whole lot of effort. "Tell me, Faith."

"Yes! Now let go!" She wrenched free and reached for her door handle.

"If you get out of this truck, I will only come after you." It was all she could do not to flinch at the rage in his snarling words. "Let's hope your little sister still has her camera rolling. Maybe we'll go viral."

Faith turned to glare at him, her eyes narrowed. "Are you serious, Cord? Really?" Her words dripped with sarcasm. "You're going to chase me down in the church parking lot?"

"Serious as a heart attack, Faith. If that's what it takes. And I assure you, I can run a whole lot faster than you can."

"Tell me something I don't know," she snapped. "Last time you left, you ran outta here so quick, you left skid marks across three counties."

"I didn't run!" he protested loudly. He hit the dashboard with his open palm, creating a loud smack that rivaled the fan-to-the-mic technique Trudy had used inside the sanctuary. Faith flinched. She wasn't afraid of him; at least, she didn't think she was. But then, she couldn't imagine being in his shoes right now. Truth be told, she'd be a raging mass of emotions, too, if she'd just learned that she had a nine-year-old daughter.

Cord pinched the bridge of his nose and squeezed his eyes shut, hard. "I didn't run. I didn't even walk away," he said again, his voice low and quiet, and all the more menacing for it. "I left for college. I left to play football, to go to college. I left to get my education and pursue a career," Cord ground out, turning shadowed eyes on her. He took a deep breath and added, "I wanted to give you the world."

"You still don't get it, do you?" She could feel an invisible wall going up between them, but she could not let herself be weak, soft. Her eyes stung with unshed tears, but she found the courage to look at him anyway. His jaw tightened visibly beneath his clean shave, and a vein in his neck throbbed hard and fast, telling her his heart was racing in time with hers. "I didn't want that life, Cord. I didn't want what you were pursuing." She waved a hand toward the front window where her father and Jasmine were just now exiting the church. Yvette, Levi, and Nona were right behind them. "This is my life. This is my home. These are my people, and I didn't want more than this."

"Really? Because that's not what you said to me all those years ago," he shot back. "We talked about it all the time, leaving together. You said you'd go anywhere with me. You said you loved me."

She kept her mouth closed; they had talked about leaving, and she had said she'd leave with him. And oh, how she'd loved him. But that was before Jasmine.

"I would have given it all up if I'd known how you really felt," he added, his voice softening just a little.

"Given up all of what? Football? University? The money?" She tried to keep the scathing tone out of her words, but she felt it cut through, anyway. "College girls?"

"Yes," he replied without hesitation. "Everything."

"Well, that's easy to say now that you don't have anything to lose anymore." The moment the words were out, she wanted to snatch them back. Her cruelty shocked even herself. She could only imagine how hard it must have been for Cord to lose his football dream because of injuries. It must have devastated him. But she clung to the renewed anger and resentment that fueled it; she hadn't realized how deeply the pit of her bitterness went.

After several moments of silence, Cord spoke again, his jaws clenched in an obvious effort to restrain himself. "Why didn't you tell me?" His pain was like a hot poker probing her heart.

Everything had changed the summer after high school. Instead of spending a couple of blissful months at Whispering Hills Ranch, Cord had only been able to visit for a few days around the Fourth of July before heading off to football camp. Perhaps it was the knowledge that they had so little time together that spurred them on, but those seventy-two hours in the sultry heat of a Kentucky summer had been spent in a frenzy of emotions and hormones. Their last night together, they'd finally given in to temptation and consummated their relationship. Cord had left early the next morning.

At first, they'd called each other every day, whenever their schedules allowed. Caught up in the afterglow of making love for the first time, they fed off their unrelenting need for each other that was made all the more palpable by their forced separation. But as the long days of that busy summer slipped by, the calls became fewer as they found it more and more of an effort to find things to talk about. It was as though that one night under the stars, that blissful awakening of what had once been forbidden, had slowly and subtly eaten away at the foundation they'd built together up to that point. By early August, the phone calls had turned to texts, and the few times they did speak, Faith felt the miles between them all the way to her soul. She rode a roller coaster of emotions, one minute lashing out at her younger sisters, the next breaking down in tears over something as commonplace as the birdsong that greeted her in the morning. All she wanted was to see Cord again, to make sure the light in his eyes still burned for her. She needed his arms around her and his voice whispering in her ear that everything would be all right.

Because Faith had begun to suspect that there was a reason her period was late.

Cord had promised he'd be back before school started. He'd promised he'd spend a few of his last free days of August in Plumwood Hollow with her.

But Cord never showed. She learned via cryptic text that something had come up, a change in the practice schedule or some equally reasonable explanation. Her response was also cryptic: *Okay.*

The following morning, she'd driven over to the Wal-Mart in Muldoon, purchased two pregnancy tests, and in the cleanest bathroom stall she could find, she learned that she was indeed going to be a mother.

She took the second pregnancy test three days later at home, just to be sure. Faith spent the next few weeks coming to terms with the fact that she was going to have a baby. She also realized that if the child was going to have a father, she needed to talk to Cord, no matter how busy they were.

She wrote a letter telling him she missed him and needed to see him. If he couldn't get away to the hollow, she'd make the five-hour drive to visit him on campus. A week later, Cord texted, telling her his schedule was too full to leave any time soon, and that he didn't feel good about her making that drive alone, but maybe he could get over to see her during the Thanksgiving break in a few months.

Faith knew then that things would never be the same between them.

She ran her hands through her hair, then turned to face him. She swallowed hard, willing away the tears that were gathering at the back of her throat. "I tried," she managed to get out. "I wrote to you, remember? I told you I needed to see you. You brushed me off, so I came to see you anyway."

"Oh, Faith," he murmured. Something in his eyes told her he already knew what she was going to say next.

"I hardly recognized you, Cord." She held his gaze, no longer caring if he saw the tears threatening to spill over. "And you weren't... alone."

"Oh, Faith," he whispered, bringing both hands up to cover his face. "I'm so sorry."

She'd brought Hope and Charity along, which meant telling them her secret on the long drive there. It wasn't because she needed them with her when she told Cord about the pregnancy, but to keep her company on the long ride home again. Some dark, whimpering thing in her heart told her she would, indeed, be returning to Plumwood Hollow without Cord.

When they arrived at his dorm, Cord had been too busy with the pretty girl in his arms to notice the three Goodacre sisters standing outside the expansive plate glass windows of the lobby. When the couple ended their long embrace with a quick kiss and then headed up the stairs, arms still draped around each other, Faith had turned without a word. Fortunately, the shuttle that would take them back to the parking structure was still loading a group of passengers, and flanked by her equally shocked sisters, they managed to catch it just in time. Once on the road again, Faith had climbed in behind the wheel and cranked up the radio too loudly for conversation. They'd all sung along at the tops of their lungs until Faith broke down so badly she had to pull over on the highway where she emptied her stomach while her sisters stood by in helpless sympathy.

By the time they made it back to Plumwood Hollow, Faith was dry-eyed and determined to get on with life the best she could.

Hope and Charity made a pact with her that they would do everything in their power to make sure their niece or nephew would know nothing but love and security and happiness in his or her life. Out of some sense of possibly misplaced loyalty, Faith made them promise to keep the pregnancy a secret until Thanksgiving. If Cord showed up, she'd tell him first. She had no delusions that the relationship could be salvaged, but she wanted to give him the opportunity to decide what part he'd play in the baby's life.

If he didn't make an appearance, that would be her answer.

Faith knew she wouldn't be able to hide her misery from her father until then, so that evening, she told him she and Cord were taking a break from each other. He'd reacted in a very uncharacteristic display of affection, putting his arms around her and hugging her hard, which only served to bring on her tears again. Jed had dragged his big, scratchy thumbs across her cheeks, peered down at her with glistening eyes of his own, and told her the words she'd wanted to hear from Cord. "Everything will be all right."

Thanksgiving came and went, and Cord didn't show, nor did he call to explain what kept him. That Saturday, Faith rose long before anyone else, brewed the morning coffee, and was waiting for her father when he awoke to start his day. To her great relief, Jed had taken her news about the pregnancy in stride, hadn't argued with her plans to raise the baby without a father, had agreed to let her take over more of the responsibilities around the ranch in exchange for allowing her to continue living at Seven Virtues. Then he'd hugged her again and assured her that he loved her and was proud of her for doing right by his first grandchild.

Although she had no doubt Cord had quickly filled her absence in his life with pretty college coeds, his absence in her life took a little longer to overcome. Once her daughter was born, however, it got a little easier. She had the prettiest girl in all the world in her own arms.

Jasmine Caroline Goodacre stole her mama's heart from the moment she first fluttered in the womb, and when Faith held her tiny, sweet baby to her breast for the first time, she knew that God was in the business of blessing and restoration, not punishment and condemnation. The tiny, squirming, squeaking bundle of joy filled her empty heart with a whole new kind of love, a love that enabled Faith to set aside her heartache over Cord and focus on being the best mama she could be to her baby.

Now, after all this time, here he was, stirring all those unresolved emotions up again. Emotions she'd thought were long dead and buried. She'd never quite understood the notion of love and hate being two sides of the same coin, not until now.

"It wasn't exactly what you thought, you know," he began.

She turned to face him straight on. "Really? I may be just a country bumpkin, Cord, but I'm not so naive that I didn't recognize what was going on when I came to see you, to *tell* you about the baby that day. I knew things had changed between us long before that visit. I don't think I was even surprised. Brianna, right? Isn't that her name?"

"It wasn't like that—it wasn't because of us." But he sounded like a kid caught with his hand in the cookie jar. "And I never, ever thought of you as a country bumpkin."

"Didn't you almost marry that girl?" Faith asked, ignoring his last comment. "Word was that you two were pretty serious. What happened?" But she already knew the answer to that. She'd heard from the gossip circles that his on-and-off again college girlfriend had stuck by him only until he retired from his very short football career.

"Look," Cord began, holding her gaze, his eyes pained, but sincere. "I messed up with her. It was flirting, and it meant nothing to either one of us at the time—"

"It meant something to me, Cord," she interrupted, then added for effect, "At the time."

"You're right." He squared his shoulders and started again. "I compromised. In so many ways, Faith. I was a self-centered, egotistical, young jackass who thought the world revolved around me."

"Sounds about right," she muttered.

"Sounds exactly right. And by the time Thanksgiving rolled around, I knew I'd taken a thousand wrong turns away from you, and I was too ashamed for you to see me the way I was. You'd know right away that I didn't deserve you." He shook his head as though disgusted with himself all over again. "I didn't know how to go back to the guy you'd fallen in love with, so I stayed away."

Faith sighed. "You never even called." It wasn't a question. "I never heard from you again."

"I know. I know." He nodded his head slowly. "I can't tell you how badly I missed you, Faith. I knew I'd screwed up and didn't deserve you, but that didn't stop me from needing you. I wanted to make things right between us, but I didn't know how. So I just stayed away. Kept my distance." He paused for a moment, and then in a quiet, serious voice, he said, "I was—I *am* so sorry for hurting you. For hurting us. For abandoning us."

Faith nodded, not quite sure how to process what he was saying. Because he hadn't been sorry enough to come talk to her face to face. Not in ten years. He hadn't been sorry enough to make their relationship a priority, to fight for her. Either that or she simply hadn't been worth his time. "Honestly, Cord, even if you had come to see me that Thanksgiving, I don't think anything would have changed. Your apology might have appeased your guilt and shame, but there's no way I would have been able to trust you." She sighed, and her shoulders drooped, her rage leaving her suddenly and completely deflated. "After that disastrous and oh, so revealing visit to your campus, I wasn't about to coerce you into coming back to me because of a baby."

"It wouldn't have been coercion." Cord leaned in, reaching across the console, but not quite touching her.

She shook her head. "There's no way it wouldn't have been coercion of some kind." When Cord didn't argue, she took a long, slow breath, and let it out in a rush. "In the end, I chose you, but you didn't choose me. In the end, you chose football and Brianna, but they didn't choose you."

"I don't even know her name," Cord whispered.

Please don't cry. Please don't cry. But one tear, then another, spilled over to sear hot tracks down her cheeks. "You never looked back, Cord. If you had, even just once, you would have known about her." Her last words came out just above a whisper. "I'm not the one who left. I—we've been here all along. And her name is Jasmine. Jasmine Caroline Goodacre."

Cord's face crumpled as her words had their intended effect. Finally, he spoke. "What can I do to make things right between us, Faith? I want to be a part of your life again. I want to be in Jasmine's life." His last words came out on a gulping sob. "I have a daughter—we have a daughter."

FOURTEEN

Jasmine.

In his memory, he heard Faith whisper the word as they lay on their backs, gazing up at the night sky through the hole in the hayloft roof. A light breeze swirled around them, the sound of crickets and katydids playing their tunes, the fragrance of night blossoms filling the air. "Jasmine. Can you smell it?" She'd sighed euphorically, then added, "I'll always think of you and this night when I smell jasmine."

He imagined he could feel his heart breaking all over again.

"No, Cord. I have a daughter." Faith's words brought him out of the past abruptly. Her voice wasn't harsh, but he heard the ring of steel in it when she claimed possession of the little girl. He could almost see the line she was drawing in the sand between them. "You and I have a lot to sort out before—if ever—that changes to... to include you." She lifted the hem of her skirt to wipe away the telltale moisture on her face, inadvertently flashing a few inches of pale thigh at him as she did. Then she smoothed the fabric back down, straightened her shoulders, and turned her amber ale eyes on him. "Jasmine is the most important person in my life, and she's on her way over here with my daddy as we speak. You should know that the way you handle the next few minutes will likely determine the course of our future."

Cord shook his head in growing frustration and anger, trying to get his emotions in check, but failing miserably. One minute he was on the verge of breaking down and crying like a baby, the next he was ready to take a bat to something. One moment he wanted to drag Faith across the console between them and hold her like a child in his lap, and the next he wanted nothing more than to tell the woman how certifiably crazy she was. Apparently, now was one of those moments. "No, Faith." He tried to keep his voice calm, tried to keep the sudden burst of rage in check as he caught sight of the girl who was a stranger to him. "You've kept me from her long enough. That was your decision, not mine. I may not have come back to the hollow the way I should have, but you knew where to find me. You knew how to reach me. You could have written. Called. Heck, you could have texted."

"I tried," came her defensive reply.

"You didn't try hard enough."

"Well, neither did you." She smacked the steering wheel, then yelped quietly and tucked her hand between her knees, clearly in pain. Served her right.

"You think I'm going to stand by and let you keep making my decisions for me? Whether you like it or not, she is mine. I have a right to know her. She has a right to know me." His voice rose in volume as he slapped his chest in emphasis. "You have robbed me of my daughter, and her of a father, and I will not stand by and let you steal another second from us." He reached for the door handle; he'd suddenly had enough. Too much.

"Please."

The single word made him freeze. He held his breath and began counting backwards from twenty. He refused to look at her, but instead, kept his eyes riveted on the approaching duo as Jed nodded at something the animated girl said.

"Cord, I'm begging you. Not now. Not here."

He tightened his jaw, not wanting to back down. He didn't take his eyes off his daughter. *His daughter.*

"Please." This time, it was something between a whisper and a whimper.

He let out the breath in a rush. "Fine. I'll play the deadbeat dad for now—"

"That's not what I meant...." Her words trailed off.

"Well, that's what you've made me out to be," he ground out. "Whether you meant it or not."

She lowered her gaze but said nothing.

That's right, Miss Goodacre. You have no leg to stand on. "I'll go along with your ruse for now," he continued through gritted teeth. "But I'm not leaving here today until we get some things sorted out."

She shook her head. "I can't stay. It's Sunday, Cord. We have our big family dinner, and I—"

"And I have a daughter with you," he interrupted. He let the words hang in the air between them for a few moments, then went on. "We can do this here, or we can go somewhere private and do this without an audience. You choose."

When Jedediah Goodacre looked up from his conversation with his granddaughter, and his eyes landed on Cord in the front seat of Faith's truck, the man stopped short, the movement so sudden, the girl holding his hand let out a cry of alarm. "What is it, Grampa?"

Cord wasn't at all surprised when the rancher turned on his heel and steered the girl back toward the church.

"Who is that man in Mama's truck?" Jasmine's question rang out, and in the driver's seat, Faith flinched.

He watched the pair hurry back the way they'd come, Jasmine darting curious glances over her shoulder at them, until they disappeared inside the sanctuary. He offhandedly wondered what story her grandfather would sell the girl.

But not more than thirty seconds later, Jed re-emerged alone from the building and headed back across the parking lot toward them.

Cord, however, wasn't going to wait for Jedediah Goodacre to come to him. He pushed open the passenger door and rounded the hood of the truck just as the man drew near. He was limping, Cord saw, something he hadn't noticed when he'd walked slowly with his granddaughter.

"Mr. Goodacre," Cord said by way of greeting, his hand outstretched.

Jed stopped in front of him, sized him up for about two seconds, then took his hand in a firm grip. "Cordell Overman. I heard you were back in the hollow." The man had a rancher's voice, one of those deep rumbles that evoked images of campfires, branding irons, and long hot days spent driving cattle. The kind of voice that made you stand up straight and polish up your Yes and No sirs.

"Yes, sir. I am." Cord's response was out of respect, not due to intimidation. At least, that's the message he tried to portray by not lowering his gaze or stepping back, even when the older man moved in a little too close for comfort.

"This fellow bothering you, Faith?" Jed kept his gaze locked on Cord.

"It's all right, Daddy," The quaver in Faith's voice belied her words of reassurance. "We're just talking."

"You're not the only ones," Jed said, and sure enough, when Cord glanced over in the direction of the church lawn, he saw they had the attention of several people. "Here to start rumors about my daughter again, are you, Mr. Overman?"

"I'm not here to start anything, sir," Cord countered, lifting his chin a notch. "In fact, I believe I'm here to finish things. Something I should have done years ago." He lifted a hand in a quick sweeping gesture to encompass the parking lot. "Something I would have done had someone—*anyone*—in this tight-lipped community bothered to tell me that I had a daughter." He had to push the last few words out past the lump still lodged in his throat, as it hit him like yet another sucker punch to the gut that everyone—*everyone*—in the hollow knew he was Jasmine's daddy before he did. Had Uncle Judge known, too? The thought made his stomach churn.

"Don't get smart with me, boy." Jed took a step closer. "And don't confuse protecting our own with being tight-lipped."

Folks at the grocery store, the bank. Bink's comments about Storm Chaser getting loose at Seven Virtues. Even Reverend Treadwell. They'd be having words, Cord and the good pastor, that was for certain.

He dipped his head and clenched his teeth together—something he seemed to be doing a lot of today—willing his temper under control. It wasn't like he was going to fight the old man, and certainly not in the church parking lot on Sunday morning. "I meant no disrespect, sir," he finally said, biting back the rest of his thoughts clamoring to get out.

"And I meant every word I said. We protect our own." Jed tipped his head so he could look past Cord to Faith. "Did he tell you he is, indeed, buying the Flanner place, Faith?"

Cord closed his eyes and ground his teeth in frustration, his lips pressed into a thin line. Maybe he'd haul off and deck the man after all.

Behind him, Faith's truck roared to life. "No, Daddy, he didn't," she called out through her open window.

Cord spun and rounded the hood to the driver's side, then reached inside her open window to grab the steering wheel with one hand, the other on the door frame, ready to launch himself into the truck bed if need be. "Hold up, Faith."

"What are you doing?" Her question was asked with such ridicule, Cord almost let go.

"We have to talk. Today." He didn't want to cause a scene, but apparently, she had no such reservations, so if he had to, he'd go along for the ride. Literally.

"You're joking, right? You think I'm going to just peel off and leave you in my dust, or something?"

"I don't know what to think, Faith. I don't know what to expect from you anymore." If she rolled her eyes any harder, they might fall out of her head.

"You're right about one thing; you don't know me anymore," she retorted, the telltale flush in her cheeks telling him he'd hit on a nerve. "This isn't high school, you idiot. Get in the truck. Let's go get this over with." She leaned forward so she could see around him. "Daddy, can you look after Jasmine for a while when you get home? And don't hold dinner for me. Maybe Charity can put up a plate for me, though." Then she thrust her chin in the direction of the church entrance. "Abby's got her phone out again. You need to slap that child, Daddy."

She could always make him smile, and right now, as he chomped down on his bottom lip to keep one at bay, Cord really disliked that about her. He turned back to face Jed and held out his hand. "Good to see you, Mr. Goodacre. You have a beautiful granddaughter, if I do say so myself. And I apologize about my bull breaking through your fence last Sunday. Binks told me all about it."

For one brief moment, Cord thought the guy wasn't going shake his hand. But finally, he did, squeezing his knuckles so hard it made Cord's eyes water. Shooting a dead-serious look at Faith, her father called out, "You need help burying the body, you just give your old man a call." Then he nodded at both of them and walked away.

Cord glared after the man for a moment, then made his way back around to the passenger side of the truck. "You know, I've really missed your old man," he muttered sarcastically, slamming the door a little harder than necessary.

Faith snorted rudely. "Better buckle up, City Boy. I'm a ticked off country girl in a big bad truck, and there's a long stretch of winding road between here and the place I'm taking you."

Had they been seventeen again, he would have teased her for trying to be tough, but the set of her jaw as they cruised slowly through the busy parking lot made him think twice. He buckled up.

"Hey, you two!" A woman with a toddler on her hip waved, but Cord didn't recognize her. With their windows open, there was no escaping the few souls brave enough—or ignorant enough—to call out greetings as they passed.

"Sunday drive for old time's sake?" Roger Platt called out, thumping the passenger side door. Cord just nodded at him; the man really was a fool.

Abby and Prudence stood on the church steps, Abby's phone aimed right at them, her guitar case at her feet. Prudence just watched, a troubled look on her face. The rest of the Goodacre sisters were nowhere to be seen. They must be keeping Jasmine distracted inside until Jed returned. Cord glanced into the side view mirror and saw the rancher making his way back through the milling churchgoers.

He was fairly certain they'd just officially become the talk of the town.

For a while, they didn't speak, and at first, he didn't mind. But as the silence between them grew, so did the emotions he'd been holding in check in front of her father.

Finally, unable to keep it in a moment longer, he said, "You know, I thought losing you was just about the worst thing that could ever happen to me." He didn't care if he sounded vulnerable. He didn't care if he made a fool of himself. This situation was a whole lot bigger than any feelings or emotions or pride. "But now? Why didn't you tell me about her, Faith? I understand you were angry—you had every right to be. But to not tell me about our baby?"

After a few moments of silence, Faith said, "Put yourself in my shoes, Cord. From the things you said to me and the way you treated me, I knew things were turning sour. And then I find you wrapped around someone else? Talk about confirmation." Her voice hardened a little. "I couldn't do that to you. I knew you wanted to play football. I knew you wanted more than this." She flung her hand in a wide arc inside the cab, gesturing wildly at the land around them.

Cord jerked away so as not to get hit and thumped his head on the rear cab window. She didn't seem to notice how close she'd come to decking him, nor the grunt of pain he just emitted. He reached up to massage the back of his skull gingerly. "I wanted you, too."

She shook her head but didn't look at him. "I knew I'd be okay here, that I'd never have to do this alone if I stayed here in the hollow. I knew it would be hard, but I also knew I could do it, and you'd be free to follow the dreams you'd worked so hard to achieve." Was she purposely goading him? If he hadn't seen her tears, he'd think she was cold as ice.

"I wanted you, too, Faith Goodacre," he said again, this time more slowly, more deliberately.

"Stop saying that. You sound like a broken record."

"It's true whether I say it or not." He needed her to hear him, to know what was in his heart. "I messed up so badly; I know that. But if I'd known, I would have moved heaven and earth to figure out a way to get you back. I would have chosen you over all of it."

"But you didn't." Her voice sounded pinched; he couldn't tell if she was angry, sad, or both. "Words are empty until you fill them up with deeds, Cord."

"And you didn't tell me about our daughter!" he exclaimed, his voice rising in frustration.

"I shouldn't have had to tell you. You should have been here. You left and didn't come back!" Now she was yelling, too.

He shook his head. In a way, she was right. Nothing he could say would make her believe him, even if he was telling the truth.

Well, he didn't want to waste time arguing. He wanted answers. "Fine. I left, okay?" He leaned out his open passenger window and yelled, "You hear that, Plumwood Hollow? I left Faith Goodacre!" Then he threw himself back into his seat, hard, hitting his head again. "Ow!" He scrubbed the spot ferociously this time, allowing the pain to fuel his anger.

"Keep doing that. Maybe it'll knock some sense into that brick of yours."

"You are such a—" He bit the foul word off when she snapped her head around to shoot daggers at him. She stepped on the gas as she did, creating an angry squeal of rubber on asphalt, sending them hurtling along at breakneck speed. "Watch the road, Faith!"

"Scared? Don't worry. I could drive this stretch blindfolded. I'd rather watch you make an idiot of yourself." She shifted in her seat so that she was turned even more toward him, accelerating all the while. "You were saying?"

Cord closed his eyes and lowered his voice to speak as calmly as he could. "Faith, please slow down and watch the road." He hesitated a moment, then before he could talk himself out of the impulsive move, he reached over and rubbed the back of his knuckles down the bare skin of her upper arm. "Please."

Faith jerked the steering wheel so hard the truck swerved, the back tires fishtailing wildly. Without forethought, Cord slapped a palm flat against her chest, as though by his own strength and will, he could keep her from face-planting into the steering wheel. The motion thrust him forward so that he banged his forehead against the windshield.

In another moment, she'd righted the truck and was slowing to a stop on the side of the road. By the time she'd turned off the ignition, her door was open. She knocked his hand away and practically fell out of the cab, quickly putting distance between her and her truck. And him.

Cord stayed where he was and let her storm off. His forehead throbbed, but he didn't think he'd have anything more than a bruise for a couple of days, thanks to the seatbelt she'd insisted he put on.

But his chest? Now that hurt bad. His lungs burned with every breath, and his heart ached with every contraction, not from the sudden stop or the shoulder strap that had locked tight to hold him in place. No, his pain was caused by the misery between him and the woman who'd just about killed him. The woman whose heart he was here to win back. "How's that going for you, man?" he muttered, willing his pulse to return to normal.

He could see her in the rearview mirror, several yards behind the truck, pacing back and forth along the side of the road, arms crossed tightly over her chest.

How were they going to mend the broken places between them? How did they bridge the chasm of nearly a decade of hurt and bitterness between them? And where did Jasmine, the one piece that would link them together for the rest of their lives, fit into all of this?

Or maybe the better question was where did he fit into all of this? Because as far as he could tell, he was the missing piece in their lives.

Faith was right about one thing. He'd left. For whatever reason, good, bad, justifiable or not, he'd left. And now there was an empty place in their lives that only he could fill.

Whether Faith wanted to admit it or not.

FIFTEEN

Faith's whole body trembled as she paced, and she squeezed her arms tighter around her middle. She felt like she might shatter into a million pieces if she let go. What had she been thinking, driving like that? And she'd called *him* an idiot. "I could have killed us both," she whimpered, her voice trembling, too. "Oh God, what is wrong with me? This isn't like me. What do I do?"

She glanced back at the truck, half expecting Cord to be making his way toward her—half hoping he was?—but he remained inside the cab.

What was he thinking? Was he hurt? She'd heard the thunk of his head against the windshield.

She pressed her open palm against her chest where Cord's hand had been only minutes before. How many times had she done the same thing to Jasmine? To whatever sister happened to be occupying the passenger seat next to her? That instinctive protective gesture... how many times had she hit the brakes for one reason or another, and simultaneously thrust out an arm to prevent her daughter from slamming into the dashboard?

Cord hadn't yelled at her; he hadn't grabbed the wheel. He wasn't thinking of himself in the crisis, but of her.

Faith closed her eyes and stopped pacing, a sudden overwhelming sense of certainty washing over her. She had to stop this. She had to figure out a way to set aside her own selfish emotions, her own fears, her ridiculous need to be in control. Because as much as she didn't want to acknowledge it, in spite of the years she'd spent pushing the knowledge to the back of her mind, the fact remained that Cordell Overman was indeed Jasmine's father. Then there was the other truth she was dealing with; she still had a thing for the boy next door who was now, apparently, the rancher next door.

It was time to face this head-on.

She took a deep breath, squared her shoulders, and returned to the truck. Cord studied her in silence as she climbed back in and gripped the steering wheel for courage. "I'm sorry," she finally said. "That was all kinds of stupid, and I'm sorry."

"Forgiven." His voice was quiet, calm, and remarkably steady compared to her own.

"How's your head?" she asked, braving a glance at him. She winced when she saw the red mark just below his hairline. "Yikes. That looks like it's going to leave a mark."

"Only for a day or two, I can assure you." He rapped his knuckles on the top of his head. "Hard as a brick."

Faith rolled her eyes and looked away. "I am sorry, Cord."

"What about you?" he asked. "You okay? Did I hurt you?"

He was asking if he'd hurt her? "I—I'm fine."

"I didn't mean to smack you so hard." He held his big hand out, palm up, then waved his fingers at his own chest. "Sorry."

Faith looked down and was surprised to see some lingering redness above the neckline of her dress, right where his hand slammed against her sternum. She shook her head. "No, no. You didn't hurt me, Cord. You were protecting me. From myself, it seems." She rubbed at the spot. "This isn't from you. My chest gets all blotchy when I get all worked up."

"Good. I'm glad." Then he chuckled. "I'm glad I didn't hurt you, not that you get all blotchy."

"Thanks." Now she was smiling, too.

"Actually, I take that back. Seems like a good way to gauge whatever mood you're in." He shot her a cheeky grin. "Now I have an excuse to stare at your chest."

"Cordell Overman!" She flung her arm out and thumped him right over his heart.

"Ouch," he said, rubbing the spot as though deeply wounded.

"Now we're even."

Cord pointed at his forehead, one eyebrow raised in challenge. "I think you still owe me."

Faith's shoulders drooped a little, and she looked away. "You're right. I'm not usually like this. All over the place and out of control." Her shoulders drooped a little, and she added, "I'd like to blame you for it. Like I said, you get me all riled up."

"I'm more than willing to take the blame, Faith." Cord's expression grew somber, too, and Faith was grateful. She felt extremely vulnerable right now, letting him in, even if it was only in increments, and she needed to know that he grasped the gravity of their situation.

She shook her head. "I'm not asking you to. I'm just saying that I have a hard time letting go of the reins, you know? And for a long time, I've been the one holding them." She knew that was vague, but she was still trying to put all her newly dug up emotions into some semblance of order, so finding words to explain them to him was a little like looking for needles in a haystack. She sighed and picked up the keys from the console where she'd tossed them. "As awful as it makes me sound, I'm really struggling with the idea of you being in Jasmine's life."

Cord didn't say anything for a few moments, and Faith toyed with the keys nervously before he finally spoke. "Maybe we should start with the idea of me being in your life first," he suggested softly, maybe even tenderly, and her heart squeezed tight in her chest. "Then we can work on Jasmine together."

"I—I can't quite see what that looks like, Cord. And to be honest, the notion of it just about scares the life out of me."

He stayed quiet again, but she could tell he was processing her words. To give him time, she pulled her seatbelt on and started the truck up, then pulled back out onto the road.

They drove the rest of the way in silence, but she didn't mind. She'd decided where they were going, and it both terrified and excited her.

SIXTEEN

Cord mulled over her words, understanding full well that they were as honest as she could get, but they hurt nonetheless. He had no trouble imagining her in his life; how many times had he dreamed of her, longed for her over the years? Ever since Frankie made him the offer on Uncle Judge's property, it had been the prevailing thought in his mind. It was so real to him; he didn't have to close his eyes to picture them together, he and Faith at Whispering Hills. He'd even conjured up a couple of kids who'd help them turn the big old Flanner ranch house into a big old Overman family home. And Jasmine? From the moment he'd first realized she was his, one of those kids had suddenly begun to look a whole lot like the daughter he had yet to meet. She was like a jump start on those dreams.

He knew well the route they were on and assumed Faith was taking him back to Seven Virtues where she felt the firmest footing beneath her. He didn't blame her for wanting that. She was being asked to rewrite just about everything in her life.

But when she pulled off Carpenter Road and headed up the lane to Judge Flanner's place, he frowned. She didn't stop in the driveway, either, but veered off instead on one of the dirt roads that led toward the property line between Whispering Hills Ranch and Seven Virtues. Where were they going?

Suddenly, he knew. His pulse jumped erratically, and he turned to look out his window, not wanting her to see the thoughts careening through his mind, should she happen to glance over at him. Surely, they'd be written all over his face.

A few minutes later, she pulled up in front of the old hay barn and parked. For several seconds, they both just sat there, staring out at the abandoned outbuilding. It looked even more dilapidated since they'd last been there together, but through the large door hanging at an angle from a single hinge, he could clearly make out the loft inside. The ladder they'd rounded up from one of the storage buildings on the other side of the property was still there, too, leaning against the framework as though waiting for them. The sight of it made his gut clench—the last night they'd spent there had been the single most memorable of his life. Why had she brought him here, of all places?

As though she'd read his mind, she murmured, "Maybe this was a bad idea." But then she opened her door and slid out of the truck. Not bothering to see if he followed, she walked toward the barn's entrance and peered inside.

Cord got out more slowly, willing his heart to stop hammering against his sternum. He'd been by the structure several times since coming back to the hollow, but he'd yet to set foot inside it. For some reason, he couldn't bring himself to do it. Had he simply been waiting until they could cross the threshold together?

Images flashed like movies through his mind, making his blood run hot in his veins. This was, indeed, a bad idea.

"What are we doing here, Faith?" He stopped several yards away from her and crossed his arms, hating the way his body betrayed him. He fought a fierce urge to take her in his arms and kiss her, to make her remember, and remember some more, just the way he was. They couldn't stay here, not with everything so volatile between them.

She turned around to face him, and the sight of her standing there, framed in the doorway, their past brought to life in the barn behind her, took his breath away. "You are so beautiful, Faith," he said when he could find his voice. "So very beautiful to me."

She lowered her gaze and crossed her arms, self-conscious under his admiration. When she spoke, he had to hold his breath so he could hear. Obvious confusion furrowed her brow. "My daddy told me he thought you knew. About the baby. About Jasmine."

The words hit him with such force that he staggered. "No, Faith." He moved forward, stopping only a few feet from her. His legs might be unsteady beneath him, but his voice, thank goodness, came out strong and true. "I didn't know. If I had known, I would never, never have stayed away."

"But he said you two talked." Her voice was so small. She kicked at a pebble lodged in the earth near her feet, knocking it loose. It skittered to a halt in front of him.

Cord furrowed his brow in confusion. He had received one phone call from the man the week after Thanksgiving, and Jed hadn't called to talk, at least not with anything but the business end of a shotgun. In as few words as humanly possible, her father had made it abundantly clear that if Cord so much as set foot on Goodacre ground any time in the near future, Jed would consider it a threat to the safety and security of his family, and Cord would likely lose at least one of his kneecaps in the process.

"He said you wanted to make things right."

Suddenly, it dawned on him what had happened. There had been another conversation, one that even now made his stomach turn. Cord closed the distance between them in a few quick strides. He wrapped his hands, ever so gently, around her upper arms. "Faith, look at me."

She shook her head, but he saw a single tear roll down the slope of her nose and drop to the ground at her feet.

"You have to believe me. I didn't know about the baby." He slid his palms down her arms, tugging until she uncrossed them and let him take her hands in his. She still didn't look at him, but he sensed that she was yielding. "But maybe I know why he thought I did."

She frowned and rubbed her tear-dampened cheek against her shoulder, but she didn't try to pull her hands from his.

"Faith. Please look at me."

"I can't." Her words were barely more than a whisper. "I—I'm listening, though."

It would have to be enough. "I came to see him right before school started."

"What?" The tone of the single word told him she wasn't faking her surprise. He couldn't believe the man had said nothing to his daughter about that fateful visit, but clearly, she was completely in the dark.

"I knew things had gotten off between you and me, and I had no doubt that it was because of what we'd done, because of the way we'd compromised. I knew we couldn't go back, but I wanted to make things right, and I could only think of one way to do that." He considered his words carefully. "I ended up with just one free day, Faith, not nearly as much time as I'd hoped for, but I came out here, and I went to him first."

Faith shook her head slowly. "You were here? That August? You talked to my dad?"

"Yeah. I was. I did. I came, just like I said I would."

"He didn't tell me," she whispered. Then she lifted her confused gaze to his. "Why did you see him and not me?"

Cord sighed and shook his head, rethinking everything in light of her not knowing he'd been there. "Might as well go for broke," he muttered. He had nothing to lose at this point, certainly not his pride.

"I don't understand." She lowered her gaze to their clasped hands.

"I came here armed with my heart on my sleeve and a ring in my pocket, and I told your daddy I wanted to marry you."

"You what?" She jerked back, stunned, her eyes wide, but he didn't let go of her hands. "Marry—marry me?" Her voice rose high and almost frantic.

"I asked him for his blessing. I came here to propose to you."

"No," she said, shaking her head. "No, that's not possible. He never told me anything about that. He would have told me, Cord. You're lying." She twisted her hands-free of his and crossed her arms tightly in front of her, turning away from him toward her truck.

"Faith," he said, his voice raised above her rant. Afraid she'd get in her truck and drive away, he circled to stand in front of her. "He wasn't honest with you, then."

She jerked back and frowned. "My daddy wouldn't lie to me, Cord. You know him better than that."

He did know her father. He knew Jed was an old-school conservative rancher who thought America was a paradise second only to Heaven, who read his Bible daily and went to church every Sunday, come Hell or high water, as Faith put it, and he raised his children to do the same.

He also knew Jed to be a man blindsided by his own weaknesses and fears—weren't all men?—and one of Jed's greatest fears was that of losing his daughters to unworthy men. Cord knew exactly how Jed felt about him; the man had told him that day in no uncertain terms.

"You want to marry my daughter, boy?" Jed hadn't waited for a response. "Marriage is hard work. It's the hardest work a man will ever do. The most rewarding, too, if you do it right. But believe me, it's not about meeting each other halfway or even somewhere in the middle. It's about giving and giving until you think there's nothing more to give, and then you give some more. It's about burning yourself out for the woman you have sworn before God to love and cherish and protect. It's about honor and justice, about earning your worth as a man."

"I know, sir. I know. I know all about hard work and sacrifice. I love her, and I want to marry her. I'll marry her now, today, if she'll have me."

Jed had simply laughed. "You and your trust fund and your summers playing ranch hand? You wouldn't know hard work if it jumped up and bit you in the hindquarters. You've had everything in your life handed to you on a silver platter, and now you want me to hand my daughter over to you, as well?" Jed had chuckled again, a sound like wind in a bone tree. "No, Mr. Overman. I will not give you my blessing." He was walking away before he even finished speaking, his head still shaking.

Frantic, Cord had called after him, "But, sir! I don't want to be without her. I need her."

Jed cut him off. "Listen, young man. You need a security blanket, not a wife. Why don't you come back in a decade or so, after you've got some adult living under your belt? Maybe when you're ready to settle down and get serious about something other than having a good time. If you're still in love with my daughter, maybe we can have this conversation again. Not because I like you personally, mind you, but because I know you come from good people."

Stunned by the rejection he hadn't expected, Cord had opened his mouth to reason with the man, but words of desperation came out instead.

"We're already married in the eyes of God, sir. I only want to make it right in the eyes of man."

Time had stood still, then Jed cleared his throat, gravel against steel. "If I weren't a religious man, you'd be dead, boy. How dare you come onto my property and make your demands. How dare you try to force my hand into giving you my eldest child whom I love more than life itself." With each statement, he took another step closer. Cord stood his ground, but for the first time in his life, he fully understood what it meant to shake in his boots. With little more than a foot of space between them, Jed said, "You are a disgrace, boy. I could care less about my own pride and dignity, but you have dishonored my daughter, yourself, and above all, God. You go play frat boy with someone else's daughter, you hear? Faith isn't some trophy wife you can add to your collection. Her home is here in this hollow. She's a deep roots girl, and if you truly loved her, you'd know that already."

Now, standing in front of the only woman he'd ever wanted to marry, Cord didn't relay all the sordid details of that conversation to her, but enough so she would know what had happened. He smiled sadly and said, "I didn't know you were pregnant. That's the God-honest truth." Then he grimaced. "But I did tell him we'd slept together. That we were already married in the eyes of God."

She gaped at him, her mouth opening and closing as she fumbled for something to say.

"I know, I know. Stupid." Cord raised both hands in surrender. "Stupid because it totally backfired on me. I thought telling him was me manning up. I thought he'd realize how serious I was about you." He released a short, sardonic laugh. "Suffice it to say; he was not impressed. He essentially told me I wasn't good enough for you, that you deserved better."

Faith started to protest, but Cord kept talking.

"And maybe he was right. I wasn't good enough for you. And you did—you do—deserve better. But only because I was young and untried, Faith. Not because I didn't love you enough."

She finally got her voice to work again, although it came out more of a croak than anything. "What happened? You left without seeing me."

Cord grimaced and nodded. "Yeah," he said on a miserable sigh. "I was angry. My pride—my stupid pride had been reduced to a pile of ashes. I schlepped my way back to school where I took it upon myself to become everything your father already believed me to be. And no," he said, holding up both hands to halt any protests she might throw at him. "I am in no way blaming your father for my behavior. I claimed to be a man ready to take a wife, but I acted like an immature child who didn't like being told no."

It was difficult not to try to defend himself, but it wouldn't make any difference now, anyway. How could she possibly know how devastated he'd been by her father's—and by proxy, *her*—rejection of him? How could she fathom the blow his young manhood took that day as he drove away under the dark cloud of Jedediah Goodacre's judgment and recrimination. Too ashamed to see Faith, he'd ducked out of Plumwood Hollow, red-faced and cut down to size. Angry, and yes, shocked that things hadn't gone the way he'd planned, or as Jed put it, that things hadn't been handed to him on a silver platter. He'd shown up on campus raring to go, chomping at the bit to prove his worth to anyone who would give him the time of day, and he'd succumbed to the ready temptation of a myriad of pretty eyes and pouting lips that were willing and available every time he turned around.

Wrong? Yes. He'd had no desire to pursue a real relationship with any of them, not even Brianna Peters at the time. But his bludgeoned ego, his battered pride, had responded like a champ to their attention. It was good to be wanted for who he was, and that was all he'd thought about at the time.

"You should have asked me," Faith said in a quiet voice. She wouldn't look at him, but she wasn't trying to escape him anymore. "I was an adult. Old enough to make my own decisions. You should have come to me."

Cord nodded, but that decision he was quick to defend. "I wanted to do it right, Faith. I'd already done so much of it wrong, starting with that night here, and then the phone calls that only fanned those flames and focused on the wrong things in our relationship. I got consumed, didn't you? It was tearing me up inside. I wanted to make it right, and I told him that." He hesitated only a beat before adding, "I stand by that, even now."

She said nothing for several moments, then lifted her gaze to his again. "Why didn't you come to see me at Thanksgiving like you said you would?" she asked.

Cord frowned, carefully considering how to answer that. Hadn't he already done enough to make her father look like the bad guy in this whole ordeal? He didn't need to tell her about that phone call, too. "I wasn't man enough. Like I said, I didn't want you to see the person I'd become. I was ashamed. I was embarrassed, and to be honest, I was afraid of what I'd see in your eyes when you looked at me. I think something in me believed that as long as you didn't know how low I'd fallen, there might still be hope for us one day." He smiled slightly. "Slim, but there."

Faith's head kept moving back and forth, her eyes shining with misery. "I still don't understand why he never told me this. You're right; he did lie to me. He's been lying to me this whole time."

Cord shook his head. "No, Faith. I don't think that's quite right." Because she knew nothing of the conversation between Jed and him, Cord saw things from a different perspective. "He was protecting you, don't you think? It's what parents do. Isn't it the same thing you've done with Jasmine by not telling her about me?" Before she could answer, he added, "The most tragic part about that is the part where you both felt you had to protect your children from me."

Lord have mercy, that hurt more than he thought possible.

"Oh, Cord," she whispered, her shoulders sagging. "What a mess we've made of things."

Cord swallowed hard and gestured in the general direction of Seven Virtues. "He was right, though, wasn't he?" he asked. "This is where you belong. I know that now." Then he added, "I think I knew it back then, too."

"You still should have asked me," she said again. Then she lifted her chin and stated, "You never asked me."

He hesitated, not wanting to contradict her, but he wasn't going to stand silent about something so important. "That's not true, Faith." He kept his tone gentle. "I asked you. Right here. Right there." He pointed past her shoulder into the barn. "That night—" He took a steadying breath. "That night when we—when I—" Why was it so hard to say? "I asked you to marry me that night. I asked you to be my wife, and to come with me, to do life with me, no matter where it took us. Have you really forgotten?"

"I thought...." Her voice trailed off, but she lifted her eyes to his and tried again. "I thought we were still dreaming, Cord. I didn't know you meant it. Not for real, anyway."

She didn't know he'd meant it? She didn't know how absolutely real it all was to him? He swallowed the lump that rose in his throat. "But you said yes."

"I did."

"I meant it, Faith. Every word, every moment." He clenched his jaw tightly, choosing his words carefully. "And I was under the impression that you meant it, too."

They'd made love up there in the loft, the diamond-studded cobalt sky winking down at them through a gaping hole in the roof above them. It was the first time for both of them, and they'd called it their wedding night.

"I did," she said again, her voice a hushed whisper.

"I don't understand." It was his turn to be confused. "As far as I was concerned, we were married that night. With everything in me, I meant it," he repeated, then added, "I still do."

"Cord, please don't." The way she said his name made his chest hurt as it had earlier in the truck.

"I was wrong, Faith," he acknowledged again. He shoved his hands in his pockets, aching to pull her to him, to soothe away the fear she was hiding behind, the fear he'd planted. He wanted her to hear his words, to know his heart, and if he touched her, he might not be able to get them out. "I'm asking you to forgive me. I want another chance for us. And now, with Jasmine, there's even more reason to try. Please." His eyes burned with unshed tears of his own. "Let me prove you wrong about me this time," he said, then shook his head. "No, let me prove that I'm right for you. That we belong together. All three of us, Faith."

She said nothing for several moments, and although it almost killed him to do so, he waited. He'd laid himself bare before her; now it was up to her to make the next move.

Finally, *finally*, she spoke. "You asked me what we're doing here. Why I brought you here." She turned away from him to face the empty barn behind her. "I haven't been back here since you left. But this place houses some of the best memories of my life—"

"Mine, too," he declared, then grimaced when she pressed her lips together. "Sorry. Go on."

"It also represents one of the most devastating times in my life, Cord. Not just the end of my childhood, but the beginning of a very different future than the one I'd hoped for. The one we talked about sharing."

He wanted to chime in again, to tell her he understood, that he, too, suffered the losses she talked of, but he kept his mouth closed. *Let her speak, man.*

"We compromised here, Cord." She lifted her gaze to the hayloft. "We broke promises we made to each other, to God, to ourselves. We changed the rules, and that changed us."

After several moments, he moved to stand beside her. "I know." It had been the most incredible night of his life, more amazing than he'd ever dreamed it could be, but by morning, Cord knew that what they'd done, what they'd shared, as perfect as it had seemed while it was happening, was tainted by compromise and justification.

She sighed deeply beside him, and he realized she wasn't finished. He closed his eyes and braced himself for more, sensing that he wasn't going to like whatever it was she had to say.

"We both made the decision to participate in an act that had the potential to create a child. I wasn't alone in that, Cord. Which meant we both should have taken responsibility for whatever happened as a result of that decision." She lowered her gaze and once again, crossed her arms, as though strapping on a shield to protect her heart. "We slept together. Why wouldn't you wonder if I was pregnant? Why wasn't it just as much an obligation to you to find out one way or the other as it was mine? You never even asked."

"If you'd only told me—" he began.

"If you'd only asked," she said, cutting him off. "But you didn't. You weren't here, and I had to find out alone." She sniffed delicately, and even though she kept her face averted, he saw the tears that trickled down her cheeks.

I didn't know! He wanted to raise his fist and shout the words, but he remained silent.

"I faced it all alone, Cord. The shame, the gossip, the reputation, my daddy's broken trust and broken heart. I thought I was going to die without you. There were days—weeks, months—I didn't think I could do it, when I believed my heart would simply stop beating." She swiped at her cheeks, and stepped inside the barn, moving around the open space, her fingers brushing lightly against the support beams, along the rough surfaces of the vertical plank siding that made up the walls of the small outbuilding. She smiled when she found the amateur painting of the red daisies on the wall beneath the loft. Much of it had faded or completely worn away, but she traced the faint lines with her fingertips. Her voice rose a little as she continued. "You know what, though?" She grinned at him over her shoulder, a bittersweet look that hurt him to see. "I'm still here. My little old heart just kept right on ticking. But I'll never forget the first time I felt our baby move inside of me. It was like this secret joy in the midst of my misery. And every time she kicked or flipped or hiccupped—" she smiled at him again, this time her eyes bright with something more than just tears. "—I stood a little taller. I got a little tougher and grew a little stronger, and by the time the doctor laid that tiny squeaky angel baby in my arms, I knew I was going to be okay. We were going to be okay." She stopped when she reached the ladder that led to the loft but didn't look up. Instead, she looked at him. "We've been more than okay, Jasmine and me. We're a family."

He nodded, not exactly sure how he was supposed to respond. He wanted to argue again, that if she'd told him about the baby, he'd be part of that family, too. But he was beginning to understand things from her perspective. He had, in fact, wondered about a pregnancy; he knew the possible consequences of their actions. But he'd also reassured himself that if there were one, she'd let him know. When no word came from her, he assumed....

Faith crossed the dirt floor and held out her hands to him. Surprise quickly turned to hope, and he took them, his heart in his throat as she lifted her beautiful eyes to meet his. "Cord, you are asking me to take down the life I've built for Jasmine and me, all the way down to its very foundation, and to rebuild it with you in the blueprint. You do have the right to know your daughter, and she has the right to know you. But having the right to something doesn't make it right. Do you know what I mean?" She bit her lip, her expression serious, and then continued. "I want you to know that I *am* willing to rebuild with you *if* you're staying. I need to know that Jasmine can count on you to be here for her, no matter what happens between you and me."

"I'm not going anywhere. I promise." He squeezed her hands gently, marveling at how right—how familiar—they felt cradled in his. "This place, Whispering Hills, is mine now. Or it will be when the sale closes."

Faith nodded. "Yeah. We should talk about that at some point."

"Anything you want to know." The idea of talking with Faith about his plans for the place made him almost lightheaded with happiness. He wanted to tell her everything, to see her eyes light up and to hear her opinion on all his ideas.

"A dude ranch, Cord? Really?" She shot him a disbelieving look.

Cord snorted. "What are you talking about? Who said anything about a dude ranch?" Then he rolled his eyes. "That's what people are saying? Geez. The rumor mill is alive and well in the hollow, I see."

Faith eyed him skeptically. "So, does that mean it's not true? Because you know how gossip goes. There's always a little truth to the tale."

He let go of her hand momentarily to cross his heart. "I solemnly swear that I am not opening a dude ranch at Whispering Hills." He laced his fingers with hers again. "Uncle Judge would rise up out of his grave if he thought as much." He stepped a little closer to her, relieved when she didn't back away. "I'd love to include you in on the blueprint of my life here at the ranch," he said, using her analogy from earlier.

She smiled up at him, a little shy, a little tentative. "Let's start with us first, okay? Then maybe we'll move on to bigger projects."

Cord's breath hitched. "Us? As in you and me?" Did he dare hope?

She hesitated, then said, "I don't know. Yes. I guess. Yes." She giggled nervously and squeezed her eyes shut. "I'm sorry. I'm not usually this indecisive." She took a deep breath and lifted her gaze back to his. What he saw there made his heart sing. "The other day, you said you were going to try to win back my heart."

"Yes." He nodded slowly. "I am. That's my plan."

She giggled again. "You clearly do not struggle with indecision."

"No. Not where you're concerned, Faith."

"Do you want to know how you can do that?" she asked, a slight tremor in her voice. He felt it in her hands, too.

"Please. Yes." There was nothing he wanted more.

"Slowly," she said. "This rebuild may take me a while, and I'm not sure how Jasmine is going to adjust to all of this. She may be an even tougher nut to crack than I am, you know? So, I need you to take things slowly. With both of us."

"Slowly," Cord said. Now that he'd had some time to get past the initial shock of finding out he was a father, he was able to look at things a little more objectively. This was what he wanted, wasn't it? He'd come back to the hollow for just this. Faith Goodacre. A place to call his own. And now, there was Jasmine, too. He could do slowly.

In spite of what folks around here seemed to think of him, he hadn't really expected everything to simply fall into his lap. He may have dreamed it might happen that way, sure. But after talking to his parents, and after doing a little soul searching over the last week, he could say, with a clear conscience, that he had no illusions about it being easy. What he did expect was that he was going to have to work hard for the things he wanted in this community, in life. And that didn't scare him at all. He was good at hard work. He wanted to earn what he got. And truth be told, he liked knowing that he'd have to work hard to win Faith's heart.

So yeah. "I can do slowly."

She took a deep breath and blew it out between pursed lips. "I'm nervous, Cord." Her next words came out a whisper. "I don't know why, but I'm so afraid."

Cord slid his hands up to her shoulders, and then gently pulled her against him, wrapping his arms around her. She stepped into his embrace without hesitation, and his whole body thrummed with the surge of emotions that welled up in him. "You gotta have faith in me, baby. In us. You're not alone anymore." He rocked her gently side to side, murmuring against her hair. "I'm here now. We'll do this together."

"Together," she echoed, resting her cheek against his shoulder, her arms sliding tentatively around his waist.

Cord couldn't remember ever hearing a sweeter word.

SEVENTEEN

It was like coming home after being gone far too long. Held against him, his crooning words in her ears, his chin resting against her temple, he even smelled familiar to her. Not the cologne he wore; she didn't recognize it. He'd graduated to something a little classier than the Axe body spray all the guys wore in high school. But underneath the synthetic fragrance was all Cord, that essence of him that triggered memories of moonlit walks, driving dusty roads with the windows rolled down, and late-night swims in the lake after too many hours in the summer sunshine. Faith closed her eyes and breathed him in, listening to the steady rhythm of his heart beating inside his chest, willing her own to slow down. Willing herself not to tumble headlong back in love with this man.

Then again, she wasn't sure she'd ever stopped loving him.

Every time she looked at Jasmine, she saw Cord's eyes looking back at her. A tilt of the head, an impish grin, the arch of a brow in challenge. Even though Jasmine had never met her father, she was so like him. Sometimes the resemblance brought Faith profound joy, while other times, seeing him in their child every day, made her heart ache for all that they'd lost, for what might have been.

Was it foolish to hope that they could build a future together after all the heartache between them? Was it as simple as picking up where they'd left off? It couldn't be, could it? So much had changed in the last decade. She was the head of a household now, a mother. Adulthood forced people to adjust and grow and flex, and motherhood brought on complexities of its own.

No, they couldn't go back, but maybe, if they took it slowly, they could go forward from this place.

Finally, Faith lifted her head and leaned back to look up at him.

Cord returned her gaze, his eyes alight with expectation, with happiness, and yes, she could see it now, with the same love she'd seen in them all those years ago.

When his hand slid up her spine to cup the back of her head, and when he lowered his mouth to hers, she didn't pull away.

The kiss was a gentle exploration, a testing of the waters, his mouth moving tenderly against hers. She sighed, and his arm around her waist tightened in response.

When he lifted his head, a smile tugged up one corner of his mouth. "I have missed you, Faith Goodacre. Lord, how I've missed you." Then he stepped back, releasing her from his embrace, but taking both her hands in his again. "Slowly," he said, as though reminding himself of their agreement. Then he raised her arms above her head, spun her around so she was facing away from him, and drew her back against him in a loose embrace so they were both looking out toward Whispering Hills Ranch. "See all this?" he said, his murmur against her ear sending ripples of pleasure up her spine. "This is where I belong," he said. "Coming back here was like coming home again. I've been gone too long, Faith. Far too long, and it's good to be home."

Her breath caught as he said the words she'd been thinking only moments before. "I've missed you, too, Cordell Overman," she whispered, resting her head back against his shoulder, amazed to be standing in the circle of his arms again.

"What comes next?" His voice was quiet, calm, but the question he asked was loaded. "When do I get to meet my daughter?"

Faith flinched. She couldn't help it. He must have sensed her withdrawal because he let her go when she stepped away from him. She immediately felt a sense of loss without his arms around her.

Faith thought she'd been ready to introduce them today. She thought she could handle it. But nothing had gone the way she'd expected, and she needed to regroup. To regain control of the situation. She was a mother, for Pete's sake. "I need some time, Cord."

He straightened his shoulders, and his chin came up in resistance, but she reached out and twined her fingers with his again, needing that physical connection.

"Hear me out, okay?" She waited until he nodded, then she continued. "Motherhood changes a person. Loyalties, priorities, purpose. They all get rearranged when that child is handed into your care." She pointed through the trees toward Seven Virtues. "Everything I've built next door is for her. Every moment of my life has been dedicated to making sure she knows she's loved and provided for."

"I know you, Faith," he declared. "I know it's been a long time, but I still know you. It's the way you've always operated. All or nothing. That hasn't changed."

Faith nodded. "I'm an all or nothing girl; you're right about that. So you should also know I'm not going to renege on my word. But she doesn't know you, Cord. She doesn't know any—anything about you." She stumbled over her words, hating the flicker of pain on his face. "I'm asking you to go slowly for her sake as much as for mine. You're going to need to court her, I think."

"I can do that," he said, without hesitation. "I want to court you both." He snorted softly. "In fact, I think I'm going to have to court your daddy, too. I have a feeling I'm going to have my work cut out winning him over."

"Daddy's mellowed over the years," she countered. "He might surprise you and end up being your biggest ally."

"Really? So, he wasn't serious when he said he'd help you bury my dead body if you needed it?"

Faith smiled but shook her head. "Oh, he meant it, all right. Notice he didn't offer to help kill you, just to help dispose of you if it came to that. Seriously, though, he's the least of your worries right now." She grinned at him. "That said, you should at least try to get him on your side. It'll go a long way in Jasmine's book, too. He's the only father figure she's had."

Cord nodded, then said, "I don't want to wait to meet her, Faith. If you aren't ready to tell her about us, then would you be willing to introduce me as the guy moving in next door? That would be innocent enough, wouldn't it?"

It seemed harmless enough in theory, but when she looked up at him, she knew it would never fly. "Innocent, my foot. Not if you're going to stare at me like that. Good grief." She felt her cheeks grow warm with embarrassment. "Even Jasmine won't fall for the guy next door line."

Cord grinned down at her. "Like what?" He cupped her jaw in his big hand, his fingers curling gently around the column of her neck. "Like I'm a starving man and you're a smorgasbord of every single one of my favorite dishes?"

Faith laughed out loud and pulled away, suddenly afraid he might try to kiss her again. "Yeah, something like that. Seriously, Cord."

"Well, maybe introduce me as your high school sweetheart, then. It's the truth, and it would explain the drool." He swiped dramatically at his chin.

She shook her head anyway. "Let me think about it while I take you back to your truck, okay? Come on." With a last look at the old barn, she turned to go, but their hands were still linked, and he pulled her back to him. He tipped her chin up and rubbed a thumb across her bottom lip before lowering his mouth to hers again.

This kiss was more intense, more intimate. No testing of the waters this time. It was full of promise. Hope. Of reawakened passion. He tipped her head up higher and pressed soft, sweet kisses along her jaw and then back to her mouth again.

Everything seemed to stop and speed up at the same time. Faith gave in to the sheer bliss of it, relishing in the searing pressure of his lips against her flesh. Then with a sigh, she pushed him away and held up her hands between them. "Stop," she said, her pulse racing, her breathing quick and shallow. "I can't think when you do that."

Cord stepped back and dropped his hands to his sides where he looped his thumbs in his pockets, but he was grinning like the Cheshire Cat.

"Wipe that smug look off your face," she said, poking him in the chest. "Or I'll do it for you—eep!"

He was quick; his hand shot up and his long fingers wrapped around her wrist, pulling her close again. "There's only one way you'll get rid of this smile." His voice came out a little ragged. Apparently, she wasn't the only one affected by that kiss.

"Whoa, city boy." She laughed breathlessly, flattening her palm against his shoulder to keep the space between them. "Slowly, remember?"

He reluctantly let go, but the grin was still just as bold and smug as ever. "Slowly."

"Come on." She moved quickly so as not to give him the opportunity to grab her again. She didn't think she'd have the will to break away from him another time.

Once more, she was grateful for the wide middle seat console between them. She kept both hands on the wheel except for when she shifted gears and focused her attention on the road ahead of them. Even so, she could feel him watching her, and every muscle in her body seemed to twitch and tingle like she was sitting too close to an electrical circuit board. The few times she worked up the courage to glance his way, she inevitably found his smoky eyes on her, his expression so intense it made her hot all over, even with the windows rolled down.

About halfway back to the church, Cord reached over and ran the backs of his knuckles down her arm, just like he'd done on the way out to the Flanner place, his touch once again sending a jolt through her. She jerked the wheel slightly, then without looking at him, she said, "The last time you did that I nearly ran us off the road."

"I know," Cord said. "Call it living dangerously. I just needed to touch you."

After a moment's hesitation, Faith scooted a little closer to the console so she could rest her forearm beside Cord's, then tucked her hand in his, lacing their fingers together. They rode in silence the rest of the way.

EIGHTEEN

Cord's truck was the only vehicle still parked outside the church when they pulled in, and Faith pulled up alongside it and turned off her engine. She shifted in her seat so that she was facing him, and he studied her openly. In a million small ways, she'd changed. Her lips were still full but more defined than he remembered them. The color of her eyes still made him think of amber ale, and her dark lashes still set them off in sharp contrast, but there were fine lines at the corners that crinkled prettily when she smiled. Her cheekbones were more pronounced, her neck long and slender, her collarbones both delicate and sharp at the same time. She was more voluptuous in ways she hadn't been as a teenager, and yet there was a sinewy leanness about her that gave evidence to her long hours working her daddy's ranch. Cord had heard about Jed's accident, and how Faith had stepped in to take care of the place while he recovered, how she'd turned the flagging ranch into a thriving business.

"So, here's what I'm thinking," Faith began, without preamble. "I know I'm asking a lot of you, Cord, but would you be willing to give me a week? I want to try and pave the way a little. To clean up a little after today. I know I'll get a barrage of questions when I get home since I left with you, and my family did bring up your name on Mother's Day."

"They did?" he said, lifting a brow in question. "I'm almost afraid to ask why."

"Daddy found out from Reverend Treadwell that you'd paid me a visit." She screwed up one side of her face. "He was just curious as to why he hadn't heard it from me."

"I see."

She snorted. "You sound just like him."

Cord looked at her in confusion. "I do?"

"Like the pastor, not like my daddy," she explained with a goofy grin. "He always says 'I see,' when he isn't ready to share what he's really thinking."

Cord laughed out loud. "You don't know the half of it," he told her, recalling his somewhat frustrating conversation with the man last week. He didn't want to get sidetracked from the issue at hand, though. "Why a week? I don't want to wait that long."

Her smile faded. "I am going to tell her you're my high school sweetheart if you're okay with that. Especially since we're going to..." She waved a hand back and forth between them. "You know. Start. Or restart. Or whatever." She shot him a pleading look. "I just need a little time to talk to her about you. About what you were to me back then. And about why you've come back."

Cord didn't like the direction this plan of hers was going. He understood the impulse to try to ease into the truth with Jasmine, but he didn't like it. It felt dishonest to him, and after all the years they'd lost because of withholding information from each other, it bothered him that they were considering doing the same thing to their daughter. Besides, he wanted to be a part of those conversations. He wanted to tell Jasmine about how much her mother had meant to him, too. "Do you know why I've come back?"

"I do. You're buying your uncle's place." She tapped a finger on the steering wheel, but it was more out of nervous energy than impatience, he was certain. "I don't need to give her a ton of details. Believe me; she'll be happy someone we know is taking over Whispering Hills. She's been begging me to buy it because she doesn't want a bunch of freaks moving in next door. Her words, not mine."

"Too late for that," Cord said with a self-deprecating chuckle. He couldn't wait to meet the girl, to get to know her. But he held up a hand to stop Faith before she went on. "While I am, indeed, buying Uncle Judge's place, that's not the real reason I'm here." He eyed her pointedly.

Faith's cheeks flushed; Lord, she was beautiful. He could feast his eyes on her all day.

"I know, I know," she murmured. "But that's a detail I'm not yet prepared to give her," she said with a sheepish grimace. "I need the week, not just for her, but for me, too, Cord. This has all been kinda sudden, you know? For both of us."

"And finding out I have a nine-year-old daughter is kind of sudden for me, too."

Faith sighed and lowered her hands to her lap, lacing her fingers together tightly. "I know. I'm sorry." She lifted wide, sincere eyes to his. "I'm sorry, Cord. I should have done this all so differently. Not just today—"

Cord reached over and stroked her arm again. "Stop. Let's not do that to each other, okay? Or to ourselves. We've already decided to move forward. Let's not go back." He said the words as though he meant them, and the honorable and noble part of Cordell Overman in him did. But there was another part of him that stomped around, fuming in the background. He'd missed so much of Jasmine's life already; he didn't want to miss another day. Another minute. Another second.

"Thank you," Faith whispered, then squared her shoulders and continued. "I'd like you to join us for Sunday dinner, if you'll come. I can introduce you at Seven Virtues where she'll be most comfortable. And that way, if she gets overwhelmed, she can find refuge."

Cord cocked a questioning brow at her.

"Sometimes she just needs to disappear so she can process," Faith explained.

"Sounds like someone else I know," Cord said, trying to remain optimistic. But he didn't like the solution she was suggesting. Sure, in some ideological world it sounded pleasant enough. At the moment, however, he had a hard enough time imagining sitting down at the table surrounded by Faith's posse of sisters all sizing him up, weighing and measuring him the way Prudence had, and Jedediah Goodacre glaring at him from across the pot roast. Adding Jasmine to the mix would be like strapping chum to his chest and jumping into a shark tank without a cage. "I don't really see that going down the way you're hoping it will," he countered. "How about a compromise?"

After a few moments, she said, "I'm listening."

"Here's what *I'm* thinking. How about you introduce us today. I can come over right now. I've been meaning to get over and talk to you and your daddy about my plans for Whispering Hills, anyway, and that would be a good excuse to do so, without putting any pressure on Jasmine." The name sounded so strange on his lips, yet so familiar to him. So right. "Then I'll step back for a week, and you can do whatever it is you need to do between now and then." He kept talking even though she was shaking her head. "That way, she'll know we're okay." He gestured between them. "The last she saw us, we weren't exactly getting along. Validated by your father whisking her away from the scene like that." He grimaced as he recalled the look on the child's face when she noticed him in the truck with her mother.

"I don't know." Faith's brow furrowed with concern. "I feel like I need to prepare her."

"Why? Are you worried about how she'll take it? Or are you worried about not being able to control the situation?" He didn't intend to sound cruel, but this was Faith they were talking about, and the Faith he remembered had a tight-fisted grip on all the loose ends in her life. The look on her face told him he'd hit a sore spot.

"Please, Cord," she said again. "I know my daughter. Our daughter," she corrected, sending a little thrill of pleasure through him, despite his unsettled emotions. "She's like me when it comes to surprises. We don't do well with them, and I expect she'll need some time to adjust. Rushing this isn't going to help."

And there was the crux of it all. Sure, he could insist on doing things his way, but like Faith said earlier, just because he had the right to make demands, didn't make the demands right. She knew the child; he didn't. Cord wanted Faith to trust him; maybe he needed to trust her, too.

"Think about it this way. You can talk to Daddy any time this week. Clear the air between you, catch him up to speed on Whispering Hills. Then you can focus on Jasmine during Sunday dinner, knowing you've already got Daddy on your side. It will be a good opportunity for you and Jas to start getting to know each other on safe ground. Her territory, you know?

Maybe tell her a little about your plans for the ranch—she's so curious about what will happen there now that Judge is gone."

Cord frowned, remembering a thought he'd had earlier. "Did my uncle know about Jasmine? That she was mine?"

Faith didn't answer right away, but finally, she turned a pensive look on her face. "He never came right out and said so." She brushed some imaginary lint off the console between them. "But I think maybe he did. Your aunt died only a few months after Jasmine was born, but she took us under her wings. She was very kind to me, Cord, and there was a period when kindness toward me was in short supply. Particularly when I just started showing." She smiled softly, her hand resting subconsciously on her abdomen.

The idea of anyone being cruel to her in his absence—because of his absence—made him a little sick to his stomach. "I'm sorry I wasn't there," he said. It wasn't just a platitude, either. He meant it. He wished with all his heart that he could go back in time and do things differently.

"I'm sorry, too," Faith said with a sad nod. "You know, your aunt did the same for us when my mom passed away. She was always over here, fluttering around, making sure we had food to eat and clean clothes, checking on baby Abby and poor, sad Daddy. At twelve, I believed I could handle everything on my own, and I thought she was kinda bossy and nosy, but looking back, she did things for us that I didn't even know about. I got to thank her the second time around." She choked up a little as she spoke, and Cord reached across the console to brush her cheek with his knuckles. "She got to see Jasmine, and for that I'm glad. She was truly an angel, Cord. She looked after us—all of us Goodacres—as though we were her own, right up until she got sick. We did our best to return the love until Judge moved her to Louisville."

The summer after Cord's freshman year at UK, Aunt Betina had been diagnosed with pancreatic cancer. She died less than three months later. There'd been a memorial service in Plumwood Hollow, but because her family came from Louisville, that's where her funeral was. Cord had just begun his sophomore year and had only made it to the family service.

It was during that weekend in Louisville that Uncle Judge had offered him a job on the ranch. "Finish your education, Cord, then come on back to the hollow where you belong. I'll have a job waiting for you."

Now that he thought about it, it hadn't been a job offer at all. It had been a chance for Cord to do the right thing. At that moment, he had no doubt in his mind that Uncle Judge had known about the baby, and had assumed that Cord knew, too. Without passing judgment, his uncle had offered him an opportunity to redeem himself.

And Cord had passed it up for football. *I didn't know.* The words thrashed about in his brain, but they were losing their clout. Like Faith had pointed out, he'd never bothered to ask, either.

Ten years. It had been nearly ten years since he'd been back to Plumwood Hollow, nine since Jasmine was born. He supposed he could wait another week. He nodded slowly. "Okay. We'll do it your way. I'll wait until next Sunday."

"Thank—"

"On one condition," he continued, cutting her off. "I want to see you every day this week."

"No," she said, shaking her head, her eyes crinkling with laughter. "No. That's not possible."

He grinned, recognizing the panic in her expression. Not because she was afraid of him. Nope. Because she was afraid of what he stirred up in her. "And why not? We're next-door neighbors now."

"No!" Her voice rose, and she gripped the steering wheel, frowning at him. "I'm busy. It's a busy time at our place. We're—we're busy."

"So... you're busy?" he asked, his eyes wide with feigned innocence.

"Shut up." But one side of her mouth quirked tellingly at his teasing. "And yes. We're weaning the fall calves this month."

"I can help," he said agreeably. "I remember how to separate calves from their mamas."

"That's not how we do it. We start with nose tags and then separate them about a week later after they're weaned."

Cord shrugged. "Hey. If I can band bulls with the best of them, I'm sure I can learn how to put a nose tag in." He'd seen the devices and knew how they worked—a plastic flap inserted into the nose that prevented a calf from getting to the teats—and he wasn't surprised at all that Faith used them, especially when she explained why. According to her, weaning the calves off the milk, but allowing them to stay with their mothers through the process, caused a significantly less amount of stress on the animals, which in turn, made for healthier herds.

It would benefit him greatly to see the process as he was planning to eventually incorporate it into practice at Whispering Hills. "I'd love to help."

"But I don't need your help."

He cocked a brow at her and nodded slowly. "I see."

She rolled her eyes at him. "Jerk."

"All you have to do is ask," he sing-songed.

"And that will never happen."

Cord chuckled knowingly. "I figured as much. Which is why I'm not waiting for you to ask. What time does Jasmine go to school in the morning?"

"No." She pointed her finger and narrowed her eyes at him.

"Great. I'll be there at nine o'clock, sharp."

"Cord." She crossed her arms and glared at him.

"Faith." He crossed his arms and glared back, trying not to laugh. Finally, he lowered his arms. "Fine. You're busy. So, you tell me; when can I see you again? Are you free tonight?"

She shook her head slowly. "I think I need a little time to process—" she waved a hand back and forth between them. "—this."

"Okay, so not tonight. How about tomorrow? Tuesday?" He said it in a lighthearted tone, but he wasn't joking. He'd spend every waking moment with her if she'd let him; hopefully, one day, every sleeping moment, too. He hardly dared believe where they'd ended up after today, and there was no way he was going to give any ground at this point. "I am not waiting until next Sunday to see you."

'I don't know, Cord. Like I said, I'm scared. Slowly, remember?" She looked up at him, her eyes beseeching.

He didn't immediately speak; she looked like she had something else she wanted to say. Sure enough, she opened her mouth, closed it, then started again.

"How—how did you know? That she was yours. Mine. Ours." She rushed through the pronouns, tripping over herself to find the right one. "I mean, she's petite for her age. And she looks a lot more like Hope than she does me, don't you think?"

"Her eyes are mine," he said without a moment's hesitation. "When she turned around in that pew and locked eyes with mine, you could have knocked me over with a feather. It was like looking through old photos of myself, except she's a heck of a lot prettier than I ever was." He shook his head, once again bereft at the reminder that he'd missed out on so much of his daughter's life already. But he bit back the resentment his words stirred up and reached across the console to cup her chin. "The way she holds her head, the shape of her ears, the stubborn set of her jaw. Those are yours." He stroked the pad of his thumb along her jawline. "The way she studied everyone around her, the way she looked directly at me, weighing and measuring me, the same way you did the first time I met you...." His thumb brushed over the curve of her bottom lip again, and Cord lowered his gaze to her mouth, forgetting what else he was going to say.

But when he leaned in for another kiss, Faith withdrew, pressing back against the driver's door. He'd have to practically crawl over the console to get to her lips now.

"I have to go." She swallowed visibly and glanced away from him, color suffusing her cheeks. "It'll make it difficult to do so if you start that again."

He grinned, even though she wasn't looking at him. "Start what again?"

"Stop teasing me," she whispered, covering her face with both hands. "Man, I feel like I'm sixteen all over again."

"So do I," he said, reaching over to wrap his long fingers around one of her wrists. He pulled her hand away, then tucked it into his own. "Look at me, Faith."

It took her a moment, but she turned slightly and peered at him from between the fingers of her other hand.

"I want to start that again. I want to start kissing you and never stop. I want to kiss you until you can't think straight. Until you can't breathe right. Until you can't come up with any word except 'more.'" Without breaking eye contact, he lifted her hand and pressed his lips into her palm. She shivered, and it made him want to thump his chest and grunt triumphantly. "But even more than that, I want to do whatever it takes to assure you that your heart is safe with me. That you can trust me with it. I'm not leaving this time. I'm here to stay. This is my home. You are my home."

She licked her lips, and for a moment, he thought his heart had stopped. "Well, you seem to have the whole can't-think-straight-can't-breathe-right thing down since I'm having trouble with both at the moment." Her eyes shone with what he hoped was happiness. "But we have to save the more for another time. I really do need to go. Without you attached to me," she added with a giggle, lifting their clasped hands between them.

"Let me bring you lunch this week," Cord said, not letting go. "You pick the day and the time. I'll be there."

He could tell she was waffling, so he waited. "I think you should start by talking to my dad. Clear the air there, and then we can talk about lunch, okay?"

Cord nodded. "I can do that. I'll give him a call as soon as I get home and get that set up."

"Sounds good. Now will you give me back my hand and get out of my truck so I can go home and eat already? I'm starving." When she tried to pry his fingers loose with her free hand, he grabbed that one, too.

"Faith Goodacre, will you just say yes to lunch with me so I can give you back your hands and get out of your truck and let you go home and eat? You must be starving. I know I am." He started pulling her toward him, very slowly. "Time and day."

He let her work one hand loose. She opened her mouth to argue, but he spoke first.

"Time and day," he cajoled.

"Fine," she gave in, breathlessly. "Eleven thirty. Friday."

He let go of her, a satisfied grin spreading across his face. He could wait five days. Heck, he'd waited ten years already. That didn't mean he couldn't try for better. "Wednesday," he countered.

"Friday."

Thursday?"

"Take it or leave it, Mr. Overman. Lunch next Friday. That is, if you're still in town that long."

Cord grimaced. "Ouch." But he nodded, still thrilled that she was willing at all. "I'll be there with bells on."

Faith snickered. "Please don't. You'll scare the cows." Then to his surprise and delight, she leaned across the distance between them, cupped his face in both hands, and kissed him sweetly. "Welcome home, Cowboy."

NINETEEN

SHE WAS GOING TO make him fight for every moment of her time and attention. And he was going to make every moment count.

But he had his work cut out for him in more ways than one. He was amazed at how quickly the procurement of the ranch had gone, once Frankie accepted his offer, but unfortunately, the purchase of the property was not the biggest hurdle he was facing. It wasn't even the second, third, or fourth biggest hurdle. After spending the last several days getting the lay of the land, Cord was surprised and saddened by the state of disrepair he found. Uncle Judge had let things go, and Frankie assured Cord that his father had never said a word about needing help.

According to Binks, the two old men had done all right together. "But I'm telling you, young squire; Judge should have handed this place off years ago. He might still be around today if he had." Binks shook his head, something he often did when talking about the last several years on the ranch. "That man, God rest his soul, was as stubborn as the day is long, and no matter what I said to him, he just didn't have the good sense to know when to say enough was enough."

"Was he out of money?" Cord asked, feeling insensitive and intrusive, but he couldn't wrap his mind around why the place was in the condition he found it unless it was a financial one. Binks might not know for sure, but he'd been around since what Cord now thought of as "the glory days" when the ranch was bustling with activity year-round.

"It wasn't that," Binks said. "No, not that." He sighed deeply, the lines in his forehead deepening into furrows with his frown. "Judge is—was—a proud man who didn't like to ask for help."

It was Cord's turn to frown. "He didn't seem to have a problem asking for help in the past. This place used to be crawling with folks he hired on, depending on the season's need."

"Ah. But that was back when he didn't think he needed help. There's a difference between hiring on folk to do work you know you're capable of doing yourself and hiring on folk because you no longer can." Binks leaned back in the sturdy kitchen chair and took a long swig of his coffee.

Was it something in the water around here that made people so reticent to admit they needed each other?

Binks added, "Judge had been slowing down for years. But then, haven't we all?" He shook his head again. "I think when he realized he was asking men to do things for him that he could no longer do for himself, he just started shutting down."

"Didn't Frankie—"

"Judge wasn't about to ask Frankie to come home, Cordell." Binks toyed with the handle of his coffee cup as he spoke, his gnarled fingers trembling just the slightest bit.

Cord realized his uncle wasn't the only one who struggled with the pride of a hard-working man coming to the end of his days. Clearly, there'd been a lot resting on Binks' shoulders for several years, not just since Judge's passing.

"He was proud of that boy, grateful for the years his son spent defending this fine country. He knew Frankie would try to convince him to up and sell, or the boy would give up his own career and come back. Judge wasn't willing to consider either option. So." The old man lifted his eyes, lined and hooded by years spent outdoors, and looked sadly into Cord's. "He did nothing. He just waited and prayed for the good Lord to help him make up his mind about what he was gonna do." Binks shrugged and pushed his empty cup toward the middle of the table. "Truth is, young squire, I don't believe Judge would've wanted to die anywhere else than here on his land. This wasn't just his home; it was his life. That old codger is the heart and soul of this place, Cordell, and he always will be. Don't you forget that, no matter what you have planned for this place."

Cord didn't miss the glisten in the old man's eyes as he spoke of his longtime friend. And that's what they'd been, Binks and Judge. Lifelong friends. "You have my word on that."

Hearing Binks talk about Uncle Judge and his pride resonated with Cord. His own pride had kept him from getting out earlier, from letting someone—anyone—know how much he was struggling. It had it been hard to even admit it to himself.

Last November, a few weeks before Thanksgiving, Cord sat behind the wheel of another rented car, driving late into the night, a half-drunk cup of coffee in the console beside him. He was on his way back to Lexington after wooing yet another young man into coming to UK. It had been his last stop on his circuit, and although he'd successfully convinced the family that his alma mater was the place for their boy, he'd wanted nothing more than to get the heck out of the small town that reminded him so much of Plumwood Hollow.

He'd seen himself in that young man, in his naive hope and anticipation for a future in a sport that was supposed to bring fame and riches into his life. What he didn't understand was that more often than not, the sport chewed up kids like him and spat them out at the other end, physically and emotionally handicapped in ways that few ever talked about. His thoughts went round and round as he drove, mile after mile slipping away beneath his tires until he started to wonder why he was trying to convince these young men to leave families who loved them, and girlfriends who wept tears of both pride and despair over knowing that their futures would forever be changed.

Cord just wanted to go home, but he had no idea where that was anymore. It certainly wasn't the small, but expensively furnished apartment he rented. His bed might be large and comfortable, there might be plenty of good food in the cupboards, but it was a place to sleep and eat, not a place to live. Sure, his parents were always thrilled when he visited, but to Cord, their mansion in Louisville felt more like a museum of his childhood rather than his home anymore.

In his heart, home to him had once been Whispering Hills Ranch.

No, home to him had once been Faith Goodacre. And that home had crumbled to the ground by his own doing.

Several hours later, he'd snapped awake as he careened off the side of the road, swerving in time to miss a utility pole, then fishtailing into the darkened landscape lit only by the half-moon overhead. The car came to a halt with the back left fender crumpled against a boulder, and the back brake light busted out. It had taken Cord another half an hour before he was steady enough to pull the vehicle back on the road, grateful that it was still drivable.

By the time he pulled into the closest roadside motel, it was in the darkest hours before dawn, and Cord, too, found himself in a very dark place of the soul. He ended up staying in that motel, locked in the room, for almost a week, questioning everything about his life. He didn't answer his phone, he didn't check his emails, and he left the room only when he needed to eat. In that drab, stale space, he realized he had two choices. He could continue doing what he was doing and die just a little more every day, or he could walk out of that motel room, head back to the university, turn in his resignation, and live.

He chose to live. The coaching team did their best to convince him to stay; his recruits were almost always winners, and the Wildcats had been at the top of their game, due in part to Cord's ability to find players who fit the Wildcat formula. He agreed to give them six more months, to get them through the next draft season, and then he'd be done.

Now, here he was, the soon-to-be owner of a run-down ranch with a whole lot of potential, sitting across the table from the one man who knew the place better than Cord did. And for the first time in too long, Cord was excited about what lay ahead.

As though reading his mind, Binks tapped the table with a gnarled fist. "So, what's on the agenda for the next couple of weeks? I know you're still waiting on the sale to close, but you're not planning on waiting to start the work around here, are you?"

Cord shook his head. "No, sir. I'm diving right in. But this week will be pretty quiet—just you and me. I'm still taking stock of things and getting a handle on what's priority. But I've got a contractor coming in next week to take a look and give me some quotes. The big barn I plan to keep intact - clean it up a bit - but from what I can tell, the two smaller barns are safety hazards. If he can save them, that would be my first choice, but I'm thinking at least one of them may have to come down. There are several outbuildings I'll have him take a look at, too. I'm thinking of converting a few of them to cowboy cabins since some of them haven't been in use in years. If the price is right, I'll make those priority, and once they're ready to move into, I will move out to one of those as I plan to do some major work on this house. I'm hoping having this place empty will expedite the renovation here as they won't have to worry about us being underfoot." He lifted a questioning brow at Binks. "I know you've been in the foreman's cabin for a long time, my friend. You ready for an overhaul or do you want me to keep my hands off the place?" If Cord wasn't mistaken, Binks' cabin still had an original pull-chain toilet with an elevated tank that might have been installed before the man was born.

Binks nodded slowly, taking it all in stride. "What contractor you plan on using?" he asked. His tone was casual, but Cord wasn't fooled. Community loyalty was second to godliness in Plumwood Hollow, and Cord wasn't foolish enough to stir that pot.

"John Maddox. Actually, I'll be working with Skid and Ernie on this one."

Binks tapped the table again. "John and his boys are welcome to come take a look-see and tell me what they think. I've been making do, but the place could stand a few upgrades."

Maddox and Sons Construction was as local as he could get, and although the company had no real competition in the hollow, the Maddox men prided themselves on being the best builders this side of the Mississippi River. Their work stood up to the test, and Cord hadn't considered going anywhere else. Skid and Ernie, not quite two years apart, were several years younger than Cord, but they'd crossed paths during those summers Cord had spent on the ranch. John wasn't near ready to retire yet, but these days, he handed off the larger projects like this one to his boys, and the brothers were thrilled at the prospect of getting their hands on Whispering Hills. Because of the rumors, the guys had taken to calling it "The Dude Ranch Project," especially since they knew how much it goaded Cord when they did.

Word had gotten around quickly once he'd started canvassing for help, and everywhere he went, he found himself trying to explain away the term, but to no avail. Folks greeted him with, "Hey there, Cord. How about them Bengals?" followed by a casual question about how things were going with him and Faith Goodacre. Since Bengal pride was alive and well in Plumwood Hollow, all he had to do was say, "Who dey?" to get a "Who dey think gonna beat the Bengals? Nobody!" in response. He wasn't quite so sure how to answer the Faith question since he still wasn't exactly certain of how it was going himself. When he kept it vague, the inevitable response was along the lines of, "I'll bet she and Jed have something to say about you opening a dude ranch next door." Cord smiled affably at the comments, realizing that part of the ribbing was the community's way of testing his motives.

By the middle of the week, Cord thought he would go crazy if he didn't see Faith. He'd been by to speak with Jed on Monday—the man had offered him a cup of coffee on the back porch while they talked. Faith, of course, had been nowhere to be seen; presumably out with her cows, or even more likely hiding in the woods, knowing he was there. The talk with Jed had been one of few words and a lot of nods and grunts, but when Cord rose to leave, Jed stood and gave him a firm double-handed handshake.

"Welcome back to the hollow, Cord. I expect I'll be seeing you regularly around our place in the days to come."

Cord had nodded, smiled, and said, "I expect you will." It was, for all intents and purposes, Jed's version of a blessing, and it had taken Cord all his willpower not to launch himself off the top step in celebration. Two down—kinda—and one—the big one—to go. It struck him as ironic that his biggest hurdle in the Goodacre family came in the smallest package.

He could hardly wait until Sunday.

Today, however, he had to see Faith. He didn't want to take her from her work; he just wanted to see her, to let her know he was thinking about her, and to find out if she'd been thinking about him, too. He wouldn't even have to ask; he'd be able to see it in her eyes, he was certain.

Which meant he needed to see her eyes. Now.

Cord headed to the horse pasture armed with a carrot and a lead line, but even before he'd ducked through the rail fence, Capitan was headed toward him, calling out a welcoming whinny. The horse, thrilled by the treat, nudged Cord affectionately while he slid the harness on the big animal, then they headed back toward the barn to saddle up.

The two of them had quickly grown reacquainted with each other again, and as he rode the animal down the paved drive toward Carpenter Road, he couldn't keep the smile off his face. From atop the horse, the property felt like a kingdom to him, his kingdom. "Which makes me a king," he said with a chuckle. Capitan nickered softly, possibly in agreement, but Cord wouldn't be surprised if the beast were laughing at him instead. He didn't care.

"Fine. I'm a white knight on a fiery steed." He leaned forward and patted the horse's sleek neck. "And we're off to pay homage to the queen next door." Then he shook his head at his fanciful thoughts. If his Bengal brothers could hear him now, they'd have no trouble believing he'd had one concussion too many.

Cord straightened his shoulders and lifted his chin, then reached up to draw the front of his hat lower over his forehead. "There," he growled. "Manly enough, you think, Capitan?"

Ten minutes later, he was heading up the gravel drive of Seven Virtues Ranch. He knew Faith wasn't at the house, not at this time of the afternoon, and if she was, indeed, starting the weaning process on her calves, then he knew where to find her. He veered off toward the small cattle barn and the paddocks and cattle chutes behind it, and sure enough, as he approached, he could hear the stress bawling of babies and mamas temporarily separated from each other. When he rounded the barn, the sight that met him made him pull up short in his saddle.

With the help of Jack, who circled a small group of cattle, keeping them tightly knit with short, sharp yips and ankle lunge now and then, Faith and Watson threading her way through them, expertly separating the half-grown calves from their mamas. The mamas were moved into a paddock where they milled around calling to their offspring, and the youngsters she herded into a narrow chute. One of the twins, Courage, he thought, let two calves pass by at a time, then pushed a swing gate closed behind the pair, forcing them into a narrow alley. The front calf inevitably tried to lurch through the other end, trapping himself in the headgate, where Justice waited with a nose tag at the ready. Like putting in a clip-on nose ring, she slipped the plastic flap into place in the calf's wide nostrils, talking in soothing tones all the while, then tugged on the flap gently to make sure it wouldn't go anywhere. She took her time giving each calf a once-over, checking eyes, ears, and teeth before calling out stats to Courage, who had circled the short alley and was writing things down on a clipboard. Once satisfied the calf was in good shape, Justice pulled down on the lever that opened the headgate just long enough to let the first calf through, then closed it quickly as the next animal pushed into place. The calves with flaps in place milled about in a small holding pen until there were four of them, then one of the girls would swing open the pen gate to let them into the paddock where they were reunited with their mamas.

It was like watching a well-oiled machine in action. The sisters hardly said a word to one another, their attention focused on the task at hand, working efficiently and expertly to cause as little stress on the animals as possible. Even as he watched, Cord could see that the work was made so much more efficient by the help of many hands, but the whole operation could be manned by one person, if the need arose. He might have to start out that way, so he was mentally taking notes. It was simple and well-organized, no less than what he'd expect from Faith Goodacre.

"Hey!" One of the twins noticed him and lifted a hand in greeting. Faith glanced over her shoulder, then pulled up short, making Watson whinny in surprise. Apparently, he was the last person she expected to see.

"Ladies," he said in return, tipping his hat in greeting. "Just dropping by to check out the operation." With a wink at Faith, he added, "Since I haven't been asked to help."

"Good timing," Justice said, a calculating grin on her face. "This is the last of today's lot, and then we're calling it a wrap." She turned to Faith. "Hey, sis, maybe Cord can help you get this group back to the herd so

Courage and I can get going." Without waiting for an answer, she crossed the paddock toward Cord, Courage close behind.

Cord dismounted, but he waited for them to approach. He didn't dare look at Faith, lest she come up with some excuse to cut and run on him. "It's good to see you two," he said, flashing them his signature half smile. It was habit now, the grin he'd practiced in the mirror back in college, the one that never failed to get a smile in return.

They'd been thirteen, maybe fourteen, when he was last here, and he remembered them well. Full of the kind of energy and bravado required for anyone who performed daredevil tricks on horses, the girls still glowed with that same verve. They no longer looked so much alike, but the similarities between them were heightened by the way they communicated, almost as though they knew what the other was thinking without having to say a word.

"It's been too long, Cordell Overman," Courage said, but her words were softened by a grin. "What on earth kept you?"

Cord chuckled as he gave each of them a quick hug in greeting. "Would you believe... football?" he asked, a wry grin on his face.

Justice, winking boldly at him, held up both gloved hands for his inspection. "Would you believe that I didn't just rub calf snot down the back of your shirt?"

Cord closed his eyes and let out a disgusted grunt. "You're not kidding, are you?"

"She isn't," Courage assured him. "But then, consider it part of your initiation back into ranching."

"Or back into our good graces," Justice quipped. "The key word there is 'part', Mr. Overman."

"But it is really good to see you again," Courage said. "It's about time."

And with that, the two girls strode off on foot, leaving him alone with Faith, Jack, their two horses, and the twenty cow and calf pairs milling about in the paddock, waiting for whatever came next.

TWENTY

Faith stayed back, watched him interact with her sisters, biting back the laughter that wanted to roll out of her over the way they'd put him in his place. Another part of her wanted to beg them to stop, lest he decide sticking around to fend off her sisters wasn't worth it.

Jack, on the other hand, had no such reservations, and when he realized nothing was happening with the cows at the moment, he quickly made his way over to see the newcomer, too. Cord crouched down to greet the dog, who dropped to the ground and went belly up in front of the man. Faith rolled her eyes at the animal's shameless adoration.

Abandoned by her sisters, and now by her dog, she made her way toward him. "Want to help me get these cows back to their paddock?" she asked, knowing the question would surprise him nearly as much as his showing up had done to her.

Cord stood and removed his hat, then held it to his chest in exaggerated wonder. "I would be honored to help you," he said, dipping his head in a slow bow, but not taking his eyes off her.

"Then saddle up, city boy. Let's go." She watched as he swung up onto the back of the black Morgan, even though she knew it probably made him a little uncomfortable. She noted the slight hesitation of a man still getting accustomed to sitting a saddle, the careful handling of reins that didn't hang loose enough in his hands, and the way he held his body tall and stiff, not yet one with the animal beneath him. But that would come, she knew. She had no trouble conjuring up the memory of Cord riding hell-bent across a pasture alongside her, his head thrust forward over the neck of this same horse, his body barely bouncing in the saddle, elbows wide and knees close. He'd remember, just the way she did already.

"Come on, Jack," she called out to her dog, sliding off Watson's back to open the gate. "Let's get this done!" Jack, always ready to be put to work, leaped to his feet and circled the milling cows with a volley of excited barks.

Within moments, she was back in the saddle. "You take that flank," she called out to Cord. "I've got this side, and Jack will bring up the middle. This should be a piece of cake—they just want to go back to their buddies and eat. We'll be switching paddocks early today, so we don't add more stress to these cows by making them move again in a couple of hours. You can watch how we do that, too."

Judge Flanner still practiced traditional grazing, and the condition of his pasture compared to hers was evidence of the fact. She hoped Cord would take note and adopt the mob grazing system she used. Sure, his herd was significantly larger than hers, but then, so was his ranch.

She took her time getting everyone settled, explaining each part of her process, from how she calculated the size of the paddocks according to the numbers and needs of the cows, what kind of wire and stakes she used, to the pros and cons of operating her ranch the way she did. Cord listened with rapt attention, taking it all in. He asked good questions and made thoughtful observations, as they checked the water stations and followed up with a quick perimeter check for fencing issues. Without even realizing it, they'd slipped into easy conversation, the ranch work lending them middle ground.

She wasn't in any hurry—she'd thought she'd be doing the nose tags herself today, but the twins had offered to help at the last minute, so the task was done in short order. She loved working with Justice and Courage. The sisters had a way with the large breed animals, partly because they were fearless around them, but Faith thought it was more than that. The twins were so accustomed to reading each other and the horses they rode and trained with, almost like a cerebral form of communication, and it translated just as well with the cattle as it did with horses. Hope had that same magnetism, and although Faith liked to think she had a bit of it, too, she knew she loved her animals more than they loved her. But she was okay with that. In some ways, it helped her keep things in perspective. Losing a cow or a calf was tough, and no rancher ever got through a loss without some kind of heartache. But Faith seemed to be able to see the big picture more clearly than her sisters, and that simply made her a better rancher.

She finished rolling up the leftover wire and strapped the spool to the back of her saddle before getting back on her horse. Glancing over at Cord, she was struck by an uncomfortable thought. He hadn't loved her as much as she loved him at one time, too, and he'd broken her heart because of it. Maybe, just maybe, he was the reason for her reservedness. Oh, she'd always been a loner, needing time to herself to recharge, but that all or nothing girl he'd referred to the other day? These days, she took a lot of pushing and pulling to step out from behind the wall of self-preservation.

Could she trust him not to break her heart again?

How would she know if she didn't give him a chance to prove himself?

"Thanks for your help," she began, as she drew up alongside him and the two of them started across the pasture toward the dirt lane that circled the pasture to take them back to the house. "I appreciate it."

"You're welcome," he said with a grin.

"What did I take you away from today?" she asked. What she really wanted to know was why he'd shown up here at all. Since Sunday, she'd secretly hoped he'd make an appearance before Friday, and when her father told her Cord had stopped by to see him Monday afternoon, she'd been surprised by the wave of disappointment she felt at having missed him. Knowing her father had welcomed him back had her certain Cord would come by on Tuesday, and once again, she'd berated herself for looking for signs of him every time she stepped outside.

Today, she'd forced herself to stop...and today, he'd made his appearance. Was he here to see her?

"Nothing pressing," he said. They rode slowly, Jack meandering through the grasses ahead of them, following his nose wherever it led him. "I just wanted to see you, Faith. I tried to stay away, but—" He smiled endearingly. "You can see how well that worked."

Faith nodded slowly. "Well," she began. Her throat tightened up, almost as though fighting to keep the words from slipping out. She moved a little closer so that their knees bumped. "I'm glad you came by. I've been wanting to see you, too." She shot him a sideways glance, and her heart skipped a beat at the look on his face. He opened his mouth to speak, but she said, "Race you to the lane," then she bumped her heels against Watson's sides and shot forward.

"Hey!" he shouted after her, but she heard the playful note in his voice and laughed out loud. Jack let loose an echoing bark, and Faith followed that with a whoop.

It was stupid, she knew, challenging Cord to run his horse like that. But her bold admission had left her feeling terribly vulnerable, and she needed an excuse to put distance between them. She wasn't surprised, however, when she glanced over her shoulder, to find him not far behind her, Capitan responding well to Cord's encouragement to pick up the pace.

It was a short dash, really, but she reached the lane far enough ahead of him to be able to turn around and watch him. The look of exhilaration on his face told her without words that he'd missed the thrill of a good run on horseback. She sighed at the sight of him; his head tipped forward so his hat wouldn't go flying, the wind billowing his shirt around him, as he raced up the slope of the pasture toward her.

He was beautiful, that was all there was to it. He was no longer lanky and lean the way he'd been in high school; he'd put on a good thirty or forty pounds, easily, all bulky muscle that made the shoulder seams of his shirts snug, and the sleeves tight around his biceps. Long veins ran up the contours of his arms, and her fingertips itched to follow the lines of them. His hair was just long enough to curl slightly at the nape, but he wore the top combed back away from his forehead, and the other day, when he'd been without a hat, Faith had thought she'd seen a little gray at the temples, something that made her knees weak.

He slowed his horse as he drew near, and she held out a hand to him. When he took it, she pulled him toward her, and without giving herself the option of overthinking it, she kissed him, knocking his hat off in the process. He didn't seem to notice. It was just a quick, happy kiss, but when she leaned away, he didn't release her hand. The horses stood patiently, as though they knew their two humans were trying to figure things out, and when Cord said, "Do that again," Faith didn't hesitate. She tugged her hand free of his and reached up to grab the front of his shirt, instead, pulling him toward her. The sound of pleasure he made against her mouth had her pulse racing even more than the run across the pasture had.

Finally, she pulled back and let go of his shirt, then nudged Watson forward a few paces so she could slide off his back. "Your hat," she said, hoping she didn't sound as breathless as she felt. "I'm sorry." She picked it up and held it out toward him just as he swung his leg over and dropped to the ground himself.

In two quick strides, he had his arms around her and was hauling her up against him. She squealed with laughter but lifted on her toes to meet his kiss, reaching up to cup his face in her hands, her fingertips sliding through the short hair at his temples. Yep, there it was, the sunshine glinting off the silver. Her laughter quickly softened to sighs as she leaned into him, letting the strength of his arms hold her up.

When she straightened, Cord's eyes opened to meet hers, and he smiled so sweetly, so like Jasmine, that Faith thought her heart might break, but for all the best reasons.

"I don't want to ever stop kissing you," he whispered. "Not for the rest of my life." He reached up to smooth a wayward curl back behind her ear; her hat had fallen off in the process, too.

"I think I could handle that," Faith whispered back, brushing her lips against his as she spoke, not quite a kiss, but perhaps just as intimate.

Suddenly, she heard barking. Jack barking. In the distance. His joyful, "Someone's here!" bark.

Caught up in the camaraderie of the last hour spent with Cord, Faith had forgotten—she'd forgotten!—that Jasmine and Abby would be home from school at any time, and her daughter would certainly come looking for her. She stepped abruptly from Cord's embrace, practically pushing him away from her.

"What is it? What's wrong?" he asked, his expression filled with concern.

"Jasmine," she whispered, bending quickly to snatch up her hat and return it to her head. Watson had stayed right close to her side, and she hoped against all hope that the horse had blocked the view of anyone who might be coming up over the rise. *Lord, if Jasmine had seen them kissing....*

"Oh." Cord's eyes grew wide as it occurred to him what she was saying. "Oh! What time is it?" He reached into his back pocket and dug out his phone.

"Quarter past three," Faith muttered. "I have to get back." Panic tingled just under the surface of her already heated and hypersensitive skin, and she did her best to keep it at bay. At that moment, she heard the roar of one of the ATVs; whoever was on it would likely meet them on the lane coming up from the barn. "Looks like you're going to get your wish after all. That's probably Jasmine."

"She rides the ATVs alone?" He shot her a look that made Faith frown.

"Uh, yes. She's nine years old, Cord. She's been riding that thing since she was four or five." She reached up and patted his cheek, perhaps a little harder than necessary, but she didn't like the look of censure in his eyes. "Don't worry; she wears a helmet." Then she hauled herself up into the saddle and commanded him to do the same.

Sure enough, just as Cord was getting situated on Capitan's back, the smallest of the four-wheelers came around the bend ahead of them on the lane. "Hey, mama!" Jasmine hollered when she saw them. "Hey, Mr. Overman!" she added with a wave.

Cord turned another wide-eyed look on Faith. "How does she know who I am?"

Faith grinned over at him. "Everyone knows who you are. You're the talk of the town, Mr. Overman. New guy. Single. Hot. Just bought the biggest ranch in the hollow. Sunday morning altercation with one of the Goodacre girls. What's not to talk about?" She nudged her horse forward.

A moment passed, and then he called after her, "So you think I'm hot?"

Faith thought her heart might burst out of her chest at how happy she was in that moment.

TWENTY-ONE

Jasmine pulled up in front of her mother, a huge smile on her face. The child expertly maneuvered the four-wheeler on the narrow lane, Jack cavorting around her, somehow staying clear of the machine. Cord grinned like a… well, like a proud papa. Yep. That was his girl.

She hit the kill switch on the machine, and peering around Watson, she shot Cord a smile, squinting one eye closed against the bright afternoon sun. "Hi. I'm Jasmine Goodacre."

Cord doffed his hat and held it to his chest in an effort to slow his pounding heart. "I'm Cordell Overman. Nice to meet you, Jasmine." Today, her name rolled off his tongue like it had been born there.

Jasmine turned back to her mother. "Aunt Justice said you were moving the cows early today, so I thought I'd come help."

"We're finished, baby. We were just riding back." Faith turned to grin at him over her shoulder. "Weren't we, cowboy?"

"Which am I? A city boy or a cowboy?" Cord asked, unable to decide which of the two gorgeous ladies to look at. He couldn't get enough of either one of them.

"On that fine horse, and after helping out with my Dexters?" Faith shrugged. "I supposed one might consider you a cowboy."

"I heard you were one of those hot shots from the big city who just comes out to the hollow to play dress up." Jasmine planted a hand on one hip in the sauciest pose he'd ever seen on a little girl.

"Jasmine," Faith said, "Stop that."

Cord laughed outright. "Lord, have mercy. Did your mama tell you that?"

"No," the child shot back with a little head bob. "I have eyes in my head. I also have eyes in my heart, just like my mama, and we can tell things about people."

"Jasmine!"

Cord's brows shot up. "Really? Then you should know that I—"

"Don't worry," Jasmine interrupted him. "I know you're for real. I was just giving you a hard time, cuz that's what I do to people I like." She shrugged, a motion that was so like her mama's it made Cord's pulse kick. "And even if I don't wind up liking you, well, I gotta love you, since you're my neighbor and all."

"Jasmine Good—"

The girl rolled right over her mother, too. "You know that verse in the Bible about loving your neighbors? We're good at that here in the hollow, so you don't have to worry." She unclasped her helmet and took it off, then fanned her face with it. "It's hotter than Grampa's seat cushion out here, Mama. Why are you two just standing around? I mean, look at you. Your cheeks are bright red."

"Jasmine Caroline Goodacre!" Faith squawked.

Cord laughed so hard he thought he might fall off his horse.

Jasmine stared up at her mother with a shocked expression on her face. "What did I do? Why did you use all my names just now?"

"I needed to get your attention, baby," Faith said, shaking her head in wonder. "You got on a roll there, and I didn't think you were going to stop. Did Yvette not show up at school today or something? Did you not have anyone to talk to?"

"She was there," Jasmine said with another shrug. "But I did get in trouble for talking, just so you know. I'm sure Miss Apple-butt is going to be calling you again."

Faith tipped her head to the heavens and lifted a hand as though begging for intervention. "Seriously, Jas? Do you know how sad Miss Allenbaum would be if she heard you call her that? She loves you."

"I know." The child hung her head, dragging the word out. She rested her helmet on the fuel tank in front of her. "I'm sorry. She just made me mad today. She embarrassed me in front of everyone."

"She did?" Faith frowned down at her daughter. That didn't sound like the sweet teacher she knew. "Or were you embarrassed because you got in trouble?"

"I guess a little of both. I was kinda ticked off because Smelly Delly was teasing me again. So, I drew a picture of him when I was supposed to be working on my math paper, and Miss Allenbaum asked me what it was."

"Oh, Lord. What did you draw?" The line of Faith's mouth told Cord she knew it wasn't going to be good.

"Nothing really bad. It didn't even look like him. It was just the way I see him with my heart."

"Jasmine."

"Fine." The child threw her hands in the air and rolled her eyes. The sudden motion knocked her helmet to the ground, and she clambered off the machine to fetch it. "It was a pile of cow poop with a couple of dung beetles digging around in it. That's how he looks to me, because he's mean. And not just to me, either. He was mean to Vetty today, too. Calling us names."

"Oh, baby," Faith said, dismounting and crossing to her daughter to wrap her in a hug. "Did you tell Miss Allenbaum he was bothering you girls again?"

"No," Jasmine snapped, but she looped her arms around her mom's waist and laid her head on Faith's chest. "I'm not a snitch."

A few moments passed, then Faith leaned back to look down at her daughter's face. She smiled tenderly at the girl. "Did you bring the drawing home with you? I want to see it."

Jasmine giggled. "I did. Miss Allenbaum said I had to show it to you." She reached up and covered her mouth as though trying to keep in a secret. "She doesn't know you have a framed collection of all my dirty drawings."

Faith chuckled softly. "Please don't call them that, Jasmine. That means something completely different. They're naughty. Disrespectful. Rude."

"But funny. You know they are," the girl retorted with another head bob.

Faith let out a sound halfway between a guffaw and a snort. "I can't argue there. But if you ever tell anyone how much I love that disrespectful artwork, that, my child, I will deny whole-heartedly."

"What about him?" Jasmine asked, tipping her head toward Cord. "We just told him."

Cord winked at her. "I'm on your side. I love dirty drawings. Sounds like Smelly Delly is a piece of work."

"You're telling me," the child shot back, rolling her eyes so hard her whole head moved with them. Then she slipped out of her mother's hug, threw her leg back over the ATV, and buckled her helmet back on her head. "You just made me super sweaty with that hug, hot mama. I need a drink."

Cord watched the exchange between the two with so many mixed emotions that he couldn't lay a finger on any single one. And it scared the living daylights out of him. It was like standing at the edge of a bottomless pool of water after stumbling endlessly through the wilderness. Desperate to get in, to drink, to be washed clean, but knowing he might also drown in it. He could lose himself in these two if they let him in, and if he went under... Well, he could think of a worse way to go.

They made their way back to the house, the motor of the ATV making conversation almost impossible. When they got to the equipment barn, Jasmine disappeared inside, assuring them she didn't need help.

"Sounds like someone else I know," Cord said as they headed toward the horse barn.

Faith rolled her eyes at him. "Wow. Really? After I asked for your help with my cows today?"

Cord nodded slowly. "You're right. I take that back. Except she does remind me of you, Faith."

"That's a good thing, right?"

"It is. A very good thing."

"Good. Because she reminds me of you, too, Cord. Every time I look at her, you're there looking right back at me." She smiled sweetly at him, and Cord felt himself sinking a little deeper into that bottomless pool of her.

"Thanks for not being angry with me today. I mean, for being here when she got home. That wasn't my plan, you know. I was just going to come by; see your face." He shot her a rather wicked grin. "Maybe sneak a few kisses in when no one was looking, then head on home again."

"I couldn't have planned it better," Faith admitted, then she asked in a tentative voice, "You good with that for now? Are you still okay with me not telling her about this, yet?" She waved her hand between them. "I've already told her we dated in high school, but that's as far as I've gotten. She was more interested in what you're planning on doing with the ranch than anything else right now."

"I think what happened today was a great start. A little more time is good with me." He glanced over his shoulder to make sure the girl wasn't within earshot. "It's crazy Faith, what's going on in my head right now. I mean, I can't figure out how to feel about her. It's all over the place, like a wild roller coaster ride. Does that make me a bad—a bad—not a natural—Whoooo!" He reached up and rubbed the back of his neck.

"Father? Daddy? Parent?" Faith teased, but her voice was gentle, kind. "Honestly, if you weren't a little freaked out at the idea of being a dad, then I'd be worried. I've had her for nine years, and I still get freaked out on a regular basis."

"Thank you," he murmured. "I appreciate you saying that."

They entered the cool barn, waited a moment for their eyes to adjust, then dismounted, but when Faith asked if he wanted to unsaddle Capitan and stay for dinner, he shook his head.

"I've got to get back. I told Binks I'd be gone for about an hour. It's been far longer than that." They stood together in silence for a moment, the horses patiently waiting. Finally, she stepped forward, rested a hand on Cord's chest, then pushed up on tiptoe to press her lips to his. He slid his free arm around her waist and pulled her gently to him.

Jack came bounding into the barn, warning them of Jasmine's approach. Faith ducked her head and stepped back just in time.

"You guys still haven't even taken off your saddles?" she exclaimed from the barn door. "What have you been doing? Sheesh."

Cord chuckled and reached down to give Jack's scruff a good scratch. "We were just talking about what a remarkable kid you are," he said.

"That's what my Grampa says about me. I'm already nine years old, you know." She moved to stand at Capitan's face, casually stroking the horse's neck. It was obvious to anyone that she'd been raised in a barn, in the best sense of the term. "I just had a birthday last month. Too bad you missed it. It was a sunshine day, so we had a ginormous slip and slide on the hill over there." She pointed through the barn door to a rise just beyond the large kitchen garden. A couple of shade trees linked limbs over a picnic table and a swing set, a lone tire swing hung from a huge oak nearby, and he thought he could tell where the lawn was still recovering from the partiers.

"I wish I'd been here," he said with a nod. "If I'd come back to the hollow a little sooner, I would have been. My loss." He shot Faith a meaningful look, but she dipped her head to avoid meeting his eyes. "I hope you'll invite me to your next party," he said to Jasmine.

"You know it!" Jasmine quipped without even hesitating. "'Specially since you're rich enough to buy Whispering Hills. You probably give great presents."

Faith made a strangling sound. "Jasmine! Oh, my lands, child. I taught you better than that."

Jasmine shrugged. "I figure if he knows the truth about my dirty drawings, he can probably handle the truth about other things, too."

"You know, I thought it was the mother's job to embarrass the child," Faith said, reaching over to tug on her daughter's hair. "You and your mouth are going to find yourself in a heap of trouble someday, young lady."

"Oh, my mouth gets me in trouble every day already. I'm used to it." She moved to give Watson some affection, too. "Do you need any help, Mama? I can start filling the feed bags."

"No, sweetie, but thank you for your offer. I know you've got homework. You go on inside before you say anything else to show off your breeding." Faith softened her words with a quick squeeze of her daughter's shoulders and a peck on the top of her head.

"I hate homework," Jasmine grumbled. "I'd rather muck out stalls any day." She squared her shoulders and lifted her chin. "I guess I'll be seeing you around, Mr. Overman. If I survive my homework to live another day."

"Go. Get out of here," Faith said, patting Jasmine on the backside. "I'll be right there."

"Bye, Jasmine. It was really good to meet you, and I can hardly wait to see you again." He removed his hat again, and she grinned cheekily back.

"You've got good manners for a city boy," she quipped, then dashed outside into the afternoon, calling for Jack to join her.

"Wow." It was the only word he could find. "Just, wow."

"Yeah," Faith agreed from the other side of Watson. Their eyes met over the backs of the horses; they'd ended up with the two animals between them, like a subconscious effort to keep their distance.

"I'm going to head out now," Cord said.

"Yeah, I've gotta get inside and help with homework."

Neither of them moved. Watson nickered and nudged Faith's shoulder.

"Okay. I'm leaving."

"Okay."

"We still on for Friday?" he asked, although he had no reason to think she'd changed her mind. He'd take any excuse to linger, though.

"Yeah. Friday." She ducked under Watson's neck and moved to stand between the horses.

"I might need to stop by tomorrow for... *something*," he said.

"Okay," she said with a nod, then ducked under Capitan's neck, too, until she stood directly in front of him. "I'll be here. I may even have that... *something* you'll be stopping by for."

"I see," he said, grinning down at her. It took all his willpower not to touch her.

"I have... *something* for you now," she began, barely above a whisper. "It might help you remember the something you're stopping by for tomorrow."

"You do?" Cord's pulse raced, and he felt a little short of breath, but he held his ground, waiting to see what she'd do.

"I guess if you don't want it, I can save it for tomorrow." There was that shrug again; then she started to turn around.

Cord lurched forward and grabbed her around the waist, drawing her back against him. He buried his face in her neck, and she laughed when her hat fell off again, before turning in his embrace and wrapping both arms around his neck.

He cupped the back of her head and wound his fingers in her hair, tugging slightly so she tipped her head higher, and he kissed her until she was breathless, until he thought his heart might explode.

Until someone cleared their throat.

They leaped apart like two teenagers caught making out past curfew.

Cord squeezed his eyes shut for just a moment—he knew who stood framed in the barn door—then moved to stand in front of Faith to give her a moment to collect herself. "Sir."

"I'd like a word with my daughter," Jed Goodacre said, standing with his feet wide, his thumbs looped in his pockets. He wasn't a small man, and he still wore his working man image well.

Cord nodded. "Yes, sir. Would you give us a moment?" Faith pressed her forehead into the space between his shoulder blades. He could feel the slight tremble coursing through her.

Jed just stood there for a few moments, and Cord slid a hand behind his back to keep Faith there. Because they weren't two teenagers caught making out after curfew, and he wasn't going to stand by and let Faith's father make either of them feel guilty for finding each other again. He sensed the battle going on behind him, but to his relief, she stayed put.

Jed crossed his arms over his chest, making him look bigger and broader. "Tread wisely here, son. My sentiments haven't changed much over the years where my daughters—and now my granddaughter—are concerned. Hurt them, and I hurt you. That's just the way of it." He spun on his heel and started back out of the barn. Without turning around, he said, "I'll be in the kitchen when you two are finished, Faith."

TWENTY-TWO

Faith covered her face with her hands as Cord turned around and pulled her into an embrace. "It'll be okay," he whispered, clearly concerned for her. But she wasn't trembling with nervousness; she was doing her best to hold back the hysterical giggles that had started the moment her father cleared his throat.

When Cord leaned back to look at her, she let loose and laughed until her stomach hurt. "Oh, my lands," she gasped out. "You should have seen your face, Cord. I thought you were going to have a heart attack on the spot."

"*My* face?" He leaned back even more. "I thought you were freaking out behind me," he said. "I could feel you shaking."

"I was trying not to laugh, Cord," she countered. "That's the funniest thing that's happened to me in a long time. Besides Jasmine, that is."

"She is a funny kid," Cord said with some reservation.

Faith shook her head at him, still giggling intermittently. "Hey. We're full-grown adults here. So, my daddy walked in on us making out. Embarrassing, yeah, but no big deal, okay? I mean, we could have been a little more discreet. It is his barn."

Cord chuckled. "Okay. I guess I worried for nothing."

"No!" Faith slid her arms around him and hugged him tightly, laying her head against his shoulder. "No, you were protecting me, Cord. That was cool. Thank you for letting me hide behind you." His actions reminded her of his automatic gesture in the car when she'd slammed on the brakes, how his hand had shot out to block her. "You're rather heroic, you know."

"Thank you," he said, and she smiled to hear his voice rumbling familiarly under her ear pressed to his chest. It was deeper than she remembered it, but it was still Cord.

"You're welcome. Now on your horse. Get out of here before you get me in real trouble. And you better come by tomorrow for that something. Don't let my daddy scare you off." She pushed away from him and ducked around to Capitan's other side before he tried kissing her again.

For a moment, it looked like he wanted to say something more, but then he stepped into the stirrup and swung up into the saddle. Faith noticed him grimace a little as he settled in.

"Saddle sore?" she asked, making a point to be kind. "Been a while, huh?"

"Yeah," he admitted. "I think my brain remembers it a little better than my body. I'm feeling muscles I forgot I had."

"It'll get better, I promise," she said, patting his thigh. Then she reached up and tugged gently on the front of his shirt, drawing him down for one last, quick kiss. "Bye, now. It was good to see you."

"It was good to be seen by you," Cord said in response.

Faith gave Capitan's flank a gentle smack, and the horse moved forward. She watched them go, her whole body buzzing with pleasure and anticipation for what was ahead.

She made quick work of tending Watson, released him into the corral with some of the other horses, then headed inside to face her daddy. She knew he wasn't angry. Or rather, if he'd been angry, she would have known. But she had a feeling she knew what he had to say to her.

Sure enough, the moment she stepped inside, Jed stood and pushed his chair in. He'd been sitting beside Jasmine, reading a book while she did her schoolwork, keeping her company. "Will you walk out to the garden with me, Faith?" he asked. "Abby!" He didn't exactly yell, but his voice rose loud enough to be heard throughout the house.

Abby poked her head around the door frame, one earbud pulled out of her ear. "What? Oh, hey, Faith. You wrap things up nice and tight with that Cordell Overman?"

"Abby," Jed warned.

"Actually, yes, we did, indeed." Faith approached her father and slipped an arm through his. "Didn't we, Daddy?"

"You girls are going to be the early death of me. Have you no shame?" But he didn't pull away, and when Faith giggled, he looked down at her with a speculative smile. "Now that's a sound I haven't heard in a while."

"Like, never," Abby retorted. She crossed to the fridge and took out a pitcher of sweet tea. "You sound like a schoolgirl in love."

"How would you know what that sounds like, Abstinence?" Faith asked, trying to redirect the conversation before Jasmine picked up on what exactly they were talking about. "Been to any gun shows lately?"

Jasmine snickered behind her hands, apparently following along attentively, but said nothing.

"Will you keep an eye on Jasmine while I step outside with Daddy?"

"I don't need a sitter."

"Fine. Will you keep Jasmine company while I step outside with Daddy?"

"Only if we can spy on you from the kitchen window," Abby shot back. "If Daddy's taking you out to the garden, you must be in trouble." She drew the two syllables out.

Jasmine's eyes grew wide as she looked back and forth between her mother and grandfather, but Faith held up a reassuring hand. "I'm not in trouble, Jas. We just need to talk shop without interruptions for a few minutes. Do your homework, and I'll be back inside in a flash."

With her arm still linked in her father's, she led him outside and down the porch steps toward the garden path.

"So that's how it is, hm?" His question was direct and without preamble. "Once again, it would have been nice to hear it from you, first."

"Well, Daddy, you kinda did hear it from me first." She squeezed his arm. "I mean, I didn't say the words out loud, but think of it as a pantomime. A silent film version of 'This is how it is.'" She lifted a hand to cover her mouth, the laughter bubbling up again and threatening to spill over.

"Good grief, child. Get a hold of yourself." He spoke sternly, but she didn't miss the twinkle in his eyes.

"I'm sorry, Daddy. Sorry," she whispered, her hand still over her mouth. "I don't know what's wrong with me."

They'd made it to the garden gate, and he held it open for her. "Your sister may be right," he said.

"I know, I know. I'm acting like a giddy little schoolgirl." She stood aside so he could get around her.

"No," he said, leading the way toward the tomato plants. She should have known that's where they were heading. "The part about being in love."

Faith stopped abruptly, the giggles suddenly gone. Her father didn't seem to notice, but instead, began poking around under the tomato vines. "Don't you think it's a little soon to call it love, Daddy?" Faith asked in a small voice.

He didn't look at her, but said, "Do you know that it takes about ten to twelve weeks for a tomato to go from seed to bloom?"

Faith started forward again, with her arms crossed around her middle. "Yes. I know that."

"And once a bloom sets fruit, it only takes about three or four weeks for the fruit to ripen to maturity."

Faith nodded, realizing her father wasn't exactly expecting an answer.

"But it's the few days between blossom and fruit that are the most important. If those flowers aren't pollinated, there will be no fruit. The flowers will drop off and produce nothing." He crooked a finger at her. "Look. This is what I'm talking about."

She moved in closer to look over his shoulder. Jed held his hand under a bract of small yellow blossoms. One tiny green ball was forming inside the shriveled petals of one of the flowers.

"Is that your first tomato?" she asked, catching a little of his excitement.

"As far as I know. But the point is, that this is the important time. Right now. This is when the blossoms get fertilized so they can set fruit. This is when the bumblebees work their magic. This is when we need to offer as much help and assistance as possible, so the plant will do what it is supposed to do. Make tomatoes."

Faith nodded.

She had no idea what he was getting at.

"Make tomatoes," she echoed, because clearly, he was waiting for her to say something. "Right."

Jed straightened and turned to look at her. Then he chuckled softly. "You're not following, are you? Floating a few too many inches off the ground, I think."

"I'm trying," she said, sounding a little childish. "What are you getting at?"

Jed sighed and stepped closer to her, then pulled her into an uncharacteristic hug. He was not a demonstrative man by nature, so the embrace was unexpected. "The way I see it, Faith, just like my tomato plants, the seed of this thing between you and Cordell Overman was planted a good ten to twelve years ago, and with him coming back to the hollow to stay, well, things are blooming." He stepped back, his hands on her upper arms, and looked her in the eyes. "You can't be timid with tomato blossoms. Not if you want them to produce." He let go of her and pulled a battery-operated toothbrush from his back pocket.

Faith smiled when she saw it. Daddy had started using the toothbrush trick several years ago, and it had increased his tomato production dramatically.

"Some folks will shake the plant. Some will use a tiny brush and try to delicately brush the pollen from one flower to another. But the best pollinator for tomatoes is the big, black bumblebee, and you know why, right?" He didn't wait for her to answer. "Because it's not gentle. It's clumsy. And it vibrates like a miniature Harley Davidson." He held up his toothbrush. "So does my handy dandy toothbrush here."

"Okay," Faith began, biting back a smile. She couldn't help it. Her daddy was too easy to tease. "So, you think I should rub up against Cord some more and none too gently?"

He straightened and closed his eyes, his nostrils flaring as he inhaled slowly. "Do you want me to die of heart failure right here in my garden?" he asked when he opened his eyes again.

Faith bumped him with an elbow to the ribs. "You always said you wanted to be buried here. That would save us a step."

"No, I do not want you to rub up against that boy, Faith Louise. Look what happened the last time you did that." He waved a hand in the general direction of the kitchen where she was certain Jasmine languished pitifully over her homework.

"Daddy!"

"What? You can be crass, but I can't?" Then he shook his head. "Never mind. I'm trying to give you an object lesson here, so zip it, and give your old man some respect."

Faith nodded, drawing her fingers across her lips like a zipper.

"What I was trying to say," he began, "is that this isn't the time to be timid. Don't get me wrong; you need to be wise—use the right tools, and make sure they're not weapons, mind you—but don't wait around, hoping things will work out the way you want them to."

Faith frowned, not wanting to interrupt him, but too curious to keep her mouth closed. "As you saw in the barn, we're not really waiting around."

"I'm not talking about you two."

"Oh." Her eyes widened, and she darted a glance over her shoulder at the house. "Oh. You mean Jasmine."

"I do." He held up his toothbrush again. "You need to be fearless with the truth right now, Faith. Putting it off isn't going to help; this is the time. Don't wait, hoping things will turn out the way you want them to. She needs to hear about her daddy from you, not from one of her friends. Or even worse, from that little Del kid." He switched the brush on, then reached over and tapped a blossom with it. "Jasmine is a lot tougher than you give her credit for."

Faith had grown serious again as her father spoke, knowing his words to be true. "I know. But you're right. I'm scared."

"It's all right to be scared," her father said, glancing at her over his shoulder as he moved the toothbrush from flower to flower. "Do it afraid."

"I know," she groaned.

"And do it soon," he added.

"I know," she said again.

"Tonight would be good."

"I know." It was barely a whisper.

Silence fell between them as Jed worked his way through the rows of plants. From the other end of the tomato patch, he said, "It's good to see you all lit up, Faith. It doesn't happen often enough."

Faith smiled and nodded. She *felt* lit up.

"That boy better do right by you this time around," he added. "You deserve it."

"Thank you, Daddy. I love you."

"Love you, too, Faithy." He waved his toothbrush at the house. "Go on. Your daughter needs you."

Faith turned around to see Jasmine standing on the porch, her hands on her hips in her 'I have had it up to here' stance.

"There's my girl," she murmured to herself with an odd mixture of relief and weariness.

TWENTY-THREE

Friday morning dawned hot and humid, and Faith was already sweating bullets before she got her first cup of coffee down, although some of that might have been due to Cord's pending lunch date.

He hadn't stopped by yesterday after all. Oh, he'd called and explained that he'd gotten in over his head on a project and couldn't get away until after dinner. But Faith had told him no on the evening thing, mainly because she needed to talk to Jasmine. He said he understood and promised to make it up to her on their lunch date, but it didn't change the fact that she felt stood up.

Which, in turn, planted a tiny seed of doubt in her mind, making it difficult to fall asleep that night. This morning, the seed had taken root, and she could feel it growing inside her, especially as the day unfolded into one minor fiasco after another.

She'd chickened out on telling Jasmine about Cord on Wednesday night, using the excuse that her daughter rarely had much homework by the end of the week, and it would be better if they had more time, just in case the news didn't go over well. Thursday nights were typically more flexible, so she'd promised herself to make it a priority.

But of course, things didn't go as planned. Out of the blue, Hope showed up with a bottle of wild cherry cordial and a homemade lemon Bundt cake. Hope explained that Chet was out of town on a business trip, and because she was bored, she'd made the cake, then realized she'd eat the whole thing herself if she didn't find someone to share it with immediately. There weren't even any crumbs left by the end of the evening, and when Faith tucked Jasmine in later than usual that night, she'd silently apologized for letting yet another day slip by without telling the girl about her daddy.

When she and the twins came in from feeding the horses, ready for Charity's hot breakfast, she was dismayed to find that Jasmine had fallen back to sleep, and Faith had to revert to threats to get the child moving. Grumpy and uncooperative, Jasmine pushed every button her mother had, turning Faith into a short-tempered, clumsy wreck, admittedly more frustrated with herself than anything. She dropped a half-full cup of coffee, splattering the brown liquid in every direction, and breaking her favorite mug. Jasmine had given it to her as a birthday gift a few years ago, and her daughter was practically inconsolable over the destruction.

Which distressed the girl even more. "I can't go to school looking like I survived a meth lab explosion!" she wailed, gesturing dramatically at her red and blotchy face.

"Heaven help us, child. Where did you come up with that?" her grandfather asked, clearly appalled, but Faith could see his mouth twitch as he did his best not to laugh.

"It's not funny, Grampa," Jasmine declared, covering her face with both hands. "You have no idea how grueling it is to be a nine-year-old girl. If anyone sees me looking like this, I'll simply die of mornication."

"Mortification, Jas," Faith corrected her from where she stood at the sink, helping Prudence with the dishes.

"Mortification. That's what I said," Jasmine snipped, shooting her mother a narrow-eyed look.

"Mortification? Grueling? I didn't even know nine-year-old girls used words like that." Jed ducked his head to hide his smile behind the morning paper he was reading.

Finally, Abby took the girl back to her bedroom to freshen up, promising her she could borrow some concealer and face powder to hide the telltale blotchiness.

"Please remember she's nine!" Faith called after them as the two girls disappeared down the hall. She sighed and looked over her shoulder at her father. "You shouldn't antagonize her."

He lowered the paper. "Antagonize her? I complimented her, that's all. She is quite remarkable, that granddaughter of mine," he said with a chuckle. "I wonder how Cord Overman is going to measure up in her eyes."

"Daddy!" Faith nearly dropped the plate she was drying as she spun around. The rest of the room went silent.

"Oh. You didn't tell her yet?" His tone remained casual, but there was a serious glint in his eyes that made Faith feel like a child again. He already knew the answer.

"No. I was going to last night, but Hope showed up." Ugh. It sounded like a lame excuse, even to her own ears.

"Well, then I guess I'm curious as to when that might happen, seeing how it's likely going to affect us all." He took a long sip of his coffee, then folded his paper and set it aside. "This conversation with your daughter is long overdue."

Prudence, dear Prudence, stepped close to Faith and slipped a supportive arm around her waist. She said nothing, but Faith leaned into her little sister, grateful for her kindness. The twins sat across from each other at the table, exchanging looks that held whole conversations between them.

Charity leaned back in her chair so she could see Faith better. "You're seeing Cord today, aren't you?" she prompted, even though she already knew about Faith's plans with him. Ever the peacemaker, though, Charity was doing her best to help Faith out. "Maybe you guys can come up with a plan today. Or are you wanting to talk to her yourself, first?"

Faith crossed the room to peer down the hall, relieved to see Abby's door closed tightly. Turning back to her father and sisters, she said, "I will talk to her tonight. I promise. I'm going to take her with me when I move the cows, and maybe we'll go for a ride out to Mom's garden."

"What are you going to tell her?" Prudence asked in her characteristically direct but gentle nature.

Faith shrugged half-heartedly. "Well, I already told her he was my high school boyfriend, so I figured I'd let her know we're seeing each other again."

The room went silent again, and then Jed spoke up. "That's it?"

"How do you think it's going to pan out when Jas discovers that your old boyfriend who is now your new boyfriend also happens to be her da—"

"Hey. Hey!" Faith cut her off, her voice raised. "Can we at least try not to make it happen before school? We've already met our quota of meltdowns for the day."

Justice held up both hands in a defensive motion, but added, "I don't think she'll be very happy if you aren't up front with her from the get-go. No matter how you do it, it's going to be a big bite to swallow, and if I were her, I'd want it all in one shovelful."

"Yes, well, you're not her. And you're not her mother, either. It's my decision."

"Unless someone else does it for you," her father said, his eyes never leaving Faith's. They were kind, but firm. "Sunday's coming," he said again. "And folks are primed for another showdown."

"They're taking bets over at Schooners," Justice mumbled. Across from her, Courage shook her head and slashed a hand back and forth in front of her throat.

"Bets? On what?" Faith asked, appalled at the idea. "Courage?" she asked, turning to the other twin when Justice didn't answer. "What is she talking about?" Schooners was the local diner where both girls worked a couple of shifts a week.

Courage sighed and shot another reproachful look at Justice before saying, "Some are betting you two will be married before the year is out—"

"And pregnant," Justice interjected.

"Justice Goodacre," Jed said, smacking his palm on the table. "Show some respect."

"I didn't say they'd already have a baby, Daddy, just that they'd be married and expecting one. Nothing disrespectful about that." Justice ignored her father's narrowed eyes and gestured at Courage to continue. Faith stood frozen, a hand over her mouth as she listened.

"Some are betting you and Jasmine will run him out of town before the year is out," Courage said with a shrug of one shoulder. "It's about fifty-fifty right now."

"And who's getting the kitty when it's over?" Charity asked. "Because I think Faith deserves every last penny of it."

"Not helping, Charity," Faith squeaked, finally managing to get her voice to work. "This is horrible. People are horrible." She went back to the sink and set the plate she still held in the dish drainer. Her hands were trembling, and she was afraid she was going to drop it. "It's no one's business but our own. Who are they to toy with people's lives that way?"

"It's everyone's business, Faith," Jed said, making her turn around in wounded surprise. "You have not raised your daughter in a vacuum. You have the final say over that child, yes, but that doesn't mean it's no one else's business. This man coming back to the hollow after all this time is bound to stir up a bit of a storm cloud, and we're all going to be exposed to what comes of it, whether you like it or not. It's only reasonable that folks want to know what to expect."

Faith ducked her head and crossed her arms over her chest, squeezing tightly. When Prudence laid a hand on her shoulder, she shrugged it away. Finally, she lifted her gaze to meet her father's. "I don't know what to expect myself, Daddy."

Just then, the door flew open at the other end of the hall, and the chatter of the two girls indicated that all was right with Jasmine's world again. At least for the moment.

"Tonight, then," Jed said, pushing up from his seat at the table. "We'll count on that." Turning to the two schoolgirls as they entered the kitchen, he said, "You two ready to go? Would you give me a ride down to the front gate, Abby? I have a replacement part for that busted hinge. I can walk back." They said their goodbyes, and then he herded them out the back door ahead of him.

THE REST OF THE morning hadn't gone any smoother for Faith. Even Jack had abandoned her at some point, romping off across the field toward the house as though he'd had enough of her foul mood and fake curses for the day. She'd forgotten to turn off the electrical current and got zapped pretty good when she went to tighten a section of the border fence. The cows had somehow managed to kick over the water trough, and when she righted it, she discovered a gurgling puddle of water beneath it, which meant a broken water line. She returned Watson to the barn and took an ATV out instead, carrying her toolbox and shovel lashed to the rear rack behind the seat. The repair went surprisingly quick, but on her way back, she drove too close to the edge of the lower pond and ended up nearly tipping over when the back tire sank in the muck. It had taken all her might to push the machine back up the bank, and she was splattered with mud from gunning the motor too hard, setting the back wheels spinning in the mire. Her jeans were soaked to above the knees, and her boots sloshed as she climbed off the quad in the storage barn and started toward the house just after eleven. She wanted a shower something fierce before Cord arrived.

Maybe he would be caught up in another project and would be late. Or maybe he wouldn't be able to make it at all.

She couldn't decide whether she liked that thought or not.

But Cord, blast him, was already there waiting for her on the back porch, looking fresh as a daisy. Clean-shaven, he wore a crisp blue button-down shirt tucked into his jeans, and what looked like a brand-new ivory felt hat on his head. And Jack, traitorous blackguard that he was, lounged happily on the porch at his feet. Cord stood quickly and removed the hat when he saw her approaching, his smile faltering only a little at the sight of her. Jack, too, got to his feet and ambled down the steps to greet her with slobbery kisses and happy tail whips.

"You're here," she said, knowing she sounded more miffed than pleased. But pleased, she was. In spite of her sorry state, he was a sight for sore eyes, and the way he looked at her made her pulse jump.

"Wild horses couldn't keep me away," he replied.

"Nice hat," she said, stopping at the bottom of the steps.

"Thank you. I'm hoping you'll call me cowboy again." He held it loosely in one hand the way a man does when he's accustomed to holding a cowboy hat, his fingers and thumb resting in the grooves of the crown of it, then returned it to his head. With a crooked grin, he drew the side of his forefinger along the front of the brim the way Sam Elliott did in his iconic hat tip in *The Big Lebowski*. They'd watched the movie together long ago and had both been oddly fascinated by it.

Faith couldn't help smiling at his obvious attempt to cheer her up. "I think the bar is winning this round," she said, referring to a line in the movie. She held her arms out to the sides. "I'm a mess. Can you give me a few minutes to clean up? You're welcome to come inside and wait. It's probably cooler."

"You look good to me, Miss Goodacre."

"Really?" She cocked her head, and then headed up the steps toward him. "How about a nice, wet hug?"

Cord laughed and backed away. "Fine, fine. You win. Go get your shine on, and I'll wait inside. I wanted to have a word with your sister, anyway."

Faith stopped mid-stride and turned back to face him. "Which one? I've got six of them, you know."

He grinned and looped his thumbs over his belt as he watched her. "I know," he said. "I'm after Charity today."

Faith lifted an eyebrow but said nothing. She toed off her boots, then reached down to tug off her soggy socks. She didn't dare track in whatever she'd brought back with her from the pond.

"About work," he clarified. "Go on. I'll tell you all about it when you come back." He pulled open the screen door and stood back to let her go through ahead of him.

Charity glanced over at them from where she stood at the kitchen sink. Faith sometimes wondered what on earth her sister found to do in the kitchen all day, but Charity seemed to find satisfaction and fulfillment in the culinary masterpieces she concocted. Like a scientist in a lab, the woman could take the most random ingredients and combine them to make a meal fit for a queen. "Hey, you two. Holy smokes, Faith. You fall into the lake or something?"

"Pretty much," Faith began, then waved away her own words. "You don't want to know, trust me. I'm going to go tidy up a little, but this guy here wants to talk to you about something." She gestured with her thumb over her shoulder at Cord, then disappeared down the hall.

Not quite fifteen minutes later, she was showered, dressed, and starving. She'd washed her hair, but let it hang down her back to dry, certain Cord wouldn't mind her wet locks. Then she started back toward the kitchen, pausing when she heard her name.

"Faith is a tough cookie, Cord. So is Jasmine. You have your work cut out for you."

"I know that, Charity. It's one of the things I love about her."

He loved her? And he was telling Charity this before he told Faith? She reached behind her and closed the bathroom door with a solid thunk, opened it again, and started humming softly, giving the two in the kitchen a heads up that she was on her way back. Their conversation ended abruptly.

"Ready?" Cord asked, standing when she appeared in the doorway. "Food is already waiting for us. I thought we'd head over to the creek for a picnic. Put our toes in the water." He eyed her feet in the clean socks she'd donned. "I'll take mine off if you take yours off."

Faith rolled her eyes and Charity let loose a hoot of laughter.

Charity had the most contagious laugh, one that usually started quiet, and then bubbled up like root beer poured over a scoop of ice cream, until everyone around her was laughing along with her, even if they had no clue what she found so funny. It wasn't as common these days, not since she'd received the devastating news of her husband's death in Afghanistan just over a year ago. He and several others in his troop had been the victims of a suicide bomber, a young woman who approached their vehicle asking for help for her and her baby. Except the bundle strapped to her back was full of explosives, not a child. In fact, more often than not, her laughter would turn to tears, almost as though the release of any emotion at all triggered her grief, but everyone was quick to comfort and cover for her. They all missed Theo; he was a good man, a good soldier, and he'd loved their Charity to distraction, just as she'd loved him.

"Oh!" Charity said with a start. "I have something for you two." She bustled to the fridge and brought out a tall glass bottle with a hinged swing top stopper. "Ice cold redbud lemonade," she said, wrapping it in a clean kitchen towel and handing it to Faith. "Did you remember to pack glasses?" she asked Cord.

He chuckled and shook his head. "No, I brought a couple of bottles of sarsaparilla and some water bottles, but I didn't think to load any cups." He shot her a hopeful look. "Can I snag a few from you?"

Before he was even finished speaking, Charity was holding out two drinking jars with handles to him. "The only way to drink redbud lemonade," she said. "Mason jars."

The walk was quiet as they headed toward the small creek that meandered through the narrow grove of trees between their properties. They both seemed to sense the gravity of what they were doing, in that this wasn't really a casual picnic, or even a first date. This was more like the official start of a reunion between two people who were still so strongly attached that being in each other's proximity made the air around them practically spark with electricity.

There was no doubt in Faith's mind that they were charging headlong into a future together, but what that future looked like was still so unclear. She worried about her daughter with such fierceness that part of her still wanted to send Cord packing, just as half the folks at Schooner's thought she would. But another part of her wanted him to drop to one knee today and promise to love and cherish her and Jasmine for the rest of their lives.

If he left again, she knew she'd survive. She'd done so for the past decade already, and as much as she hated the idea, there was comfort in the familiar, even if the familiar was the pain of a broken heart.

But if he stayed, that would mean she'd have to choose to trust him with her heart the way he wanted her to, and that was proving more difficult than she'd thought. Oh, she still loved him, yes indeed. She'd gotten past that hang up during the course of the week. His visit—his sweet words and even sweeter kisses—had confirmed that. She loved him, and she yearned for his love in return.

But loving Cord was easy. Ask all the women who'd draped themselves all over him over the years. Trusting him was the difficult part. She'd learned the hard way that trusting Cord came with a price that she wasn't sure she was willing to pay again.

When they rounded the barn and moved out of a direct line of sight from the house, Cord reached over and laced his fingers with hers. As though sensing her disquiet, he didn't say anything, but just held her hand as they walked, and before long, Faith began to relax, the awareness of him beside her so achingly familiar. Finally, she broke the silence between them.

"So, tell me what kind of work you were talking to Charity about," she said, hoping the impersonal topic would help ease them into casual conversation. She didn't want to jump right into the meat of things, at least not until they'd gotten past the awkwardness of being alone together again.

"I asked her if she'd be interested in a part-time job doing some cooking for me. There's going to be a lot going on at the ranch over the next couple of years, and that means a lot of hungry mouths to feed. I could make everyone bring their own food, but I'm thinking it might be more neighborly to provide a midday meal to the crews. I heard your sister did some catering, and I want to hire her."

"That sounds like a great idea," Faith said with a nod. "Did she go for it?"

"We didn't get that far. I won't need her right away, so she's got some time to think about whether or not she wants to commit to something so long term. I told her we'd talk next week when I have a better idea about when the construction crews are going to start coming in."

The conversation turned to Whispering Hills, and they talked quietly, enjoying each other's company. The glasses in Cord's other hand clinked softly as they walked, a disjointed percussion accompanied by buzzing insects in the midday heat, and the thrum of a far-off tractor or some other farm vehicle. Jack sauntered along beside them, his panting breaths pacing the rhythm of their matched strides, their booted feet scraping the dirt, reminding her of the sand blocks she used to rub together in music class back in elementary school. This was the music of home to her, and when a cow lowed in the distance, answered by a chorus of others, she couldn't hold back the sigh of contentment that escaped her. Was this what happily ever after felt like?

"It's a nice day," Cord said as they approached the trees. "Hot, but nice." He squeezed her fingers gently, tugging her a little closer. "You love it here, don't you?"

She nodded, not looking at him. "I do. This is the home of my heart, Cord." Especially now that he was back and walking hand in hand beside her. "Everything I could possibly need is here."

TWENTY-FOUR

Everything she needed? Did he dare hope that list included him? He was, indeed, here, wasn't he?

"Everything I need is here, too," he ventured to say, his voice low and carefully modulated. It was true, so why try to deny it? "I have always loved this hollow, and our two ranches especially." They'd reached the tree line, and he ducked to avoid catching his hat on a low-hanging limb. When he straightened, he found her gazing up at him, and he stopped abruptly. As though she'd been expecting it, she turned toward him so that they were facing each other.

Without breaking eye contact, Cord set the two cups down on the ground at his feet, then took the lemonade from her, the chilled bottle practically sizzling against the heat of his palm. He set it down next to the glasses, removed his hat, and tossed it to the ground as well. Then he drew her even closer until she had to tip her head back to look at him. "You are home to me, Faith."

She swallowed audibly and let her eyes drift closed when he released her hands and skimmed his fingers up her arms and over her shoulders until he held her face between his palms. "You are my home," he whispered before he lowered his mouth to hers.

It started out as just a caress, a gentle quest at first, but then her arms slid around his waist, and she leaned into him with a tiny, breathless sigh. He groaned low in his throat, opening his mouth against hers, his tongue delving between her lips to taste her sweetness.

Why had he waited so long to come home? What had kept him away from her all this time? From them. From what was, and what could be between them. The questions shot like random sparks through the rising fog of passion in his brain, but for the life of him, he couldn't come up with a single sensible answer. What a fool he'd been to stay away.

He buried his fingers in her hair, cradling the back of her head as he explored her mouth with his own, his other hand drifting down her back to rest possessively against the base of her spine, pressing her even closer to him. Their bodies fit together exquisitely, her soft curves melding into his hard lines as though they'd never been apart.

When the kiss finally ended, he didn't lift his head, but rested his cheek against her forehead, relishing in the telltale sounds of her rapid, shallow breaths. Her hair smelled like some tropical drink, and he couldn't tell whether the throbbing pulse in his ears was his racing heartbeat or hers was. "Faith," he murmured. It was too soon, he knew it, but he didn't want to waste another moment of their lives. "I love you, Faith. I've always loved you; you must know that."

She didn't respond in words, but instead, lifted her hands to cup his face the same way he'd done hers. She gazed up into his eyes for a fathomless moment before rising on tiptoe to press her soft lips to his again.

Jack, who'd entertained himself by marking every tree in a ten-foot radius while he waited for them, was ready to move on. Not caring that he was interrupting something important, he thrust his cold nose against the couple's legs, wedging his wriggling body between them. With a laugh, Faith pulled away from Cord and reached down to ruffle the dog's ears.

"Sorry, boy. You're not used to anyone else kissing me, are you?" She crouched down with her arms open, and Jack stepped close, then lifted his front paws to her shoulders and laid his head against her neck. "Oh, Jackman, I love you."

Cord frowned at the ridiculous jolt of jealousy that shot through him. It was a dog, for Pete's sake, not competition. But Faith's declaration of love for Jack had come so easy, and Cord wanted to hear her say those same words about him. To him.

It occurred to him, then, that her undivided attention to her dog at the moment might be a cover for the overwhelming emotions they were both feeling. He rubbed his palm across his mouth in an effort to wipe the frown away; he should be celebrating. He should be thumping his chest with both fists. He should be raising his voice in some primal victory chant, not pouting like a little boy because the girl he liked really liked her dog.

He scooped up the lemonade and both glasses in one hand, then reached out to Faith with his other. She took it and let him help pull her back up, then grabbed his hat from the ground and plunked it on his head for him. "Looks good on you, cowboy."

They headed down the little footpath toward the small creek that meandered back and forth along the property line. Cord had been surprised to find the trail so easily—if he didn't know better, he'd think it was still being used. But Faith had assured him she hadn't been to the hay barn in all this time, so he chalked it up to wild animals.

The day was hot and humid, even under the shade of the trees, and their palms were damp where they pressed together, so he didn't mind when she let go. They said nothing more until the picnic spot he'd chosen came into view.

"Cord, this is gorgeous," Faith said, coming to a standstill and lifting both hands to her cheeks. He'd spread a blanket out on the bank of the little stream and had positioned a wooden crate in the center of it. On top of the crate was a piece of plywood covered in a square of buffalo plaid fabric. In the middle of the cloth sat an authentic picnic basket, complete with gingham lining and a flip-top lid. Nearby was a large blue and white cooler with two towels folded neatly on top.

"The basket was Binks' idea," Cord said, suddenly feeling self-conscious and a little silly. "He said my aunt used it all the time when Frankie was younger. Said the family never took a picnic without it and suggested I carry on the tradition."

Faith beamed up at him. "So, we're family, are we?"

Cord nodded without a moment's hesitation. "We are. And thanks to Jasmine, we're the real deal." He reached over and took her hand again. Lord, how he hoped to make it official before too much longer. The more time he spent in Plumwood Hollow, the more he felt the years that he'd let slip away.

To his relief, Faith didn't argue, but let him lead her to the blanket where she sat. When she started to toe off her boots, he knelt in front of her and slid them off for her, then set them aside before pulling off her socks, cupping her heels in his big hands as he did. Her cheeks flushed pink at his ministrations. "I'm glad I took a shower," she said self-consciously. "You wouldn't have wanted to touch those puppies an hour ago."

Cord just grinned at her as he rolled the cuffs of her jeans up a few times, enjoying the heat of her skin under his fingertips, the curve of her calves, the delicate bones of her ankles. Then he dropped to the blanket beside her and divested himself of his boots, too. "Come get your feet wet," he said, rising up and once again offering her a hand. "The water is really clear today." It had rained yesterday morning, which always muddied the stream with runoff from the banks until everything settled again.

But Faith leaped to her feet, a wicked grin on her face, and darted past him. "Race you!"

"Hey!" he shouted but caught up to her just as she splashed into the water, Jack right on her heels. How many times had they done this very thing those summers together, dashing into the trees, tossing boots and socks onto the bank, and then splashing through the stream, purposely dousing each other in the process?

"Mercy!" she gasped. "It's frigid!" Then she bent over, hands together, and scooped water in his direction, splattering him thoroughly.

"Oh, ho-ho!" He launched himself at her just as she turned to escape up the other bank, and caught her around the waist with both arms, dragging her up against him. Shrieking with laughter, she braced her hands on his forearms in an attempt to pry them loose, but to no avail. She kicked at his legs, splashing them both in the process until he swept her legs out from under her and caught her up in his arms. She was heavier than he remembered, but he liked the way she felt held against him, the bump of her womanly hip against his belly, the way she clung to him, both arms around his neck when he threatened to drop her.

Without warning, she slid her fingers up into the short hair at the back of his head and kissed him, her mouth curved in an open smile against his, her laughter still bubbling up out of her. The kiss grew feverish, their hunger for each other eclipsing even the joy of their shared memories. Cord stumbled out of the water with her held high against his chest, then crossed to the cooler and sat down with her on his lap. The kiss went on and on, time standing still, the sounds of the gurgling stream, the faint breeze rustling the leaves overhead, the hum of insects, it all melded together into background music, a soundtrack of their lives.

Finally, Faith pulled away with a sigh, and rested her head on his shoulder, pressing her face into the curve of his neck. He could feel her breath against his flushed skin, and when she tenderly kissed the throbbing pulse just under his jaw, he shivered.

"I can't stop kissing you," she whispered. "I don't want to eat. I don't want to sleep. My cows can fend for themselves, as far as I'm concerned. As long as you keep kissing me, none of that will matter."

Cord chuckled softly, and she lifted her head.

"What?" She still whispered, and he couldn't tell if she was suddenly shy or still so breathless, she couldn't find her voice.

"I guess I got the 'more' part down now, too."

"More," she said against his mouth. "More."

He obliged her.

TWENTY-FIVE

By the time Faith made it out of the trees, her lips felt swollen, her eyelids heavy, and her skin was tingling with currents of electricity that seemed to spark and sizzle along every nerve path. She'd refused to let Cord walk her back across the pasture to the house, instead insisting that he go home. She didn't think she could handle walking docilely beside him; they could hardly keep their hands off each other.

It truly was like being in high school again, the mad, endless kissing, the hands that wanted to be everywhere, the restraint required to keep those same hands in the safe zone. When Faith had slid her fingers up under the hem of his shirt to touch the fiery skin of his back, Cord had gone rigid for just a heartbeat, but it was enough of a reaction for Faith to remember how easy it would be to cross the lines again.

Cord was like an opiate to her system, lulling her into a stupor that made it difficult to remember her own name. By the time she made it back to the house, she was anxious to grab her hat and get on her horse. She needed a fast ride to clear her head.

She was relieved to find no one in the kitchen when she pushed inside. She hurried through the room and down the hallway to the large bedroom she and Jasmine shared. On the wall over her dresser was a large oval mirror, and as she passed by it, she caught sight of herself and jerked to a halt. "Good grief," she muttered, reaching up to smooth her hair. She wasn't pretentious when it came to her looks, but the girl who stared back at her, as Abby would say, was tore up.

Her mouth was indeed swollen, and the skin around her lips, along her jaw, and up and down her neck looked raw and irritated. It had been a long time since she'd really kissed a man, and she'd just spent the last hour trying to make up for lost time. Cord may have been clean-shaven, but even so, that much friction was bound to leave a mark. She stifled a giggle at what she'd say to her daddy if he saw her face right now. Her shirt looked rumpled, like she'd slept in it, and she frowned when she found that she'd lost one of her earrings, a teardrop garnet stud. She hurried across the hall to the bathroom, making certain to lock the door behind her, then soaked a washcloth in cold water, and pressed it to her jaw and neck.

Finally, when she was satisfied that she was at least presentable, she headed back outside, grabbing her hat off the hook as she pushed through the door. The twins were just coming in from a practice session with their horses, and they shot her matching grins as they passed. "Looking good today, Faith," Justice quipped. Courage elbowed her in the side.

"Thank you, ladies," she replied, refusing to let anyone squelch her euphoric feelings. That would come soon enough, she knew, once the day wound down, and she had her talk with Jasmine. For now, she would take advantage of what time she had left to wallow in her well of emotions.

Lovely emotions.

Love emotions.

Love.

Oh, how she prayed Jasmine would love Cord as much as she did. Maybe not today, but soon.

Two hours later, she discovered how much her daughter did not love Cord Overman.

Abby's warning text came as Faith finished settling the chicken tractor in its new location for the next several days. *Heads up, sis. Jas is on a tear. Someone at lunch told her CO is her daddy-o. We are not in Happy Town today.*

While Faith had been frolicking about in the woods with Cord, Jasmine had been receiving news that would change her life forever. Faith's heart plummeted to her toes. *Oh, Lord, what do I do now?* She had fifteen minutes to figure it out. By the time Abby pulled in and parked, Faith was no nearer a solution, and when the passenger door flew open and Jasmine practically launched out of the vehicle, Faith knew she was in for a whale of a thunderstorm.

"Mama!" Jasmine was calling for her before she even got to the porch steps, her voice raised and shrill. Any other time, Faith would have reprimanded her for talking to her in that tone, but today, she believed her daughter had every right to be livid. "Mama!" she hollered again, then looked up to see Faith seated at the patio table waiting for her.

"I'm here, Jasmine."

"Is he my daddy? Is he?" The girl's eyes were red-rimmed and puffy, like she'd been crying for hours, and the pale skin above her neckline was blotchy and red, the same way Faith's looked when she got all worked up.

"Can we go for a walk? Or a ride? Maybe out to Grandma's secret garden?"

"No! You tell me now!" Jasmine demanded, and then covered her face with her hands as her shoulders began to shake. "Never mind. I'm not stupid. I already know he is because you didn't say no." Then she turned around and dashed off across the pasture.

Jack, clearly understanding this was not a game, followed close on her heels, but his tail was lowered, and he didn't bark with excitement the way he usually did when the two played together.

Faith rose and followed her at a walk, allowing the girl to have a little time on her own. She knew her daughter, and as much of a people person as Jasmine was, she was enough like her mother that when things got out of control, the last thing she needed was consolation or comfort. At least not right at first.

"Smelly Del," Abby said when Faith asked her what happened. "I guess he started chanting 'Big Daddy Overman' at her when she went out to the playground at lunchtime. At first no one realized what he was even shouting, but finally one of the playground duty ladies stopped him because it was obvious that he was taunting Jasmine, regardless of what he said. When the lady asked him what the chant was, he explained loud enough for everyone around to hear that Cordell Overman was Jasmine's daddy and that you, dear Faith, were... well, the word he used meant a woman of loose morals. To put it nicely." Abby explained.

"That little—"

"Go ahead. Say it. I'll pull a buck out of the cuss jar and pay you if you do. He deserves it," Abby snarled. "That kid has been nothing but a turd muffin in Jasmine's life for too long. What is wrong with him?"

Faith sighed and rubbed her forehead. "Honestly, Abs, it's not his fault. His mother is a bitter, unhappy woman, and I'm sure Del's behavior is a direct result of that." Marty Lender, Del's mother, wasn't just bitter and unhappy herself, but she preferred that everyone around her be bitter and unhappy, too. And if that wasn't the case, she was the kind of person who did everything in her power to make it happen. It didn't surprise Faith that young Del Lender behaved similarly. The mother bear in her wanted to rip his throat out, sure, but that same instinct made her wonder what was going on in his little life that made him so angry and hurtful. She hoped he was okay—she'd have to ask the teacher next time they spoke.

Which would likely be this afternoon. She checked her back pocket to make sure she had her phone with her. Knowing Miss Allenbaum, she would call to speak to Del's mother first, and knowing Mary Lender, that phone call could turn ugly pretty quickly, and might take a while to wrap up. Which was fine by Faith; she had a daughter to love on right now, and a phone call assuring her teacher that Jasmine would be fine was low priority.

She found Jasmine sitting in the tire swing that hung from the huge oak tree at the top of the rise where they'd had her birthday party. When Jasmine saw her approaching, the girl spun the tire so she was facing the opposite direction and otherwise, refused to acknowledge Faith.

"Baby," Faith began, feeling even more helpless when she caught a glimpse of the tears still streaming down Jasmine's cheeks. "Sweetie, I'm so sorry you had to find out the way you did."

"So it is true," the girl snapped. "You're a liar, Mama. That's all there is to it."

"Hey. No name calling, Jas. That's not how we do things around here." But her daughter was right.

"Fine. You lie. Maybe not about everything, but you lied about this my whole life. That's a long time."

Hadn't she said the same thing about her father just the other day? Why had she put off this conversation for so long? "It is, baby. And you're right." Faith drew nearer and rested a hand on the girl's shoulder. Jasmine shrugged it off, rotating the swing around just a little more so Faith couldn't see her face.

Faith took a steadying breath, fighting back the tears that were building behind her own eyes, then returned her hand to Jasmine's back. She gave her a gentle push that lifted the girl's foot off the ground and set the tire swinging. When Jasmine didn't immediately balk, she kept pushing her, until the girl moved back and forth in a long pendulous arc. It was almost like rocking the child, but in a way that gave them both the space they needed to process through the situation they found themselves in.

A good ten minutes passed before Jasmine started dragging her toe on the ground to slow the swing. Faith stopped pushing and moved around so she could look at her daughter's face. "Why didn't you tell me about him?" Jasmine finally called out, her voice wobbly from crying. "I didn't think I had a daddy, and I was fine with that," she wailed. "But I do."

"Oh, Jas." Faith took hold of the tire swing with both hands and brought it to a stop. She crouched down in front of it so Jasmine wouldn't have to look up at her. "I thought I'd never see him again. I thought we would never see him again."

"Why not? Why did he go away? Didn't you guys love each other? Were you mean to him?"

"No, baby. No. I wasn't mean to him, and yes, we loved each other very much. But we were so young, and he didn't live here. He—he had a whole different life from us, and I didn't want his life, and he didn't want my life back then."

"That's dumb. If you guys loved each other, you would do anything for each other. That's what you always say to me." Jasmine still wouldn't look at her, but at least she wasn't spinning away from her anymore.

"I know. And you're right. We didn't fight hard enough for each other back then." Faith's thighs were beginning to burn, so she stood and reached out to cup her daughter's face. "I wish we'd done things differently, Jasmine. So many things. If I could go back and undo things, I would go in a heartbeat. But I can't, and I don't know what to do except to start here. You can ask me anything, baby, and I'll tell you. I'll tell you anything you want to know."

"But will it be the truth? What if I ask something you don't want to tell me? Like about sex or something."

Faith chuckled softly. "It will be the truth, Jasmine. Even if you ask me about sex or something." She tipped her head so she could look her daughter in the eye. "Do you want to take the quad out to Grandma's secret garden? I go there when I need to sort things out, did you know that? I know Grandma isn't there, not in real life; she's waiting for us in heaven. But when I need a mom to talk to, that's where I feel closest to her. We can swing by the house and grab some of Aunt Charity's redbud lemonade and a snack to take with us."

But Jasmine shook her head. "I don't think I'm ready to talk right now. I think I need some space."

"Okay," Faith said, her heart lurching to a stop. "I'll go sit at the picnic table, and when you're ready, you can join me there."

"That's not what I mean. I need to be by myself." Jasmine rotated the swing away from her mother and rested her cheek against the curve of the tire, her shoulders drooping as she draped her arms around the rope to hold on. She looked so sad and forlorn, and her next words broke Faith's heart. "I don't want you here."

Somehow, she managed to swallow the lump in her throat so she could breathe again. "Okay," she said, trying not to let her daughter hear the tears that were all but strangling her. "I'll be around close to the house. I have my cell phone with me if you want to call me."

Jasmine nodded, but she said nothing more.

"I love you, Jasmine," Faith murmured, then started down the slope toward the house.

"I love you, too, Mama," came the girl's weary reply.

By the time she made it to the house, Faith was weeping openly. She'd said it to Cord just the other day; what a mess they'd made of things. Fearless Faith, her daddy always called her, and yet, she was the most fearful person she knew. Every moment of her life was spent holding on too tightly for fear of losing control. Looking too closely, for fear of missing something. Being too careful, for fear of getting hurt. She was so tired of being afraid all the time.

In the kitchen, Abby, Charity, and Prudence were sitting around the table talking quietly, and when she burst in, they looked at her with worried questions in their eyes. Charity leaped to her feet and rushed toward her, arms out, her expression crumpling in sympathy. "Oh, Faithy," she murmured as she wrapped her arms around her.

For a moment, Faith froze. Her instinct to push away her sister's comfort almost overwhelmed her, but wasn't that exactly what had gotten her into this situation in the first place? Cord was right; she didn't know how to ask for help, not when she really needed it. She closed her eyes and wrapped her arms around Charity's waist and let herself fall apart in her sister's embrace. Prudence tucked a paper napkin into Faith's hand, then wrapped her arms around them, too. Abby joined them a moment later.

"Where's Daddy?" Faith asked after blowing her nose. "I think Jasmine is going to need him."

"At Hope's," Prudence told her. "It's Friday, remember?" Hope's assistant left at noon on Fridays, and Jed had taken to helping out in her vet clinic Friday afternoons. He liked animals well enough, but the sisters were pretty sure he volunteered his time each week because he was a concerned father keeping an eye on his daughter.

"Right," she whispered, taking another napkin from Prudence. The group hug began to break up a little, but the three girls stayed close around her.

"Where's Jasmine?" Abby asked, propping a hip against the edge of the table.

"She's out at her tire swing. She needs some space," Faith explained with a sad smile for her youngest sister.

"Sorry," Abby said, a grimace marring her pretty features.

"Oh, Abs, I wasn't blaming you." Faith reached out and hugged her hard. "But usually, it's us needing space from her, you know? I think this is the first time she's pushed me away like this, and it feels like torture, knowing I'm not the comfort she needs right now."

"Do you think I should call Cord?" Prudence asked.

Three pairs of eyes turned sharply in her direction.

"Maybe she needs to talk to him," Prudence said in response to their silent questions. "I mean, she's hurting because she's learned about him, so maybe he's the best one to help her through this."

"I don't know," Faith began.

"Seems pretty risky to me," Charity agreed.

"Seems pretty spot on to me," Abby said. "Want me to go next door and see if he's around?"

For a moment, Faith almost went along with it, but then caution overruled the idea. She shook her head. "You both may be right, but let's wait on that. I think I need to call Daddy. Maybe he can come home. If anyone can get her to open up, he can."

"I can go fill in at the clinic if Hope needs help," Prudence offered. "I haven't been over there in a long time."

"I'll call Daddy while you get ready," Abby said, whipping out her phone and tapping Hope's number.

"I'll get a pot of coffee brewing and make a batch of cookies," Charity said, hugging Faith one more time. "Nothing clears the air like the smell of java and peanut butter oatmeal cookies. Dad and Jasmine's favorites."

Abby pulled out a chair while she waited for someone to pick up on the end of the phone. "Here, Faith," she whispered. "Take a load off."

Faith sat in humble appreciation as her sisters buzzed around her in their desire to take care of her. It felt so nice just to hand the reins over to someone else for a change, to let everyone else figure out how to fix what was broken. And they were surprisingly good at it, too.

She listened in silence while Abby explained to their father what had happened that day, her words efficient and effective. Within minutes, she was off the phone, a comforting smile on her face. "He's heading out now—Hope told him not to wait, that she'd be fine until Pru got there."

"Thank you, Abs."

Abby shrugged. "It's cool. It'll all be okay, sis, you'll see. Want me to go check on her?"

Faith started to say no, but then changed her mind. "Can you do it without her knowing?"

Abby released a scoffing snort. "My middle name is Clandestine." Then she cocked her head, narrowed her eyes, and pressed a finger to her chin. "Actually, that would be bomb. Abstinence Clandestine Goodacre. Has a certain ring to it, don't you think?"

Faith surprised herself by laughing, in spite of the painful circumstances.

"She laughs. My work here is done." Abby dropped into a dramatic bow and then ducked out the door to go spy on Jasmine.

A moment later, Prudence bustled into the kitchen dressed in a pair of cutoff shorts and a floor-length crocheted kimono style cardigan over a pale pink tank top. She slipped her feet into a pair of red cowboy boots with turquoise stitching, then grabbed a to-go cup, tossed in some ice, then filled it with redbud lemonade from the fridge. "This is the best stuff, Charity. Nectar of the gods, I'm telling you." She threw her arms around Faith. "I'm gone. I'll be praying."

"You smell yummy," Faith said, hugging her back. "Thank you."

True to her word, by the time Daddy walked into the kitchen, the coffee was ready, and the first batch of cookies was out cooling on a rack.

"Hey, Daddy. Sorry about this," Faith began, but he silenced her with a gentle hand on her shoulder.

Abby sauntered in moments later. "She's still just sitting in the tire swing, spinning it around super slow. Hope she doesn't barf. She's all yours, Pops." Then she headed off down the hall toward her room, her phone in hand while she industriously texted someone about something.

While Jed poured fresh coffee into his travel mug, Charity found a plastic cup with a lid and a straw and filled it with lemonade for Jasmine. She packed several cookies into a plastic container, along with a couple of napkins, then tucked the lemonade and cookies into a small plastic bin for easy carrying, leaving room for Jed's coffee mug. "Here you go, Daddy. You're our hero."

TWENTY-SIX

"Boy, you got it bad." Binks leaned against the fence rail and studied Cord with narrowed eyes. "You been digging that same hole for a good quarter hour. You hoping to strike oil or something?"

Cord looked over at the sound of the old man's voice, but it took a moment for his words to register. He felt the grin settle into place again. He'd been grinning all afternoon. He glanced down into the post hole and shook his head. "Dang. That's deep."

"You're not good for much like this, young squire. I think I see bluebirds fluttering around in circles above your head."

"I think I hear them," Cord said with a good-natured chuckle. He set the post hole digger aside and wiped his forehead with his shirt sleeve. It didn't help much; it was hot and humid, and the manual labor had him sweating and dirty. His mind, however, was a million miles away—or rather, it was about a quarter mile away, still playing with Faith at the stream where they'd had lunch together several hours ago.

Had they eaten anything at all?

"Enjoy your picnic lunch, did you?" Binks asked, reading his mind.

"Best lunch I've had in a long time," Cord said with a satisfied nod. He reached for the steel water thermos tucked into the tool bag on the ground and took a long swig of cold water. "Faith loved the basket."

"I figured she would," Binks said with a nod. He picked at a splintered section of the rail, his gnarled fingers moving deftly over the wood. "You met that girl of hers yet?"

Cord took another drink, screwed the lid back in place, then shot the old man a sly grin. "My daughter?"

After a moment, Binks nodded slowly. "I guess you have, then."

"I guess I have then," Cord echoed. Not facetiously, no. In fact, he said it with a great deal of pride in his voice. "She's quite a girl, isn't she?"

"That she is," Binks agreed. "Just like her mama. That Faith Goodacre is the King Midas of ranching, Cord, and don't you forget it. Everything she puts her hand to is pure gold. She's helped out a lot of folks in this hollow, teaching them how to care for their land better, how to make the most of what they got. You know, at one time, your uncle had it in his mind that you and she might make a life together here at Whispering Hills. I think he hoped she'd bring a little life back into this place."

Cord nodded and told Binks about the job his uncle had offered him. "I think you're right. I believe he was offering me the chance to do right by them without forcing my hand. He was a good man, Binks. A good man."

"But you opted out," Binks stated, although Cord recognized it for the question it was. "Not ready to be a daddy."

"At the time, Faith and I weren't even speaking. I knew nothing of the child."

The older man straightened and frowned. "She never told you?"

"I never asked," Cord stated. "It's my fault as much as it is hers. But we're sorting through all that and seeing what we can make out of things where they are now."

Binks nodded slowly, contemplatively. "Seems you're doing a lot of that lately. This ranch," he added by way of explanation. "I figure you're just now beginning to realize the size of the chunk you've bitten off. You really planning to stick around?"

It was Cord's turn to straighten, his expression sober. "I'm here to stay, man. That's not negotiable. How I'll manage to make this place work? That may require some major finessing, but I'll figure it out somehow. This is my home now, and as long as you want to be a part of it, it's your home, too. But you should know that I have every intention of doing exactly what Judge Flanner intended. If it takes moving Heaven and Earth to do so, I aim to make a life together with that Goodacre girl next door and the daughter we have between us, so you can set your mind at ease."

Binks pushed away from the fence and nodded in the direction of the house. "I've got a pot of your aunt's chili on the stove in the big kitchen. Should be ready in an hour. I don't make it like she did—no one can make it like she did—but it's hearty and has a good kick to it, and it'll stick to your ribs. You come on in and have some when you're through here."

Cord watched the man saunter away and smiled with contentment. Aunt Betina's cowboy chili was renown in these parts, and the fact that the foreman had cooked up a batch just for the two of them was about the same as if he'd given Cord his blessing. He made quick work of filling in the hole back to the right depth, mixing up the quick set concrete he'd brought with him, then setting the new pole in place. "About a million more to go," he told himself, but he wasn't too worried about it. He'd hired a guy from a farm across town to bring his tractor and auger over to dig the rest of the post holes for him, but after lunch, he'd been too wound up to go back to work in his makeshift office. He'd needed some manual labor to clear his head, and there was nothing like digging and shoveling to get the job done.

Back at the house, he washed up and hurried to the kitchen just as Binks was dishing up a couple of bowls of the meaty stew. "Cornbread, too?" Cord asked, eyeing the golden cake in the iron skillet. "You're going to spoil me, sir."

"Too late for that," Binks chortled. "And I had nothing to do with it."

The two men ate in comfortable silence, enjoying the air conditioning that offered a reprieve from the sweltering heat outside. Cord hadn't realized how hungry he was and said so when he got up for seconds. He returned to the table with his full bowl and took a bite. "This is good stuff, Binks."

"Thank you, young squire." The foreman pushed his bowl away and sat back in his chair, looping an arm over the back of the seat next to him as he watched Cord eat.

It suddenly occurred to him that Binks might have an ulterior motive for the delicious meal. He took a long swig of cold water and met the man's gaze. "What's on your mind?" he asked, and then took another bite of chili.

Binks didn't even bother feigning ignorance. He nodded slowly, cleared his throat, and then said, "Rodeo. Ever thought of it?"

Cord frowned and shook his head. "Rodeo," he repeated. "Not sure what you're getting at."

Binks nodded again. "This property, young squire. There's a heck of a lot of it, and we haven't been utilizing an awful lot of it for some time now. Even before things started winding down around here. That western pasture used to be hay, but it's gone back to the wild in the last six or seven years. Think about it. There's easy access off Carpenter Road; folks wouldn't have to set foot on any of the rest of the property to get to it. That's enough acreage for several arenas and a sizable stadium, one that would suit just fine for folks in these parts. A buddy of mine tells me the SPRA is looking for a new site that's more centralized in this region. There's that fairground over in Placer they're using right now, but it's not meant for a rodeo, and the locals complain about the noise and traffic so much they've been talking about shutting it down altogether. You could sponsor them here, lease a section of Whispering Hills to them, let them foot the bill for the work, and once the rodeo is up and running, you get your cut off the top without having to lift a finger. It would sure help in offsetting some of the costs you're incurring fixing up this ranch, and it would certainly set to right any notions folks have of you being a city slicker playing cowboy. Bring the rodeo to town, son, and you're everyone's hero."

The longer Binks talked, the less Cord thought about the bowl of food in front of him, and by the time the old man came up for air, Cord's mind was working in overdrive.

Rodeo. Bring the rodeo to Plumwood Hollow? Why not?

Rodeo. The word rolled around in his head. Rodeo.

Saddle bronc riding. Bull riding. Bareback riding. Steer wrestling. Team roping. Calf roping. Breakaway roping. Barrel racing. Trick riders. Cattle auctions and livestock competitions.

Why hadn't he thought of it himself?

Rodeo. He nodded slowly, then looked across the table to find Binks moving his head up and down with him. "Yeah," he said, the word coming out long and low.

"Yeah," Binks echoed, still nodding.

"Rodeo." Cord tapped the table the way Binks did. "You're a genius, sir."

Binks grinned and waved a hand at the barely touched bowl of chili in front of Cord. "Eat up, young squire. Your soup is getting cold."

After the dinner dishes were washed and put away, Cord headed straight to the shower. Half an hour later, he was dressed and ready to call on his neighbor. He wanted to tell Faith all about what he and Binks had brainstormed over, and there was no way he could wait until Sunday. Not over the phone either; he wanted to watch Faith's eyes light up with the same kind of excitement he felt coursing through his veins.

He dug his cell phone out of the pile of assorted items on the dresser and dialed the number he already had programmed in his phone. It was the landline—he hadn't thought to ask Faith for her cell number—but he knew it still rang through to the Goodacre home. Sure enough, after the third ring, someone picked up.

"Hello? Prudence speaking." He smiled at her oh, so proper greeting.

"Prudence, it's Cord. How are you?"

"Oh. Hi, Cord."

Cord frowned at the hesitant note in her voice. It didn't bode well, especially coming from Prudence. "Is everything all right?"

"Well, it's been a rough day around here," she said candidly. "Jasmine found out you're her daddy from someone at school. Someone who isn't a friend. Or family."

"Oh." Cord's stomach lurched. "Oh."

"Yeah."

His thoughts went flying in a dozen different directions. Should he do something? Go over there? Talk to Jasmine? To Faith? To Jed? Did he need to go beat someone up? What was a daddy supposed to do in this situation?

"So, listen, Cord. I think now isn't a great time. I'll let Faith know you called. You're still planning on dinner with us on Sunday, right? Things should be right as rain by then."

"Wait. No. Yes, I mean. Yes, I'm still planning on Sunday dinner, but what about right now?" he asked, not about to let her hang up on him. "What can I do? Should I come over?"

"No, no. That wouldn't be good." Prudence remained calm, but he could almost feel the tension zinging through the telephone wires. "Now isn't a good time, Cord. Maybe try calling back in the morning if you don't want to wait until Sunday."

"But Prudence, I can't just leave it like this. What can I do?" He could only imagine what was going on over at the Goodacre place and he didn't like the direction his thoughts were taking. "Can I speak to Faith?"

Prudence sighed softly. "Faith is asleep right now, and Jasmine isn't speaking to anyone in this family right now. That includes you, Daddy Cord. My father is sitting with her, and that's the best thing for everyone right now. I'm asking you to understand that this is a fragile situation right now, so please do not come over tonight. I'll let Faith know you called, and I'm sure she'll call you back in the morning if you'd like her to."

"Yes, yes! Please," he murmured, leaning his hip against the dresser as he spoke. The room was the same one he'd used all four summers he'd visited the ranch back in high school, but it seemed so much smaller to him now. The single bed had a sturdy iron frame and an old-fashioned floral comforter over faded flannel sheets. The dresser looked like something out of the seventies with its bulky drawer pulls and blocky, angular features, and the lamp on the bedside table had a fluted shade that was definitely too pretty for a guy's room. But it was comfortable in its familiarity, and now, with Prudence's last words echoing through his mind, he had little choice but to call it a night. It was early, sure, but he had no desire to go out to Schooners, or the Smokehouse, not now, knowing his girls were hurting.

As he slowly undressed, he began to pray. For Faith and Jasmine, for his relationship with them. He thanked the good Lord for the ranch and all the possibilities that it brought with it. He asked for patience and wisdom, and for the chance to become the kind of father to Jasmine that his father was to him. That Jed was to his daughters. That Uncle Judge had been to Frankie.

While he slipped into his pajama pants and headed to the kitchen for a bowl of ice cream and a glass of water, he thanked God for a foreman like Binks, a man who deeply cared about Whispering Hills and the legacy his old boss had left behind.

While he washed the dishes and locked up, he thanked God for Plumwood Hollow, for Glory to God church and Reverend Treadwell and Trudy Huckster.

As he brushed his teeth, he thanked God for Jim, Skid, and Ernie Maddox, who would be here bright and early Monday morning to give him a better idea of what he was getting into.

While he lay in bed staring up at the random trowel pattern in the plaster ceiling, he prayed about Faith Goodacre, thanking God that she wasn't just beautiful and single, but that she was receptive to his pursuit...then he prayed even more fervently that after tonight, she still would be receptive to it.

"Lord, please don't let this be a roadblock or a dead end. A pothole, even a detour, I can handle. But not a dead end, Lord."

TWENTY-SEVEN

Faith awoke with a start, her heart racing, panting in ragged breaths. "Oh, Lord," she groaned, rolling to her side and curling into a ball around a pillow as she willed the fight or flight adrenaline rush away. "Help." It was the only prayer she could think of at the moment, but she knew it would do just fine. It was the one thing she needed most, the one thing that was hardest to ask for, and the one thing the good Lord above wanted to do for her more than anything. As Cord liked to say, all she had to do was ask.

"I'm asking now," she murmured into the pillow she'd drawn up to her face to block out the rays of early morning sunshine. "Jasmine and I need your help something fierce, Lord."

She sat up suddenly, then closed her eyes and breathed slowly as a wave of dizziness washed over her. When she opened them again, it was still morning. She glanced at her bedside table for her watch, then realized she hadn't bothered taking it off the night before. It was almost nine o'clock!

With a gasp that had her heart kicking up a notch again, she threw off the covers and scrambled out of bed, not bothering to change out of her flannel pajama bottoms and an oversized tee before rushing out into the hallway and to the kitchen. "Jasmine?" she called out. It was Saturday morning, and she had no idea where her daughter was. When was the last time Faith had slept in so late?

"Hey, Faith," Charity said as Faith barreled into the room, arms akimbo. "She's out with Abby playing with the kittens in the barn." But Charity's sad eyes told Faith a whole lot more than her words did. "We decided to let you sleep as long as possible since you were up so late last night. Pru and the twins took care of the horses this morning for you, and Daddy is out prepping some of the fields for next week's planting." She glanced up at the clock on the wall. "He was already gone by the time I got up, so you might want to check on him."

In other words, check on Daddy, not Jasmine.

"She's still not talking to anyone?" Faith ran her fingers through her wild hair, then eyed the empty coffee pot. Ever the hostess, Charity didn't even ask; she simply went about starting a fresh pot.

As yesterday afternoon progressed into evening, Jasmine had gotten more and more withdrawn, refusing to even speak to Jed. "Everyone in this whole stinkin' family knew, and no one thought they should tell me?" she wailed to no one in particular as she marched through the house on her way to the bathroom.

"I didn't know until Mother's Day," Abby called out after the girl, her youth making her reckless in the face of Jasmine's wrath. "I was totally freaked out, too," she added when Jasmine spun on her heels to glare at her.

"Are you lying like the rest of them?" Jasmine asked with narrowed eyes, her hands on her hips.

"Nope. Ask your mama."

Faith sat across the table from Abby going over the accounts. It wasn't something she needed to do today, but she wanted to stay close to the house, just in case, and working out in the barn had made it too easy to step outside to check on Jasmine every five minutes. At one point, her daughter had hollered out, "That's not giving me space; that's spying!" So, she'd finished up the task at hand and headed inside to stuff her face with peanut butter cookies and cold milk while she found other ways to stay productive.

"I'm not asking her anything right now." She shot her mother a scathing look.

"Suit yourself," Abby had said with a shrug, then popped her earbuds into her ears. Faith had a feeling the teenager wasn't listening to anything at all, but the props had their intended effect. Jasmine had nodded, disappeared into the bathroom to use the toilet, then marched back through the kitchen on her way outside again.

"I'm still mad at you, cuz you knew for almost two weeks and didn't tell me, but I guess I can talk to you," Jasmine said before pushing through the back door.

Abby shot a questioning look at Faith, who nodded gratefully. "I'll bring cookies," Abby called after the girl as she got to her feet and snatched up the half-empty plate from in front of Faith. To her big sister, she said, "You'll puke if you eat any more of these."

An hour later, Faith headed off to the pasture to move the herd, waving off Prudence's offer of help. She could use some space of her own, not because she was angry, but because she felt so helpless. Part of her wanted to step in and pull the Mama card, the one that demanded her daughter behave, the one that would mete out some form of disciplinary action of Jasmine didn't shape up. Another part of her felt deep sympathy for the girl, watching her from afar as Jasmine peeled back layer after layer of the facade she'd been living under. The girl was sharp and aware of far more than most nine-year-olds, and the longer she thought about the situation, the clearer things became. And the more upset she got.

When Faith had left her at the tire swing, she'd been certain Jasmine would come looking for her after fifteen minutes of being alone. But once it occurred to the child that it wasn't just Faith who'd kept the secret from her, she'd initiated a family-wide silent treatment, refusing even to speak to her grandfather.

So, when Jasmine agreed to let Abby into her self-imposed bubble, Faith was relieved on several accounts. It meant she didn't have to worry that the child would do something dangerous, like run away. It also meant that Jasmine felt she had an ally in a house that seemed like it had turned on her. She'd slept in Abby's room with her, too, which was a far cry from her original plan to camp under the porch with Jack. It broke Faith's heart, but she knew her daughter's heart wasn't faring so well, either. Surely, a good night's sleep would help to set things right again.

But now, with the morning half gone already, and Jasmine still not speaking to her, Faith wasn't so sure. "I can't believe I slept so late," she said, smiling gratefully at Charity when she handed her a cup of steaming hot coffee. "Thank you."

"Go get dressed and check on Daddy. I'll man the post here and make sure the girls eat."

"This can't go on much longer, Charity." Faith sipped the scalding brew carefully. "I think having Abby on her team might have been a bit like giving her permission to prolong this more than necessary, don't you? I mean, I want to give her time to process—this is a big revelation—but I feel like the longer it goes, the more it's turning into an act of punishment toward us. "

Charity dropped into the chair beside Faith and sat for a moment, studying the pattern of the wood grain in the tabletop. Finally, she said, "All I'm going to say is this. Be patient with her. Don't let her run you over but give her the space she asks for. I remember how long it took you to deal with your unexpected news, Faith, and I don't just mean the pregnancy. I'm also talking about the aftermath of that trip to UK we took together."

Faith closed her eyes and sighed deeply. Her sister was right. Faith had recovered, but it had been over a long stretch of time, and she'd spent many, many hours alone, needing the time and space quiet to allow the planets to realign in the universe of her life. "Cord is coming for dinner tomorrow after church, and I'm not going to take back that invitation. I guess she can have the rest of the day to sort through things; then I'm calling her game."

"Have you called him back yet?" Charity asked, reaching over to smooth the back of Faith's head. "Sweet bed-head," she added with a smile.

"Called who—Oh dear. I haven't. Poor guy. I'll go do that now, then check on Daddy." Faith rubbed her eyes, amazed that she still felt so exhausted, then rose to go to her room to get ready for the day.

"Cord Overman," came the abrupt voice on the other end of the line. He sounded in a hurry, or grumpy, or both.

"It's Faith. I'm so—"

"Faith? Oh, thank God," he exclaimed, his tone changing from impatience to relief. "Sorry if I sounded so short when I answered. I've been waiting for a call from your place and didn't recognize the number. I didn't want to get stuck talking to some— Never mind. I'm glad it's you." He took a breath and continued. "How is everything? How are you? Is Jasmine all right?"

"Slow down, cowboy," she said, smiling in spite of the situation. She dropped to the edge of her bed and leaned a shoulder against one of the four reeded posts of the antique bed frame. She apologized for not calling him back the night before, then said, "I can't talk long, so bear with me. Not much has changed since last night—she's still not talking to anyone but Abby, because only Abby didn't know about you."

"I'm sorry, Faith," he murmured into the phone, the rumble of his voice both stirring and soothing her at the same time. "I hate that you're having to deal with this alone."

"I'm not alone. I have my family." The second the words were out, she squeezed her eyes shut and smacked her forehead. "I'm sorry. That wasn't meant the way it sounded."

"That's not how I meant it, either," Cord said after a moment of silence. "I meant that you've been a single parent and you shouldn't have to be. I hate that you've had to be a single parent. I want to jump in and rescue you both, and I feel helpless, like one of those mama cows that are stuck out in the paddock having to watch her baby be afraid without her. I'd be bawling right now if I didn't think it would scare Binks."

"I know. I get it." She sighed and ran a hand through her hair, tugging a little too hard when she hit a tangle. "I just wanted you to know that we're still on for tomorrow if you're up for it. It may not be fun, but it'll be real."

"I'm up for it. Down for it. I'll be there. And Faith?"

"Yes?"

"I love you. I'm here for you. Just on the other side of the fence. I'm not going anywhere."

A small sound, halfway between a sob and a sigh, escaped her tight throat, and she reached up to cover her mouth so nothing else would get loose. It took her a moment to compose herself, and then another to work up the courage to respond, but finally, she whispered, "Thank you. That means more to me than you'll ever know, Cord." Oh, she wanted to tell him she loved him, she wanted to assure him that everything would be all right, that they were looking at their happily ever after together, but the words simply wouldn't come.

"Call me if anything changes," he said after a moment, only the slightest hint of resignation in his voice. If she wasn't listening for it, she might have missed it. "I have your number now, so I'll know who's calling."

They said their goodbyes, and after she hung up, she pressed the phone to her chest and murmured, "I love you, too."

TWENTY-EIGHT

BY NOON, JASMINE MADE her peace with Faith, and although it felt tentative and fragile, the little girl explained that she could forgive her mama because she wasn't the one who left. "I can't forgive that man, though," she declared later that night as they were getting ready for bed. Her eyes filled with tears and spilled over, and Faith wondered, not for the first time, if she needed to worry about Jasmine getting dehydrated. It seemed that the girl had been crying off and on for two days; it couldn't be good for her.

"How can a daddy not know his little girl is out there in the great big world somewhere? I don't want a daddy who doesn't even know in his heart that I'm alive." She pressed a little hand to her chest and whispered dramatically, "I always knew in my heart, Mama. I knew something was missing in here. Why didn't he?"

"Maybe he did, sweetie. Maybe that's why he came back here to the hollow. He says he's always known this was his home, and he wasn't even born and raised here. So, you know it has to be something else that makes him feel that way. Maybe it's you."

"Or maybe it's you. He sure has the hots for you. I saw him kiss you by the horses the other day." She rolled her eyes and feigned gagging.

Faith sat down on the bed next to Jasmine and took her hand, trying not to show her concern. She'd been certain her daughter hadn't seen anything, but she wasn't about to deny it. Jasmine wouldn't make something like that up, especially not in the middle of the current turmoil. "Did that upset you? Cord kissing me, I mean?"

Jasmine sighed deeply and shook her head. "I wasn't mad then because you looked happy so he must have been a good kisser. I'm mad now because he must be a bad daddy since he abandoned me to live the tragic life of an unwanted orphan for the rest of my days."

Faith pressed her lips together and turned her face away so Jasmine wouldn't see how hard she struggled not to laugh. "You're not an orphan, Jas. Both your parents are alive, and you've lived your whole life with me."

"Yeah, well, I feel like one. And it's that guy's fault." She flopped back onto her pillow and threw an arm across her face in a dramatic show of despair. "My life as I know it is over."

Faith stood and crossed to the dresser to grab a hairbrush and some hair ties. "Sit up, baby. Let me braid your hair." Jasmine's hair was still damp from her shower, and if they left it to dry while she slept, it would be a wild mess in the morning.

Jasmine sat up again and drew her knees up to her chest. "I don't get it. I just don't get it," she said over and over again. "How did he not know about me? I just don't get it."

Faith took her times brushing out her daughter's long brown curls, then divided the length into three strands and began weaving them together in a thick braid. "Well, Cord is coming to dinner after church tomorrow, baby. Why don't you ask him that question?" For only a moment, Faith wondered if it was fair to throw Cord to the wolves—the wolf pup, in this case—that way, but then she decided that it didn't matter if it was fair or not. He wanted to be Jasmine's daddy? Then he could jump right in with both feet. It wasn't the first difficult question the little girl had ever asked, and it certainly wouldn't be the last. If he couldn't handle it, then Faith wasn't so sure she'd want him to be Jasmine's daddy, either.

"I don't want to talk to him. Not ever," Jasmine declared.

"I understand how you feel, baby, but you will be polite to him," Faith told her. "That's not an option."

"Then I won't come to dinner." Jasmine crossed her arms over her chest and stuck out her bottom lip in a pout reminiscent of her toddler years.

"Eww," Faith said, tapping experimentally on her daughter's grossly protruding lip. "You look like you've been to the Jenners' plastic surgeon."

Jasmine jerked backward, but stopped making the face. "I don't know what that means," she said, suspicion in her eyes.

"That's actually a good thing." She tied off the end of the braid and kissed the top of the girl's head. "There. And yes, you will come to dinner, or you will make Aunt Charity and Aunt Prudence sad. They're making some of your favorites tomorrow. Ribs and potato salad and key lime pie with whipped cream on top."

For a few seconds, Faith thought Jasmine might stand her ground and refuse, but the thought of ribs, and especially key lime pie, broke through her defenses. "Fine. I'll come and eat, but I won't talk to that guy." Jasmine fell backward on the bed again and pulled the sheet up over her head.

"You will be polite, Jasmine. That's all I'm asking of you."

Except she wasn't. Several times during the worship service, Faith caught her glaring over her shoulder at Cord, who sat in the pew behind them, down near the end of the row. At one point, Faith leaned over and told her daughter that she would take her outside and paddle her backside if she didn't behave. Jasmine had lifted horrified, wide eyes to her mother. Faith didn't waver, though, and Jasmine, in turn, kept her eyes glued front and center, but she crossed her arms tightly and scowled so long, Faith wondered how her face didn't cramp up.

As they made their exit, Jasmine didn't even wait for Yvette, who was calling her from across the aisle. Instead, she pushed past her aunts and down the side aisle, pausing next to Cord long enough to say to no one in particular, "I hate people who think they're cowboys, but they're not. They're worse than stupid." Then she darted past him toward the front door.

Faith followed as quickly as she could, after offering an angry apology to Cord, for which she had to apologize as well, because she could see he thought she was mad at him. "You may not have a daughter much longer, Mr. Overman. If I get my hands on that girl before I calm down..." She left the sentence unfinished and hurried outside in search of her child.

Jasmine was already waiting in the truck, and the sight of her softened Faith's heart a little. It was sweltering hot even with the windows rolled down, and her little face was drenched in a combination of sweat and tears.

"I don't want to see him today, Mama," she wailed as soon Faith settled into the seat beside her. "I just can't. He makes my tummy hurt and my eyes water." Her words cut off with a loud hiccup, and she covered her face with her hands.

"Oh, sweetie. What are we going to do?" Faith asked, flipping up the console between them and pulling the little girl close to her side. She felt a little like crying herself. With her free hand, she stuck the key in the ignition and started the truck, then turned on the air conditioner and rolled up the windows. "We can't change the fact that he's your daddy. And he lives here now, so we can't pretend he doesn't exist. He wants to get to know you, to fall in love with you the way I have. Don't you think that's a good thing?"

"But Mama," Jasmine sobbed, her face buried against Faith's side. "I always told everyone that I never had a daddy because I was part fairy like you said. I had a magic heart like you said. Now everyone will think I'm a stinkin liar because he's here. Even Vetty will be mad at me, cuz we hate liars in our girls club."

Faith sighed loudly, berating herself again for not being honest with the girl from the very beginning. How could she have known that it would unfold like this? As tough and confident as Jasmine was, she had an acute sense of right and wrong, and when those lines got muddied, the child got lost. Now here Faith was, asking the girl to compromise her standards and to simply accept the fact that everyone in her life had deceived her about something as important as the existence of a daddy. No wonder Jasmine was so torn over this.

"I'm sorry, baby. I really am. What can I do to help make things better? I can't undo any of it, although I would if I could, but I will do anything I can to help you sort through this. I don't want you to be angry at anyone, especially not yourself. You didn't lie, I did. If you're going to be angry, be angry at me. Not yourself."

Jasmine shook her head but said nothing, her little body shaking pitifully against her mother.

"And I know you don't want to hear this right now, but Cord didn't know either, because I didn't tell him. You should be angry at me that he didn't know, not him."

"I don't want to be angry at you anymore," the little girl said, shifting so she was now practically sitting on Faith's lap.

"I'm glad, baby. I don't want you to be angry at me anymore, either." They sat that way for several minutes while Jasmine settled down, then Faith said, "How about we try to beat everyone else home? We can hide in our room until dinner starts; then if you're polite, you can excuse yourself as soon as the meal is over. Do you think you can handle that?"

Jasmine slid off Faith's lap and settled back into the seat beside her. "I don't know. Maybe I can try." She didn't sound very confident. "But I think you're asking a lot of someone like me."

"Buckle up. Let's go," she said, but Faith silently agreed with her daughter. She was asking a lot of the girl. They all were. And as badly as Faith wanted this whole ordeal to end in happily ever after, forcing it along didn't seem to be working. She knew what she needed to do, and it just about broke her heart to even think about it, but she saw no other option.

But by the time Faith pulled into the driveway behind the house, Jasmine was sound asleep against her shoulder, and no amount of bribes, threats, or pleading was enough to keep the girl awake. She was simply exhausted beyond measure after the last few days of emotional upheaval, so Faith finally gave in, tucked the child into bed, and pulled the bedroom door closed behind her just as the rest of the gang started showing up.

"She's worn herself out," Faith explained when she entered the kitchen to find Charity and Prudence already at work on the meal. "I couldn't wake her up. She'd try, but then her little eyelids would start drifting closed. I finally just decided to let her sleep. Maybe it's for the best."

"I agree," Charity said, giving Faith a quick reassuring hug. "Cord is a big boy. He can wait a little longer to spend time with Jasmine."

"For now, he'll just have to enjoy getting to know the rest of us again," Prudence added with an encouraging smile.

TWENTY-NINE

CORD DID HIS BEST to stay positive all through the delicious meal, but no matter how hard he tried to engage Faith in conversation, it was clear that she was terribly distracted. He didn't blame her; she was understandably worried about Jasmine and how the little girl was handling the news of Cord's role in her life. When he put a comforting hand on her knee under the table, she shifted incrementally away from him, but it was enough to know that things were not boding well with them. The rest of the meal, he could tell she was going out of her way to avoid any physical contact with him, not even allowing their fingers to touch when passing dishes of food around the table.

Charity was a wonderful hostess, reminding him so much of his mother, with her gentle voice and graceful manners. His confidence in her grew when he took his first bite of the ribs; the pork practically fell off the bone when he bit through the sticky crust. He hardly had to chew at all as the meat melted in his mouth. Every part of the meal had him expressing his appreciation, even the lettuce and cucumber salad, fresh-picked out of Jed's garden that morning.

"The tomatoes are from Joe's Farms," Jed told him. "Mine aren't ready yet, but he's got greenhouses, so I settle for his until I can harvest my own. I hear you're planning on having a crew or two over at Whispering Hills shortly, so if you're looking to buy good produce grown right, Joe's your man. He'll see to it that you get what you need." He tipped his head at Charity beside him. "My daughter tells me you're looking to hire her on to feed them all."

That was his opening, he realized, so he gave them a rundown of what he had planned so far. "When I worked here ten years ago, Uncle Judge typically ran around a thousand head, but even counting this year's spring calves, I'm coming into this with only about four hundred. I'm good with that, though, as I plan to cull the herd down to about two hundred this fall, keeping only the best heifers, and replacing most of our bulls. I'm purposely starting small so that I can focus on quality from the ground up. Then I'll grow the herd from there. I really do love working with the cattle, and I've been doing a lot of research into the rotational or mob grazing you've implemented here, Faith," he said, turning to look at her.

She nodded, but didn't return his gaze, focusing instead on cutting a tiny chunk of meat off the rib on her plate.

"I plan to transition into a modified version of what you're doing at Seven Virtues, essentially mob grazing on a bigger scale. I believe I can incorporate it at Whispering Hills without too much difficulty as I have a lot of unused pasture to experiment with. I'm hoping you'll give me a little guidance on the process, or at least let me wander over and watch you at work." He wanted to nudge Faith's leg, to shoot her a teasing wink, but he was getting the whole cold shoulder vibe loud and clear.

"Sound like you've given this a lot of thought," Jed said when Faith didn't respond. "I'm sure Faith would be happy to help out."

"Of course," she said, then took another bite and chewed methodically.

"Great. I'd appreciate it." What had happened? Was this standoffish behavior all because of Jasmine's reaction? Cord feared the answer was a resounding yes. What else could it be? "Anyway, once I get a better handle on the cattle, probably around this time next year, I'm buying out a horse breeder just outside of Louisville. He's retiring and selling off his stock, and because I'm taking the bulk of his operation, I'm getting the animals for a great deal. It's a little bit of a risky investment for me, mainly because I'm not a horseman by any stretch—you can ask Faith here—but I'm looking to hire on someone full time who knows what they're doing and can oversee the operation for me."

He directed his next question at Jed. Although Faith was probably the best person to answer it, he was growing weary of her abbreviated responses. "Is Seven Virtues strictly beef or do you deal in breeders with your Dexters? From what I've heard, folks seem to like those little cows."

Jed looked over at Faith, clearly expecting her to speak up, but when she continued silently downing her meal, he said, "We do sell pregnant mamas now and then, and folks buy family milk cows from us, especially when Faith works the local fair circuit."

"Our primary focus is the whole foods, antibiotic and vaccine-free grass-fed beef movement, though," Justice said, picking up where her father left off. "We work with several restaurants and whole foods suppliers, as well as private customers who purchase individual animals."

"We love them," Courage agreed. "They're a great all-around breed, especially for smaller farms and ranches. Easy to manage, easy to herd, and their size makes them perfect for families who only want a few of them."

"They're delicious, too," Jed added, holding up a stripped clean rib. "Nice work, Charity. That smoker does a fine job."

"Daddy built me a new smoker for Christmas last year, and it's amazing." Charity explained, reaching over to squeeze her father's forearm.

"If you need a good butcher, rather than sending your cows out, young Levi Valiente will come to you, did you know that? He's got a way with his knives; that's for sure. If you're serving up your own cows to your crews, he's the man for you."

"Thanks, guys," Hope interrupted, setting aside the rib she'd been chewing on. "I'm well aware that I'm eating beef, but knowing this was one of Faith's babies, and maybe one I doctored? Someone talk about something else, please."

Cord smiled across the table at Hope. "Forgive me," he said with a nod. "Anyway, my plan may seem counterintuitive, but I'm reducing everything down to only the best of the stock so I can focus on rebuilding a quality herd while I learn the ropes of full-time ranching. Once I feel like I can manage what I have, I'll expand as I see fit. Right now, I feel like I'm in over my head."

"I can't imagine taking on all that," Prudence chimed in. "You're a brave man, Cord Overman."

He chuckled around a bite of the creamiest potato salad ever. "Brash might be a better word. I wake up just about every morning wondering what in the blazes I signed up for, then the day gets rolling and I roll right along with it until I fall into bed at the end of it, amazed that I survived to tell about it. Fortunately, I have Binks. I don't know what I'd do without his patient, long-suffering guiding hand."

"I love that guy," Prudence said. "He's so cute."

Justice guffawed. "Don't let him hear you say that. He'd die of mortification. You don't call a rancher cute, Pru."

"I'll tell him you said so," Cord said with a chuckle of his own. Binks might act mortified, but he probably would get a kick out of the notion that the delightful Prudence Goodacre thought about him at all, no less as 'so cute.' "In the meantime, I'm bringing in Skid and Ernie Maddox to start renovations on just about all the standing structures on the property. The place needs a surprising amount of work; Binks has been doing a fine job of keeping up with what he has to work with, but some of those buildings need to be taken down to the foundations."

Jed nodded approvingly. "John Maddox and his boys will do right by you. They're the finest in their business."

"Wasn't one of them in school with you two?" Charity asked the twins. "I seem to remember—"

"Oh, please," Justice moaned. "Skid Maddox, yes. What a pain in the keister."

"I haven't seen him in ages," Courage said around a bite of salad. "Bomb cucumbers, Daddy. Remember his mullet, Justice?"

"That thing was awful, and he was so stinkin' proud of it. Half the time he wore it in a long braid down his back."

"Disgusting," Abby said with an exaggerated shiver. "Does he still have it, Cord? Will you sneak a pic of it and send it to me?"

The conversation ebbed and flowed around him, in spite of Faith's silent company, and Cord found himself smiling often. The dinner table at his house growing up was quiet and calm, and all his parents' attention was on him. This was so different, the way the conversation moved from topic to topic, from person to person, but other than Faith's odd behavior, no one seemed to feel left out or unnoticed, including him. It did his soul good to think of Jasmine being raised around this table alongside these women who loved each other and their father so much.

"We've all heard that the tales of dude ranches and retreat centers were just rumors, but the question bears asking. You've got a lot of fallow land right now, and with you downsizing even more, do you have something in mind for it, or are you planning on reforesting it?" Jed studied him with a shrewd look in his eyes; not antagonistically, Cord was certain, but out of curiosity that stemmed from having a vested interest. Anything Cord did to Whispering Hills would inevitably have a trickledown effect on Seven Virtues next door. He waffled for a few moments, then decided to go ahead and share the new idea with them.

"Actually, that's a good question and one I've been mulling over for some time now. Just the other day, Binks and I were talking about it, and he had a suggestion that has my wheels spinning, and I'd love your feedback." Did everyone around the table hold their breath and lean in? "He suggested I approach the rodeo association and sponsor them at Whispering Hills."

"A rodeo here?" Abby squealed before he could say anything else. "Oh, my gosh, Cord! That would be awesome!" She bounced in her seat and turned to Courage who sat beside her, grabbing her sister's arm with both hands. "You guys! Your own rodeo! Can you imagine? You could be the stars of the show." Whirling around to look at Cord again, she pressed her palms together in a prayer-like petition. "Can I do the first National Anthem there? Please?"

Cord grinned happily at the girl's response but looked over at Jed for his reaction. To his relief, the man was nodding. It was a slow, contemplative nod that told Cord he was mulling the notion around in his head, but he was nodding all the same. "That whole stretch along Carpenter would be accessible directly from the road so there'd be no reason for folks to cross private property, and the county already has water lines out there, so tapping into those would be a piece of cake. I'm thinking we could even put in an auction barn, and maybe have a mini fairground with a family focus. Rides, competitions, pageants, the works. In between rodeos, I'm thinking it wouldn't be a bad idea to host 4-H and FFA events, too. You know, support our young farmers."

Other than Abby's intermittent applause and Jed's continuous head bobbing, no one else said anything, and Cord was beginning to feel a little self-conscious about his big dreams. "I know it's a lot to think about, but if I bring in the association, it will be off my plate, and I can focus on the ranching side of things and let them handle all of that."

Prudence spoke first. "I can't watch the bull rides. I get sick to my stomach every time I think about them."

Charity reached over and put a hand on Prudence's shoulder.

Justice and Courage were staring at each other so fixedly, it made Cord feel rather unsettled. But when Justice nodded, he realized there'd been some kind of silent communication happening between them. "We've been talking about joining the local rodeo association. We've been pushing for another location for ages—the current one in this region isn't equipped for a rodeo set up, so it feels slipshod and unorganized. It doesn't garner a lot of attendees, either, probably because it's so hokey, and the locals complain about various things every year." Cord had heard the same from Binks, and it pleased him to know that others shared the same opinion the foreman did. "They've even been talking about shutting it down, which would be terrible. If you're serious, Cord, we'd put our names in today and get behind you on this."

"I can't imagine a better location," Courage added. "Carpenter exits right off the highway, and there's nothing else around us. The property across Carpenter, Daddy?" She turned to her father. "Wasn't it for sale a while back? Did anyone ever pick it up?"

"I did," Jed said, and all six of his daughters turned to stare at him.

"You?" Justice asked. "How many acres? And when did this happen?"

"I've been sitting on it for a couple of months, but I was thinking about the future and the possibility of expanding the property and maybe putting in another house. It was just too good a deal to pass up, and I didn't want anyone taking it. It's only about thirty acres, but it's good land."

"My goodness, Daddy," Charity said with a shake of her head. "Aren't you a sneaky Pete. When were you going to tell us?"

"The next time it came up," the man said, a statement so characteristic of Jedediah Goodacre that Cord had to chuckle.

"Well, that solves any dilemmas that might arise from disgruntled neighbors," Courage said, turning a beaming smile back on Cord.

But Jed hadn't yet said what his thoughts were on the rodeo, one way or another. Granted, the man wasn't known for being impulsive—except hadn't the purchase of the property across the way indicate otherwise?—and perhaps he simply needed more time to consider all the pros and cons of the idea.

"Rodeos need good vets, Hope," Abby said, pointing at her sister across the table. Hope hadn't contributed much to the conversation, either, but Cord could see her wheels were turning.

"That's true," he agreed. "Throw your hat in if you're interested," he encouraged.

"Actually," she began. "I'm more interested in hearing about your Quarter Horses. Maybe we can talk about that when you start heading in that direction."

"I think you have some sound ideas, Cord," Jed finally said. "I'm assuming you have the resources to back them."

Cord nodded. "So far, sir."

"Well, I think you could do a whole lot worse than bringing a rodeo to Plumwood Hollow."

"It all sounds wonderful, Cord," Faith said, turning in her seat so she could meet his gaze briefly. "I'm so glad Whispering Hills is in the hands of someone who loves this land and the animals on it."

"Thank you, Faith. That means a lot to me."

She nodded and looked away, but added, "And the fact that you're thinking about our community, by talking rodeo? Daddy's right about that. Tell Binks we think he's a genius."

In spite of the animated conversation around the table and the sense of accomplishment that came with the Goodacres' approval of his plans, Cord excused himself shortly after the key lime pie. It was just too much to bear sitting so close to Faith, yet having her seem so far away. He just wanted to get home and go dig another post hole or rip out a piece of siding, or something equally physically challenging.

"I'll walk you out to your truck," Faith said with a smile, surprising him with her offer. He offered her his arm, and after only a slight hesitation, she took it. The moment they were off the porch, she slipped her arm free of his, but walked beside him as they approached his truck. "Can I talk to you a minute?" she asked.

He wanted to say no. He wanted to pull his arm out of her grasp, get in his truck, and drive away. He didn't want to hear what she had to say. "Sure."

She moved a few steps away to stand beside the front wheel well. She wouldn't look at him.

"What's going on, Faith?" He held out a hand to her, but she ignored it. "Hey," he began again. "I hate seeing you like this. What can I do to help?"

She crossed her arms tightly in front of her, and then said the words he'd been dreading all weekend. "Cord, I think this is happening too soon. Too fast. Jasmine is having a really tough time with this, and I can't—"

Cord stepped forward and took her by the upper arms, ducking his head to try to get her to look at him. "Faith, stop. Don't do this. We can get through this together. We need to stick together. For her sake as well as ours."

Faith twisted slowly out of his grasp and took a step backward. "I can't. Not now. Not until she's ready. She's my first priority, Cord, and I need to be on her side right now."

"Wait a minute. Since when are there sides in this? I thought we were trying to bring all the sides together here."

"Semantics, Cord," she whispered, sounding as miserable as he felt. "You know what I mean."

"Faith," he shook his head, unwilling to accept what she was saying. "Don't do this." He stepped forward and cupped her face in his hands. "Come on, baby, don't do this."

She didn't pull away, but she closed her eyes, and two tears slid out from beneath her lashes. He brushed away the moisture with his thumbs, then bent to kiss each eye, then her cheeks, and finally, he pressed a soft kiss on her lips. He lifted his head when she didn't respond.

"Look at me, Faith. Open your eyes and tell me this is what you really want."

Faith opened her eyes, blinked away another set of tears, and said, "This is what I really want. I'm sorry," she added in a broken whisper.

He lowered his hands and stepped back. "For how long? How long do you want me to stay away? How much longer are you going to keep me waiting on the sidelines while you get to be both mommy and daddy to our daughter?"

"I need to go inside now, Cord. Please try to understand." She started to move around him, but he stopped her with a hand on her arm. She looked down at it, then lifted her gaze to his. "Let go."

"No." He stepped in front of her and pulled her to him slowly, his voice low and quiet, but tight with urgency. "No, Faith. I don't want to let go. I need you. I need Jasmine."

"Cord," she began. "Please let go of me and go home."

But he didn't. And when she started to resist, he pulled harder, unwilling to accept what she was saying. "Don't do this, Faith. I'm begging you. I love you, and I know you love me, too. I don't want to spend another day without you in my life. Without Jasmine—my daughter, Faith. Our daughter. I'm her father. Her daddy. Don't push me away."

Faith's face crumpled in despair, and she let out a pitiful sob, then he closed the space between them and wrapped his arms around her, holding her tightly against his chest.

"You are not my daddy!" Jasmine scrambled out from under the porch, scooped up a handful of pebbles, and launched them at the side of Cord's shiny red truck. "Go away! Go away and never come back! I hate you!"

She bent to pick up another one, but Jed burst through the back door and practically launched himself off the steps to stand between the girl and her parents. When the livid Jasmine attempted to duck around him, he swept her up in a bear hug, pinning her arms to her sides, and hauled her off toward the barn.

Faith brought her hands up between them and pushed him away, hard. "Please go, Cord. Please." Then she turned and practically ran after her father and daughter.

The porch door banged open again, and several more Goodacres arrived on the scene.

Cord closed his eyes, reached up to rub the back of his neck, hard, and then opened the door of his truck and climbed in.

Maybe he was wrong after all. Maybe he didn't want anything to do with this crazy, whack-job family. He turned the key in the ignition, put the truck in gear, backed out of his parking spot, and made his way down the long driveway that led away from Seven Virtues Ranch and the Goodacre family out to Carpenter Road.

THIRTY

Each morning, Faith awoke as though she were trying to drag her body through quicksand. All she wanted to do was shut her eyes and fall back to sleep. How had Cord ingrained himself so deeply in her heart again in only a few weeks? Knowing he was so close—just the other side of the tree line—yet so far away from her because she'd pushed him away was like walking on broken glass, each step sending shooting pains through her heart as she went about the daily ranching activities. While Jasmine was in school, Faith worked her fanny off in an attempt to get everything done before the child returned home so that she could spend those precious afternoon hours with Jasmine.

So, she could remember why she was enduring life without Cord in the first place.

Again.

As soon as dinner was over and the dishes washed and put away, she collected her daughter, and they made their way to their room where they read and snuggled or played games until it was time to shower and go to bed. Faith forced herself to stay awake until Jasmine's eyes drifted closed. Once the child was asleep, Faith crawled into her bed and closed her eyes, begging God to bring sleep quickly, mercifully.

Then she'd get up and do it all again.

Sunday was torture. She and Jasmine arrived as late as they dared, slipping into the end of the family pew from the side aisle just as the opening song began. She could hear Cord's tuneless droning from somewhere behind her; how could he sing at a time like this? Jasmine never once looked over her shoulder in his direction. She acted as though he no longer existed in her world. The moment church ended, the two of them slipped out before Reverend Treadwell made it to the door to greet his parishioners, hurried to Faith's truck, and made their way back to the ranch.

At first, Jasmine seemed to respond well to her mother's undivided attention, but it wasn't long before Faith started receiving calls from Miss Allenbaum that Jasmine was acting up in class or picking on other kids at the playground. The child apologized profusely, but in the same breath, blamed her bad behavior on everyone else. She insisted she'd try harder to be good, but when a call came Friday morning just after recess, Faith was appalled to hear that Jasmine had shoved Yvette out of her way, knocking her to the ground, resulting in skinned knees and lots of tears. To add insult to injury, the bullying was followed by a fit of rage at how stupid people were—courtesy of Jasmine—and Faith realized things weren't working the way she'd planned.

"What do I do, Lord?" She sat at the kitchen table alone, waiting for Abby and Jasmine to get home. "I don't know what to do."

Jack laid his head on her lap, and she stroked the soft fur on his ears. He gazed up at her with his kind, velvet eyes as though to say, "Don't worry. It will all work out in the end."

"That's the problem, Jack," she whispered. "It's not working out at all. It's so much worse than it was before." Faith could recall only one other time when she'd been so miserable. Both times, then and now, the common denominator was Cord's absence in her life.

Prudence appeared in the doorway, startling Faith, so she almost spilled the cup of coffee she was indulging in. "Maybe it's time for *you* to tell Jasmine what to do, rather than letting *her* tell you what to do," her little sister suggested, then disappeared again, leaving Faith to ponder her words.

By the time Jasmine walked in the door, arms crossed and a scowl marring her usually perpetually happy features, Faith had a plan.

It started with cancelling the movie they were supposed to see together.

"You are grounded. You will go to your room and stay there the rest of the afternoon, and you will not come out until dinner," Faith said after pulling their bedroom door closed behind them. Her voice remained level and firm. "This is not playtime. You may read one of the books I put on your bedside table." She waved at a stack of three books that were educational at best, but nothing even remotely entertaining. "Or you can write a letter to Meemaw Marcie. But we will not be going to the movies today."

The temper tantrum that followed was unlike any Faith had ever seen. Jasmine raged at her, storming around the room in such a frenzy that even when she tripped over a throw rug and bumped her head on the corner of her dresser, she only yelled louder. "I hate you! You're the worst mom in the world. I wish you were dead."

"I know you don't mean that, Jasmine," Faith said, keeping her own temper under control the best she could. "And when you calm down, you're going to feel bad about saying such terrible things to me."

"Oh yes, I do mean them!" Jasmine shot back, pointing a scrawny little finger at Faith. "If you were dead, then I could go live with my daddy, and you couldn't stop me like you did when I was born. You lied to me and told me I didn't have a daddy, but I do. I didn't even know his name until I was nine years old, and now he won't even come over here and see us anymore, because you told him to go away and never come back."

"Jasmine, I need you to calm down. That was you who told him that, remember?"

"No, no, no!" the girl wailed. "You're the liar, not me!"

A pounding knock on the door brought their shouts to a sudden halt. Jed burst into the room, his voice cutting through the air around them. "Enough!" He stopped right in front of Jasmine and bent forward, his hands on his knees, so he was eye to eye with his granddaughter. She stared wide-eyed and slack-jawed up at him, and Faith was only slightly less surprised at his interference. "Young lady, you are out of line. You are turning our home into a war zone, and I will not have it anymore. Do you understand me?"

Jasmine nodded, her eyes filling with big fat tears.

"Your mother isn't perfect, and she's made her share of mistakes, but she has tried her hardest to be the best mom she knows how to be." He thrust an arm out to point at Faith. "She has done nothing but love you and provide for you and sacrifice for you your whole life. You will apologize for saying those terrible things to her." He straightened up and glared down his nose at Jasmine. When she didn't budge, he raised his voice again and said one word. "Now."

Jasmine scurried across the room to where Faith sat on the edge of the bed and threw her arms around her neck. "I'm sorry, Mama." She buried her hot face in Faith's neck, her body trembling like a frightened little bird. "I'm sorry."

"I forgive you, baby," Faith murmured, stroking the girl's hair. She shot a look at her father, feeling the weight of his chastisement, herself.

"I'm not done," Jed said, his tone still firm, but no longer so loud. "Look at me, Jasmine."

The child straightened up, squared her shoulders, and turned to face him, although she kept one hand resting on Faith's shoulder.

"You and I will go see Yvette this evening, and you'll apologize to her, too."

"I can take her, Daddy," Faith began, but stopped when he lifted a hand.

"No, you will not. You have something else you need to do. Someone else you need to see."

Faith's eyes widened, and she shook her head.

"He is not perfect, and he's made his share of mistakes, too," Jed began, his eyebrows raised in emphasis. "You girls both need to give him a chance, and that's not a suggestion. He has come here to be in your lives, and by God, you will give him an opportunity to set things right, do you hear me?"

Faith and Jasmine both nodded, neither of them brave enough to speak.

"I love you both too much to let this continue," Jed stated. "I want peace in our home again, don't you?" He took a deep breath and let it out slowly, then crossed the room to sit on the bed beside them. He slid an arm around Faith's shoulders and said, "I miss my sweet girls."

"I'm sorry, Grampa," Jasmine whimpered, then buried her face against his chest. "I love you." She lifted her head just enough to look at Faith with one eye. "And I love you, Mama. I don't hate you. Not ever."

"I love you, too, baby," Faith said, laying her head on her daddy's shoulder. An overwhelming sense of relief filled her from the tips of her toes to the top of her head. It was almost like a band around her chest had been cut, and she could breathe again. "Thank you, Daddy. I love you, and I'm sorry I've been so miserable. I want peace, too."

"So do I," Jasmine said.

"Then let's start working together," Jed said, his voice back to his gentle rumble. "We're a family, and we need to stick together, because family is the most important thing in this world." He planted a kiss on the side of Jasmine's head. "And that includes Cordell Overman, Jasmine. He's family, too."

She turned so she could sit on her grandfather's lap and nodded contritely. "I know. I think I'm done being angry at him, too. I'm still sad, but now that my tummy doesn't hurt and my ears aren't buzzing, I think I still pretty much like him. I know Mama does. She probably even loves him and all that gooshy stuff."

Jed guffawed quietly and nudged Faith's foot with his own. "Does she?"

"Well, her happy face says so when he kisses her," Jasmine said in a silly voice, her face scrunched up in feigned disgust.

Her grandfather nodded, made an equally distasteful face, and said, "I've seen it myself, little lady. Although not enough lately. I think your daddy makes your mama pretty happy. Don't you?"

"Yeah. I think so, too."

Faith reached over and brushed a hand over to top of Jasmine's head. "I think if you let him, he'd like to try to make both of us happy, baby."

Jasmine lifted her teary gaze to Faith's. "Are you going to talk to my daddy tonight?" she asked, her voice small, but brave.

Faith's throat tightened at her daughter's obvious attempt to do the right thing. She nodded, and in a small, brave voice of her own said, "Yes, Jasmine. I'm going to talk to your daddy tonight."

"Am I still grounded?" Jasmine asked, not looking at either adult.

"Yes, you are," both Jed and Faith said at the same time.

Jasmine snickered, then covered her mouth with her hand. "Sorry. That wasn't supposed to be funny, was it?"

"No, it wasn't," Once again, Jed and Faith spoke in unison.

THIRTY-ONE

Cord made his way around the mess in the large living room, trying to get to the front door before whoever was there gave up. He wasn't expecting anyone at this time; the crew had gone home for the day, and he was ready for the peace and quiet that had fallen after they left. He ran a hand through his hair; he needed a haircut.

He needed a shower and a shave.

He needed a decent meal.

He needed a good night's rest.

More than anything, he needed Faith and Jasmine.

"Just a minute," he called when he reached the door. He fumbled in the shallow catch-all dish on the entry table until his fingers found the old key that fit the lock. Right before he opened the door, he leaned over to peer out the transom window. He froze when he saw who it was.

Brianna Peters.

What on earth was she doing on the front porch of Whispering Hills Ranch? Of his ranch. He pulled open the door slowly, frantically racking his brain to come up with an explanation for her presence there.

"Hey, Cord," she said in a melodic sigh when he finally stood before her. "How are you?"

He hesitated, then responded with a perfunctory, "Fine. How are you?"

"Can I come in? I've been dying to see this place."

"You have?" Cord wasn't liking the direction this was going. "Look, Bri. I'm not in any condition to have company right now. What are you—"

"I'm not company, silly. Let me in." She stepped forward and made to go around him, but he blocked her path, holding the door against his back.

"What are you up to, Brianna?" he asked. He narrowed his eyes suspiciously at her. "Why didn't you call first? Let me know you were coming, at least."

Brianna stuck out her bottom lip slightly, and Cord's patience waned. "I wanted to surprise you," she said, dipping her head in feigned shyness. "It's been so long since I've seen you. I came early, hoping to catch you before you ate dinner. I thought maybe we could go out tonight."

"Dinner? You, me, and Brock, right?" He made a show of peering around her. "Is he waiting in—" He broke off and glared at her. "Where's your car?"

Brianna had the grace to blush. He wasn't blind; the color in her cheeks made her practically sparkle, especially compared to how he felt these days. She looked good; he had to admit. Her long blonde hair was tied back in a high ponytail that hung straight and sleek down her back. Her brows were perfectly arched, her eyes professionally made up to look larger than life, and full lips were the color of Bing cherries. Her mouth was her best feature, she liked to say. He agreed. Her mouth was definitely eye-catching, and she knew how to use it.

She wore a short black skirt that ended mid-thigh, a loose top that looked like it was falling off one shoulder, and on her feet were her signature high heels. It never ceased to amaze him how agile she was in shoes that had her walking around on tiptoe all day long. They sure made her legs look pretty, but he couldn't get past the certainty that they had to be uncomfortable.

Brianna held up her right hand and lifted a shoulder in a resigned shrug. "Brock isn't here." Her ring finger was bare. "I had a taxi drop me off."

Cord rubbed his gritty eyes and sighed. He was being rude, making her stand on the front step while he drilled her. Obviously, she'd come with some ulterior motive, and to tell the truth, once he got over the initial shock of seeing at his door, he wasn't really surprised that she'd made her way to Plumwood Hollow in search of him. But he wasn't up for whatever game she was playing. "You can come in, Bri, but you can't stay. If you were hoping for a place to crash for the night, you won't find one here. There's an inn back in town, although they're usually full on the weekends, so you may not be able to get a room there tonight. But if you head back out to the highway and go east about ten miles, you'll hit Muldoon. They'll have a couple of hotels to choose from. My folks have stayed there before."

The disappointed expression on Brianna's face told her he'd hit the nail on the head. Then her eyes lit up.

"Oh! I know. Why don't you come with me? We can go have dinner somewhere and then find a nice place to spend—"

"Stop," Cord said, cutting her off. "That's not going to happen, Bri."

There went that lip again. Did she think that was attractive? Did anyone?

"Okay, fine," she finally said when he didn't change his tune. "What if we stop for dinner on the way to my hotel? I'll call around to find a room for just little old lonesome me while you go get ready, and then after dinner, you can drop me off, okay?" She started toward him again, and this time, he let her in, ignoring the little voice in the back of his mind saying: *Don't do it, Cord. Don't go there. Don't even crack that door or you'll be sorry you did.*

"Dinner on the way," he said with a nod. "Sounds like a plan." Binks had gone to his sister's place for supper, leaving Cord to fend for himself, and although there were some odds and ends and a few leftovers in the refrigerator, a real meal prepared by someone else sounded far better to him. "I'll be ready in about fifteen minutes. You okay to hang out until then? You can even snoop around down here if you promise to be careful. We're packing things up, and everything is a mess."

"Yay!" Brianna gushed, clapping her delicate hands together, her long manicured nails clicking together.

How different she was from the girl next door, both in the literal and figurative sense. Faith Goodacre probably wore shoes like Bri's maybe twice a year. She might even have a black mini skirt somewhere in the back of her closet. But he'd be surprised if Faith's hands ever felt as soft and supple as the hands of the woman who now stood in the middle of his living room. He grimaced. Why was she here again?

"You go shower," she told him, a coy smile on her face. "I'll wait right here, and I promise I'll be good."

THIRTY-TWO

Faith wound her way along the path between the two properties, glad for the light of the big lantern she carried. It wasn't quite yet dark, but in the woods, the shadows fell a little sooner because the trees filtered out much of the day's waning light. If all went well, Cord would drive her safely home, one arm draped around her shoulders, her nestled up against his side in the cab of his new truck.

She pushed through the last of the trees, clambered over the split rail fence, waiting while Jack scooted underneath, then cut across the corner of the near pasture to the backside of the ranch house. In spite of her trepidation, she felt like a million bucks. She wore a pair of black jeans that hugged her curves perfectly, a pale blue camisole under a white crocheted top with a wide neckline, and on her feet was a pair low-heeled kid boots that laced up at her ankle. They were pretty and feminine, but she could traverse the rough trail through the copse without any concern for her ankles.

Binks' cabin was dark, although there was a dull glow emanating from the front window, which meant he was probably at the big house with Cord, maybe still having dinner. Just then, she saw a light flicker on upstairs. Good. He was home.

She knocked on the back door. If she remembered right, it opened into a mudroom, and then you went through to the large kitchen. Certain that Binks would open the door to greet her, she was a little surprised when all remained quiet. She knocked again, then turned the handle of the door, pushing it open to let herself inside. "Hello!" she called out, relieved to find that things were as she remembered them. "Binks? Are you in here?" The kitchen, however, looked completely untouched, and Binks was nowhere to be found.

Faith poked her head around the corner and saw the glow of a light coming from the front room of the house. She followed it. "Hello? Cord?" It occurred to her that she should be at least a little cautious about venturing into a huge house like this one without being certain anyone was home, but she'd seen the light upstairs. "Cord?" she called again from the bottom of the elaborate stairway.

"Who are you and what are you doing here?"

Faith spun on her heels, her heart pounding in surprise, and almost threw the lantern at the woman standing outlined in the archway that led to the front of the house. She'd recognize her anywhere.

A sense of déjà vu coursed through her, turning her blood cold so that her hands began to tremble violently. Afraid she'd drop the old lantern, she set it on a console table against the wall of the wide stairwell. She cleared her throat and in as normal a voice as she could muster, said, "Forgive me. I knocked." She sounded ridiculous. Her brain was working in overdrive as it attempted to connect the dots before her. What was Brianna Peters doing at Whispering Hills? And where was Cord? Or Binks? "I—I guess I should have come around to the front door instead."

"Whatever," Brianna said, waving a hand of dismissal in Faith's direction. "What do you want? And who did you say you were?"

"I'm Faith. A neighbor," she said, nodding in the general direction of Seven Virtues. She took in Brianna's outfit, the fancy strappy heels, the perfect makeup and hair, and her stomach clenched violently. "I'm sorry. I'm intruding. I'll come back another time."

"Do I know you?" Brianna asked, giving Faith a slow once-over. "You look familiar to me."

"No." Faith shook her head. "Not unless you've been here in Plumwood Hollow before. I tend to stay pretty close to home. "

"Um, no." Brianna grimaced as though the thought of regular visits to the hollow was distasteful. "Not a chance."

Faith wanted to slap her. Maybe pull her hair, too.

"Did you and Cord grow up together?" Brianna tapped her full bottom lip as though trying to draw attention to it. "Wait. Aren't you cousins or something?"

"No," Faith said, not wanting to linger a moment longer than she had to. "None of the above."

"Are you sure? I could have sworn there was a cousin around here." The woman did a full spin on her spiky heels. "This place is a disaster, isn't it? I'm so glad Cord is taking me out tonight."

"I'm not Cord's cousin," Faith said quietly. Her hands were shaking, and she was afraid her knees would give out if she stayed any longer. "Look, I'm going to slip out the back door, okay?"

"Yeah, sure. Faith, right? Do you want me to let him know you stopped by?" Brianna smiled demurely, almost slyly, then approached the stairs and took a few steps up. "I should go check on him. See if he's ready yet."

"No, please. You don't need to say anything to him. I'll stop by another day. Sorry to interrupt." Her heart was pounding like a herd of wild horses, and she just needed to get out of the house now. Before Cord came downstairs and found her there exchanging words with his ex-girlfriend. Or was she no longer an ex? "You two have a good evening."

She hurried past the beautiful woman, down the short corridor the way she'd come, and back through the kitchen to the mudroom. She paused there in the shadows of the small room, a hand over her mouth as she tried to calm the adrenaline rushing through her system.

There simply weren't that many explanations for Brianna's presence at Whispering Hills, and none of the reasons Faith could conjure up made her feel any better. She made it outside before the first tear fell, but a moment later, she realized she'd left the lantern behind.

"What am I going to do?" she moaned as she glanced up at the rapidly darkening sky. She could certainly make it back through the trees without the light; even after all these years, she could probably do it blindfolded. She didn't want Cord to know she'd been there, though, and he'd recognize that lantern in a flash—he'd bought it for her at a yard sale they'd stopped by together. Could she sneak back in after they left?

Fighting back the desperate need to race home and bury her head in her pillow, Faith slipped into the shadows along the side of the house and covered her face with her hands. This was not how this night was supposed to play out. It wasn't supposed to end this way. *Why God?*

THIRTY-THREE

CORD TOOK HIS TIME drying off and getting dressed, not because he was so concerned about his appearance, but because he was deeply concerned about Brianna's appearance on his doorstep. The whole time he'd been in the shower, he'd had an overwhelming sense of unrest, and by the time he stepped out, he knew he wasn't going anywhere in public with the woman. For one thing, he knew her well enough to ascertain that she hadn't come all this way to be blown off so easily. As long as he accompanied her anywhere, she'd keep trying. Secondly, he did not want word getting back to Faith that he was seen anywhere with Brianna Peters, innocently or not. No, he'd have to go downstairs now and send her on her way.

"Dang it," he muttered, remembering she'd been dropped off. She probably had a bag somewhere, too. Had he seen one on the front porch? He'd have to deliver her to a hotel. Fine. He'd load her up, drive like a madman to Muldoon, unload the woman at the nearest hotel, and get the heck *back* to Dodge as fast as his Silverado could take him.

"You just about ready, cowboy?"

Cord paused halfway down the stairs, the endearment sickly sweet coming from Brianna. "Don't call me that," he said as she came around the bottom of the stairs... wearing his brand-new Stetson. "And please take off my hat. I don't want it smelling like hairspray."

"Well, aren't you a crabby pants tonight. You must be hungry. Are you ready to go?" Brianna didn't take the hat off, but turned to preen in front of a mirror that hung on the wall at the bottom of the stairs. "I like this hat on me. I'm going to borrow it, okay?"

"Not okay," he said, stepping up behind her and removing the item from her head. "You don't wear a man's hat without his permission, Bri." He wouldn't bother wearing it tonight; it would only egg her on. He turned to set it on the console table and froze.

In a mad rush of memories, he pictured Faith crouching in front of a row of antique kerosene lanterns on the ground, folks milling around her, everyone in search of a treasure or two. It was the kind of yard sale where treasures could be found, and she'd made him stop. "Oh Cord, don't you love these old lanterns? I've always wanted a whole ton of them lighting up my garden." He'd made her choose her favorite; then he'd bought it for her. For the rest of the day, she kept up a montage of songs about light and love, even including the old Sunday school standard, *This Little Light of Mine*. He couldn't hear that song without thinking of Faith and her antique lantern.

"Fine." Brianna puckered up at her reflection, then turned to glance at him over her shoulder. "I'm starving. Where are we going to eat tonight?"

"Where did this come from?" he asked. He hadn't seen it in ten years, and even though it had been converted from kerosene to a battery powered bulb, he would recognize it anywhere. Their initials were scratched into the base of the lantern, and he'd etched a heart into the top corner of one of the panes of glass. He picked it up: both were still clearly visible. "This wasn't here before."

"Oh, that."

Something in the way she said it had him spinning on his heel to glare at her. "Yeah, this. How did it get here?"

"Some girl stopped by. Your cousin, I think?"

His cousin? *Right.* "You mean Faith? She was here?"

Brianna shrugged. "Could have been. I don't remember her name. Said she'd come back when you weren't busy." She crossed to his side and looped her arm through his. "Come on. Let's go eat."

Cord jerked away from her grasp as understanding dawned. "You spoke to her? What did you say to her? What did you tell her?" It must have been bad for Faith to have all but fled the scene, leaving behind her cherished lantern.

Bri made a pouty face. "Don't look at me like that. I told her we were going out to eat; that's all."

Cord wanted to growl in frustration. "We're not going out to eat, Bri. I'm taking you straight to your hotel. Did you find one?" He touched the panel of glass just below the heart. It was still warm.

"Not yet. I thought I'd wait until after we got a bite to eat."

"You said you were going to make those calls while I was upstairs. What were you doing?" He was getting loud; he needed to calm down so he could deal with this disruptive woman.

"I was exploring. You said I could."

Cord took a deep breath, grabbed the lantern, set his hat on the table in its place, then gestured toward the front door. "Let's go. You can make your calls in the car. If you don't have something lined up by the time we hit Muldoon, I'll pull into the first hotel we come to."

"I need to get my bag," Brianna said, pulling away from him. "I brought it in while you were upstairs."

On the floor in the middle of the living room was a large tapestry suitcase on wheels. She'd come prepared for an extended visit. He set down the lantern, picked up the suitcase, and snapped in Brianna's direction, "Wait here. I'll be right back."

He was out the door before she could protest, and with his anger boiling just under the surface, he none too gently tossed the suitcase into the bed of his truck and strapped it down. Then he headed back inside to fetch the girl.

Part of him felt bad for his brusque treatment of this woman he'd had such a long, albeit shallow, relationship with. But he'd made it clear any number of times that there was no future for them. So, for her to show up unannounced—no, for her to arrange to be dropped off on his doorstep like an abandoned puppy—to try to coerce him into taking her in, was beyond out of line. In fact, it was time to make something else abundantly clear to Brianna Peters.

He ushered her out the front door toward his truck, his hand on the back of her arm, keeping her close so she wouldn't pull something desperate, like feigning a fall in her heels. She'd do something like that to get her way; he didn't doubt that for a moment. He pulled open the passenger side door, helped her up into the cab, careful not to look at her legs when she hiked up her skirt even higher around her thighs to get in.

"That woman? She wasn't my cousin," he said, then closed the door and hurried around to his side. "She's my next-door neighbor."

He started the truck, then continued talking about Faith as he made his way down the paved lane to Carpenter Road. "That woman is Faith Goodacre, the love of my life. She is also the mother of my daughter, and the woman I'm going to marry." He pulled to a stop at the bottom of the drive and let the truck idle, even though there was no cross traffic. "Is there any part of that you don't understand? I don't mean to be cruel; I just need to make this very clear to you, Bri."

"I understand," she murmured, her voice soft, but oozing with unsavory petulance. "What I don't understand was why you didn't say so earlier. Or why she didn't tell me so. And why were you willing to take me to dinner half an hour ago, but now you're not?"

Cord groaned. She was right. He was sending mixed messages across the board to both women. "A momentary lapse in judgment, that's all. A really stupid one." One that may have just caused a major setback in their tenuous relationship just by letting Brianna in his front door.

He wanted her out of his truck, off his property, and out of his life. He didn't wish ill on her; he just wanted to be free of her. Before he pulled out from the driveway, he said, "That's not your problem, it's mine. But in the future, if you ever show up unannounced again, if you ever decide to get dropped off without any forewarning, if you attempt to reach out to me for any reason but the most mundane and innocent—and even then, your motive will be subject to my scrutiny, be forewarned—I will make sure it becomes your problem, okay?" He'd kept his words level, calm, even though his blood was boiling.

"Is that a threat?" Brianna asked, her voice now dripping with sarcasm. "Because I don't like threats."

"No, it's not a threat. It's a promise. Because I don't like surprises like the one you just pulled on me today. Especially in light of the fact that I made it abundantly clear the last time we spoke, that we were no longer in any kind of relationship."

Brianna snorted indelicately. "You and I will always be in a relationship of some kind, Cord Overman. Either in one or in between one."

He shook his head so forcefully that he felt something pull in the back of his neck. "Your response is exactly why I'm making this promise to you right now. If anything like this happens again, I will slap a restraining on you so fast you won't know what hit you."

"You wouldn't."

"I will." He pulled out onto Carpenter Road and thrust his chin at the handbag clutched in her lap. "Make your phone calls."

THIRTY-FOUR

FAITH WATCHED AS CORD first loaded up the large suitcase, then went back for Brianna. He held the woman close to his side, a gesture so possessive and alpha male it made her want to hate him even more. To her utter dismay, she saw he had her lantern clutched in his other arm, and when he helped Bri in the truck, she overheard him tell her that Faith wasn't his cousin, she was just the girl next door.

She turned on her heel and made her way back toward the trees without her lantern, without Cord, without her heart.

Poor Jasmine. She would be devastated.

An hour later, she was flat on her back in the loft of the abandoned hay barn, staring up at the stars through a hole in the ceiling. She couldn't bring herself to go home, to face her family knowing she'd lost Cord all over again.

She'd found Jack milling about on the Goodacre side of the fence line waiting for her. Which meant that Jasmine and Daddy were likely not home yet. She made an about turn, called Jack to follow her, and they followed the dirt lane to the hay barn. Jack even climbed the ladder up to the loft; a trick Faith and Jasmine had worked with him on for weeks.

She reached over and stroked the dogs head, listening to the sounds around here. She knew better than to believe she and her dog were the only living creatures seeking refuge in the barn that night, but she hoped the two of them would be big and clumsy enough to keep the rats and other creepy crawlies at bay.

Suddenly, Jack's head popped up, and he emitted a low growl deep in his throat. It wasn't loud, but it was certainly menacing. Faith pushed up on one elbow and cocked her head to listen better.

"Faith? Are you in here?"

Cord. What was he doing here? She sat up and crossed her legs, drawing Jack close in front of her as though he might shield her from Cord.

"Faith?" He held her lantern aloft, the soft glow of the bulb casting long shadows around the rustic space.

"I'm here," she said. "So is Jack."

He disappeared from view, but a moment later, his head rose above the edge of the loft, followed by the lantern, and then the rest of his body as he climbed up the ladder into the loft beside her. Jack, thrilled to be surrounded by some of his favorite people, welcomed Cord with lavish dog kisses and tail whips. Cord hung the lantern from a beam above their heads, then turned to face Faith. He didn't touch her; he just waited for her to meet his gaze. "You are so beautiful to me, Faith Goodacre."

She opened her mouth to spout off something about Brianna Peters being beautiful to him, too, but the look in his eyes stilled her.

"I heard you came by my house looking for me, only to find Brianna Peters instead."

Faith said nothing, just stroked Jack's head.

"She was there against my wishes, Faith. She had a taxi drop her off at my front door, unannounced, and with a packed bag. This was after I told her in no uncertain terms that we had no relationship. That anything we once had wasn't authentic, anyway. And that conversation took place almost two years ago."

"She said you were taking her out to dinner tonight."

Cord nodded. "I made the mistake of compromising for just a moment tonight. I told her I'd deliver her to her hotel, and we could stop for dinner on the way. I changed my mind about that before I even came downstairs again. *Before* I saw your lantern," he added.

"I was still there when you left," Faith murmured, finding it hard to sit quietly and listen to what he was saying. It made sense, his version of things, but it didn't completely erase the last hour she'd spent in complete and utter misery. "I was going to sneak back in and grab my lantern after you left." She picked up a piece of straw and began to wind it around her finger. "I heard you tell her that I was just your neighbor."

Cord reached over and took her hand in his, unwinding the straw and tossing it aside. "Your fingertip is going to turn black and fall off," he said, lifting her hand to press a kiss into her palm. "I'm sorry you didn't hear the rest of what I told her about you." He slid a little closer, his thigh resting against hers. "Let me do my best to repeat it...." He kissed the tip of her thumb. "That woman is not my cousin; she's my neighbor." He kissed the tip of her forefinger. "That woman is Faith Goodacre, the love of my life." He kissed the tip of her middle finger. "That woman is also the mother of my daughter." He kissed her ring finger. "That is the woman I'm going to marry." Then he kissed the tip of her pinkie finger and reached up to cup her face with his other hand. "You are the woman I choose. It's always been you, Faith. I have loved you from the moment I first laid eyes on you." He leaned closer until their foreheads touched. "Do you think you could learn to love me again? Do you think Jasmine can learn to love me, too? Is there hope for me?"

"It's too late for that," Faith whispered, then she tipped her face, so her lips brushed his, and whispered against his mouth, "We already do. I love you, Cord. And it's always been you, too."

THIRTY-FIVE

THE STARS IN THE velvet sky were especially bright as Cord lay on his back on a soft blanket in the hayloft, one arm around his fiancée as he held her close against his side, the other arm around his daughter, as he held her tight against his other side. The hole in the roof was just the right size for all three of them to stare up at the beauty above them.

"I think I can hear the stars singing," Jasmine whispered. "It's not really a tune. More like they're humming to each other. Like this. Hmmmmmm." She let out a high-pitched delicate note and held it.

Faith hummed in harmony with Jasmine, their voices blending sweetly.

Cord started out around a third below that, but then his note drifted, fell flat, rose slightly, then drifted flat again.

Jack took that as his cue, and he lifted his snout toward the hold in the roof and howled plaintively, until they were all laughing and rolling around like children, tickling and wrestling, and yes, there was even a little kissing between the adults. Because Faith Goodacre, soon to be the wife of Cordell Overman, couldn't stop kissing him.

"Hey, you two lovebirds," Jasmine said, interrupting them with a poke to the ribs. "I just saw a shooting star. Know what I wished for?"

Cord poked her back, and she giggled. "A pony?" he asked.

"Nope," came the little girl's reply. "I already have one. Guess again." She drew her knees up to her chest and rocked back and forth, a happy smile on her face.

"A puppy?" Faith asked. "One like Jack?"

"I wouldn't mind a puppy like Jack," she said, scrambling to her hands and knees, then crawling between her parents and wedging herself in tightly. "But that's not it, either."

"A house of our own?" Faith suggested. "That's what I wish for." Cord turned to smile at her over Jasmine's head. He gently brushed his fingers up and down her arm.

"Nope. Besides, Daddy is already making us a home, aren't you?" Jasmine said, lifting her face to Cord's.

"That's the plan," he said, planting a kiss on her forehead. "So, what did you wish for, Peanut?"

"Well, I kinda have everything else I ever wished for, even my own grandma now." Dalton and Carmelita had just spent the last two weeks in Plumwood Hollow with them, and Jasmine had fallen in love with her new grandparents almost as hard as they'd fallen for her. "So, I think it's about time I wished for a baby. I don't care if it's a boy or a girl, so you guys can decide. But I thought it was silly to wish on a star without telling you since you guys are the ones who have to make it. So maybe you should get on it soon since it takes forever for a baby to come out."

Faith did her best to stifle her giggle, but when Cord chuckled unabashedly, she laughed out loud.

"Give us a little time for that, okay?" Cord asked, poking Jasmine in the nose. "We need to get married first."

"And figure out where we're going to live," Faith added. They still hadn't made a decision about that.

Cord slid his arm out from under both girls and got to his feet. "Stay right there, you two. I want to show you something." He swung his legs over the edge of the loft and dropped to the ground below.

"Careful, Daddy. Don't break your legs." Jasmine called out. He still thrilled at the sound of his daughter calling him Daddy. Being a father humbled and awed him every day, but the two of them were quickly adapting to each other, and now they interacted as though they'd spent every day of their lives together.

Cord scaled the ladder to find his two girls waiting patiently where he'd left them. He hoisted himself back into the loft, a cardboard tube in his hand. He held it out to Faith. "Your wish is my command. Open it." Then he took down the lantern that hung from a chain above them and settled down beside her, holding the light closer so they could see the mock-up she withdrew and unrolled on the blanket in front of them.

"This is beautiful," Faith began, a curious look on her face as she studied the 3D image of a two-story house nestled in a grove of trees. "I don't recognize it, though. When did you come up with this one?"

"Look, mama!" Jasmine pointed at a round window in the roof of an upstairs bedroom. "It has a stargazing hole just like our loft."

Faith's gaze went from the round skylight in the drawing to the round hole in the roof above them, and then to Cord, her eyes sparkling with excitement. "Is this our hay barn?"

He nodded and leaned forward to kiss her tenderly. "Right here. Smack dab in the middle of both ranches."

Jasmine pumped her fists exuberantly. "Can I have the stargazing room?"

"Read the name on the bedroom door." Cord beamed at his daughter.

"Jasmine! It says Jasmine! Mama, it's already my room even before I wished it." She threw her little arms around Cord, nearly strangling him in her exuberance. "Now all I need is a baby brother or sister, and I will have everything I ever wished for."

Faith returned the sketch to the cardboard tube and lay back on the blanket, the drawing held to her chest as she gazed up at the stars hanging like jewels in the night sky.

Cord watched her, reveling in his wife's contagious joy. Jasmine, his daughter, snuggled into his embrace and said, "You're so pretty, Mama," in as candid a compliment as anyone could give.

"Thank you, baby," Faith said, flashing a sweet smile at the girl. When she turned those dreamy liquid amber eyes on him, he said the only words that came to mind.

"And they all lived happily ever after."

***

Ready for the next book in the series?

~ ~ ~

Where There is HOPE: Seven Virtues Ranch Romance Book 2

Doc Hope is the woman to call when your pet is ailing, your cow stops eating, or your horse goes lame. She understands animals a whole lot better than she does people; that's for sure. She's sworn off men in particular since her husband walked off right before their second anniversary.

She should have seen it coming - his leaving. Apparently, everyone else did. But Hope... well, Hope hoped.

Local butcher Levi Valiente is exceptionally skilled with a curved blade and a bone saw, the tools of his trade. He's also a good man, a great dad, and he knows how to treat the women in his life. Except, perhaps, for his wife, who walked out on their family right before their daughter's first birthday.

He certainly saw it coming - her leaving. He saw it coming a mile away.

But Levi's tired of hiding his great big heart behind the shield of self-doubt he carries, and he'd like to believe that where there's Doc Hope, there's a good chance of happily ever after, too.

Hope, however, might take some convincing. The strong, silent, single father is a longtime family friend, and with her track record, she's sure she'll just mess things up for everyone.

~ ~ ~

Pick up **Where There is Hope** today, or keep reading for a sneak peek.

A Note from Becky

An Excerpt: Where There is Hope

Chapter 1

~ ~ ~

SHE WAS TOO LATE. They had waited too long to call her, and by the time she arrived on the scene, there was little she could do except to pull the dead baby from the birth canal. The first-calf heifer was on her feet and actively pushing with the contractions, but it had been a good six hours or longer since the onset of labor, and the poor girl only shuffled her hind legs half-heartedly when Hope slid a well-lubricated arm inside her.

The first order of business was to get the calf's head through the pelvic opening. The front feet were protruding enough for Hope to get the OB chains around them, but unless she got that head dislodged, the baby wasn't going anywhere. With one last effort, she slid her arm into the birth canal all the way to her shoulder, until her cheek was practically pressed against the trembling, filthy flank of the cow. This would all be worth it if we were pulling a live calf, she silently bemoaned.

There! With a forceful downward push on the calf's nose, the head shifted and engaged. "I think that did it," she said to Doug Hayward over her shoulder. "Let's get the jack on her."

The farmer was ready with the calf puller, and while Doug set the steel yoke into place against the cow's hips, Hope notched the pull chains onto the gears. Then Doug cranked the ratchet with each contraction, while Hope continued to manipulate the calf's position until finally, it was expelled onto the hay-strewn stall floor.

She peeled off the shoulder-length glove and assessed the baby for any signs of life. She already knew it was futile. There was no pulse, no response to any stimuli, and the opaque cloud over the eyes indicated the little female had succumbed to oxygen deprivation a couple of hours ago.

"Will she be all right, Dr. Hope?" Mona, Doug's wife, stood on the other side of the stall wall, a tiny baby in an infant carrier strapped to her chest. She'd stayed there throughout the ordeal, speaking low and soothing words to the distressed mama cow.

She wasn't asking about the calf, Hope knew. Doug and Mona, a young couple with a tiny homestead, two young school-age children, and the new baby, had spent their savings on Lola. She'd come to them already bred, and they'd had high hopes of getting a family milk cow, as well as a calf to sell, to recoup some of their investment. There'd been nothing left to pay for vet services, and they'd done everything they could on their own before finally conceding that they were in trouble. They'd called Hope already knowing that the best thing they could do now was to save Lola.

"She should be fine, Mona. This was tough, but it's pretty common for first-time mamas to need help. We'll treat her for any potential infections, and you'll need to monitor her for the next couple of days, but I have high hopes for her to have a full recovery." Hope stood and dragged the calf around to Lola's head, then released the cow from where she'd been tied to the stall gate so she could have some time to examine her baby.

"Will she be able to be bred again?" Doug asked as he dissembled the calf puller, careful not to watch as Lola nudged and licked the lifeless form on the ground in front of her. He was likely already trying to figure out ways to come up with the money for Hope's visit.

Hope understood their financial dilemma and didn't condemn them for it. As picturesque as Plumwood Hollow looked on the surface, there was some real need in the community. A lot of folks lived paycheck to paycheck just to keep the utilities on, and having healthy livestock providing basics, like milk and meat, was essential for survival. She could see it in the worry lines on Doug and Mona's faces, and it broke her heart to know that the couple, already in such a tight financial situation, would now have another bill to pay. Hope would do jobs like this for next to nothing, but most folks in the hollow weren't keen on that kind of charity. They understood the value of hard work, of earning what they called their own, and they had a sincere appreciation for the services Dr. Hope provided. Sometimes payment came in the form of eggs, meat, and garden produce. Other times, it might be a quilt, or homemade soaps and salves. She'd even received some home-distilled moonshine—apple pie once, and another time, peach cobbler—but her clients always paid, one way or another.

"She will," Hope assured him, circling the cow to do a final examination. "Everything seems intact, and she's alert and doing what a new mama should." She glanced over at Mona. The young woman was watching the tragic scene with tears tracking slowly down her cheeks, her arms wrapped tenderly around the child in the sling. Hope had to look away lest she succumb to the emotions she worked hard to keep at bay in circumstances like these. This family's grief was for so much more than just a lost calf.

"I will be upfront with you, Doug. Sometimes, for whatever reason, cows that have had a difficult delivery will sometimes have a harder time getting pregnant again. But Lola here seems quite healthy to me; she's been well cared for." She ran a hand down the knobby ridges of the cow's back. "You'll need to give her a little time to recover, but I don't see any reason for her not to go on and produce many fine young animals for you."

"I'll talk to my foreman about taking on some extra hours at the plant." Doug faced her with his chin high, then picked up Hope's bulky medical bag from where she'd dropped it in the corner of the stall. "You'll bill me?"

Hope eyed him speculatively. He was a sturdy country boy, probably about her age, and he'd been easy to work with, quick to respond to anything she'd asked of him, and he'd paid close attention to her instructions throughout the ordeal. "I'll bill you, Doug; that's my standard protocol. But if you're looking for extra hours, I could use your help, if you're open to it."

Mona sniffed softly and wiped at her eyes as she turned her attention on them. Doug frowned, already suspicious. "What do you have in mind?"

There was no running water in the small barn, so Hope popped the lid off a gallon jug she'd brought in and poured generous amounts of the cold water over her hands. She'd wash again more thoroughly when she had access to hot water and soap. She dried off using one of the clean towels she kept in her kit, giving herself a few more moments to make sure she was handling things right with Doug. She hadn't really thought this through, and she didn't want to make an offer she'd regret, but it did seem like providential timing.

She opted for honesty with these good folks, no matter how hard it was. "You may already know this, but, um, my husband—soon to be ex-husband—is no longer living in Plumwood Hollow." Her cheeks burned with a sudden wash of humiliation and a sense of inadequacy that seemed to catch her by surprise far too often since Chet's departure. She glanced first at Mona, then Doug. Their stoic faces showed no surprise at her revelation. Good old small-town gossip.

Chet worked from home as a consultant who specialized in creating business plans and financial statements and doing market research for small startup companies. He liked animals well enough, which was a good thing in light of the fact that Hope spent so much time with them. Because he conducted the majority of his business online, his work hours were flexible, making him available around Hope's crazy schedule so they could spend time together. It had seemed like a match made in heaven. At first, anyway.

Mona's baby, a tiny girl no more than a month old, made a sweet, cooing gurgle that melted Hope's heart. One day she might end up with a baby of her own. She was already accustomed to functioning on too little sleep and trying to care for creatures that couldn't tell her what was wrong. She'd probably be good at being a mother. She supposed having a father in the picture might be nice, too. Her oldest sister had already pulled the single mother routine, and Hope had seen firsthand how difficult it could be, even with a huge family around to help her out, and a child who was so delightful, she had to be part angel.

Start with a man who wants to stick around, then we'll go from there, she reminded herself.

"You needing someone to explain things to him?" Doug's question sounded so innocuous that it took Hope a moment to figure out what he was asking. Then her eyes widened as his meaning dawned on her.

"Oh!" Yep. They'd definitely heard about Cheating Chet. Doug was a good ol' country boy, for sure, the kind who had certain ideas about how a real man should behave. "No, no. Thank you, but that's not what—I mean, no." She shot the man a sardonic grimace. "Tempting, to be sure, but that's not really the kind of help I need right now."

He nodded but left it at that. Hope couldn't help wondering what it would be like to have a man like Doug looking out for her. A little scary, a little intense, yes, but maybe a little nice, too. As long as "explaining" things didn't involve tire irons or hunting rifles, or anything else that might wind him up in jail, she supposed, which would only leave her as alone as she was now.

She continued. "Anyway, I had started the process of recruiting a new vet right before—you know, before he left," she said, waving a hand in an impatient gesture. "We've been in need of another one—and another assistant or two, truth be told—for some time now, particularly to help during birthing season. Sometimes my dad is available to help out, but he can only do so much." Everyone in the hollow had rallied around the Goodacres several years ago when Jedediah's tractor accident nearly killed him. He'd survived, by the grace of God, but his right leg and hip were permanently damaged, and his back often caused him severe, debilitating pain, preventing him from doing many of the ranching activities he'd known all his life. Hope did her best not to let Jed do any heavy lifting, although she had to do so without embarrassing him. He knew his limitations, but he was also a proud ranching man accustomed to hard work. "But because of the divorce, I've had to put everything on hold until the air clears a little. In the meantime, I'm begging, borrowing, and bartering for any muscle power I can get."

Doug, with her medical bag and calf puller in hand, held the stall gate open for her, still not saying a word.

Mona had no such reservations. "Why do you need to wait until the divorce is final? You need help now." She came around to stand next to Doug. "Birthing season is already well underway."

Hope grimaced as she stepped out of the pen. "I know. Unfortunately, my husband—soon to be ex-husband—is trying to convince the courts that I should sell my practice and give him half the proceeds. So, it's been suggested that I put the brakes on any hiring for now."

"Dr. Hope!" Mona gasped. "That's terrible. Does he have any idea how much our community depends on you? Please tell me you're not considering it."

The good thing about being forthright is that it took Mona's attention away from the sad scene still unfolding inside the stall between the cow and her stillborn calf.

"No. I am not. I am fighting this tooth and nail. And I did not tell you this to badmouth my husband. Soon to be ex-husband."

"Why don't you just call him by his name?" Doug suggested in his hill country twang. "Seeing as how you don't really have a hankering to claim him anymore." He looked like he might have a hankering to 'explain' things to Chet whether she wanted him to or not.

"Good idea," Hope said with a nod. "Anyway, think about it. Clearly, I'm not built to manhandle anything much bigger than a miniature goat," she said with a self-deprecating grin. That wasn't quite true; she might hit five-foot-three on a good day, and only first thing in the morning before the weight of the world compressed her spine and made her shoulders droop, but Hope knew her way around large farm animals, and they were her favorite to work with. "Sometimes dealing with trouble in the bigger horses and cattle can be a bit of a task for me when I'm on my own. During the day, if I get desperate, I can have Sarah help me, although that leaves the clinic with only Patty Lynn manning the desk and taking phone calls. I do have a part-time tech, Rodney—have you met him?—but he's only there three mornings a week." Rodney also preferred working with dogs and cats and other domesticated pets, and the few times she'd taken him on farm calls with her, she'd been as worried about him as she'd been about the patient. He was great around the clinic, but out in the field, not so much. "We simply need more help. And with Cord Overman working on getting the rodeo set up on his property?" She shrugged, feeling overwhelmed just thinking about the influx of new patients to come out of that.

But because of Chet's selfish demands on something he had no share in....

Thinking of the man who had promised to love and cherish her for the rest of his life, but who seemed to love and cherish her business, instead—or the money he thought he could get out of it—always made her a little worked up.

"Anyway," she said, drawing the word out in an effort to curtail her thoughts. "I know you work full time, Doug, and you have a family." She smiled at Mona who absentmindedly stroked the top of her baby's head. "Those need to remain your priorities if you're going to help me, so I'd only call on you if it were somewhere close by, and if I really needed you. Most of the time, I can handle things with the help of whatever rancher or farmer is on hand. But sometimes, I end up at a place where I'm kind of on my own, and it would be helpful to have an extra body with a little bit of muscle on the scene. It would just be after hours, like being on call." She was blabbering. She did that when she got nervous or upset, and thinking about Chet always upset her. "Maybe once or twice a week for two or three weeks—that would more than cover my bill."

Doug nodded once, then exchanged a meaningful look with his wife.

"So, if the only reason you're considering taking on extra hours at the factory is so you can pay this bill, maybe instead, you'd consider helping me out now and then until I can hire some more help." She sounded like she was trying to sell him something. She should just be quiet and let him think. Chet had said that to her once or twice or a hundred times…

"I'll do it." The man held out a large, work-roughened hand to shake on the deal.

"We haven't even discussed how much your bill is or how much your time is worth." It didn't matter; Hope already knew she'd be shaking hands with the man regardless of the details. He'd already made up his mind.

"I trust you'll do right by me, Dr. Hope. I'll do the same by you. I'm a good listener; you can ask my wife."

"He is," Mona said, beaming up at her husband.

Doug brushed the backs of his fingers against Mona's forearm. "And I ain't afraid of hard work, ugly situations, or a little bit of bone and gore, I can assure you."

Hope laughed. "I think you and I will do just fine." Then she turned and smiled at Mona, but when the young mother stepped close to hug her, Hope held up both hands. "You don't want to hug me. I'm pretty sure there are at least five different kinds of bovine bodily fluids on me."

Mona hugged her anyway, and from the corner of her eye, Hope saw Doug smile for the first time since she'd arrived. He watched his wife and child with something that made Hope's heart ache to see.

Had Chet ever looked at her that way?

Enough! She silently berated herself. She turned one last look on the stall behind her. The cow had lost interest in the calf and was in a different corner with her nose in a trough of fresh hay.

Stillbirths always hit her hard. They were one of the hardest aspects of her job.

Hope's day didn't get any better. Sally Fields—not that Sally Fields. However, this Sally Fields liked to point out that she and that Sally Fields did share some similar features, like brown eyes and brown hair—brought in her old Bassett Hound, Burt Reynolds. Not that Burt Reynolds, either, although some in the hollow liked to point out that this Burt Reynolds and that Burt Reynolds did share some similar features, like their brown eyes and thick coats of brown fur. Apparently, Burt Reynolds discovered Sally Fields' stash of chocolate kisses in the bottom drawer of her bedside stand. "Somehow he managed to get it open just enough to pull the bag out," Sally explained in between sobs. Unfortunately, the dog had also managed to eat the nearly full bag of the dark chocolate treats, and Sally hadn't realized the cause of his horrific symptoms until she'd gone to her room to grab a pair of shoes so she could drive the dog to see Hope.

By the time they arrived, Burt Reynolds was having seizures, and because the dog was ancient and already suffered from congenital heart disease, all Hope was able to do at that point was to make him comfortable before putting him down.

Right after lunch, she was called out to check on one of the reindeer at Klaus's Christmas Tree Farm. The animal was only about nine months old. He'd been born on the farm last summer and had charmed tree shoppers with his playful antics during the holiday season. But now, having made it through the worst of the winter months, he was flagging noticeably, and for the life of her, Hope couldn't figure out why. She took some blood and fecal samples, and gave the animal a vitamin boost, but left Peter Klaus no less concerned than when she'd arrived. The man had four reindeer, and he took care of them like they were his family, so Hope didn't think it was due to mistreatment or inadequate care. She hoped the lab work would clear things up quickly.

She got back with just enough time to treat a fat hamster with a respiratory infection, followed by a cockatiel who'd been roughed up by the family cat, before she headed out on another call to Ben Crawley's sheep farm. A ewe had been discovered in great distress after having delivered a stillborn lamb, which was sad enough on its own merit. The concern, however, wasn't the lamb, but the fact that the sheep was on the ground with a prolapsed uterus hanging outside of her body, and Ben had no clue how long she'd been down. Hope found some significant discoloring of the uterine tissue, indicating it had been a while. She'd done what she could to repair the damage, but the ewe seemed to have given up already. It was common with sheep; the animals reminded her of Eeyore from Hundred Acre Wood, in that when they ran into trouble, they simply decided they were doomed and quit trying to survive. She left Ben doing what he could to coax and encourage the animal to stay on her feet. Hope wasn't sure which of the two would give up first, but she had a feeling Ben would be the only one left to tell of it come morning.

Around four o'clock, she headed across town to assess a goat buck who had gotten his horns stuck in a section of hog wire. Seeing easy pickings for the taking, a stray dog had dug under the fence to get to it and had managed to tear a pretty big chunk of flesh from the big goat's side before the farmer intervened. "I couldn't help but think of that scene in Jurassic Park," the owner said, so matter of fact that Hope couldn't tell if he was trying to be funny or not. She glanced up from examining the animal as he continued. "You know the part. It's where they tied that goat to a stake for the T-Rex's lunch."

The goat would survive, but the stray dog had met its maker, according to the farmer. Hope didn't ask for details.

She returned to the clinic only minutes ahead of a man and his two young children bringing their family dog in. The yellow lab had been hit by a car, and Hope could tell just by looking at him that the animal was shutting down. Watching the kids grieve was hard enough, but when their big, strong daddy broke down and wept behind his hands, and the kids moved in to hug and comfort him, Hope had to leave the room lest she hurtle herself into the middle of the melee and fall apart, too.

By the time she closed up and started next door to her little cottage, all she wanted to do was take a shower, eat a whole pizza pie by herself, and fall into bed. She was already exhausted, and there was no telling what the night would bring. Being only one of two animal hospitals in the county, hers was always bustling with activity, but because Hope specialized in large animals and particularly stock animals, she was in high demand around the clock, especially during birthing season. As much as she didn't want to attribute anything good to her soon to be ex-husband, having Chet around had eased her load a little. On days like today, when she was worn out, he'd field her calls so she could sleep. And he'd kept her fed when she was too tired to even remember to eat. Granted, he didn't do any cooking, so the meals were typically take-out, and his efforts were motivated more by his own hunger than by hers, but food was food, and she was grateful for it. Besides, she wasn't much of a cook herself, so she wasn't about to pick on Chet for something so mundane.

No, it was the big things she wanted to pick on him about. Or rather, the one big thing named Shelby Whitaker. And truth be told, she wanted to do a whole lot more than pick on Cheating Chet. If she had her way with him, why she'd—she'd....

"You're hopeless," she muttered. "Pitiful and hopeless." Because, truth be told, she wasn't the type to rip his heart out or throw a vase at him. No, she'd probably get all weepy and ask him why.

Which would be futile, because she already knew why. Chet had quickly grown to hate her unpredictable, round-the-clock hours. He'd come to loathe the late-night calls that pulled her out of their warm cocoon of a bed, leaving him alone with his arms empty of anything except her cold pillow. He hated how she smelled when she got home at the end of the day, and the way her scrubs and Crocs—not to mention the Carhartt coveralls she pulled on over top of everything for messy or cold jobs—made her look so frumpy. He hated that she was too tired to go out on the weekends with him. He hated that she could be called away at any moment, no matter how inopportune. Most of all, he hated that she would interrupt whatever it was they were doing and go.

It didn't matter that he knew what he was signing up for when he married her. It didn't matter that he was the one who'd changed, not her.

Because eventually, he came to hate her, which he believed gave him license to find someone to take her place.

Chapter 2

~ ~ ~

He was too late. He had waited too long, and now she was leaving for the day. Levi sat in his SUV and watched Hope pull the door of her clinic closed after her. She'd made it halfway down the sidewalk before she turned around and went back to check it, only to find it unlocked. She looked exhausted, like she could barely hold her head up, and Levi tightened his grip on the steering wheel.

He imagined, just for a second, that he held Chet Willis' scrawny neck in his hands, and he squeezed just a little harder. The fact that the man had abandoned Hope Goodacre last summer was bad enough. That he'd left her for the bit of arm candy Levi had seen him with several months ago over in Muldoon was even worse. From what Levi could surmise, the girl plastered against Chet's side was little more than cotton candy on legs. He didn't think it was possible for anyone to be that air-headed, or that sugary sweet, not in real life. Either that, or she was as much of a chameleon as Chet Willis was, using whatever worked to get what she wanted. If so, they both deserved each other.

Hope Goodacre, on the other hand—he still had a hard time thinking of her as Hope Willis—deserved a heck of a lot better than Chet Willis. Sure, the guy was inarguably a golden boy with his slick charm, fancy suits, and ridiculous curly blond hair. But Levi had a feeling Mr. Willis was the kind of man who was accustomed to getting what he wanted, to having things his way. According to Faith, Hope's older sister, Chet's gripe about how much time Hope spent with other people's animals wasn't because he worried about her welfare, but because it meant she wasn't spending time with him.

In Levi's not so unbiased opinion, Chet Willis was still nothing but a spoiled little boy.

None of that changed the fact that Hope was clearly suffering over the man's actions and decisions. Levi hoped it had more to do with the embarrassment and inconvenience he'd caused her, rather than a broken heart. On the other hand, he understood how devastating it could be to have someone you love not love you enough to stay.

He would never forget the day he came home from work to find his wife of four years, Veronica, sitting on the top step of the front porch, her packed suitcase waiting beside her. Their baby girl, Yvette, not quite six months old, was asleep in her crib in their bedroom. Ironically, Veronica hadn't slept in their bedroom since before the baby was born, but Levi had believed her when she said it was due to her hormones being completely out of whack, that she just needed time. The midwife assured them that the postpartum blues Veronica was experiencing were common and encouraged her to get help if she felt like she couldn't handle it. Levi paid close attention to how his wife behaved with Yvette, and although she remained distant and reserved toward him, he was confident that she was a good mother to their daughter. Yvette was remarkably sweet and content, and when Veronica put their tiny infant to her breast, there was nothing more beautiful to Levi than his two girls connecting so intimately and naturally.

As he approached the porch that day, he could tell Veronica had been crying for some time. Her nose was pink, and her pretty brown eyes were puffy and red-rimmed, although she'd taken extra care with her makeup to camouflage it. But the look on her face told him everything he needed to know. She was leaving, and there would be no talking her out of it.

"I need you to take me to the airport, please. I just fed the baby, so she will probably sleep the whole way there." Veronica's accent was always noticeably richer when she was emotionally charged, but that day, her words came out flat and dry. "I'll feed her again when we get there so you won't have to worry about her being hungry on the way home."

Levi had felt a strange combination of relief and horror as what she was saying sunk in. She wasn't just leaving him; she was leaving their child, too. "How long do you plan to stay away?" he asked, trying to keep his voice steady and calm.

"I won't be back, Levi." She'd stood, picked up her bag, and moved down the porch steps, heading for the truck. When he reached for her suitcase, she jerked away as though she thought he might try to force her to stay. Her reaction hurt almost as bad as her words.

"Let me at least carry your bag for you," he'd said in as soothing a tone as he could muster. He didn't want Veronica to see how gutted he felt in that moment. She needed him to be strong, even though she was the one tearing his insides out. It had always been that way.

Her eyes filled with tears again, but they didn't spill over. "I'll wait in the car while you get the baby," she'd said.

"Her name is Yvette, remember?" He hated hearing her refer to their daughter as a nameless infant, but when she climbed into the passenger side of the vehicle without saying another word, Levi had suddenly recognized what she was doing; Veronica was distancing herself from Yvette just as she'd done with him over the last six months or more.

It had been the longest, yet shortest drive he'd ever had to endure. Just like Veronica had predicted, Yvette slept peacefully the whole way there.

Levi, on the other hand, wept silently as he drove, unable to staunch the tears that ran in slow rivulets from the corners of his eyes.

Veronica sat stiff and still in the passenger seat; her focus trained on the road ahead of them.

He'd finally worked up the courage to ask her where she was going, and she hadn't hesitated to tell him. She was heading to Florida where she had a job and a place to stay already waiting for her. One of her best friends from high school—a girl who'd been a bridesmaid in their wedding—lived in Tampa, and Veronica would sleep on her couch until she could get a place of her own.

When they arrived at the airport, she asked Levi to hand her the baby, and she nursed Yvette without even looking at her. Unable to stay and witness the irreparably broken scene, Levi had taken a walk to try to process through some of the immense grief that threatened to consume him. Somehow, he'd failed his beautiful wife, and in so doing, he'd failed their precious baby girl. For the life of him, he couldn't figure out what he'd done to make Veronica prefer leaving to staying.

He returned to the truck to find her standing beside the open passenger door, her suitcase by her side, its handle extended. She'd already buckled Yvette back into her car seat, and the tiny girl waved a chubby hand in front of her, fascinated by the sounds of the wrist rattle she wore.

"I will text you when I arrive to let you know that I'm safe," Veronica had said without preamble. Then she'd lifted her eyes to meet his, the only time she'd looked directly at him since he'd gotten off work, and said, "I will be changing my phone service when I get there. I will send the baby a birthday card each year so you will have my address, and you will know how to reach me in case—in case of emergency only. Please do not come after me. Please do not try to convince me to come back. If Yvette wants to look me up when she is an adult, she can." Then she'd handed him a large white envelope. "These are our divorce papers. You'll see when you go over them that I've asked for nothing from you but the things I have with me today. Please sign where I've marked them and put them in the mail as soon as possible. There is already a postage paid envelope in there."

She'd turned on her heels and walked away without even saying goodbye.

The sound of suitcase wheels on asphalt still made him queasy, even after all these years.

Veronica hadn't left him high and dry. In the freezer back home, he'd discovered several weeks' supply of meals for him, and a bin of disposable bottle inserts filled with pumped breast milk for Yvette, enough to last a couple of months or longer. Each one was dated according to when she'd expressed it and the date it had to be used by, and it broke his heart all over again to see that some of them went back almost four months. On the counter beside the cordless phone was a list of sitters, emergency numbers, all of Yvette's medical information, and a printed out instructional on weaning an infant. The document suggested waiting until the baby was at least six months old to begin. The refrigerator was stocked with fresh groceries, and a whole shelf in the pantry held jars and jars of baby food for several different stages of development. The house was spotless, and every piece of clothing he and Yvette owned were freshly laundered and put away. Veronica's side of the closet and the drawers she used in the dresser they shared were empty.

It was more than evident that his wife had thought through her decision thoroughly.

How had he not known?

Levi had sold his truck two weeks later and replaced it with a gently used Dodge Durango. Not only did the silver SUV rank well for being safe and family-friendly, but it came with four-wheel drive and a decent amount of horsepower, which helped Levi salvage at least a tiny shred of his manhood. An added bonus was that the Durango didn't hold any memories of Veronica.

A month after his wife moved out, his mother moved in. Naomi "Nona" Valiente took over caring for the house and Yvette while Levi worked, and life had settled into a new normal for all of them.

When Yvette was one, Nona began pushing Levi to start dating again. He'd resisted at first, but somehow, word got around that he was open to the idea, and when he didn't ask anyone out, the invitations came to him. He had a good business in their small community, and he was young and healthy, broad-shouldered and strong—he had to be in his line of work—and he had a tiny daughter he was head over heels in love with, which only made him that much more endearing of a catch. According to the women he dated, he was tall, dark, and handsome with his cafe con leche skin and black hair, and it all came together to make him one of Plumwood Hollow's most eligible bachelors.

For about a year, he'd gone a little crazy over the female attention—Levi hadn't realized how much he'd missed it until he started accepting it again. He went out almost every weekend, sometimes with a date, and other times by himself, knowing he wouldn't stay that way long. He built quite a reputation for himself as a guy out for a good time, and he never had any trouble finding someone who wanted to have a good time with him.

But Levi wasn't a player by nature, and he soon realized that he preferred his simple routine to the complexities of dating games. He liked coming home in the evenings to a hot meal and the two ladies he loved most in all the world. It was his favorite time of day to spend with his horse, too, that magic hour between light and dark, when the fire of sunset burned down to charcoal, leaving behind stars like embers glowing against the dark of night. He'd much rather stay in and munch on Nona's homemade churros while watching silly movies with his daughter on the weekends, instead of dressing up fancy and trying to act like he was having the time of his life at the bars and clubs. No, having tasted it, he knew without a doubt that he just wasn't cut out for that lifestyle.

Oh, he'd made some good friends along the way; Faith Goodacre—now Faith Overman—for one. It was Jed Goodacre, a regular customer of Levi's, in fact, who suggested he ask his eldest daughter out, seeing as they had so much in common. She was several years younger than Levi, and not long out of high school, but they were both raising little girls as single parents, and according to Jed, Faith would one day take over Seven Virtues Ranch. "She has a good business head on her shoulders. You two could benefit from getting to know each other, even if you don't fall in love," the rancher had said, a wry smile on his face. Levi had appreciated the man's candor, and because he knew and trusted Jed, he asked Faith out the following weekend. She accepted, but to his surprise, she invited him, Nona, and Yvette to join her whole family—except for Hope, who was away at her first year of college—for their family night. They had dinner around the massive kitchen table, followed by popcorn and brownies in the living room while they watched a couple of episodes of Planet Earth. It had been an evening filled with laughter and camaraderie, and he'd enjoyed himself so much, he'd asked her out again.

The second date, he'd taken Faith out to dinner where they'd shared a little about their pasts, about the struggles and triumphs of single parenthood, and about their love for their work. Faith was in the process of incorporating new and still somewhat controversial grazing methods on her daddy's ranch, and although Jed was resistant to the changes, she was excited about the success of her projects so far. She listened attentively as he talked about how he got into butchering, and some of the plans he had for the future. He'd been actively looking for ways to reduce waste from his business while increasing the quality of his meat, and they spent a good deal of time brainstorming about how they could help each other in that capacity. In so many ways, they'd seemed perfect for each other.

By the end of the night, however, after a rather awkward attempt at a goodnight kiss, they'd laughingly agreed that they'd be better off as friends, a decision that laid the groundwork for their daughters to become best of friends as well.

Yvette was ten years old now, Levi was still a single parent, and his favorite place to pull up a stool—other than his own little spread—was at the counter of his butcher shop, keeping his customers happy by providing them with the best meat he could get his hands on. Not only was it comfortable in its familiarity, but the plate glass window happened to look out on the street that took folks to and from Plumwood Hollow's Animal Hospital...including the good doctor, herself. He got a pleasant jolt every time he noticed her Jeep pass by, and with her idiot husband out of the picture, he allowed himself the freedom to entertain thoughts of the woman.

All he had to do now was figure out a way to get Dr. Hope to notice him.

Levi remembered the first time he'd felt that jolt. Hope was home for the summer after her second year in her doctorate program at Purdue, and Faith had invited Levi, Yvette, and Nona over for dinner after church. He'd noticed Hope tucked between Jed and Jasmine in the church pew with the rest of the family, but when he'd first arrived at the ranch house, she'd been in her room making a phone call. It wasn't until she slipped into the seat across from him at the table, and their eyes met, that he'd suddenly lost his ability to form a coherent thought. He was pretty sure he'd heard choirs of angels singing in the background, maybe even a Mariachi band or two.

She drew him in like never before, and yet, he couldn't put a finger on anything that had really changed about her. She still wore her long hair pulled back in its usual ponytail, she still wore jeans that were more comfortable than fashionable, and she still spoke in that soothing, modulated voice of hers. Oh, he'd always appreciated her down-to-earth personality, her kind, and gentle spirit, and she was quite lovely with those marine gray eyes and full lips that should have been kissed often and well, in his opinion. But because of his relationship—platonic, though it was—with Faith, he'd maintained a respectful reserve with all the Goodacre women over the years, and on the rare occasion that Hope was home between semesters and Levi happened to be at Seven Virtues, he treated her as he might a younger sister.

Until that summer. Suddenly, he wasn't sitting across from a kid sister anymore, but from a woman, and one he was undeniably attracted to.

In retrospect, it was he who had changed, not her. He'd become comfortable with who he was and where he was in life, and although there were things he still wanted, including a wife to love and a mother for Yvette, he no longer minded waiting for the right woman to come along.

Those two months flew by for him in a blur of roller coaster emotions. He warred with the fact that Hope still had a couple of years of school left; was it fair to initiate a relationship in which they would be separated more often than not? He didn't want to distract her from her studies—she was taking an extra load so she could graduate early—and he knew long-distance affairs rarely worked out in the end. He didn't want to jeopardize anything by jumping the gun. Could he hold out? Would she? What if she met someone and chose to stay away? Impossible. Hope had too many ties in Plumwood Hollow. Not only was it her family home, but she'd worked at the animal hospital all through high school, and Doc Harper had hand-picked her as his successor at the hospital.

No, Hope would finish her degree, come home to the hollow, and take over the practice, just as planned. Two more years. Only two.

Levi could wait another two years.

He would remain reserved when she was in town between semesters and over the holidays. He would treat her no differently than he treated Faith. And he would hold his heart under lock and key until she was free to love him back.

Two years later, Hope graduated and returned to the hollow, and dove headlong into taking over from Doc Harper as he geared up to retire. She'd been home about a week when she came into the butcher shop with Jed and Faith, and for a moment, Levi had been struck speechless all over again. How he'd missed her, longed for her, and anticipated her return with every fiber of his being, and the knowledge that nothing left stood in their way—not time, or distance, or anyone else—had him almost desperate with the need to tell her how he felt. Yet there she stood before him, and he could think of nothing to say. He'd had to pry his eyes off her, and it took all his willpower to focus on the order Faith had brought in. He'd only dared glance at Hope a few times during the visit, lest he lose all capacity to think, and when the trio took their leave, he'd still said nothing, only waved like a mute schoolboy.

That day when Hope walked into his shop, Levi was pretty sure his wait was over.

Except that it wasn't.

For a while, Hope all but ignored him after that visit, often to the point that it seemed she avoided him. Sure, she was busy. Sure, she was taking over a business and making it her own. She was donning the full mantle of independent adulthood, including moving out of the ranch house at Seven Virtues and into her own place; the hospital came with the tiny cottage next door to the property. Doc Harper had used it mainly as storage, but also as a place to sleep on the nights he needed to stay on site to monitor a patient. By that fall, Hope had cleared his things out and moved her things in.

So, Levi thought perhaps it was too soon to make a move after all; maybe she needed to focus on getting established as the new resident chief before she could indulge in anything personal. He understood that. He knew how hard it was to launch a business amidst the distractions of life. He gave her space. Just a little longer, he told himself. Then she'll be ready.

But the following spring, Chet Willis showed up. Apparently, Hope had dated him during her last few months at Purdue, and when the guy realized she meant what she'd said, that she wasn't going to change her mind and stay in Indiana after graduating, he'd moved to Plumwood Hollow to be near her. Within a few months, they were married by a pastor friend of Chet's in front of a small gathering of family at a hotel in Bowling Green. Of course, Levi hadn't been invited to that, but he'd known about it because Jed had stopped by, and the rancher had alluded to his concern for his second daughter's happiness.

"He's not one of us, Levi," Jed had said with a shake of his head. "I shouldn't be voicing this to anyone, not this late in the game, but I can't quite wrap my head around what I'm feeling. I suppose it could be simply that I'm her father and no man is good enough for any of my girls." He'd complimented Levi on an especially fine pork tenderloin roast in the glass cooler, then added, "But Hope seems to care for the fellow, so I'm praying the good Lord changes my heart toward him."

Even if he had been invited, Levi would have come up with an excuse to get out of attending the event anyway. There was no way on earth he would subject himself to the misery of watching Hope celebrate her union with another man.

Besides, Levi wasn't nearly as righteous as Jedediah Goodacre. His own prayers had leaned more toward the good Lord changing Hope's heart toward—or rather, away from—Chet Willis.

Once married, Hope had softened toward Levi. They often ran into each other in the course of their days. They were both on a few town committees, they had similar political leanings, and because they both worked with animals—although she dealt with the living and he dealt with the dead—they'd grown to respect and admire each other and had become friends.

That said, in the last couple of years, Levi's prayers hadn't changed a whole lot, and although he felt guilty as sin for it now, he couldn't help being more than a little pleased that the Goodacre-Willis marriage was unraveling. He hated seeing Hope hurt, but all along, he'd agreed wholeheartedly with her daddy. Chet Willis wasn't half the man he claimed to be and didn't even register on the scale for being good enough for a woman like Hope Goodacre.

Levi wanted to believe that he, on the other hand, might be exactly the kind of man a woman like Hope Goodacre needed.

He'd take it slow; he knew it took time to recover and heal from the pain of a broken marriage. But he wasn't going to stand by while she went through it alone. Levi understood the road she was on, perhaps better than most, and he wanted her to know that she could lean on him when she didn't think she could hold herself upright anymore.

Sure, he admitted he had ulterior motives. When Hope finally lifted her head and looked around again, he wanted to be the first person she saw, and it was his hope—pun intended—that she would want him to continue being the first—and last—face she saw every day for the rest of her life. Hope Goodacre was the right woman for him, he had no doubt about it, and when she finally figured that out, he'd make sure she knew that he was the right man for her.

That had been the motivation behind his plan for this afternoon's visit. Yesterday after school, Yvette had found a kitten behind the butcher shop, and although Levi wasn't a cat person, he could understand why she'd gone a little goo-goo-eyed over the cute little furball curled up in the box in his front seat. He'd promised Yvette she could take the cat home after Dr. Hope gave it a clean bill of health. He'd intended to catch Hope at the end of her day once the last of her other patients had gone home. Then during the exam, Levi would invite her over to share in their Friday evening family festivities, just as Faith had once done for him. He thought Hope could use a little rest and relaxation, a little time away from her own house and the memories that surely haunted every room. In his home, she'd find a safe place where she didn't have to put on airs or pretend like she was okay when it was clear that she wasn't.

He should have come a little earlier. She was finished for the day, and by the looks of it, entirely done in. He wasn't about to burden her with a request to check the kitten now.

He could wait another day.

He was good at waiting, yes, indeed.

~ ~ ~

The story continues in...
Where There is HOPE: *Seven Virtues Ranch Romance Book 2*